Paige Through the Holidays

by

Ginny B. Nescott

Paige Through the Holidays

Contact Information: info@thewildrosepress.com

Cover Art by *Diana Carlile*

The Wild Rose Press, Inc.
PO Box 708
Adams Basin, NY 14410-0708

Visit us at www.thewilderroses.com

Publishing History
First Scarlet Rose Edition, 2018
Paperback ISBN 978-1-5092-2218-6

Published in the United States of America

Turning a New Paige:
A Groundhog Day Romance

Chapter One

Her tan showed she wasn't from around here. Her Southern drawl didn't help either. Snowflakes covered the shoulders of her thin jacket and dampened her hair. Her teeth chattered. All of it made her look less than the stunner she was.

Paige Myers didn't see herself as a beauty at twenty-six. Her muted light gray/blue eyes were intelligent if she glanced your way. Her body was her own without the added cup size enhancements her Southern campus sorority sisters had recommended. She even kept her own butterscotch hair color.

Paige looked around the bar/restaurant and pulled back a chair in a huff. Her mind reeled in exhaustion. February in a snow storm in some college town bar in the mountains. She was still at least an hour from her aunt's home and famished. Not at all where she expected to be. Each man was more handsome than the next and hardly a woman in sight. She had picked the place because of the name, but *Sizzle* looked more and more like a gay bar.

"F-f-fine by me," she mumbled with her Carolina accent to no one in particular. She shivered. Just a few years out of college, she had moved to Atlanta to get a job. It hadn't hurt that her boyfriend, Davis, and his whole group of fraternity brothers moved to Buckhead, too. It also hadn't hurt that he was a big blond hunk of a guy. What had hurt? He was a jerk. She'd left him behind. "Who n-n-needs men anyway?"

"I do for a start, sister." A flamboyant black-haired waiter slapped a menu and drink list in front of her and flashed a very white-toothed grin. "You eating or is this just one of those drown yourself in a drink with a cherry and make it a double?"

"D-drink, yes. Ch-cherry, no. Hot fries, hot sauce, and c-cold whatever you have on tap. Leave the menu, too." Paige wanted to sound tough, but the shiver and sugared accent took off any of the edge she tried to portray.

She shook the snow off of her jacket and huddled deeper into it.

The waiter tightened his eyes in an assessing way.

"What?" Paige said in a dismissive tone. She thought she'd left all that judgement behind in Buckhead with Davis.

"Hmm."

This time, Paige made a face and gestured with her hands in a shooing motion, her nails perfectly manicured and painted, her expensive rings glittering in the artificial light. She stared him down with tired eyes and pushed back her matted hair with another shiver, becoming aware that the snow made it look wet and greasy.

The waiter didn't move. Then he smiled. "You're not gay, but you just need a girlfriend's touch, right?"

"N-no, I am not gay. I am not anything tonight. Broke up. Hate men. Hate snow. Lost. Just hungry."

"Honey, if you were hungry, you would've stopped at a burger joint. If you were thirsty, there are a dozen other bars closer to the highways. You came here for more than a plateful. And if you are a big tipper, which I *know* you will be, you came to the right place to share your story."

When he still didn't go away, Paige gave in with a nod and a half smile to her sigh.

The waiter beamed. "One breakup special coming up. I'm adding the slider trio to your order, honey."

"Whatever. J-j-just food, drink, and I'm not t-talking." Her shiver added a stutter to her speech.

"Oh, of course not. But it's mid-week. This place might be relatively dead for the next hour or two, and me and my girls haven't done a major overhaul fixer upper in a while." He sashayed away, turned back, and said, "And you, honey, are going to be a special, fun project."

"Hey, I am not s-s-special!" Paige called out after him. With her drawl, her matted hair, and stutter, she drew attention from those close by, including the manager, who came over.

"Oh, we are all special. We're bright in our own way," he said, patting her hand in a kind but condescending way used mainly for toddlers and those with mental issues. He waited a beat and broadened his smile. She was taken aback. He just left laughing, round belly jiggling.

Embarrassment. Paige added embarrassment to the list of crap happening to her. Job lost. Boyfriend a jerk. Make that ex-boyfriend. Drove straight through and for too long. Snow, ice, without snow tires. No way was she finding her aunt's house. Not this late. Or was it early? What time was it?

She pulled out her cell phone, only partly charged since her car was packed to the top with her possessions, her charger buried in the mix. Only seven at night but pitch black from the growing storm. Less than forty-eight hours ago, she had been living with a guy, had a job, and few cares. She'd been happy. Well, happy enough. At least not cold and miserably frustrated from driving an extra six hours through a storm. Eighteen friggin' hours, half of it in bitter, horrible ice and snow.

The waiter slipped a mug of warm spiked cider in front of her. She was about to object, but the sincere expression of kindness made her stop from grousing. The drink was warm and slid down with a comfort of apples and cinnamon.

"Strong, honey, so you can be, too."

She nodded her thanks.

Paige was a realist and less of a girly girl than most of those southern belles she grew up knowing. She normally wasn't dismal. She wasn't sure what she was now. Too exhausted to be hangry. February sucks. Winter in the North sucks. Atlanta wasn't better, just warmer.

She sank back into her downward-spiraling mood. The fight with her ex kept churning in her mind. Davis… How could he? She had returned to the condo from being laid off at her job. It didn't matter that they had recently promoted her or she worked her ass off. Seniority was seniority. Laid off. Davis's first reaction was, "There go all the plans."

Did he mean a proposal? *No.* The plans were for her to chip in so they could go on an overpriced vacation with the group, meaning his fraternity brothers he constantly hung out with anyway.

She remembered her response. "That was the

surprise you mentioned at the holidays to my parents? A trip? Everybody thought you were hinting you would ask me to marry you."

"Marry you? What? With your college debt? No way," Davis scoffed.

Her mind had reeled. What had he said after he begged for her to be reasonable? Something about not worrying about the job, that her daddy could chip in. They had argued. She asked to move to a less pricey place since the rental agreement was almost up. He said no way and that he loved his Buckhead condo. His? They both paid rent. She'd dared push him further and asked if he loved her. His answer? The bastard's glib answer? "Yeah, sure. Besides, you can get a new job soon."

In that moment, she knew she needed more than a new job. She needed a new start, without Davis, but where? She wasn't quite ready to face any of her problems or showing up at her parents for the third degree. That was where the visit to her aunt came in. Time. Time to hide until she was ready to figure out her future.

She let her thoughts go numb and tuned into the conversations around her at the bar. A man with the same thick, dark hair and the same long nose as her waiter walked briskly into the bar. Older? More, something. More masculine? Striking. She watched him from where she sat, sipping the drink, eavesdropping.

"Ooh, look, it's my cousin," her waiter gushed. "All professional-looking in that fine suit."

The man walked toward them with long strides and a big smile.

A red-headed waiter paused beside her waiter, his

gaze scanning the new guy. "Hey, handsome. So, you're a *professional*? Ooh. What kind?" He wiggled his eyebrows.

"Not that kind," her waiter responded.

The man ignored the exchange and gave his cousin a hug.

"Happy Groundhog Birthday, Cuz," her waiter said, "a day early unless you stick around 'til midnight?"

Groundhog Man answered in a deeper, almost growly, voice, "Not sure if I'm staying that long, but I could have a bite."

"Ooh, better still. Bite me, baby," Red Head said and added a puckered air-kiss.

Her waiter shook his head. "Wrong team. He likes the V's."

"Eww. Too bad. Come find me if you're questioning, though." Red Head scurried off.

"Still behaving?" Groundhog Man asked.

The waiter nodded.

Groundhog Man slid some kind of envelope to his cousin. "Then this is for you."

"I can't. Shouldn't. But…thanks." The waiter's shoulders relaxed as he tucked away the envelope.

A bell dinged from the kitchen window, signaling a meal order was ready. Her waiter grabbed the plate and leaned into Groundhog Man for a few whispered words before nodding in her direction. Only then did Paige become aware she had been staring. She blushed and turned away. That much of her Southern ways were ingrained. She looked out the window pretending to be engrossed at the blowing snow and ice mix.

"Yours I presume? One breakup special, extra

fries?"

She glanced at the steamy plate set before her. The order was right, but the voice wasn't. Mr. Groundhog Man stood beside her. "I, err..."

"You need an ear, Alfie tells me. May I?" Groundhog Man pointed to the chair. He didn't wait for an answer and sat.

The waiter also approached. "Oh, honey, here's your hot sauce, and there's your ear." He patted his cousin's shoulder. "Things are picking up in here, after all. We can do something about all this"—Alfie gestured with a swirl around her face—"later. For now, he's your listener. Cute, isn't he?"

"Say anything more, and that envelope comes back," Groundhog Man said.

"I will tell on you."

Another ding sounded in the background.

"Who to?" Groundhog asked with a grin.

More dings.

"I have some handsome cousin who steps in wearing suits and looks after me every now and then." Alfie turned and nearly screeched in the direction of the ding, "I'm coming, coming, coming!"

"Atta boy!"

"Good for you, Alfie!"

"Going solo in public."

The growing crowd chided at once. Alfie laughed, took a bow, and rushed to get the next order.

"Well, it looks like you're stuck with me," Groundhog Man said. "Out with it. What's your story?"

"And I'm supposed to just spill my guts to a perfect stranger?"

Groundhog Man looked at her with a slightly

raised eyebrow. "Talk? Sure. Especially since you think I'm perfect. No guts spilling though, unless you plan on getting trashed or eating all that yourself. Then the ladies room, such that it is, is right that way." He pointed, brandishing a French fry he stole off of her plate.

"Hey!" Paige slapped his hand. He didn't drop the fry but stole another one with his other hand. She slapped him again. "That's it. I want a trade in on my appointed listener."

"Aww, sorry. Did I cross the line? Two more before my own food comes, and then I'll stop."

"Listening?"

"Stealing fries. Listening, sorry to say, I'm good at that. I happen to be that *good* guy. You know, the kind women dump on and six weeks later run off. Rebound Guy."

Paige looked at him. Medium brown eyes, sincere puppy eyes…maybe he was telling the truth. Maybe not. She didn't care at that moment. Food, delicious food, won over thought. She tucked in.

"Groundhog Man," she mumbled between tasty bites.

"What?"

"You're not Rebound Guy." She swallowed. "You're Groundhog Man. You see your shadow and for six weeks you have the woman and then they leave," she said matter-of-factly. "Groundhog Man."

She bit into a Thai slider and looked up in time to see the flinch of pain roll across his face. Then it was hidden with a smile. The kind of smile that was given in an office to a group of unknown people. She'd stung him and knew it. "Sorry."

"For you, too. When was your break up?"

She pointed to his watch. "Twenty hours and about nine hundred miles ago."

"Ouch."

"You?" She swallowed and actually slowed down and bottomed her drink.

Groundhog Man looked past her, inhaled deeply, and exhaled. "It's been awhile." He stood, took off his overcoat, his suit jacket, stretched, and sat back down.

He was slimmer than the big jerk lug, Davis Martin Greer, she'd left behind in Georgia. There was something different about the man at her table. Dang. This was the second time he caught her staring. Her blush formed again. His crooked smile told her he noticed.

To break the moment, Paige lifted her mug, waving it, in hopes of catching the waiter's attention for more to drink. Her hand whacked someone directly in the crotch as he tried to pass. She grimaced. "Oops. Sorry. So very sorry."

"Ouch. I don't go there, sister, so don't you go there either," the man said and walked away grumbling with kind of a cowboy wide-legged stance.

Groundhog Man didn't hide his laugh well.

Alfie came, carrying a tray of food and drinks. He put large shots in front of them along with a fresh mug of cider, beer, and a thick sandwich. "What did I miss?"

"Not much," Groundhog Man said. "Except my preconception of refined Southern manners just got shattered along with that guy's balls."

The waiter walked away chuckling.

Paige swallowed one more quick bite. "Maybe I should leave…"

She stood before he could say, "C'mon, just trying to make you laugh."

He rose, reaching for her, sympathy in his eyes. "Snow and ice are coming down. Didn't want to make you down, too. I'll behave. Scouts honor."

He pulled out her chair. The gesture gave her pause. Something Davis, with all his respectable background, never did for her.

She sat, with slight hesitation, taking in his full height. Something was very different about him. Italian? Native American?

Groundhog Man raised a shot glass and pushed the other to her. She took the glass, knowing the liquid would do little to keep her from talking. She planned to hold to herself, perhaps in denial of it all. Once she admitted she had lost her job, her boyfriend, and her Buckhead condo in one day, it would all become too real. Maybe she could drown it all and think about it another day instead.

Without another moment of hesitation, she threw back the shot and chased it with his untouched beer. Her eyes went wide. Her mouth opened, but no sound came out.

"Whoa. Good, huh? Never downed it in one like that. It's a double shot named after the bar, *Sizzle*."

A breathless "ha" came from her lips. She grabbed for the water and drank heavily, knowing the damage was already done, then slammed the glass on the table.

"Okay, whoever you are, that should loosen your lips. Start sinking ships, or is that too old of a reference?" He smiled. "So, what's your name, or should I just call you, Flee?" he asked with a teasing kindness to his eyes.

"Flea? As in bite and itch? Gee, thanks."

"Flee as in run away from your troubles," he said.

"I am not fleeing. I going to my aunt's." Paige looked to the window and the dark sky. The snow fell more and more. "Or so I thought. Stupid snow. Stupid sucky snow and ice."

"Wow. Harsh, Flee. Real harsh words." He raised his glass and loudly toasted, "Here's to stupid, sucky snow and ice!"

The group around them responded with raised glasses.

"Fuck the snow!"

"Fuck the ice!"

The red headed waiter added, "Fuck me!"

Lurid responses followed including, "Already did," and "Come over here and say that," along with hearty laughs.

Resigned, slightly tipsy, and smiling, Paige raised her glass, too. Maybe she needed an ear more than her stubbornness normally allowed. After all, Groundhog Man was a very handsome, dark-haired stranger. She would never see him again. She watched him out of the corner of her eye as they ate.

"Naw. Not doing it," she said firmly.

"Not doing what?" he asked, cheek filled with the warm turkey sandwich.

"I am not telling my story to some handsome stranger in a strange, icy town, in an increasingly loud gay bar the day before Groundhog Day."

"Good."

"Good?"

He took a long swallow and stole her last fry. Trying to be heard without shouting over the music, which had just pumped on, he said, "Tell it to me over dessert."

"What?" She motioned she couldn't hear.

He stood, slapped down far more money than was needed to cover the bill, and held his overcoat open to her.

Paige was confused. She was more than confused. The gesture was more chivalrous than she was used to, but the warning bells engrained in her of *stranger danger* all went off at once.

"I'm asking you out for dessert. Not for—"

"Fucking hell," a man interrupted as he entered and shook off snow before joining friends, laughing.

"What he said," Groundhog Man added. "Besides, Flee, I come equipped with a car brush and scrapper. I'm well equipped."

"Mmm, honey," the red headed waiter said as he squeezed by. "Offer still stands about a little bit of exploring."

Paige closed her eyes. When she opened them, her hands were sliding into the coat. It was warm. So warm and smelled of aftershave. It smelled of a man who had his act together. His well-equipped act together. Plus, she liked dessert, especially pie.

Chapter Two

"Donuts? What about pie?"

"Closed," he said, opening the door to the donut shop.

"Do you know what donuts do to my hips?" Flee asked as they entered.

"They make you dance?" Michael couldn't see her hips through his coat, which hung low on her, but he did make out a wiggle as she scuttled from one foot to the other for warmth. Actually, he couldn't see much until he unwrapped his Burberry scarf and shook the snow loose. They had walked the few blocks to Curry Donuts, and the ice hung on him.

"Local donut shop," he said. "Besides, it's part of the breakup special. A dozen of the best," he added, his teasing words hanging on his lips.

Was she blushing cherry red? Or perhaps the warmth of the brightly lit shop made her cheeks that color. "How is it you can make donuts sound…salacious?"

Had he known her better, his hands would have gone to her face to warm her. Instead, his eyebrows rose as did his laugh. "A vocabulary and a Southern drawl. Very enticing, Flee, as are all of these." He pointed to the case and wall of donuts behind it. "Care to pick a few?"

There. Deflected.

While she looked to the case, he took in her profile. Dark blonde with a brightness about her. Natural. Sweet. A few years younger than he was. Not bad at all.

She smiled with a flash to her gray eyes. The cold brought a pink to her tanned cheeks. "Hmm, I prefer glazed and sugar-dusted to being goo-filled."

"Ahem." A grinning high school aged boy behind the counter added his debauching grin to her comment. "What? I don't like the frosting goo, either. Some cream filling is good though."

Groundhog Man cleared his throat, and with a slight almost imperceptible shake to his head, the boy stopped midway through his squeak of a laugh. "Let's start with three chocolate-glazed and whatever our southern guest wants."

Flee pointed and gave requests. Soon a dozen donuts filled a box, and they ordered coffee and hot cocoa.

By the time she took her first sip of cocoa, she told him she had been laid off, came from Atlanta, and that her ex-boyfriend was a jerk. He sipped and noted the word "ex" had slipped in more than once. By the time the third bite of donut sugar had coated her lips, she told him she grew up in Carolina but her mother was originally from around here and was her confidante.

As she finished her first donut, she explained that her dad and older brothers were protective of her and probably would have asked her to move back home had they known. Also, that her welcoming aunt sounded more like a fictional character than a part of her family.

He listened. He sipped. He finally bit into his own donut. "Mmmmmm." His response to a soft light donut with chocolate glazing, came out in a heady growl.

Her narrative stopped. She swallowed hard.

"Oh. Sorry. These are my downfall. Here, try it," he said, pushing his plate to her, his fingertips grazing her hand. Her hand hesitated there but then turned to the box and pulled out her own chocolate glaze.

"Don't mind if I do." She bit deeply into the donut.

He smiled at seeing the flustered expression she tried to hide. "Hey, now. Those were mine. You picked all the rest."

"You said a dozen. So, the way I see it, they're all mine, and you, sir, are eating from my box."

He rolled his eyes. "You really didn't just say that."

She didn't show any sign of noticing the double meaning. "I did. Any objections?"

"None, whatsoever." None other than the rise beneath his fly. "Far be it from me to make a lascivious comment about box eating. I will, however, rectify the error." He stood up and walked toward the door, leaving Flee looking dumfounded. When at the last second, he turned toward the counter, her shoulders visibly relaxed. He couldn't help but smile. Maybe she wasn't as indifferent to him as she tried to portray.

He returned to the table with donut replacements.

"You really didn't have to do that." She gestured to the box. "Who's going to eat all those?"

He shrugged. "Not my problem. All yours. I am a man of my word and don't want to besmirch my good name."

"Which is…"

"For today and tomorrow? Groundhog Man as you so dubbed me." He placed the donuts into the box, over filling it.

"You mean I'm stuck with the name, Flee?"

He smiled and shook his head. He reached for her hand. It was soft and cool to the touch. "Care to tell me yours?"

"Paige. I'm just Paige. It's my middle name, but that's what everyone calls me apart from you, of course. You're different." She took her hand away and brushed back a fallen strand of hair.

"Thankfully." He smiled. He actually liked that she considered him apart from others.

She looked quizzically at him.

"Aren't you glad I'm not like that...whoever that lug is in Buckhead? He clearly has no appreciation of women or relationships by the way. He seems like a fool to let you go. That much I do know."

"Groundhog Man, you're just saying that to flatter me."

"No. I'm saying that because you need to understand that before we can move on. I know how it works. I only have a few hours until my birthday, and I don't want to spend that time being compared to some idiot. I want you to like me for my own idiocy."

"And your donuts. I could like you for your donuts."

He raised his coffee mug to her cocoa. "My donuts are special. Very large and special."

"Oh Pu-leeeze." Paige rolled her eyes as she rose.

"Would warm be better? Sticky? I really didn't want to go with doughy. Would tasty have done the trick?"

"I need to go to the restroom."

"Not going to be ill, are you? I wasn't that objectionable."

She just smiled and shrugged playfully. "A girl does need some relief."

He watched her move to the back of the shop, admiring the view a bit more than he expected. His snowbound, birthday weekend held the promise of getting better and better.

****

Paige looked in the mirror, mumbling to herself, "I am in the middle of nowhere Pennsylvania in a donut shop called *Curry*, coming from a gay bar, hanging with a strange man with no name. My hair is a mess. Whatever make up I had on is long worn off." She stopped her tirade in the mirror, turned, sniffed at her armpits, and shrugged. "Okay, at least I don't smell."

Lights flickered in the plain but clean bathroom as she washed her hands and face in the lovely warm water. She moved to the blower to dry her hands and fluffed her hair in the process, relishing the warm jet of air on her face. With a swipe of lipstick, she felt more herself and left the restroom.

Groundhog Man's smile widened as she approached their table in a now empty shop. A teasing flash flickered across his face.

"What? I know my lipstick isn't smeared." She sat down and waited for his answer.

He leaned forward and ran his hand over her hair, combing down a section that stuck straight out. The act, though innocent on his part, felt very intimate to Paige. Her breath caught. He must have noticed, since he leaned in further, cupped her face, and—before her mind could grapple with it—he kissed her! It was a tiny whisper of a kiss.

Paige tried to speak, but words stuck as her heart

raced.

He kissed her again. This time, his lips lingered, drawing hers to his.

She finally managed to speak, "What are you doing?"

He held back his smile, but his eyes laughed. "I'm kissing you. Like this…" Fully leaning over the corner of the table and pulling her closer, he kissed her with a deep soft moan.

Fire rolled into her. "I…I don't know your name."

"Make one up…like you did." He kissed her again.

"Paige *is* my name," she said in a hushed voice when his lips lifted off hers. When had her hands landed on his shoulders?

"*Mmmmmm*, great name." He brushed her hair back and kissed near her ear, whispering, "Love the name, Flee. Paige." He drew out her name.

To her own internal objections, she was melting. It lasted but a moment. Lights flickered notably, obviously due to the employee with his hand on the switch.

"Uh. Okay. Hey there, customers. Closing early," the donut clerk announced.

Groundhog Man let go of Paige and straightened to pull out a bill from his wallet. "I can tip."

"Okay, ten more minutes then." The young clerk smiled and stared at them.

Groundhog Man glared at the staring clerk before reaching for Paige again. She stifled a giggle. The clerk just crossed his arms.

Groundhog Man sighed. "Right." He walked firmly up to the clerk, who backed up to the wall of empty bins and let out a small eek. Instead of threatening him,

Groundhog Man slid money to him and whispered something.

The boy smiled and nearly ran to the back. The store lights went off. Street lights reflecting on the snow spilled in through the window. It threw a glow to his caramel skin, making his light brown eyes turn to an amber as he approached the table.

"Do you always get your way?" she asked suspiciously.

Groundhog Man shook his head, smiling broadly. "Not much actually. But it's close to my birthday, and I wanted to taste the cinnamon sugar on your lips."

Paige reached for her lips. "I don't have anything on my lips."

He bit into a donut, making sure to rub the sugar on his mouth, and kissed her. "Now you do."

She laughed.

"I like that laugh, Paige. Would like to hear it more, and not just for the next few minutes." He moved in close, his hands rubbing her arms, and kissed her again. She tasted the cinnamon on his lips. Their arms gravitated around each other, kissing deeply. His moan cut into her. It sent a shiver deep inside her belly. It wasn't a shiver of cold but of a need she'd suppressed. Her nipples hardened under her clothing, making her return his voracious kiss with her probing tongue. His moan deepened.

Cough. "Ahem. I really have to close, guys." The kid was back. "Boss said it's time."

"Uh huh," Groundhog Man said, but his gaze never broke from hers.

"Time to flee?" Paige giggled and broke from him and the moment. She pulled on his coat, gathered her purse, and headed toward the door.

"Aren't you forgetting something?"

She stopped and turned, still reeling from his fire-hot kiss. "Happy birthday?"

"Thanks, but that's not it." He wrapped his scarf around his neck.

"Oh, you want your coat."

"Not yet."

"You aren't expecting me to thank you for that make-out session, are you?"

He shook his head and nodded to the donut box.

Paige stepped back to the table and picked up the forgotten box. Leaning into the man who had just made her skin flush with hunger, she whispered, "Thank you, Groundhog Man."

His breath caught, and his crooked grin widened. His hand moved to her arm.

"Ahem!" The donut clerk broke in. He held out a plastic bag for the box and placed it inside. Sleet pinged against the glass window, and he looked at them. "Here you both go. Trash bags. Face and arm holes cut. You wear it like this." The clerk pulled a bag over his head and arms through the holes cut midway. "Might help you wherever you're going."

"Hey thanks, bro." Groundhog Man took the two bags the kid held out. "You're all right after all."

"Momma always said to wear protection. You two looked like you needed it." The boy let out a squeaking laugh as the three of them left the building, locking the door behind them.

"Cold! Forgot how cold it is." Paige turned her face from the wind. The trash bag at least protected her from the sting of the sleet. She held to Groundhog

Man's gloved hand with her own thin glove.

They tugged in different directions.

"Where are you going, Flee?" he asked.

"My car."

"Aren't you in the garage?"

"What garage? I parked in the square."

"You didn't."

"Did." She looked at him directly. "Why?"

A loud rumble with a booming scraping sound eclipsed his answer. The snow plow pushed through the street, shoving mounds of icy snow to the side. It moved in the direction of her car. Paige let go of his hand and ran, half stomping across the un-shoveled walks, sliding on ice covered patches, having only clogs on her feet.

He caught her easily, holding to her before the next step could send her flying. "Careful now," he said, slowing her pace.

It wasn't needed. She stood stock still and stared at the mound of snow before them. "My car's already buried."

"Your car is under all that? Sorry, Flee—Paige. It looks like it's been stuck for a while." Ice chunks and snow competed for most coverage. Her car was buried and iced in. "You're not going anywhere tonight."

She moved to the driver's side and banged at the locked door. What could be seen of the window was iced over and the lock was frozen.

"My clothes are in there." She started to scratch at the ice near the car lock. Her movements were desperate while he, too, tried the passenger side. "I will not give up." *Bang. Scratch, scratch, rub, scratch.* "I hate being such a damsel in distress. So not like me."

"I'm trying this door, too. Looks like the trunk is buried under completely and a lost cause," he called to her over her thickly covered car. "Do you have anything vital in the car?"

She rubbed her hands across the frozen window and peered in. "Not really, except Hedgy's in the front though."

"Do you have an animal in there?" he asked, shouting over the car.

She nodded and saw the look of horror on his face. "I mean no. I found my stuffed animal Hedgy when I was packing to leave. I lost him for years and just found him. When I was five…"

He moved to her side of the car, partly dodging a blast of icy wind. "Nice reunion story. Can we save it for later? The wind is gusting, and someone is borrowing my warm coat. Do you have any winter clothing in there?

"I'm coming from Atlanta. What do you think?" She attempted an expression of toughness. That façade of strength soon gave way as she thought of her predicament going from bad to dire. She was exhausted and cold with her possessions locked away under thick ice and snow. Tears edged closer.

Groundhog Man failed at unlocking her car. "I think I am freezing, and you are coming with me."

She was bordering on panic, which translated to a thickening of her drawl. "I am not that kind of a girl."

"You might not be, but you will be a frozen kind if we don't get inside soon." He smiled warmly, puffs of his breath visible in the cold. "C'mon. There's a sofa in my room. I'm about five minutes that way in a B & B. You can figure it out from there."

She nodded and took a deep breath. It was a mistake. Instead of clearing her head, her breath froze her lungs, blocking further thought. The bitter cold took hold of her. He was right. She desperately needed to be in a warm place.

He put his arm around her, guiding her. She took one last look at her buried car, memorizing its spot as the snow kept falling. Music still poured out of *Sizzle* nearby. He held tight to her as she clung to her purse and donuts, the only worldly possessions she had at that moment. That and his coat and a plastic bag over her head that smelled vaguely of donuts and pot.

Chapter Three

Paige stirred, curling against something, awareness only half creeping in. She fought exhaustion to assess where she was. And that was in her panties and bra, in a bed—a gorgeous bed. She was nuzzling something warm and large. Not something, she realized but a someone. She was in a bed with a stranger beside her!

She quickly rolled away, clutching the comforter, suddenly very awake. Her mind reeled. It was still night. She looked over at him as he slept. Groundhog Man. Handsome Groundhog Man.

Her thoughts flashed back to the trudge in the snow, the dripping coats and wet shoes left near the kitchen to dry. The bed and breakfast! She recalled the mansion was incredible even in the dim light, all the dark antiques, curtains, and stained glass, though she'd only had a glance on the way to his room.

When they had arrived in the room, the curtains were open, lights on, showing a deep red brocade on the walls, scattering of ornate, walnut furniture pieces, and a bed suited for royalty in plums, crimsons, and purples. Enchanting. But she'd been too wet and cold to take it all in.

"And you expect me to just jump into bed with you?" Paige remembered asking.

"Expect? No. Hope? Wildly. Think you will?" He wiggled his eyebrows and turned to take off his suit jacket.

While Groundhog Man had his back to her, she had made her move. And that move was to run to the bathroom.

"That depends," she had said through the bathroom door.

"On what?"

"Hotel availability elsewhere…and…" She peeked through the crack of the bathroom door. She closed the door again. "And what you look like under your robe."

She remembered giggling and locking the door before he could enter and standing in a hot, hot shower, with him knocking on the door demanding for her to save some water. She remembered opening the door in her underthings and shirt, staring at him. He was wrapped in a robe, shivering, moving to the shower, a hint of his smooth chest showing.

She must have fallen asleep before he even came out of the shower. The long ride and missed night's sleep had taken a toll on her.

Paige turned to look at him now. In the dim light from the window, his skin wasn't tanned but of slight olive tone. She took in the image of his long nose, large brow, broad cheeks, and that hair…so thick and dark. Her finger nearly touched his lips, but she stopped and a smile came to her.

His eyes peeped open. "Hey, Flee. Don't they teach you in the South not to stare?"

"Name's Paige. And what happened to hotel availability?"

His arms reached out to her. "Notta one, except this room."

"Did you even check?" Paige shifted, but he moved

closer, spooning her.

He pushed back her hair and inhaled against her neck, sending a shiver through her. "Nuh uh. Do you want me to?" He kissed her neck, nuzzling her against his body.

Without pulling away, she tipped her head slightly and kissed his smooth skin. "You should. Mmm. Remember I don't do one-night stands." She sweetened her words with her thickened Carolina tone.

He turned her and half leaned over her, wearing nothing more than PJ bottoms. Groundhog Man kissed her and then again, deeply, lingeringly, moaning. "The way I see it, nobody is standing."

She chuckled, then the smile disappeared. "I don't even know your real name."

"Bob." He kissed her forehead and smirked.

"That's not your name, is it?"

"No." He kissed her eyelid. "Ted." Then her other eyelid. "Tim." His hand slid to hers, interlocking their fingers, and brought it to his lips, smiling. "Joe."

She tightened her face to the mock tough one and drawled, "Were you just going through a list of short names?"

"No." He smiled, let go of her hand, and stretched as he rested on his back. "Only the three letter ones. Working my way up to four," he said with a mimicked drawl.

At that, she turned over and stole the covers.

"Okay, okay. Sorry, Paige. I'll tell you," he said in his natural, baritone. "I just liked being called Groundhog Man for some unknown reason. I never had a nickname like that." He leaned over her and whispered, "It's Michael."

She shook her head and leaned into her pillow, working on a pout.

"Michael Lukas, with a K."

She lifted her head and gave him an appraising stare in the dim light.

"Honest, Paige." He rose, walked toward the desk, stuffed two bites of a donut in his mouth, and pulled something out of his wallet. "Here. My business card," he mumbled before swallowing, his other hand not relinquishing the glazed donut. "Michael Y. Lukas. I'll put it on your purse. Nobody pronounces my middle name right. It's four syllables."

Paige rose to look at the card.

He intercepted her, chiding, "Uh, uh, uh. You have to earn my middle name."

"Fine. And you have to earn my first name," she said, her drawl extra thick. She bit a large chunk from the donut he held.

He put the remainder out of reach on the nightstand and inched closer.

"Sounds like a challenge, Flee. And I am up for a challenge." He leaned into her, making her fall back onto the bed, and crawled up, holding himself over her. "I would love nothing more than to be the best rebound lover you have ever had. We both could use it."

Her response was muffled by his lips. His delicious lips pressed to hers, still tasting of sweet donuts. She hesitated, but her lips did not.

"We're consenting adults." He bit her neck, and she sucked in a quick breath, the sound lost to a harsh gust of wind, which rattled the windows. "Not attesting to my maturity though."

He picked up the last of the donut, pretending to

feed her, but then ate it himself. The childish gesture was quickly forgotten by his next kiss that fueled her hunger.

Paige relented to her night-time desires. Her arms drew him in tighter. She drank in the taste of him, his tongue finding its way past her open lips. He was right. She needed this. Wanted this. Maybe it was the strong drink, the sleep deprivation, or the shock of her changing circumstances, but she wanted the diversion. She wanted more than that. She wanted him.

She cooed into his kiss, her palms moving over his smooth skin. He was slim and muscled. She wanted to touch every part of him.

His kisses trailed down to her chest. Michael's large hand moved onto her breast as his lips followed. He mouthed her through sheer fabric of her bra. His hands were skilled, not petting but enflaming. This was no immature Davis. This was a man's touch, and she knew it.

She felt a surge of passion so strongly that her hands moved lower on him past his muscled chest. He looked at her. She blushed in the inky light, knowing her fingertips were on the front of his pajamas. He moved his hips so that his cotton-clad length rubbed her exploring hands, silently showing his ardent consent.

Paige stroked the thickness of his cock and felt it grow firm to her touch. She felt her bra unhook and let go long enough for it to slip from her.

"Beautiful," he mumbled, nibbling her skin, massaging as he did so until he found her nipple. He tugged at one, almost with a bite and a growl. Her mouth opened with a moan, and her hand squeezed his hard shaft.

"Careful. Don't break it before we're done with it." He chuckled, the laugh turning to a groan almost instantly as his lips found her torso, his hands roving all over her body. Before she could voice an objection, he slid lower, mouthing her through the fabric of her panties. "Oh, I wanted to do this since the first time you stared me down."

He was skilled. Skilled in disarming her with his smooth determined movements. Skilled in disrobing her as he slid her panties off. Skilled in tantalizing her body to the point of begging as his hands kneaded every inch of her thighs and stomach. She was naked, wearing nothing more than the sheet now; he was still in his pajamas.

He bit her thigh and slid one finger, then another, into her pussy. When her hand reached down to his, he intercepted it and placed her hand over her head. Unfettered, his fingers drove in and out of her core as she whimpered her need in a matching, building rhythm. She gasped tiny breaths, her body struggling to get closer to his as she headed toward the tipping point.

"Not yet, Flee," he growled into her ear.

"But…"

His kiss muffled her protest. Open-mouthed, his lips took hers. His tongue plunged deeply into her mouth. Voraciously, hers followed barely stifling their moans.

"Oh, you need this, don't you?" he whispered, this time, fingering her wanton wet center with an urgent jackhammer pace. "Hold off…"

"No… P-p-please…I need to… C-c-can't stop."

"You can." He kissed her, nearly biting her lip as he tugged on it. Then his lips were gone. Finger still in her, he flicked her clit with his thumb.

She was insane with lust, barely able to watch his movements when he reached over to the night table. He bit open the condom packet with his teeth, spitting out the wrapper. Her hands found her way to his and unrolled the condom over him. It was the first time her fingers touched his cock, no cloth in the way, skin on skin.

He moaned, hand resting on hers, as if to make sure the task was done. Instead, he took her hand away, sucking on her finger, fueling his own hunger as he pressed the fingers of his other hand deep into her pussy. Lying slightly to her side, he placed her hands loosely above her head. She could've pulled free at any moment.

"What do you want, Flee?" he asked.

"You," was all she could moan.

He kissed her again, tongue diving into her mouth at the same moment he jarred her senses with a finger deep in her tender pussy. She shuddered.

"Are you sure?" He wriggled the finger, pumping into her before pulling it from her.

"Yes!" she hissed out the word, nearly screaming.

"Shh, shh, shh." He rolled on top and drove his cock straight into her.

"Ahh…" Paige muffled her cry against his shoulder.

He pulled out a fraction, slid in and out, and then drove in all the way.

Something deep inside of her broke free and shattered. She clung to him and cried out a silent scream. He paused long enough for her to gather her breath and moaned as he began to rock, sawing into her.

His face was buried in her neck, his voice rolling moans. With one hand holding both of hers, his other lifted her bottom. He drew nearly all the way out, then sank his thick shaft into her again.

"Ohh." Paige matched his rhythm, a leg curling around him. She pulled back as he did and collided with him on the down stroke. Again, and again. Waves began to grow and threaten to ripple through her.

"Ready?" he asked.

She moaned out some sound in response. Lights flashed on the street below as a rumbling sound became stronger. Instead of shaking and releasing inside her as she thought he would, he let go of her hands, leaned up, bracing himself, and pumped in and out of her in the same frenzy as his finger had before. His strong face focused on hers. His taut, muscled chest rippled with each thrust. In and out, in and out, so fast, then slow and deep, grinding at the end. And again.

She was lost. She writhed against him, breathing in needful gasps. Her eyes popped open, and everything exploded as it never had before. Her nails dug into his arms as she let out a warbled cry. He cut her cry short with his mouth on hers, quieting it to a rolling mewl, but she knew the entire B&B and half the street would have heard her if not for the snowplow. The loud crashing scrape of the street plow echoed from below.

Breathlessly, she whispered, "I want you."

He did not hold back any longer but locked deep, so deep inside her, and released, shaking, adding to her ebbing frenzy. His whole body jarred stiff as he came. Their bodies finally slowed. He kissed her again and again, then dropped down, half next to her, and pulled her to him. He gulped air, breathing deeply as she did.

Her body felt like it was floating, euphoric.

Her scattered thoughts reeled. Something it had done these past few days. *What had just happened? Incredible. How can this be so much better than with big buff Atlanta boy? It was, wasn't it?*

Breathe. She just needed to breathe.

"Wow." He grinned broadly, holding her.

She finally caught her breath. Her face felt hot, her smile, wide. "Wow, as in, dang, that Southern girl sure is good?"

"Wow as in you are loud. Too loud for a bed and breakfast, Flee."

That earned a pillow whack. And another. Not to mention a tickle in response. She started to giggle, then squeal. "I give, I give. Uncle."

He stopped for a moment. "Your first name. I know it's not Uncle. Try again." He wrestled her and tickled all that could be tickled.

"Aunt?"

"Nope." Gentler tickling with a few tickles returned. Then he did it, he tickled her feet.

"I give. I really give. My first name is Amelia. Named after some distant relative."

He stopped. She panted. Groundhog Man enfolded her in his arms, spooning her, kissing the top of her head. "Amelia. Sounds familiar. Knew I'd get it out of you. My middle name is Yotahala. There, now you know it. You can find me easily. Michael Yotahala Lukas, with a K."

She mumbled his name, stroking his arm.

"Part Oneida if you are wondering." He smiled a delicious, afterglow smile.

She turned, gave him an appraising look, mirroring

his smile. "Hmm…part Native American and a whole lot mmm," she murmured.

"As are you and then some," he said, his voice a deep whisper. "Care to share your full name, Amelia Paige?"

Paige softly stretched against him. "Hmm? Oh. Myers. As in, I met you while I was wallowing in the mire."

"Cute." He gave her a peck to the cheek.

"Just cute?"

"Can't see in this light…"

In response, she raised the pillow she was clutching.

"No." He laughed. "We'll burst the pillows if we start that up again." There was a pause as his hand roamed over her body. "Paige, you're beautiful. I'm actually amazed I have you in my arms." He cuddled her tightly and then let go. "Only, I need to take care of business." He stood up.

"In the middle of the night? You are a hard worker, Yoda."

He walked naked to the bathroom, grabbing his PJ's on the way. "Not that kind of business and it's Yota. Yotahala."

"Well, if you need something, just Yoda-hollah."

He threw something at her. It was the robe, which she gratefully put on.

She poked around the room and picked up the donut box. "Do you have anything less sweet to eat or drink in this mini-fridge?"

"Water, I think. Tea and coffee downstairs…might be a bottle of something, but the kitchen is closed."

Silence.

"Paige?" All he heard was footsteps scurrying down the stairs. "Flee really does fit you," he said to no one.

Chapter Four

Suddenly famished, Paige headed to the kitchen. Maybe she was making up for the lack of food on the long trip. Maybe she just needed to process what had just happened. In any case, a snack was her answer and the kitchen her means.

The kitchen was lost in time with copper pots hanging over a re-modeled large pot belly stove, something straight out of the early 1900's. Donut box in hand, she turned to a cabinet, afterglow blocking any forethought, and opened it for sneak inspection.

"Ahem. Excuse me," came a deep startling voice.

"Oh, I..." Paige turned, feeling heat creeping up her neck, one hand holding the robe to make sure it was closed, the other gripping tightly to the donuts. The cabinet door stayed open as a tell-all to her snooping.

"The kitchen is closed."

"I'm sorry. Really." She turned to leave.

"Wait." The man yawned and sighed. "I'm the proprietor. Did the snowplows wake you up, too? You're not the only one who came down here."

She nodded, not wanting to out and out lie to the man who looked somewhere between exhausted early middle age and who-can-tell.

"Donut?" she sheepishly asked, holding out the box in recompense.

"Curry's?" the man asked.

She nodded again.

"My favorite. I'll trade you for that midnight snack you must have been hunting."

"Deal. Do you have anything to drink?" Paige asked, thinking tea.

He pulled out some crackers, cheese, carrots, and a bottle of wine. He uncorked it with a pop. He poured two glasses and filled water glasses as well. They sat, small plates in front of them, hers savory, his sweet.

"Ever since I rolled into Pennsylvania, I seem to be hungry. Why is that?"

"I could say the cold but who knows? You might have heard that couple going pell-mell in one room, too. Ignites the snackies for me every time." He gave a hearty laugh.

Paige blushed hot as fire. She knew he knew but said nothing. "This is one of the most handsome bed and breakfasts by the way, and I only saw it at night."

He thanked her for the compliment and told the story of the original brewery family owners and his subsequent restoration efforts. A story he obviously knew by rote, but his telling was warm and familiar, as if he were talking to family. A non-dysfunctional family. He asked about her accent without pressing for details. Snacks were shared, and wine was toasted to health and sleep. She might not have had any answers to what was happening in her life, but she was content and sated.

"Well, goodnight. I'm sure I'll see you sometime in the morning, Mr. Hagers," she said with a lingering sleepiness to her words.

"And most likely during the day. Didn't you hear the forecast? This is only part one of the storm.

Groundhog Day is sure to be a doozy. Bet they'll give a travel advisory again."

"Travel advisory?"

"Yes. I heard it on the news and radio. We need to stay off the roads unless it's an emergency. Gives time to clear up those poor shlubs whose cars are now buried in snow, too. Glad to have the pleasure of your company an extra day."

That was news to Paige. She would definitely need to contact family tomorrow before they started to worry. She turned to leave. "Unfortunately, I'm one of those shlubs."

"Yikes. Oh, and don't forget to set your clock radio alarm to our local station. There's a surprise in the morning, Miss, uh, Miss…"

"Amelia Paige." Why had she done that? She never gave out her first name.

"Really? We have a room by that name. Which one are you in?"

"Not sure. All crimson and purples, just up there."

"Well, I'll be. That's the Amelia room."

"You have to be kidding."

He shook his head. "Nope. It's really the Amelia room. It was named after some distant relative from about the turn of the century. No brewery connections to my knowledge. Too bad. I suppose it was a popular name back then. Still a pleasant coincidence, don't you think? Guess it was meant to be." He raised his glass.

She shrugged and answered him with a smile before turning to leave again.

"Oh, you forgot your donuts." He pushed the box toward her.

"They're all yours. And thank you."

"Remember to put on the local music station."

She nodded and beamed at him one last time before hurrying up the thickly carpeted stairs with rich dark wood rails. She returned to the room, thinking *"Meant to be? Nothing is ever meant to be, is it?"*

After setting the alarm to play the radio station Mr. Hager mentioned, Paige dropped the robe, slid into bed beside her Groundhog Man, and kissed his cheek. "Is this room, meant to be? Are we meant to be?"

He shifted, spooned around her, and mumbled in his sleep. "Mmm hmm. Meant to be sleeping."

She yawned. Maybe he was right. Then again, maybe both men were right. She snuggled in tight to his warmth and fell asleep soundly.

****

"I got you, Babe! I got you, Babe!" As the song ended, a voice came over the radio, "That's right folks. It's Groundhog Day. You voted. We will be playing at least part of that song on the hour, every hour today. Happy Groundhog Day! A big screen viewing of the movie will be shown tonight at…"

Paige reached over and pushed some button on the radio alarm. *Click!*

She stretched, still exhausted. The sky was dark. How early was it? Not early. Already ten in the morning. She patted the covers. No Groundhog Man. The long drive without sleep and the events of the last few days claimed her. She rolled over, yanked up the covers, and fell back asleep.

"…say we're young and we don't know."

"Huh?" Paige reached for the noise and the button, but the alarm clock fell and kept playing, louder now. The familiar lyrics blasted until she could scramble to reach the clock.

Click!

"Great. Now that song's going to be playing in my head all day. Thanks, Mr. Hager." Paige stretched again and sat up fully this time. Eleven a.m. His side of the bed wasn't even warm anymore. She looked around the room. Unfamiliar but enchanting with flocked crimson wallpaper, Victorian ottomans, and brocade lace. She climbed out of bed and dragged her hand over the deep rose velvet of the settee. Walnut and mahogany furniture pieces made it feel like a movie set. One in which, she was underdressed. No hoop skirt. In fact, no clothing at all. She never walked naked back in Buckhead. Somehow, she enjoyed it here.

"Michael? Michael Yadalotta?"

No Groundhog Man. If he were within ear shot, he would have definitely responded to that tease of muddling his middle name.

Paige poked about the room further. His computer was closed on the desk, and his was luggage close at hand. She stretched and balanced, even bending to a few yoga moves and finishing with a smile at how well she slept. How unusually well.

A small tray of tidbit snacks was on a table. She had plans for those after freshening up. Opening a few drawers on the desk, she found his charger. Her phone was dead, and that charger looked to be the right kind. She plugged in her phone and readied herself. The snow and ice had already started again. Today, would be a very interesting day, and she wanted to be part of it.

A half hour later with the tray of empty dishes in her hands, Paige left the room, closing the door but leaving it unlocked. She had dared to look inside his luggage and removed a sweater. She also took some wooly looking socks. Without her shoes, which she'd left somewhere downstairs to dry, the stripy socks were the next best choice.

She was a mish mash of fashion, her jeans and shirt under his sweater and socks. Her panties were MIA. Something no Southern girl would normally allow, but without luggage, she had no choice. She'd loosely braided her dirty blonde hair but didn't have a tie so she wrapped the end in dental floss. The look? Anything but model-ready but hopefully huggable on her small frame.

As she padded down the stairs, voices drifted up. She stopped to listen, squatting with the clattery tray still in her hands.

"Glad the simple breakfast was to your liking," said a jovial woman's voice.

A man murmured something. Was that Groundhog Man?

"Of course, no problem with staying the extra day, Mr. Lukas. I had no idea you had your fiancé with you. Months ago, you mentioned one," the female said.

Paige tried to hear more but their voices grew quieter. Fiancé? What was Groundhog Man saying? The woman laughed, startling Paige enough to clink a dish. She rose and nearly fell trying to get her bearings as she walked down the thickly carpeted stairs.

"Here she comes now, uh…trippingly." Michael, her handsome Groundhog Man, looked so fitting, standing in slacks and cashmere sweater by the ornate fireplace, cellphone in hand and earbud in one ear. GQ? Something more international with his skin tone.

Paige held tight to the tray as it wobbled in her

hands when she saw him.

"Oh dear, let me take that from you," the kindly woman said. "You didn't have to bring that down, but this old thing does appreciate it."

"You're not old," Paige and Michael said in unison. Paige's cheeks flushed a bit.

"How about I put this in the kitchen and leave you two alone for a moment? Come in when you're ready for a coffee, though, since I don't have the afternoon station set up yet." The woman beamed, cheeks rosy, hair gray, breasts full and threatening to bump into everything on the tray as she walked to the kitchen, hips swaying.

Paige looked at Michael, who removed his ear bud, and without hesitation, pulled her into his arms in an alcove of the room. He broke the *next-day* ice with a tender morning kiss, and she with a hug of satisfaction.

"How's my sleepy head?"

"Rested now." Paige couldn't help smiling.

"I know. I took conference calls down here since I didn't want to wake you."

"Sorry. Normally, I'm a pretty early riser. I think driving through the night got to me. Plus, someone woke me up last night."

"Oh? I thought it was the other way around. Maybe it was the snowplow. They can be *so* loud." Before she could object, he kissed her again. This time, his arms drew her tight to him, and he took full advantage of the hidden alcove.

Her hand wove into his silken dark hair as he held her. The kiss deepened. Something tugged inside her, and she melted to him until he broke from the kiss.

"I have more calls and business, Flee. We can tend

to your car after the storm slows down. Mind if I have a little time upstairs to work?"

"Uh-huh." Paige said dreamily.

He gave her a strange look.

With a deep breath, she came back to reality. "I mean, no, go ahead. I'll keep myself busy. Oh, I borrowed your charger, if that's okay."

"That sweater looks familiar, too."

"Want it back?" Paige teased with a giggle, tugging at the light toned grayish sweater.

"If it were my sweat pants, I would have said yes, just to see what you would do." He smiled as he toyed with her braid, eyeing the dental floss-tie invention. "It looks good on you by the way, Flee. Is this a Southern thing, or do you just look good in most things?"

"You're just flattering me so you can have your way with me."

"Hardly. If I were having my way with you, you would not be clothed at all and you would be making sounds much different from that little giggle of yours." He touched her face and kissed her with his now familiar soft moan. His phone beeped, he inhaled and exhaled, shaking his head. He clicked the button on his earbud. "Lukas here. Shoot…"

He motioned something about taking the call and flew up the stairs, Paige watching his every move.

Chapter Five

"Hello," Paige said, drawing out the word with her accent as she entered the kitchen. The woman was swallowing a bite of something and nearly choked. "Sorry for interrupting. You said something about coffee?"

"Come on in, sweetie. Have a seat. I'm Jenny, but everyone calls me Cookie. Not very inventive, but I still like it." The woman appeared to be in her late sixties and wore her age happily. "I'd offer you a donut, but that was the last."

"No more donuts. I am all dough-nutted out." Her drawl thickened whenever she met new people.

"Then let me get that coffee going. Or is tea better?" Cookie opened a cabinet.

"Either. I'm Paige by the way." Paige saw that the cook was rubbing and wringing her hands as her grandmother had. "Here, let me help you." She pulled out a couple mugs instead of the more expensive, delicate cup and saucer sets Cookie had been reaching for. "I like these better anyway. Would you join me? Michael has some work to do upstairs."

"Love to, but I need to finish these dishes first," Cookie said over the running of the hot water in the sink.

"Don't you have a dishwasher?"

"Yes, but, this cold, icy weather gets to me."

Cookie held up her hands, wiggling her stiff fingers.

"My grandmother used to soak her hands to ease her joints, too. She had arthritis as long as I knew her. Smart woman. She passed over a year ago."

"Sorry to hear that."

Paige nodded. "I'm going to visit my aunt about an hour away from here, to help clean out and fix up my grandparent's home to sell. Mom says Auntie isn't making much progress so I might be the kick in the butt she needs."

The two fell into relaxed chatter, both washing in warm sudsy water until the dishes were done. Coffee mugs were filled. Paige added extra whole milk, something she never did at home—watching her weight—but she felt as if she were on some kind of vacation.

She eyed a deck of well-worn cards. "Do you play Gin?"

"Plain or Rummy 500?"

"Rummy 500 if you have time. It's been so long since I played it. Unless you cheat."

"I can try not to," Cookie said with a wink.

Soon, the cards were shuffled and dealt. Rounds swung in and out of each's favor. They spoke more, where Paige was from, her accent, Michael's birthday, and then Cookie asked the inevitable questions about being engaged to him.

Paige looked up. "I'm not really his fiancé. I'm not sure what I am. Maybe his rebound and he's mine? You're not going to kick me out, are you?"

Cookie laughed. "Not hardly. He is a prince though. Known him for some time. From how he looks at you, though, and the way you two went at it this morning, there might be something there, don't you think?"

Paige blushed. "You saw?"

"Only a peek. Okay most of it."

"You are a cheater."

"Learning to be. Gin. Again." Cookie gleefully wrote down the score. "So why does he call you Flea? Is there something cleaning wise we should know about you?"

"Ha. Ha. He means flee as in run away. I sorta just left Atlanta because I lost a job and ditched my immature ex-boyfriend in Buckhead in the process." Paige realized what she had spilled so readily to yet another stranger. "I think I said too much."

"Tut. Not hardly."

"I… Well, I didn't mean to shock you about leaving one guy and then going with…" Paige pointed up, implying her Groundhog Man and the bedroom.

"Shock? Ha. You ever hear of Woodstock? I was there. I had many a man in my time and still do when I get the chance." Paige's eyebrows shot up at her confession. Cookie waved her off. "So, you slept around a bit, big deal." Cookie leaned back in her chair.

"I didn't sleep around." Paige defended herself. "Only a couple college guys before Davis came along, and we moved in together in Buckhead."

"That's it? You're, what? Twenty something?"

"Twenty-six."

"By your age, I must have had a dozen lovers come and gone." Cookie stared off in thought. "More. It was a different time back then. No Snapchat, Twitter, Swiper, or anything like that. Free love. Now it's all digital, isn't it?"

They both held to their mugs, silent for a moment. Then Cookie asked, "So what happened in Buckhead?"

Paige explained how Davis had been upset about missing out on a vacation with pals when she lost her job and how he had then confessed to having no marriage intentions, blaming it on her college debt. "I was packing up to move out when I thought he was coming around. He said, 'Don't move out now.' I stopped packing and asked why not. He had the nerve to say the game was about to start! The jerk."

"I would have kicked him," Cookie shared.

"We Southern girls don't kick. I stomped on his foot…accidentally." She got Cookie laughing at that. "You know the sad part of it all? When I asked if he ever loved me, you know what he said?"

Cookie shook her head.

Paige mimicked Davis's voice with only the slightest hurt to the words, "'Course I love you, bae. We all do.' Like I was just part of his fraternity and some vapid replaceable girl. *Greerster*, as they usually called him, worried more about sport scores and going out with the group than being with me. And…"

Cookie listened. Her sympathetic eyes encouraged Paige to continue.

"…and I guess I let him. I think I liked the idea of being with someone, especially someone my brothers and family liked. I wonder if I really understood or connected with him. He wasn't ever right for me, was he?"

Cookie seemed to let the thought sink in. She looked up at Paige with sincerity pouring from her and shook her head. "No. Or at least it doesn't sound like he was *the one*… I could joke with you and tell you to make up for lost time. That's not you, is it? Just that, whatever is happening with you and Mr. Mc Handsome upstairs, that might be special. My eyes don't lie to me about the chemistry you two share. He's a rare breed. One of the good ones, I suspect. Maybe you two…well, who knows."

Cookie shook out of whatever deep thought she had. "Anyway, shoo, Paige. Go kiss that new man of yours and have yourself some fun. Let Atlanta slide to the past."

Paige rose, took a few steps, then came back and hugged Cookie. "You're a good woman."

"Don't let that get around. And here." Cookie dug in the fridge and handed Paige a simple sandwich and a granola bar from the counter. "Doubt anybody's making deliveries with this weather. In case you and birthday boy miss lunch—make that, I hope you miss lunch."

Paige would make sure she did. She ran up the stairs, not fleeing from something but running toward something. She still stumbled, though, on the thick stripy socks, completely forgetting her shoes.

Chapter Six

Perhaps being bolstered by her conversation in the kitchen or just seeing Michael, Paige's heart raced as she entered the room. He had his headphones on and was working at the desk on the far side wall, staring at his laptop. The wind picked up outside again, leaving a burnish of ice coating the windows facing the street. His profile was lit, revealing his strong cheekbones, long nose, and firm chin. He was masculine with an authentic Native American air to him, something that made her want to touch him.

She put down the meager lunch and tiptoed up to him, approaching from behind and reached over him. She nuzzled into his neck, slid her hands languidly down his arms, and drawled, "Happy Birthday, Groundhog Man!" She placed a loud kiss on his cheek with a "Mwwah," and pulled back.

Only then did she see the image on his computer screen of a board room full of people dressed in corporate attire. The people were laughing, and from the closeness of his earpiece, she could hear chuckles and a few comments.

"Oh, it's Michael's birthday."

"Happy birthday."

One of the men snickered and called him Groundhog Man.

Paige cringed.

Michael tried to keep to the point, but she felt him stiffen. And not in a good way. "Okay, thank you. Just wanted to make sure all of you were awake with that diversion."

The man at the head of the table spoke with a booming voice, loud enough that Paige heard him through the earpiece, though she had ducked out of view. "Let's review to make sure the rollout goes smoothly. Need to keep this *grounded* and don't want to *hog* up any more of your time."

The board room joined the man in light laughter.

Paige's cheeks burned with embarrassment. Michael's coloring flared, too. She mouthed "sorry" before grabbing her cell phone and running from the room.

What had she done? She had no idea, but she knew to hustle out of harm's way and fast. Having two older brothers taught her that long ago.

Michael's coat was hanging downstairs and her shoes were tossed nearby, but without her purse and wallet, she had to stay put. The snowfall with whipping gusts confirmed it. The soft settee looked inviting in what appeared to be a parlor or living room of sorts filled with ornate pieces, carved flourishes on furniture, and a beautiful fireplace. It was empty. This would be her new hideaway while Michael finished his work. She hoped he had a sense of humor. His workplace seemed to at least. Hopefully, it was still his workplace after the little show she'd accidentally put on. Thank heavens she'd had on clothes.

Gripping her charged phone, she turned it on for the first time since her grueling car ride from Atlanta. Nine voice messages, fourteen texts, and she wasn't going to even think about emails. First, she sent texts to her mother and aunt, telling of the delay due to the storm and that she was safe in a friendly bed and breakfast. Assuming the roads were clear, she expected to reach her aunt the next day at her grandparents' home. She added a second text to her mom and said she loved her and not to tell Dad yet. She also reminded her not to let Davis know where she was as they had both agreed.

The fun part started as she listened to the voice messages. The first one was from Davis. It almost tugged at her heart strings when he'd begged her to come back only to have him say something of her taking the laundry. Delete. Voice messages from Davis continued.

"Hey there, Paigey. I know you are working off steam because you lost your job. So, uh, take your time. But think about heading back soon. Next month's rent is due in a week—"

Delete. The next one, too. Not to mention she hated being called "Paigey." They only got better.

"You took the lamp! I liked that lamp. I know you bought it, but it goes with the other furniture pieces you bought. You should—"

Delete. She was not about to hear what she should do.

"So, I texted you and you aren't answering. Not so cool. I'm not sure what the lock thing on the dishwasher is and where the soap goes. At least you could—"

Delete with a giggle. She'd explained that to him so many times. He always had played dumb so he didn't have to do chores. Serves him right. The next message was priceless.

"I get it. You left and took your clothes without sorting or folding mine. You took my sweatshirt. You know the one you bought for me but wore because I didn't like it? That's okay I guess. But my jersey? My favorite lucky jersey? I need that for Sunday if my team's gonna win. Come back and bring my jersey with you, Paige, or I will call your parents."

Her laughter turned silent at the part about her parents. "Jerk. Idiot. Pig."

Thankfully, the next message was from her mother.

"Honey, the lug your brothers and father like called. I deflected him, saying I knew you'd disappeared. When he complained about some god-awful friggin' jersey, excuse my French, I told him you must have taken it because it reminded you of him. I told him to be strong and to look up how to run the dishwasher and washing machines on YouTube. Honestly, I don't know how you took care of that baby for so long. Then again, your father wasn't much better in the beginning. Speaking of which, he's heading home. Gotta rush. Remember to exercise. Love you."

The next voice message was from Chrissy. Odd. She was the blondest but hadn't been the friendliest of their buddies, at least not to Paige. She had the thickest most insincere drawl.

"I'm here now with Davis, and he seems very upset, Paige. Not nice of you to run off. I'm making him dinner. He is such a sweet guy. I don't understand you. Not to mention, you seemed to have taken his favorite pan of yours. You could have left that—"

Delete.

"Oooh. Jerk. Idiot. The whole lot of them," Paige

said to the wall clock.

"Called your home. Your mom answered and said she didn't know where you were. Your dad is traveling. Did you go with him? Tell him I'm sorry to upset him… Can he still give me those tickets he promised?"

Delete. Texts were next. The first text she didn't delete.

At least we should talk, when you're ready.

Then more texts followed.

Will you come back if I tell you I'll think about marrying you? That's what JoJo, Stan's fiancé said. She might be right. Talk to me when you are ready.

"Really? Absolutely unbelievable," Paige told the fireplace. She read the next text aloud as if telling a story, and answered it as she went. "'Miss you, Paige. You're probably just at Cailey's since she won't talk to anyone.' Wrong, she's away on business overseas. 'I get it. You are punishing me for something.' Wrong, again. Leaving you because we don't fit."

There, she said it. No matter what happened with Groundhog Man. The truth just slipped out. She and Davis didn't fit. Not now and not with each other. She paused and shifted, letting it all sink in. She finally made it to the last text from Davis.

Called your oldest brother and told him that you were pouting off somewhere and told him to send you back along with all the items needed, especially my jersey.

At that, Paige stood up and started to pace to work off steam. She kept saying things aloud, taking a few steps between each. "Never going to see that jersey again." Pacing steps on the antique Persian carpet. "Do your own wash." Stomping steps. "What a Jerk." Fast stomping steps. "Idiot…jerk. Jerk who's an idiot." Paige stopped walking and stared at the settee. "What was I thinking? Not even that great in bed it turns out!"

"Whoa." Groundhog Man stepped into the room wide-eyed at the revelations she spewed to the parlor furniture. Heated, she swallowed hard, but instead of backing down from her tirade, she doubled down. Holding up her phone, she brandished it. "He's a jerk! An idiot. A baby who needs his jersey blankie and doesn't even know how to care for himself."

"Uh, and the bad in bed part…your ex and not…" He pointed to himself and shook his head with a grin.

"No, not you. But then how would I know if we only did it once?" At that, her face flamed as it did so frequently near him.

"C'mon, Flee." He took her hand. "You can continue your tirade and explain it all to the furniture upstairs. I think the parlor heard enough."

"We all did," called Mr. Hager from the other room. "Glad to know you aren't bad in bed though, Michael."

Groundhog Man laughed. "Thanks. Practice makes perfect."

"Nice warning. I'm putting on the music…loud."

Paige followed Michael upstairs, leaving behind his coat, her shoes, and her frustrations. They had some practicing to do.

Chapter Seven

As soon as the door closed, Groundhog Man clicked the lock and moved to Paige. The sound of the lock signaled something inside her. With it, she knew what was coming but momentarily froze at the realization.

Michael didn't. His hands slid down her arms as his gaze locked on hers. One hand quietly reached for hers, pulling the cellphone out of her hand and putting it on the side table.

"What about—"

He did not let her finish her sentence and kissed her.

"Mmmfff."

He kissed her again, silencing her. Then his hand slid around her waist under the cashmere sweater. He pulled her tighter to him, walking her backward to the bed. He caressed her supple skin while his lips parted, tongue pressing deep into her mouth. The kiss burned heated need into her. His fingers reached to her makeshift ponytail, holding her open mouth to his, kissing her more deeply. Her arms moved around him, hesitations long since melted away. She returned the fire of his hunger, grinding into him, moaning.

He whispered, "You were saying?"

"Was I?" Her voice came out foggy.

He nodded slowly, letting go of her, and sat on the

bed, patting the mattress with that luring smile. "But first, aren't you too warm?" He motioned to her clothing.

It was her turn to smile and nod. She pulled his borrowed sweater over her head, slightly loosening her make-shift braid in the process. His locked, heated gaze urged her to continue. She unbuttoned her blouse, and that fell from her shoulders landing on top of the sweater. The hazy daylight of the winter storm shined on her tanned skin. He reached out, pulling her to sit on the bed. His warm hand slid around her back.

"Are your calls and meetings done, Groundhog Man…Michael?"

"Yes. For now, it's just me, you, this room…" He kissed her neck. "That storm…" His hand inched back around, fingers spread wide as he touched her stomach. "And something that needs attending to. After all, it's February 2nd…"

"I already told you happy birthday, but that didn't go so well."

"Care to try again?" He undid the dental floss tie to her hair and shook the braid free, running his fingers through her hair. "Lucky for you, I am a forgiving man…eventually. Mmmmmm."

He kissed her lower on her shoulder, fingers dipping to the edge of her bra.

Paige tugged the sweater off his body and added it to the pile of discarded clothing. She undid two buttons of his shirt, but he stopped her.

"Happy birthday?" She kissed his nose. "Better?"

He shook his head. She straddled him in her jeans and bra, unbuttoned one more of his buttons, and looked at him. One of his eyebrows raised up.

She leaned and whispered, "Happy birthday." She kissed his cheek. "Better?"

"Closer."

She finished unbuttoning his shirt, ran her palms under his, across his taut chest, and kissed him slowly on the lips, drawing his body to hers. "Happy birthday, Groundhog Man. Too bad I don't have a gift for you."

"You don't?" His hands skimmed down her back and landed on her jean bottoms.

"Ice." Kiss. "Snow." Kiss. "No chance to even buy you a cake. Did bring a sandwich though."

"I noticed. It was from Cookie for after." He groaned, rocking her against his throbbing bulge.

Her eyes rolled closed, and she murmured, "After?"

"Mmm hmm. After we warm up the bed. I have an idea for a gift. How about you take my birthday spanking for me." His hand softly lifted and landed on her unsuspecting ass with a pop. He repeated the toying swat with his other hand on her other cheek."

"But it's *your* birthday. I should be spanking you."

He shook his head. "The way I see it, Flee, you owe me a gift, not to mention recompense for that earlier little event during my video conference…"

Light tap, tap.

"It was a warm greeting," she countered.

He pulled her in and kissed her with a sudden, poignant deep open-mouthed need. It took her by surprise and sent her reeling. Mmm. She returned the kiss, and tendrils of longing flew through her as she unconsciously rubbed her pussy into his crotch, the seam stitching poised perfectly.

"You'd do it? Take a spanking as your birthday gift

to me?"

"Mmm hmm," she replied in a heady trance.

He smiled, and before she knew what was happening, he spun her, angling her so her face was resting on a pillow on the bed and she was ass up across his lap. He leaned over her, hand rubbing her back. "I'll go easy, Flee. Relax and hold the pillow."

Paige twisted. "I don't know about this."

"Shh, just relax. If it gets too much, just say…what was that stuffed animal? Hedgehog?"

"Hedgy."

"Okay, say, Hedgy. But don't say it mid-set of strokes. Okay?" Before she could say anything, he continued, "Let's see, I'm thirty-one and one to grow on."

"What about the four already?"

"Thirty-three it is. No more complaints."

Tap. Tap. Tap. Rub. Tap. Tap. Tap. Rub.

He barely touched her with each patting stroke. More playful than anything. As the patterned repeated, Paige relaxed and wriggled her bottom to his touches.

"Not bad, is it?" he asked, his voice low and lusty.

"Not at all."

"Uh oh."

"Uh oh?"

"I lost count, Flee. Let's start again."

"Hey!" The pattern of tap, tap, tap and rub to each cheek through her jeans repeated. Paige didn't complain that his swats became slightly firmer than the previous light pats.

"How about we take your jeans off?"

"Okay." Paige climbed to her feet. "But that was eighteen. No pretending you lost count again." She pulled off her jeans, blushing when she realized she was without underwear. She stood before him in her bra and his socks, hands hiding her lower parts.

His eyebrows shot up, and his eyes glazed over.

She shrugged. "My undies are in my iced-in car. Didn't think yours would work on me."

He drew her into him and kissed her again, then helped her back across his lap. It became clear to her that her lack of panties was working well on him as his cock stiffened under her belly. One hand rubbed her ass, and one roamed up her back, relaxing her.

He paused and built the anticipation by molding her cheeks in his hands. She wriggled against the warmth of his experienced touch.

Suddenly, a firmer tap landed. Tap. Rub. Firmer tap, tap. Rub. His hand raised higher, coming down playfully but with an edge. Smack, smack. Pause. Smack.

"Hey." Paige squirmed, kicking her sock-covered feet before the next stinging smack landed.

Groundhog Man sighed. "Flee, I told you not to interrupt the set. Now, we were at eighteen."

"No, no, no. We were at twenty-two."

"Okay twenty-two, but we go straight through then. No stopping. Hold on. Here goes."

Whether it was the warning or that she was naked bottomed across his lap, Paige's heart raced and something odd was happening inside her. Her breathing huffed in little gulped gasps as his strokes began. The firmness of each landing smack was randomized as was the spot, until he hit three in a row with a *thwack*.

"Yowww." Paige kicked, reached back, and rubbed herself, surprised not to feel heat on her cheeks.

"Oh Flee, you were so close."

"That one stung."

"A lot?" His hands rubbed and kneaded her thighs softly.

Silence. "No, actually."

"Good. Not my intention, Flee. We need to redo the last ten, okay?" To urge a yes from her, his hand moved between her legs, cupping her pussy. He groaned as he squeezed her there.

"Ohh." Paige moaned.

"Sounds like a yes to me, but I'm warm." He helped her stand. He disrobed completely and turned down the bed covers. She took in the full view of him. Smooth olive skin across his sculpted chest. Toned body without being overdone. He gave no protest to her stare but nodded to her bra. She unhooked it and added it to the stack of clothes. He looked down at the socks she wore questioningly. She just smiled and shook her head. He laughed and pulled her back over his naked lap, his distended cock more than a distraction.

"Here goes, Flee. Ready?"

She nodded.

He waited.

Her breathing deepened.

He still waited.

"Yes. I'm ready. Ready for your birthday spankings."

"Good. Remember to keep it quiet." His fingers brushed between her legs.

"I wasn't that noisy...ouch!" Her head went to the pillow. He did random hard thwacks interspersed with the light smacks, building speed and intensity. Her legs kicked up, and the fire somehow shot deep inside her core. Nerve cells ignited, sending unexpected tingles quivering into her belly. The heat of her skin pulsed through her. Not fully understanding why, she was wet and desperately ached for something. That something was his thick cock inside her.

Without a moment's hesitation, he turned her over onto her back on the bed. His warm hands cupped her achingly swollen breasts, kneading as he kissed and nibbled his way to her nipples. She was crazed with need, drawing his head to her soft flushed skin, encouraging his touches and bites.

His smooth, strong hand rubbed down her belly and finally reached the juncture of her thighs. She wriggled toward his touch. Slowly, teasingly, his fingers brushed her small trimmed patch in front of her mound. She was in anguish for relief. His mouth smothered her lips with a fiery kiss at the same moment his fingers tugged a nipple. Then and only then, did Michael slide two fingers to her mound, opening her and sinking into her achingly wet core.

She cried out with a shudder. A dam broke loose inside her. His hungry lips stifled the noise but not the frenzied bucking of her hips. She squeezed and rode his fingers, begging him.

"Please," was all she could mouth.

"Please what?" Michael teased.

"Please take me, Michael. Drive up deep into me."

With her begging need voiced, he pulled his fingers from her with a lustfully glazed smile and shifted enough to reach for a condom. He bit it open.

Paige's breathing was nothing more than ragged gulps, chest rising with each gasped breath. He barely had the condom on his rigid cock before she pulled him to her. She was raw with need for him and he for her.

Michael sank into her wet pussy, driving almost fully into her as her legs wrapped around him. Fire shot through her instantly. She convulsed around him but wanted even more. She was frantic, biting his neck and bucking up to meet his colliding stroke. And the next. And the next. Raw hungry lust poured out of her and was met equally by Michael.

His rocking pulse became a fast frenzy, his hands interlocking with hers. Then he pulled out nearly all the way and kissed her. "Look at me, Flee."

She nodded, her eyes opened wide.

"Ohh…Flee…my sweet Paige." He called out her name in a long drawn out song. With that, he drove into her, hard and deep.

Everything surged within her, and she exploded with him, her mouth open, her back arching, her body shaking, gripping…so lost. She willed her eyes open and gave voice to her release in a wailing, "Ahhhhh, Michael!"

His mouth moved to hers, unable to quiet his own grunting cry.

Eventually, their breathing slowed and the waves pulsing through Paige trailed off.

With a final shudder, he brought her with him as he rolled to his back, enfolding her to the crook of his arm. "Wow."

"Uh huh," Paige answered, breathless. Neither spoke. Neither quipped. For a time, the only sound was the ice pellets occasionally hitting the window.

The clock radio cut the peaceful lull with a shout, "I got you, Babe!"

She laughed, and his chest shook with a chuckle

against her.

They didn't move to turn off the song right away, neither wanting to break the moment. Eventually, his hand reached over to hit the button. Eventually, the cover was pulled over them. Eventually, they twisted together in a wordless cuddle.

Paige sighed, nuzzling into Groundhog Man. He kissed her forehead, actions speaking louder than words, as they rested.

Chapter Eight

"Hello?" Paige said to her cellphone. The ringing didn't stop. She put down her phone and hit a button on the clock radio. Still ringing. She shook Groundhog Man. "Yours."

In response, he turned and pulled her to him. "Mmmmmm. Mine. Best birthday present."

She tried to pull free. "No. Your cell keeps ringing. Is it important?"

That stirred him awake, and he padded naked to the desk. She leaned up in bed. Her eyes followed him, still taking in the fact that he was her... Even in her thoughts, she didn't dare say lover.

The sun was still up, such that it was, overshadowed by clouds. Early evening? She heard him clicking on his cell.

Groundhog Man stood nude talking on the phone as he looked at Paige. "Hey, Cuz. Heard you called. Yeah, we were busy. I mean I was busy..." He grimaced at the laugh that must have come from the other end of the call. "Can't believe you completely shoveled out her car. Perfect birthday present."

Groundhog Man smiled and gave Paige a thumbs up.

"You the man! Yeah, I agree, would have been easier if we waited a day, but she... Uh huh. Yup, we need to move it to the garage so it won't be ticketed and towed. Hey, is *Sizzle* open tonight?" He waited for the answer. "Then what is? Uh huh. Yes, that Indian place. More of a college hangout, but the food is great. Wait, let me put you on speaker."

"Hey there, Miss Breakup Special. So, you and Cuz are getting along? How's his—" *Cough.* "—listening skills?"

"My skills are fine. Any more from you and I might not treat you to a free dinner."

"All right, Cuz." Alfie said. "Hold your horses or whatever you're holding. I'm taking you up on dinner, but only if I can bring a girlfriend, too."

"Girlfriend? You're gay."

"So's he. Meet us down by the car in fifteen."

"Too soon. I need to get ready," Paige interjected, rising out of bed and sorting through clothing.

"Honey, I'm starved, and dressing to impress is something you don't need to do with me. You were such a depressed lump yesterday. You can't possibly look worse," Alfie said over Michael's phone.

Michael inhaled and let out a deep groan. "I can attest that she looks mighty fine as she is."

Paige rolled her eyes. She held a random pile of clothing.

"She just needs to bundle up a bit more."

She started to throw on clothing.

"You're both naked, aren't you?" Alfie said. "Birthday or no, please hustle. I'm starved from all that excavating and shoveling."

Click.

"I'm starved, too, and I didn't do any lifting," Michael announced. "Well, not too much."

That earned him a face full of clothing.

****

With sidewalks only half cleared, Paige and Michael rushed to meet Alfie, opting to sometimes walk in the streets. The wind was milder now, and Michael was happier wearing his coat this time. Paige was smarter this time, too. She wore layers, borrowing his sweater and hoodie, which was long enough to look almost skirt-like under her jacket. Her shoes barely fit over the thick fresh socks she stole from him. Her hair was twisted in a knot, which she pinned up with a binder clip, all temporarily hidden under the hoodie.

As they approached her car, her pace quickened, making her slide on slick pavement. She didn't fall, though, with Michael holding her arm.

"My car, my clothes, my things!" she drawled thickly.

"My arm! One more near spill and you will be twisting my arm off."

"Sorry." The apology came with a giggle.

After a commotion of greetings and plans for who should drive—Paige since the seat couldn't be pushed back more—and who navigated—Alfie since he was thin, could hold the boxes, and still squeeze in the front seat—they began the process of rocking the car free from the diagonal parking spot. With a shove from the three men, it finally backed up. Alfie piled in, precariously. Paige sat determined but white knuckled at the wheel.

"See you two at the restaurant and don't forget the wine, Cuz!"

"Hey, I thought it was your turn," Michael called out.

Alfie pretended not to hear. "Quick, drive, Paige."

"Which way?"

"Right. Left. No. Just go."

With fumbled directions and finally locating a spot in the garage a few blocks away, Paige parked. She rifled through her car, grabbed a small bag, and stuffed in a few items.

"I know you need your things, Paige honey, especially to change out of whatever the hell this is you're wearing, but trust me, you are overdressed for dinner, and if we don't go soon, I will eat whatever the heck I am holding here."

"Hedgy."

"Hedgy?"

"You're holding my stuffed animal from when I was little. I think it might be a hedgehog, and when my brother—"

"Honey, that story needs to be shut down." Alfie closed and locked the door, pulling her in the direction of the restaurant.

"Oh, save it for later?"

He shook his head. "How about save it for someone else."

Paige laughed. "Poor Hedgy. Nobody wants to hear his story."

"I can think of many other stories I would love to hear though. Especially ones involving a certain birthday boy and you. Hope you two are playing nice, because I don't shovel for just anybody. Walk faster, girl. That's my stomach growling."

"Is that what I heard? Seemed kind of windy."

"I plead the fifth."

****

The restaurant might have had simple décor, but

the food was divine. The four of them sat at a square table, boy-boy, girl-girl with the red headed waiter from *Sizzle* playing the part of the other girl, or so he had said.

"Call me Red," Alfie's friend had explained to Paige when they'd first settled in.

"With a name like Rutherford, you have to," Alfie added.

Red blushed, his face all the more crimson against his carrot-red hair. Michael was about to speak. Red cut him off. "Before you ask, the carpet matches the drapes."

"I was just going to ask you to pass the pitcher of water, but good to know."

Several dishes were ordered, all meant to be shared. Naan bread came early at Alfie's pleading, but all shared in the gobbling of the warm bread, so much so, that another one was ordered. Michael produced two bottles of wine to choose from, both with funny names—If You See Kay and Big Red, which had a picture of two roosters and the word "cock" hidden in red.

"I picked them out," Red announced.

"I get the bottle with the cocks, but what's with the biker chick on the other?" Alfie asked.

"Read the label out loud twice and fast." All four laughed at the sounded-out explicative the words produced. Both bottles were opened and even shared with a table close at hand.

"Time for Twenty Questions, starting with Birthday Boy," Red suggested after several gulps of wine.

"We'll be here all night. How 'bout a few

questions directed to each instead," Groundhog Man suggested.

After a quickly bantered negotiation, the plan landed on six questions each, with the ability to plead the fifth on one question and to start with basic questions first. Groundhog Man had only one older married brother. When asked, Paige divulged that she had two siblings, both older brothers, so she knew how to fight and when to run.

Dishes were passed. The tandoori chicken landed on Paige's plate twice. "What? I told you I had older brothers. This is seriously delicious chicken. Didn't anybody else have brothers or sisters growing up?"

"Yoo hoo. I did. I had an older sister," offered Red. "Who else could I steal makeup from?" He continued between bites of curried vegetables. "And I didn't just use the makeup for dolling up. I needed to hide the bruises when I got beaten up in high school. Daddy would never have understood."

Paige dropped her fork. Alfie and Michael swallowed hard.

"That's terrible." Paige reached for his hand.

He pulled his hand away, leaving her unsure what to do next until she noticed he wiped his hand on his napkin and returned it, giving hers a squeeze. "It's all right, honey. What doesn't kill you makes you great at makeup."

She couldn't help but laugh, the others joining in the relief Red just allowed them to have.

"I thought it made you stranger—I mean stronger," Alfie added with a chuckle.

"Same difference. Besides, I learned to live with the hard stuff." Red was the first to laugh at his own double entendre. He then turned to Paige. "Okay, my turn to ask. Full name, worst and best nicknames ever."

Michael leaned in. His amber eyes interested and focused on Paige.

"Amelia Paige Myers, but everyone calls me Paige. That's partly because of the nickname I hated. Amelia Squealia." That brought chuckles, and one oink from the group. "Wrong kind of squeal. I was sort of a tag-along to my older brothers when I was little. I guess when things got too rough, I would run off and tell Daddy on them." She paused. "As for my best nickname…Flee," she said, looking at Groundhog Man.

Michael's hand travelled to her leg.

"Like the creepy biting thing?" Red looked repulsed.

"Flee as in run away or maybe run toward? Is that too corny?" By now, she was blushing again, heat from his hand on her adding fuel to the embers.

Michael picked up her hand and kissed it.

Red sighed. "Honestly, too bad your cuz is into heteroville. He's just my type."

"Dark haired, handsome-ish?"

"No. Male." Both Alfie and Red laughed, their gazes locked and holding long enough for the laugh to drift to a smile, a warm assessing smile. Red was the first to break eye contact. "My turn to ask this Groundhog Man a question."

"Mo, it's mot," Paige tried to say, finishing a mouthful of food heavy with sauce that produced a fire in her mouth. She grabbed her water.

"Ask him a tough one," Alfie said.

Paige took a big swallow of water, losing her chance to do the asking.

Red stared at Groundhog Man and asked, "Why did you break up with your ex? What happened there?"

"Oooohh jugular," Alfie said.

"You can plead the fifth. Alfie did earlier," Paige offered, fanning her mouth.

"When?"

"Parking lot," Paige reminded him. "That kind of gas doesn't come from cars."

"She's right. We all got to let it out sometime," Alfie said with a laugh. "So, Cuz, you pleading or letting us have it?"

"I'll answer."

"Oh, goodie. He's going to let us all have it, not just you, sweetie." Red patted Flee's shoulder. She nearly spat out her bite of *tandori*.

"Ahem."

They looked at Michael, Paige in rapt attention.

Michael took a swallow of wine. "Susan, my ex and almost fiancé, was a corporate manager, an exec of sorts, and older than me by a few years. I was smitten by her. She taught me plenty, but she was always what Oneida call 'a'e', you know, distant in some way. We were together for a while—"

"I'll say," his cousin interjected.

"One day," Michael continued, looking everywhere but at Paige, "she just announced she was going to take a job in Europe within two weeks. Not an assignment or trip. A position. No discussion. She welcomed me to follow. Looking back, it all happened so fast and unilaterally. Just when I called her to say I thought I could make a transfer work out, she told me it was all right, don't. She'd already moved on. So, I didn't break it off. I was dumped, big time, and over the phone."

71

Paige's jaw dropped. She tried to process what Michael had divulged. Before she could offer any sympathy, Red spoke up, "That's not big time. Heard lots worse. Remember Tranny Franny?"

"Who?" Alfie asked, looking confused.

"You know, the one who wore the whole Fran what's-her-face outfit for the Bouffant Blow Out party at *Sizzle*? Fran…Fran Dress-Her—"

"Oh yeah. Had the whole New Yaawwk accent down, too."

"Well, she got pissed off and dumped him right on stage in the middle of her act. Franny took her wig off and threw it at him, too. Hurt him. Who knew she had a jar holding up the whole bee hive? Anyway, sounds like this ah-eh…ah-ay whatever…distant thing Susan bitchy exec had, well, she wasn't right for you and you didn't even have a jar-filled, smelly wig thrown at you."

There was a pregnant pause at the table.

Alfie laughed first and raised his wine glass. "Here's to wigless endings."

They clinked and sipped.

"Mmm. Here's to If You See Kay wine," Michael added.

They clinked, some chugged.

"Here's to exes staying exes," Paige offered and swallowed hard after the clink, thinking of how it also applied to her. Michael looked right at Paige for the toast and took an extra sip.

They returned to their plates. Perhaps it was the building heat from the wine, along with the spice from the food, but Paige chose that moment to remove another layer of clothing, tugging off her borrowed hoodie, and shifted Michael's sweater into place. Forks stopped mid-air.

She looked at them and drew her hand to her face, patting it, feeling for crumbs. "Uh, is there something I should know?"

"What on God's green earth is that thing on your head, girl?" Alfie demanded.

Michael just held back his laughter, eating a mouthful of *biryani*. He held up his hands in innocence.

She reached up and squeezed the twisted hair knob on top of her head. It was roughly the size of a tennis ball, held together with the makeshift clip. "It's my hair twist-knob. You said hurry so up my hair went."

"Well, dial it down. Did they teach you nothing in the South?"

Red came to her defense. "Oh, I get the whole updo thing, but a binder clip?"

"Well, I nevah…" Paige put on her thickest drawl and biggest smile as she stood up. "No touching my *Khuza*-whatever dumplings or chicken *pandoor*-hooey while I'm gone. Gentlemen, if you will excuse me." She turned and sashayed to the bathroom, feeling their gazes follow her.

She returned with her thick hair twisted up in the back, still held by the binder clip with the ends bouncing as she walked. "Better?"

All three men mumbled something, heads down, staring at their food.

"What did I miss? Hey, I'm down all three dumplings. We Southern women take dumplings seriously. Who stole them?"

Each of them pointed to the other. Michael uncharacteristically squirreled food in his cheeks and gave her a smile she gladly returned. She did a double take and eyed him suspiciously. He did not, however, return the last bite of dumpling.

Wine glasses were filled once more. Eventually, their bellies were, too.

Paige, while not behaving daintily, still attempted some decorum, even when Groundhog Man's hands touched hers or when his leg *accidentally* rubbed against hers for a few minutes. His reassuring touches were as welcome as their delicious meal.

When Twenty Questions continued, Alfie admitted his dad kicked him out when he found out he was gay. Alfie had moved in with Michael, who took care of him even when his now ex-girlfriend objected to having another person around. "The only bad part about living with this guy here was that he refused to share his clothes for any reason."

Paige smoothed her hand over the soft cashmere of Michael's sweater that she was wearing and saw him in a new light. Michael had loaned his clothes to her without any fuss. He took her in, expending effort on her. Not only that, he cared for Alfie. Really cared for him and took his own generosity in stride.

She let the conversation flow around her, barely listening as she studied Michael. There was a depth of concern and pride when he looked at Alfie and even Red. He was just supposed to be a rebound, but all of it made him more alluring. He was an adult. A caring, very masculine, very hot, adult.

His hand patted her leg again. The simple gesture of his touch jarred her from her wandering thoughts. A familiar warmth rushed up to her face, and she rejoined the group's discussion.

Red had been speaking. "We all learn from our

past even from that bitch, Susan. Excuse me, *executive* bitch. Michael, you must have learned a lot from her." He crooked an eyebrow to make sure the double meaning wasn't lost.

Alfie laughed.

"What? I meant business acumen, board room behavior," Red falsely corrected himself.

Paige turned to Michael with a questioning expression.

He shrugged. "Maybe. I don't quarterly report and tell."

Laughter continued as they lingered at the table.

In the next lull to the conversation, Paige said, out of the blue, "I'm going to miss calling you Groundhog Man after today." She stared at her plate, toying with her leftover food. Not ready for the evening to end, she began to mindlessly build something on her plate using the rice and bread.

"Don't worry, honey. You can call him that every year," Red blurted out, followed by, "Ouch. What? They look cute together is all. This here girl was just giving them a teensy shove."

"Don't put him on the spot. He's paying for dinner," Alfie corrected with a smile.

Red nodded. "Right." He triple-snapped his fingers with sass. "Bitch, you be done calling him names after today. Cute cake though." He indicated Paige's plate "Love what you did with the naan, curry rice, and that green stuff. Capsicum I think they called it."

"Really there's a food called cum?" Alfie interjected. "Even I don't want to touch that line."

They all looked at what Paige had created. She had stacked the extra naan bread, over the last of the rice, making it look like a miniature cake. She pushed it to Michael. "Happy birthday, Groundhog Man."

"We need a candle," Red announced.

The manager found one and put it into the mini-naan cake, adding impetus for a loud and off-key rendition of the birthday song. Others in the restaurant joined in. Michael blew out the candle.

"What did you wish for?" Alfie asked.

"He can't tell you, or it won't come true," Red huffed.

"It already did. You are all here with me," Groundhog Man said.

"Eww...now I am going to be sick," his cousin said, rolling his eyes.

"Ex-nay . on the complain-ay. He's paying for dinner, remember-ay?" Red reminded Alfie.

"I meant awwwww..." Alfie corrected and offered to cut the cake.

"Wait, let's get some photos first." The candle was re-lit and selfies taken with the four of them. They quickly shifted, traded phones, retaking and forwarding photos, including one where Michael was puffy-cheeked, as if he had a hard time blowing out his candle. The last two photos were with just Groundhog Man and Flee.

Alfie cut the cake and placed tiny slices on their plates. They ooh'ed and aah'ed over the bits as if it were the finest birthday cake. The bill was paid, goodbyes were said, and they stood outside the restaurant door.

"Hard to believe," Alfie said to Paige, "that just over twenty-something hours ago, you plopped down at my table, a depressed mess, and now look at you. Well, apart from the caught-in-a-storm fashion thing, you're all glowing. Am I good at this Breakup Special thing or what?"

"Right, like it's all *your* doing," Groundhog Man said as he gave his cousin a bro-hug.

"So glad you admit it." Alfie waved and left with red-headed Rutherford, arms linked.

Chapter Nine

The wind picked up. A fitting end to the Groundhog Day storm. Paige and Michael headed back to the bed and breakfast, carrying her small bag of gathered possessions, a wine bag, and some antacids. They walked happily but quickly past darkened shops, dodging a puddle ringed with ice.

"What a perfect evening," Groundhog Man exclaimed.

A truck turned the corner and splashed them with salty, cold ice.

"You were saying?" Paige tried to brush off her clothing, which was covered with chunks of gray ice, embedded with dirt and street salt.

"I was saying, what a perfect evening…for a hot shower." He laughed despite the fact his overcoat was now in serious need of dry cleaning.

Her response was to pull him to her by his splattered coat lapels. She kissed the smile right off of his face. "Race you."

****

For the second evening in a row, Michael and Paige entered the bed and breakfast in the dark. For the second time, they hung wet coats and scarves in the appointed location, taking over the empty hooks. For the second time, they kicked off their wet shoes and onto the boot tray. This time, though, they both rushed up to the room, without any nervous anticipation. Just anticipation.

As soon as he unlocked the door, she ran past him into the room, quickly shedding her bag and clothing. He simply locked the door, undid his pants, and unhurriedly removed his clothing under the dim light of one side lamp, watching her. The faster she tried, the more she fumbled, tugging at her jeans.

"You're distracting me," she said with a giggle but was still the first into the bathroom. She struggled and tugged at the binder clip twisted in her hair. Entering the room, he reached behind her and deftly unclipped it, tossing it aside.

"You may be in the bathroom first again," he said, his voice deepening as he continued. "The difference tonight is, I'm joining you."

He pushed the door closed with a click and countered her light-hearted air from the race with a methodical determination. He was simmering with something different, something more sensual and pulse-building and wanted her to feel it. He moved his arms purposefully around her, pinning her to the closed bathroom door.

He took her lips lightly with his.

"I'm going to touch you, Flee…" He opened his mouth slightly as he nibbled on hers. "All over."

She blushed beet red.

"Mmm…smooth. Your skin is so smooth." Her words followed her hand, moving up his chest and neck.

"Not all of it." Michael rubbed his grizzled chin against her palm when she touched his face. Though his body was relatively hairless, his face was not. He hadn't shaved since the morning. Her gaze settled into the simmer he already felt.

His hands flowed over her. They instinctively knew where to go to pleasure her but teasingly did not as he kissed her, open-mouthed. He leaned onto the door, his weight on one hand. He slid his other hand between their bodies, palm to his stomach so the smooth of the back of his hand brushed her belly. It was ever so slightly distended from the meal they had eaten. He rubbed his chin stubble to her neck and then kissed her roughly. At that moment, he eased his hand upward and gripped her breast.

The soft supple roundness to her breast was perfect. Just the right size. He cupped and squeezed it, unable to resist letting his thumb brush against the nipple. It swelled to his glancing touch. He rolled it between his thumb and finger, watching her close her eyes. He moaned against her ear and heard her breath catch.

Shifting his body even closer to her, he rubbed his belly against her, feeling her soft skin and taut nipples against his bare chest. He reached behind her and grabbed her ass.

Her eyes fluttered open.

"Your pert little ass is cold but not even pink, is it, Flee?" he said after he tipped his head to look behind her. Though it had been so lightly spanked earlier, no signs of reddening remained apart from the flush on her face. He squeezed her cheek, fingers toying close to the center. He kissed her tenderly and felt a shiver roll into her.

She rubbed her bottom against his hand as her hands splayed on his back. He loved the way she massaged the muscles under his shoulder blades. She was pressed against the door for support as he kissed his way down her neck, mouthing and nibbling. Her eyes opened. He followed her gaze and turned to see she had been looking at his ass in the mirror across the room. His legs were spread enough to match closer to her height, giving her more of a show. That brought a smile to his lips, soon to vanish when she kissed him.

He tasted the salt of her skin and mix of the spices left on their pallets from dinner. The scent of tandoori and wine lingered. The luscious tastes and smells added to his hunger.

Her cold-skinned shiver stopped him. He broke from the fire of their embrace.

He blasted the shower, and they stepped in, hot spray hitting their bodies. The warmth of the water sent them to a dreamy, sweeter place. There was almost an innocence to their touches as they actually cleaned each other. The banter of the evening transformed into murmurs, tender exploration, and with it, a newly building sensuality.

His moans were soft and slow as he lathered her hair. He massaged her scalp, letting the lather slide down her neck and back. He watched it, fingers playing with it. He let the water wash the lather from her hair. The creaminess of the conditioner had him pulling closer to her, sliding the gel not just in her hair, which was darkened by the water, but over her breasts, her nipples. Her coo gave voice to her pleasure.

"Flee… You feel wonderful, Paige," he whispered, her nickname and real name interspersed.

"Mmm, you do, too, Michael." She had found a puffy sponge and filled it with a luxurious soap. She turned toward him and drew the sponge down his chest. He relished the feel of the squishing sponge sliding down his front, leaving a trail of eucalyptus-mint scented suds. As she squeezed the spongy loofah, it spilled sudsy water of glistening warmth. It felt erotic. Slow and pulsingly erotic. Each stroke elicited moans from them.

He took the loofah from her, filling it again, and tilted his head. "My turn, Flee." He drew out her name in sigh.

He stood back enough so she couldn't touch him but could only feel the heated spray of the water. Her hands moved to cover her pussy as she faced him. He stepped closer and positioned each of her hands on the corner walls behind her.

He rolled thick suds over the front of her beautifully formed naked body, savoring the sight. He trailed the sponge over her arms, her neck, and down her underarms and sides. Slowly. Carefully, wickedly slowly. He added more soap and washed down her outer legs and up her inner thighs. With a squeeze of the sponge over her mound, the suds intoxicatingly trickled down between her legs and over her clit.

He exhaled at the visual of her soaked body undulating before him. It sent a bolt straight into him, hardening his dick into an almost painful thickness. His balls tightened. He wanted to touch, to taste, to drive into her then and there.

With a groan, her hands flew from the wall to his waist and chest. The sponge dropped to the floor of the shower, and his finger slid deep inside of her tender folds. His tongue plundered inside her mouth with a lust-filled hunger as his finger pulled out and sawed back into her pussy. She responded with a bursting passionate kiss, breaking only to breathe in a deep lungful of eucalyptus-filled air.

"I want to be here," he said. "Deep inside you, Paige."

"Yes. Please. Now. Oh, Michael."

He could tell she was on the edge. Her pussy pulsed with slickness as he touched her. He knew he needed her wet for him to fit inside her, especially since shower water could wash away her own moisture.

Paige scrambled to help him tear the packet he'd placed close at hand. The task was derailed when she took his hardness in her hands and soaped his length. He arched into the wall and her body as she pumped him. Whatever demure shyness she had vanished as she watched her hands move on him.

"Flee…stop…" He pulled her hands from his cock and took several breaths while he unfurled the condom on his throbbing erection.

She looked at him. And he at her. Water cascaded over her front and his back. Time stopped. It was a fraction of a minute, a second, the image emblazed in his memory.

Her moan broke the stillness. He cupped her face and kissed her deeply, one hand pulling her tender body tight to him. Instinctively, her foot rose to the lip of shower ridge, opening herself to him. He rubbed his shaft against her hungry pussy, her own natural moisture only slightly diminished by the flow of water. His other hand never left her face, and the pressure of his grasp pulled her gaze to his.

He gave a questioning tilt to his head. She responded with the tiniest nod. With that, he thrust upward into her. His shaft drove part way into her core.

Her eyes opened wide with her sighed groan. "Oh."

He was controlled. Had to be. Ever so agonizingly slowly, he rocked and moved deeper into her. With each stroke, he moaned in her ear. Her body relaxed and joined in the building rhythm, accommodating him more and more.

"Yes...mmmmmm."

Her coos made him lose just that edge of control. He finally drove all the way in, lodging himself inside her. He kissed and bit her neck, muffling his groan into a growl.

Soon that urgency of raw need propelled him to the lunging strokes he craved. Words were uttered. He thrust deep within her, flesh locked to flesh. She accepted him. More than that, her body pressed skin to skin, rocking again and again. He bucked into her, driving them both to crest of an achingly bursting crescendo. He exploded inside of her with a white-hot eruption, losing any sense of self.

She cried out with a long and visceral cry, her body arched into him and her pussy twitching and clenched tight on him. She shook and nearly fell. He held her until awareness crept back into both of them. Soft kisses caught water from the spray of the showerhead.

"Wow, Flee. If I didn't know better, I would think we need another shower after this."

Paige let out a laugh, breathless, already re-soaping her skin as he did the same, this time washing his own hair.

Their movements were slow and relaxed. They floated, still flushed, they accepted each other's kisses and touching little pecks. He finally turned off the water and helped her step from the shower. She dried herself in long sweeping movements before tucking a fluffy towel around her.

"Hey, Amelia, Squealia, got noisy again, didn't you?" He wrapped himself in the terrycloth robe.

She giggled, suddenly not minding the nickname at all. Maybe that Michael was the one to cause the squealing or simply that coming from him made the nickname more of an endearment. Yep, might have had something to do with it.

Chapter Ten

The sound of the blow-dryer muffled Michael's words when he left the bathroom. Had they ended with something like "love you" or "loved this?" Both rang true, but Paige would not admit that to herself. She stepped from the bathroom, her hair feeling fluffy, returning to its normal fullness. She expected to sink into the bed with him or at least cuddle.

She did not expect what she saw. Groundhog Man grousing, wearing jeans and pulling on a sweater, mumbling about computer failure preventing reports and re-doing something.

"Sorry, Paige. Any chance you can run downstairs and get me a coffee? Looks like a not-so-pleasant birthday surprise."

She didn't object to his having to complete the work late at night. She had been driven like that before and quickly stepped into sidekick mode, something Davis never did for her nor did she ever need to for him. She found a blouse in the bag she'd confiscated from her car but unfortunately, no pants. She reached into his luggage, stole his sweat pants, and rolled up the bottoms.

After a quick trip downstairs, she returned, holding out a large coffee cup. "It might not be too hot. I put milk in it. Hope that's okay."

He said his thanks and gave her the briefest non-inviting smile before returning to the keyboard and swilling the coffee. Though she had already slipped into the velvet chair, he mumbled toward where she previously stood, never taking his eyes from the screen. "Looks like I can't take off all of tomorrow as I'd hoped. Maybe part of it. I need to get this out to circumvent a two-week delay for the team."

"Uh huh. At least you got a shower in. Besides, afterglow's not what it's cracked up to be these days, right?" she teased.

"Right...right, right. Can't believe this crap happened," he said, clicking away, headphones on. Then he swore and his fingers flew. The reflected light from his computer screen showed a mix of frustration and angst on his face. She knew that look. Not from Davis, who was anything but hardworking. She knew that look from her father. It was definitely one that said, "leave me alone." So, she did.

Paige tucked her cold feet under her on the chair and pulled out her cell phone, which she had silenced during dinner. More messages and texts. Didn't they know she was in hiding? She deleted texts from Davis readily and answered others. She gave reassurances to a few worried girlfriends, assuring them she would call after settling in on her family project with her aunt. She felt a twinge of guilt at avoiding long explanations, but it felt so comforting to hide away with her Groundhog Man.

Her man? She shook that thought away or at least shoved it aside when she put her phone to her ear to hear her last voice message.

"Hey Sis, Davis Greer called looking for you. Sorry about losing your job and some special vacation.

For what it's worth, Davis is a nice guy, but a bit young if you know what I mean. So, uh, call if you need something. Otherwise, find a spot and job before Dad makes his little girl move back home. And no, not ratting you out to Dad or Davis. That's your job, Paiging Amelia Squealia. Haaa haa. Love ya, Sis.

"Love you too, bro," she whispered to her phone, silencing it and putting it aside.

Her cold toes stole her attention. She tiptoed to Michael's suitcase and found his last pair of socks. She thought trade-sies were in order. She wrote out a note, signed it, and slipped it deep into his luggage. In doing so, her hand hit on a bottle of wine with a screw top that looked like a racing gearshift.

With a soft chuckle, she pulled it from his luggage. He had his work plans. She would have her own plans for the rest of the night—warm toes, TV, and a sip of red. She settled in, watching the last of a movie, toes wiggling, sipping wine.

At midnight, the clock radio popped back to life, the announcer's voice overpowering the TV. "Almost midnight. Last time for this song today…"

Paige turned off the television and stood more shakily than intended. She gave in to the replaying of *I Got You, Babe*, softly singing and dancing along with it. She smiled and looked at Groundhog Man, her voice rising in song. She told herself not to divert his attention. He had to get on with work.

Then it all hit her at once. *It's over tomorrow. This magical storm-induced mini-heaven tucked away in a bed and breakfast is over tomorrow.* Her face went slack.

She hadn't realized Michael was watching her, but

he must have read something in her expression. He pulled off his headphones and joined her in the song.

Taking her free hand, Groundhog Man sang, "Then put your little hand in mine."

Her smile returned at his silliness, and she reached for the wine. She sang further lines of the next verse into the bottle like a microphone.

They took turns with the next phrase of the song. Her Groundhog sang the last bit in what must have been his real voice, ending with a whispered word, "Babe."

The announcer's voice came on, "Well that's it folks. Groundhog Day is over. Hope you all had a great one, and if not, there's always next—"

She clicked off the clock radio and brushed away a tear. "But we don't."

"We don't what, Flee?"

She didn't answer. Emotion clogged her throat.

He moved closer and looked at the wine bottle she held. Touching her arm, he turned the bottle. The label read, "Stop Running Away, Cabernet."

He pulled it gently from her hand and put it down. "You were drinking that? I bought it when you were parking your car and hid it. It's my housewarming gift for you."

Her words slurred slightly, "Yesh. Why not? It says to stop running away, but it has a twist cap like a gear shift. Encouraging just the opposite." She pulled away slightly. "Vacation's over tomorrow. It's all over, Michael. You have work. I was just a diversion. Your rebound lover. I don't have you to 'love me so.' What was I thinking? I can't handle a one-night stand."

Paige bit hard on her lip to keep from crying.

"Huh? Oh Flee, no. That's not true." He gingerly

brushed back her hair. "No, not one night. We are two nights going on who knows how long."

"And that's better, how?"

"It's better because we keep going," he said, gently moving in close.

She pulled away abruptly and unsteadily. Slurred words flew out. "Do you have any idea how many times…we—" Paige's voice dropped to a whisper. "Made love?" Her voice picked up in volume. "You're just loving me and leaving me. Did you see the time? Midnight. You're Michael now. No more Groundhog Man. You disappear. It sucks. It all sucks. Shouldn't have feelings. Not supposed to happen. Not now."

Michael was quiet.

Paige didn't know what to make of his silent observation. She sat heavily on the bed and cried. "Michael, I just had a one-night stand in a hotel. What does that make me?"

"Shh, Flee." He sat beside her on the bed and brushed a tear from her face. He tried to lighten her mood. "It's a B and B." She almost smiled, but her sob caught, so he continued, "There's a big difference, one is more homey and friendly." He gave a reassuring smile and tried nudge her out of her funk.

She stared at him.

His arm slid around her. "Technically, we had a two-night stand. You're in the clear." He pulled her close to him.

"Clear? I am clear as mud. Snowy, icy, muddled-up mud, clinging to a stranger who is my lover from who knows where. It dawned on me that you traveled here, to this area. That means you don't live near here."

"Neither do you," Michael retorted.

"That's the problem."

"How's that a problem? Look, we'll figure all this out after we've had some rest."

"Why are you so…so…self-assured?" She spat out the word as if it were suddenly a horrible quality. "And so calm, so…glib about this?" She pulled her arm away from his.

"Older, wiser?" He tried not to smile. "Less red-wine filled?"

She glared in response.

He tried again. "Because I got you, babe, and baby, you got me? Oh, Flee, c'mere. This isn't what either of us expected, but…" He tilted up her chin and looked into her eyes again. "I want to work this out. I want to be with you."

"I do, too. Just don't know how. I have no idea where I'm going." There. She said it. The real problem or, at least, another facet of it.

"Oh, Flee. Paige. Look, you're heading to your aunt's, your grandparents' house, however you look at it. I am in the area for another month or two. Can we continue and see where this goes?"

She wanted to say yes, but she couldn't control the skeptical twist of her frown.

"Flee, I want it to go somewhere, too."

"For what? A month or six weeks like the others? Or are you going to be like your fiancée and transfer?"

"You know that isn't fair, Paige. She was older and did a number on me. It wasn't six weeks. You don't know."

She answered with a quiet chagrin to her voice, "No, I don't. I'm sorry." She turned and wrapped her arms around him, holding him tight, crying on his shoulder, her thoughts mixing together.

"I'm feeling…well…scared and amazed and…oh, I'm so damn confused." She suddenly stood and paced. "All of this is happening so fast. And I don't swear. Daddy would have my head if he knew I f'ing swore."

"I won't tell."

"Damn well better not." She almost smiled.

"Hmm, you swore again." He picked up her phone. "Look, this contact button says Home. Should I push it?"

"Give me that back," she demanded.

He held it up high.

"Real mature, Groundhog Man," she complained but was smiling, his playfulness infectious. She reached over head for her cell.

"Hello?" A voice came over the phone, surprising them both.

"Oh, Mom, hello." Paige yanked the phone out of Michael's hands and glared at him. He returned a cheesy grin. "No nothing wrong. Didn't know it was late. Mmm hmm. Got stuck in a town in PA… Uh huh… Yes. Tomorrow if the roads are clear… Yes. Of course, I remembered to floss and eat veggies. No. A break up is no reason to stop taking care of my body. Uh huh. Take antacid if I eat something hot. You know me and liking a bit a flavor."

By now, Groundhog Man was grinning and pointing to himself at the word *flavor*. She shooed him away, trying to dodge his passing tickle. She squeaked.

"What? Nope, I can't say I miss Davis. Not one bit, surprisingly. Okay. Goodnight Mom. Oh Mom," Paige paused and ended the call with, "I love you." She reflexively turned, when, at that same moment, Michael stepped into view. She happened to be looking straight at him when she spoke the last words to her mother.

Her breath caught. She blanched at the implication that those words could have been directed to him. *Had he heard her?*

He gave no indication but moved to her and held her gingerly. Exhaustion won over her battle of emotions and wine drinking. She held onto him, easing her full weight against him. He rocked her gently, and his hand brushed down her hair. She relaxed to a sweet lull as he rubbed her back. They hugged for a while before he turned down the bedding. He tucked her into bed, climbed in next to her, and gave her whispers of kisses. It filled her with a heady haze. Not sexual but one of warmth and caring…contentment. Her breathing relaxed and deepened.

She was nearly asleep when Michael whispered, "I'm confused, too, you know. I'm supposed to be the mature one. And here I am, falling for you." In a barely audible whisper, he said, "One day I want to hear you say those words to me."

Somewhere in a half-waking dream, she absorbed the whispers from her lover. An incredible lover, in the dark night, in an elegant bed and breakfast, in a small, snowy city. Whispers of promised love.

Her mind replayed a mantra of the words, "Michael" and "meant to be."

Chapter Eleven

Morning came. It came with a harsh brightness to Paige. The storm had passed, and the temperature warmed slightly. Icy surfaces reflected light all the stronger. She rubbed sleep from her eyes and heard a tapping noise. She looked over and saw that Michael was still working hard at his managerial or technical task of some sort.

She looked down. She was still in the clothing from last night. Hung over, her head was foggy at best as pieces of the night came back to her. Not just the fun dinner or the lingering delicious shower, but the wine and…oh no…their discussion.

Knowing she had to look like death warmed over, she dashed to the restroom to freshen up and to give her reflection a good talking to.

"This whole time, Michael was, well, incredible," she told herself as she squeezed toothpaste onto her toothbrush, finally using her own toiletries. "Really increbibble." She spat out the toothpaste and rinsed, then looked at her complexion. It did glow a bit. She smiled and began brushing her hair. Her dopey grin vanished, and her eyebrows furrowed. "But he said all those nice things because he had to. Ya put 'im on the spot. He did seem genuine, though."

Her brush strokes lengthened, and her face brightened. She stopped in mid-stroke of the brush and shook her head. "Nope. He just thinks you're a vacation, a dalliance, a dream." Paige sighed a school girl sigh and put away the brush. "What a dream."

"No, no, no, missy! Dreamy or no, you need to move on." She started to floss but stopped with the string in her mouth. "You just had too much truth juice last night."

She rinsed again and did her makeup very lightly as she preferred. Even with the *talking to* she gave herself, deep down, she knew she wasn't convinced. Groundhog Man had stolen her heart. She'd need it back and soon. Well, sometime, at least.

Returning to the bedroom, Paige tried not to be obvious as she collected her things, but Michael looked up from his laptop and waved her over, taking off his headphones. "Morning, sweet stuff."

She looked at him, not sure what to make of the newest nickname. He clicked something and stood up, rubbing his hands together and smiling. More new things.

"Um, sorry for the *Cabernet* show I put on last night."

"Nothing to be sorry for." He pulled her in close and hugged her tightly, kissing her forehead. He said something that sounded like, "Ya way lo hottie" followed by "Let it go."

He kissed her lips. "Mmm. Minty. Are you okay, now?" He leaned back and looked into her eyes with those sincere amber-brown eyes of his.

Inside her, every ounce of her being wanted to scream, *No! I'm not okay. I haven't a clue what the F is going on, but I want to be with you and not leave.* Instead, she took the high road and managed a few words, "Sure. Fine. Just need a sip of coffee or tea. Your project's done?"

"Will be. I know we need to check out soon, so I'm rushing to get this phase done. A guy's gotta do what a guy's gotta do." The computer bleeped at him. "Excuse me." He looked excited, sat down, and put his headphones back on. She let him work.

She had texts and messages waiting on her phone but ignored them after seeing most were from Davis. Dressed in her overly worn jeans, she looked for something warm to wear on top. While she had a few things from her car, she just didn't have the right clothing. She found his sweater on top of his luggage and pulled out the last of his socks.

She motioned to Michael, "Can I wear this again?"

He nodded and returned to his web cam meeting. She had little to gather and did so quickly. Since he had told her the wine was her gift, the sentimental part of her told her to take the bottle. Screwing the cap on tightly, she shoved it in her bag. She looked about the room. The exquisite room. Their room.

With an inhale and steady exhale, she stuffed away dreamy thoughts of the last two nights. Reality hit as harshly as the glaring sunshine.

She interrupted him again. "You said we have to check out. Going to get breakfast first. Okay?"

"Sure," he answered quickly with that business smile and turned back to the computer.

"Leaving now. Bye, then."

All she got was a wave.

Momentarily, she was dumbfounded. Was he really shooing her away? It would have crushed her if she dared let it. She couldn't. She was raised to be a strong, bright woman. She had a soft exterior and an inviting drawl, but she could be hard as nails if need be. She left Davis and Atlanta. She could handle this. Or so she told herself as she pulled closed the door to her namesake, Amelia's room.

She scoffed as she walked down the stairs, "Meant to be all right. Meant to be a rebound."

Chapter Twelve

There was a knock on the bedroom door some minutes after Paige had left for breakfast. Michael opened the door, "Did you forget and lock the door, Flee? Oh, hello, Mr. Hager." His shoulders slumped.

The proprietor stood before him and laughed. "I know I'm no hot twenty-something, but you don't have to look so glum. Hate to trouble you, but we do need the room."

Michael ushered him in, barely looked at the bill he was given, and began stacking his orderly work. "Oh, sure. Lost track of time. Had an urgent business issue while Paige had some breakfast. Just wrapped up. Any chance for a bite to eat maybe on the way?"

"Paige asked Cookie to save you a sandwich before she left."

"She left? Wait, who left?" Michael stopped gathering his papers. He turned to Mr. Hager, "Paige left?"

"Sure, left a bit ago. Sweet girl, that one. Sorry to see her go."

"What do you mean she left?" Michael's heart lurched.

Mr. Hager shrugged. "Well, she had coffee, ate something, hugged Cookie, and left. I even got a hug for giving her directions."

"When?" It suddenly felt difficult to breathe.

"After she ate."

"I mean, what time did she go?" Panic gripped Michael.

"Oh, fifteen-twenty minutes ago."

"I have to go." He began randomly jamming what had been meticulous papers into his briefcase.

"Yes. That's what I have been saying. I need the room." Mr. Hager watched as Michael began throwing his things together, dashing from one spot to another without accomplishing much. "Is something wrong? Did you lose something? Don't tell me you expected her to pay part of the bill?"

Michael gave him a look to say that wasn't it at all. "I did lose something. My Paige, my Flee. She fled."

"Your who? What?"

"She left me. She panicked on us and left me. I want her back."

"Oh. Well, hurry man. Go get her." Mr. Hager told Michael the directions he had given to Paige's grandparent's hometown while he helped put items in Michael's suitcase and Michael loaded his computer.

"You told her to go through that pass? Why? She doesn't have snow tires or all-wheel drive."

"She should have said so. All she asked was for the shortest route."

"Southern remember?" Michael scolded and apologized in the same breath. Then he rushed part way down the stairs with his computer bag.

"Forget something?" Mr. Hager called after him from the room doorway.

Michael patted his pockets. "No. Don't think so."

"How about your luggage?"

"Oh, right. That. Thanks." Michael rushed up the

stairs, handed him the computer bag, and took the suitcase. He began to run down the stairs again.

"Try again, Mr. Lukas."

Michael looked up. Mr. Hager brandished the computer bag and the bill. "Right."

He left his suitcase on the lower stairs and ran back up to the landing to take his computer bag from Mr. Hager. He turned with a nod of thanks.

"And payment?" Mr. Hager said, stopping Michael in his tracks.

Michael fumbled with the bill and dropped the pen. "Heck, is the credit card on file okay?"

"Yes, sure, just go."

"Oh, and tip. Can you throw in my usual tip?"

Cookie came around the corner and called up to him. She had already lugged his case the rest of the way. "He sure will." Michael joined her at the bottom of the stairs. "Here's your sandwich, Mr. Lukas, and a to-go coffee. Paige asked for extra milk in it. Might want to tell her you prefer just a splash of cream when you see her."

"If I see her. If she'll see me."

Cookie's eyebrows shot up. "Sure hope so. Wait a moment." She pulled a scarf off the hook and put it on him. "I think you forgot one more, little thing."

"Right." He hugged her and gave her a kiss on the cheek.

"Not what I meant. But thanks." She pointed to his feet and the boots right next to him. He handed over the items for Cookie to hold and stuffed his feet into his boots.

Mr. Hager couldn't hold back his laughter. "Never saw you like this. You must have it bad."

"No. For once, I have it *good* and don't want to lose it."

"Don't go with that line. Not the best," he advised.

Michael didn't have time to disagree. He grabbed all his possessions and flew to the door with a wave.

Cookie called after him, "I hope you enjoyed your stay."

The last thing he heard was, "From the looks of it, Cookie, my dear, I think he really did."

****

Paige concentrated on the road as she left town. Though mostly cleared, ice patches riddled the roads. It was treacherous going. Her car fishtailed, making her reduce her speed. Visibility wasn't the best with all her possessions stuffed to the brim. It also didn't help that her phone pinged continually with incoming texts and messages. Davis's latest strategy seemed to be to flood her phone until she finally picked up.

She had reached to turn off her distracting cellphone, only to have it fall out of her hands and ricochet under the passenger seat behind the boxes. Annoyingly, her cell phone continued to ping, though far out of reach.

"Fine." With determination screwed in place, she turned on the radio to muffle the sound. The radio went to static. She had been smart enough to refill her tank. Why hadn't she been smart enough to load any CD's?

As the elevation grew, so did the ice patches on the road. Her phone rang again and again.

"That's it!"

She found a small place to pull over. Parking the car, she turned off the engine. The area she'd chosen had a deep drop off to the right and a rock wall to the on the other side of the road. She unbuckled, dove head first under the passenger seat, reached past wrappers, pushed aside a box, and fished the floorboard until she found her phone.

Before she could sit back up, she unlocked her phone, clinging to the avalanche of her belongings. Grunting, she screamed to the caller, "I'm driving on a dangerous road. I'm not talking to you so stop calling. I don't want to ever see you again."

Silence.

"Are you sure?" came the voice, sounding crushed.

Crushed but deep, and without a twang.

Her brain took a moment to click into gear and register the voice. Not Davis.

She gave a soft utterance, without any words. "Oh."

"Paige?"

"Michael, is that you?"

"Yes. Are you okay? I have been calling and texting you. I was trying to tell you there's a much better road to your aunt's. It's a few miles longer but much safer without all-wheel drive."

"You called?" Feeling numb, she slumped where she lay across possessions, resting her face on the cold fabric of her little Hedgy. "You have my number?"

"And you have mine, I finally realized. From the shared photos at dinner."

She tried to take it all in. He called. He cared. A car pulled in to the same overlook. She stared at her phone. "You care."

"Oh, Paige, of course I care. I followed you. I want something back."

"Your sweater?"

Michael's laughter came over her cell. "Not even close."

"It's warm though." Paige let out a soft laugh. She had to laugh, or she might tear up. A tap to her foggy driver side window startled her, making her bolt upright and her possessions topple. The phone jostled from her fingers, and she dropped it again. "Dang."

She dove again and heard his laugh. Only it didn't just come from the floor of the car. It came from her fogged driver's side window. She pushed the button, lowering the window half way. Michael was standing there!

"No, Flee, I followed you, because I want *you* back."

"You do?"

He nodded. "I do."

Paige's heart raced. He wanted her. Not a two-night stand. Her fingers flew to the door panel. She found the latch and nearly whacked him in the stomach as she opened her car door. He jumped to the side just in time.

She threw herself out of the car and directly at Michael, there on the slim, paved rest-area, with cars and trucks zooming by. His arms, open, coat spattered, and cellphone still gripped in his hand as she pinned him to her car. He took but a second to pull her in tight. There was no kiss, just a crushing hug that lingered.

He leaned back and looked into her eyes with a profound relief.

An eighteen-wheeler drove by, blowing its loud horn. Two men yelled out the window, "Kiss her!"

The words echoed off the cliff-face across the road. The last syllable trailed off as the truck went around the bend.

They did as the mountainside seemed to instruct. Though it started as a sweet reunion kiss, desire spread between them almost instantly. His amber eyes flashed with a smoldering lust. Lips brushed lips, need tugged on need. Pausing only for half a breath, they kissed again, a deeper, longing kiss that sent tendrils of welcome heat through her body.

The kiss intensified. Fire ignited and rolled inside her core. Her hands sank under his open overcoat, and their bodies shared each other's radiating heat while surrounded by chilled mountain air. He groaned into her open-mouthed wanton kiss. He plunged his tongue in. She mewled. Honks of passing cars added their own echoing noise. "Get a room!"

The kiss finally broke. They shared a chuckle.

Paige brushed his road-sludge-stained coat. "I missed this. It's only been hours, but I missed this," she said as she took in a deep heady breath, her exhale condensing in the cold air.

"My coat? It's yours." There it was, his melt-you, warm smile and laugh.

She had no words, just her own soft laugh.

"Oh, my sweet Paige, my sweet fleeing Paige. Any chance you can stop running or, in today's case, fishtailing away? Let's turn around."

She moved to do so, shifting her stance in his arms so that she faced the road.

He laughed harder. "No. Your car. Turn around and follow me. Let's get off this road. I'll get you to your aunt's safely. I started out as a process engineer, after all."

He opened her car door for her. Her lips brushed

his cheek before she sat. After belting herself in, she said through the half-open driver's side window, "Engineer, huh? Then you're in a heap of trouble. One of my brothers is an engineer, and I have plenty of engineering jokes at the ready."

Michael's eyebrow shot up. "Oh, well, I have lots of unemployed jokes, but..." He paused for effect. "None of them work." He laughed.

She groaned and couldn't close the window fast enough but found herself laughing, too.

"Not a good one?" he asked through the frosty window.

She pretended not to hear, shrugging. As he returned to his car, she said, "The joke was just meh, but you, Mr. Groundhog Man, are definitely incredible."

"Thanks." The voice came from somewhere vaguely under the seat.

"Hey. You weren't supposed to hear that." Paige shouted to her phone somewhere on the floor of her car.

"Remember to follow me," his voice still came through the lost phone.

"Do you always have to lead?" Paige asked, fumbling through the possessions littering the floorboard for her phone.

"Definitely not."

"Good, because if you do, it's going to be hard to be a strong-willed, self-assured, got-it-together Southern girl."

"You forgot to mention bright, hot, impetuous, funny-dressing..."

She finally grabbed her phone and turned it off. There would be plenty of time for quips later. She savored the most welcome thought. There would be a later with Michael. He was no rebound. He was the real thing. Her very own Groundhog Man.

Paige's car swerved slightly as she turned around to follow him. It was an action befitting her state. She'd swerved from her life path, but if that kiss and those nights together were any sign, it was a detour worth taking. She was turning a new leaf, a new mission, a new place to live, and unexpectedly with it, a new man. She couldn't be happier.

She fishtailed her way to a new start. If Groundhog Man was any indication, it was going to be a jaw-dropping ride.

A Paige in Cupid's Book:
A Valentine's Day Romance

Chapter One

Two cars pulled up to the old Victorian farm home. Amelia Paige Myers followed the smooth large, black SUV with tinted windows until it came to a graceful stop on the ice and snow-covered roadside. She fishtailed past, driving the over-packed, smaller car without snow tires, and turned into the ice-slick driveway, bouncing off a snowbank. She braked abruptly only a few feet into the drive, seeing that the rest of it hadn't been cleared of the several-inch coating of snow.

Paige let out a huge sigh. She was twenty-six and far from Atlanta and completely unfamiliar with winter driving. After pouring her concentration onto the white-knuckle drive on the slick mountain roads, she was at finally her aunt's house, which was to be her home for the following weeks. Her next thought was of the incredible man who dropped everything to lead the way on those roads—her Michael, her handsome rebound Michael, her know-what-he's-doing Michael. Was he really hers? If so, for how long?

She shook her head free from that worrying thought. No time for that. It was cold, and she couldn't wait to see her aunt and the home she had last visited as a child.

Michael Yotahala Lukas stepped smoothly out of his black car, both he and his expensive overcoat having their share of salt and road-dirt stains from earlier mishaps. He was striking, tall, lean, long-nosed, dark-haired with a slight caramel color to his skin.

"You made it." His expression showed relief in his smile as he walked with firm strides toward her.

She stepped free from her car, which had been stuffed to the roof with her possessions. "Of course, I made it," she said with a distinct Carolina drawl. Her words puffed cold as she spoke, but she smiled warmly to Michael.

He readily put his arm around her. "Who needs snow tires, all-wheel drive or even unobstructed view for that matter?"

"You do if you plan on living with me for a while." The interrupting voice boomed from around the bend of the driveway.

"Aunt Linney!" Paige turned away from Michael just as he had bent to kiss her. Though, just an hour earlier, they had embraced and shared kiss after heated kiss at a rest stop on a winding mountainside pass.

"Hey." He moaned, his face hinted at a distinct pang of rejection.

"Sorry." Paige grinned and reached up to peck him on the cheek before running toward her aunt with open arms for her reunion hug. She was hampered by the thick snow to an awkward stomp as she trudged through it wearing only clogs.

Her aunt was somewhere in her early fifties and somewhere thirty plus pounds extra with a sometimes-stoic air. She was not stoic now. With cold-nipped rosy cheeks, she beamed at her.

"There's my favorite niece," her aunt called out with a gravel to her voice.

"I'm your only niece," Paige replied happily at the mantra the two had always shared.

Linney Smith's hair was a rich brunette, several shades darker than Paige's hair, which ranged from honey blonde to dirty wheat-colored, depending on the amount of sun she'd had. Paige had had plenty of sun recently. Linney had not. Her hair was cut in a style that could only be described as, "it will grow in soon."

In a hearty rural Pennsylvania accent, Linney said, "Sagey-Paigey, how's my strong-willed, southern squirt doing?" She gave Paige an even heartier hug.

"Not as strong-willed as you might hope. I ran away from Atlanta when I was laid off," Paige said.

"I don't know about that. Your mom and I thought it took a lot of courage to pile up and drive up here to help me fix up this old place."

"Maybe." Paige looked up at her grandparents' home and did a double-take. It was far more worn than when they had been alive. "Whoa. Now I can see why you said it was courageous. This house isn't anything like I remembered."

"They let it go for quite a piece. Happens with illness hitting the elderly. Just locked the doors and left it alone in the end. Squatters didn't help. The snow's hiding more than a paint problem. Got our work cut out for us."

Paige nodded, shielding her eyes from the bright sunshine reflecting off the snow. She took in the view of the home. It looked neglected, cold, and gray especially with the window shades drawn. The triangle of roof over the middle of the attic sported a broken, boarded circular window. She huddled closer into her thin jacket and noticed Michael had kept his distance, his computer bag in hand. She motioned for him to come closer.

"Working on this place should help you put Buckhead behind you," Linney said. "And I don't mean the condo. I mean that lug David… Davis…Dookey, whoever you lived with. That blockhead came off lazy and about as smart as the football he loved."

"It was Davis. Davis Martin Greer, but you're right. He's a thing of the past," Paige said through her chattering teeth.

"Thank heavens. And I suppose this one is the future?" Linney tilted her head and eyed Michael with a critical stare as he approached.

Paige chuckled. "This is—"

Her aunt cut her off with a wave of a hand. She scrutinized the dark-haired, strong-bodied man and said something to him in Mohawk language.

He shook his head. "Part Oneida." He followed with, "*Natuhkwa* Michael Yotahala Lukas, with a K, but Paige calls me *Kanaskwiyo Ukwe*." He shrugged at her aunt's surprised look, then nodded, chuckling. "Groundhog Man."

"His birthday was yesterday on Groundhog Day. Only fitting that I called him that," Paige interjected in her own defense. A shiver added to her teeth chattering. "Not for anything, when did you learn Oneida? I thought Uncle Roger was part Mohawk."

Her aunt started to usher Paige toward the house. "He was. Lucky I didn't skin him alive Mohawk style when I left him." She explained for Michael's benefit, "I found him with that…*kalyo tanu yanit*. That *yonhehti*!"

Paige's eyebrows shot up. "Don't know what it

means, but it can't be good."

"Terrible animal. Bitch," Michael said with heightened emphasis matching her aunt's. Both women glared at him. "What? Just translating."

Paige laughed. "So, Aunt Linney, it still doesn't explain the Oneida."

"You know I'm a nurse. I've been working in hospice. It helps for communication to learn a few words of various languages as they come through at such a trying time. There must have been an Oneida community or suburb nearby since several spoke it. One woman was without family, and she...well, she taught me. Sweet thing, that one. Was old as the hills and wrinkled as a prune, but um..." She paused in reflection. "*Iyo...Iyo...*"

"*Ukwe?*" Michael offered.

Aunt Linney shook her head. "More than good woman. Soul. Beautiful, good soul. She hung in there longer than anybody expected, and I stayed with her. She actually helped me through the divorce with Can't-keep-his-pants-up Roger."

Her aunt stood on the front porch, more of a stoop since it had only half a roof and the remaining part hung on a precarious angle. The railings were mostly missing, having long fallen over. Stomping her feet, she swung open the door, "Well, welcome to Dusty Haven. Your hoarding paradise for as long as you can take it."

"Oh, Michael, don't listen to her. It can't be all that bad."

It was worse.

****

Paige took in the view, or the lack of it. Though the bay windows in the living room faced a vista of a sloping meadow, the window seat was obscured with several collapsing boxes and old cartons. The walls might have seen paint forty years earlier, all dulled to a dirty tone except where paintings were removed and wires hung loose.

A handful of newer grocery store boxes were clustered in one corner of the foyer as if to ready to fight against stacks of yellowed magazines and newspapers piled up six feet thickly throughout what might have been the living room. A handful of disheveled furniture pieces were unburied from their surrounding rubble and newspaper walls.

"I made a lot of progress in here," Aunt Linney proudly declared. "You could barely walk in here before. Took forever to get the house out of probate. Some squatters broke in while the courts took their time. Still have rooms upstairs and down where you can't see the floor."

Stunned, Paige said, "So this is squatters doing, not Grandpa Benny and Grandma Ida's?"

"More of a combo. That's the trouble. We need to weed out the heirloom from all of this. Treasure from the trash."

Michael nodded, his hand wiped the dust off an antique frame holding a picture of a wedding couple that had been taken over a hundred years ago. Paige moved to his side. Several other sepia-toned photos were stacked on the rickety mantel begging for attention.

"Okay, okay. Before you two go sentimental treasure hunting, there's shoveling to do, outside this time, and a car to unload. I vote you two do it," Aunt Linney said, shaking them out of their stupor.

Paige still shivered as she looked questioningly at her Aunt.

"I'll get some soup going. You can use my spare boots, and, uh, just add socks or newspaper since your feet look smaller. Here, take my coat, too." Linney handed a heavy oversized parka to Paige.

"I can shovel. Michael has work. He just helped me find my way here," Paige said, with a thicker drawl emerging from her discomfort at putting Michael on the spot.

Both Michael and Aunt Linney sighed. "Is she always like that?" he asked.

"Nah…worse."

"I do have a work crisis, though." He looked at this watch. "Any chance I can plug into your Wi-Fi and start another report running before shoveling?" Michael scanned for outlets.

"What Wi-Fi?"

"No Wi-Fi?" both Paige and Michael asked, Paige, in amazement, Michael with deflation.

"Nope. Limited cell reception, too, at least with my carrier." Aunt Linney plunked down a pair of oversized boots in front of Paige.

"Is that why you never texted or called me back?" Paige watched Michael turn and press button after button on his phone.

Aunt Linney just shook her head. "Nope. I'm old school. Not into texting. Just real phone or emails. I was wondering why you didn't call me. You must have been trying to reach my cell. Gotta find that thing. It's out of battery and hiding. Your mom called though and mentioned you made it to Pennsylvania at least."

"I drove through the night. Weren't you even

worried about me driving alone or getting into trouble during the icy storm the other night?"

"Nah. You might have grown up in the South, but you have tough Pennsylvania farmer blood in you— Dornheim blood. I saw how you handled your older brothers. You usually have your wits about you. Smart enough to dump Buckhead dork, so I don't have to worry much about you, Paige. You've always been prepared and careful, if not orderly."

Michael let out a snort. His hands went up in defense at Aunt Linney's scrutinizing look.

Paige grinned. She couldn't really argue with Michael's objection. She might never have met him had she been the normal, hard-working, over-scheduled person she was in Atlanta. Her mind flashed back to how they met in an icy snowstorm just a couple days ago. Michael had been in town on business when she landed at *Sizzle*, a gay bar in a college town, after driving through the night. He'd been thrown at her and taken her underwing as part of the "Breakup Special" his gay cousin manipulated.

She and Michael spent a whirlwind of nights sequestered in his room at a bed and breakfast. Snowed in, they were plunged into the circumstance, and now, even a glance at his smile made her long for the rebound to continue to something more, much more. She worried that walking into this hoarded, decrepit home would change things.

Paige snapped out of her concerns and back into the discussion.

Michael was defending his reaction. "She's bright, yes. But…prepared and orderly? No snow tires and did you see how her car's packed?" He plugged his computer into a wall socket and pressed something on his cell.

"Not yet. It's too far down the driveway," Linney responded. "That's why you both need to get to work while the sun is shining." She turned to Michael. "And what the hell did you just do?"

"I set up a temporary Wi-Fi hotspot. It'll chew up my data plan, but this way I can test the reliability of…" Michael stopped at Linney's glazed expression.

Paige nodded as if to urge him on.

Her aunt just looked cross-eyed at him, grunted, and left the room.

"Go on," Paige encouraged. Light spilled in from the front door window pane, bouncing off his dark hair.

Finally, with privacy, he moved toward her. "…reliability of the perimeters set. They have to be in close range." He pulled her in tight, hugging her through the fluffiness of the borrowed coat. Her eyes locked onto his rich amber ones. They were golden brown in the center with a rim of chocolate brown, all of which was much brighter in the reflection of the snow. She drank in their delicious intensity.

"Uh huh," Paige whispered. "Very close range."

Without hesitation, he pulled her into a deep hungry kiss. *That* kiss. The one that drew a soft moan from her. Her hand moved to his face. The feeling of the slight grizzle to his chin sent her body a flashback to when he was with her in bed, entwined and pulsing. His kiss sent tendrils of longing through her. Another moan escaped her lips as she returned his deepened kiss.

"Oh brother," her aunt exclaimed, reentering the living room and dropping a second shovel. "And here. I brought extra gloves to keep you two warm—like you need it." She tossed the gloves and walked toward the kitchen with a waddle and a laugh.

"Shovel?" Paige asked, offering the red scoop-shovel to Michael.

"Now that's a nickname I haven't been called before." He took the shovel from her. "And no *plow* jokes or I stop."

She almost said something but stopped and mimicked a zipped lip.

"After you," Michael said with a groan that sounded very much like an animal sound. A very ill-behaved animal. That earned him a snowball almost as soon as they stepped back outdoors.

****

"Owwwww. What the hell was that?" Michael pulled a limp lump with inch long spikes from Paige's car and flung it into the snow. "It bit me."

He began to yank out the needles from his gloved hand and wrist. Two or three hours earlier, he had been warm and spike-free. A day ago, he had been curled up around Paige in a gorgeous bed. A week before that was just a blur. That was before Paige had fled Atlanta straight into his life and no longer seemed to matter much.

They had shoveled the winding driveway, pushing the heavy snow to the sides, potholes making the smooth strokes rougher. Only a few snowballs were thrown when they began. He couldn't help it. It had been so long since he was with someone playful other than family. She was a handful years younger than his thirty-one and energetic.

So, when she pegged him with a snowball a third

time, he had to prove his own stamina and show her the proper way to dunk someone into a snowbank. He tossed her into a mountain of the fluffy stuff and followed her into the snow drift, kissing his way out any retaliation. He even had helped her up. She had reached to brush off snow from his hair but instead smashed a fistful on his head.

She had tried to run, but her boots flopped, so he caught her near the tree line and pressed his body to hers, his overcoat opened up enough so that he knew she could feel everything that was surging through him. Then, as she fell backward into the birch, the tree shook loose a mountain of snow on top of them, sending them chasing again. She escaped and hopped into her car.

Oh no. Is she going to flee again like she had this morning?

He had jammed his reports into his computer bag and fled from the bed and breakfast to follow her in his company car. Just before she reached the most dangerous part of the mountain road, he caught up with her, kissed her within an inch of his life, and had her follow him on safer roads. He had no idea how long his work projects would keep him in the area. What he did know was that he didn't want their time to be over, at least not yet.

His panic at her leaving again calmed to a sigh of relief when she pulled her car up to park closer to the front door.

"Unloading time," Paige announced with a bright, enthusiastic smile and hoisted a box. She was nothing like his ex who'd been older, demanding, and continually serious.

Paige was fascinating and, from what he could tell,

able to handle what was thrown at her and still keep her sense of humor. Her sexy, playful nature drew him in. Compared to his exacting ex, who had treated their relationship as if it were another task on her managerial to-do list, Paige hadn't pushed expectations on him. She even seemed to relish his assistance. Still, the sting from his breakup a year ago made him cautious. Very cautious if he reflected on it.

He watched Paige's movements as he followed her inside with each load from the car. His reflection on her took on a whole new facet with the fluidity of her backside wiggling up the steps. That made him think other thoughts, naked-under-the-covers thoughts, which let caution take a back seat, a curvy back seat.

And now, out for another load, Michael hadn't been paying attention to what he had been reaching into and was bitten by Paige's dead plant, requiring him to pluck out several hurtful spines.

"Ohh…I forgot. I must have brought Cackty, my cactus. I think it must be a victim of my move."

"As am I, it appears. Ouch." He shook his head.

She dropped what was in her arms and pulled out the last needle. "Do you want me to kiss it and make it better?"

"Yes, and then I want you to feed it and make it better. I'm starved. Let's finish fast." He lifted and carried several more garbage bags of items inside, careful to set them away from the water they dripped near the entry. Aunt Linney gave directions, usually indicating the foyer or downstairs hall since both busy workers were trailing in wet snow.

Paige had unloaded the trunk, including a second basket of laundry, which may or may not have been washed by the looks of the wadded-up clothing. Lamps, gadgets, and a small table somehow made their way out of the car in Michael's arms. The box of books had shoes thrown in with it. She carried her summer hats stacked on her head as she retrieved more items. Her business clothes were more carefully handled.

"This should be the last of it. Not big on planning this out, were you, Flee?" He picked up a rickety box with a notable, "Oof." The box rattled, threatening to break the heavy items inside.

"I just threw things together. I think that's a few kitchen items. Take it that way, please."

He did, groaning with every step.

Chapter Two

The flimsy box nearly gave way as Michael put it down with a thud on a side chair near the door of the old-fashioned kitchen. He pulled off his gloves and tucked them into his coat pocket. "What was in that?"

Paige shrugged. "Who knows? I left without taking time for organizing. It can't be the spice jars. I saw those in the first laundry basket, the one with my games and laptop. Looking back, I don't think I was so clear headed when I decided to leave Atlanta after losing my job that day."

"Any better now?" he asked with a hint of a grin.

"Of course."

"Well, let me fog it back up." His hands slid into her open coat, and his lips poised to kiss her, only to be disrupted by Aunt Linney's entrance.

Linney groaned. She was wearing an apron with huge splotches on it that read, *Schmutz Happens.* She wielded a ladle. "Do I need to separate you two? Off with your coats."

She pointed in the direction of the coat pegs before beginning to ladle out bowls of thick homemade soup. Like young children being cared for by a parent, Michael and Paige kicked off boots and hung coats near the kitchen door and even washed their hands, having been told to do so.

"That should warm you up." Aunt Linney pulled

out a plate of cheesy cornbread from the oven. It was still steaming. She laughed. "And this should cool you down." She put large glasses of water in front of them.

Paige and Michael mumbled thank you's and dove right in.

"Delicious." Paige let the warm bite of vegetable and broth swirl in her mouth.

"Great stew," Michael added between bites.

"It's okay, fast-made stew. You're just hungry from all that hard work shoveling," Aunt Linney said.

Paige just shrugged again and continued to eat, enjoying each morsel.

"Yup. You two shoveled plenty, even down the meadow. Never can say I shoveled down there on the grass like you did."

Paige joined Michael in a conspiratory chuckle, knowing full well Linney must have seen their embrace. Paige stopped eating long enough to say, "But the driveway is cleared except it needs salt."

"Kitty litter," Linney corrected. Paige looked up questioning. "Better for the land if we can use some kitty litter or sand instead."

Aunt Linney rose from the table and began to putter in the kitchen. A loud beeping noise came from the living room.

Michael scraped out the last of his soup from his bowl and stuffed a bite of corn bread into his mouth. He stood and mumbled a muffled, "Excuse me. Computer."

He kissed Paige's hair on the way out of the kitchen, dashing toward the continuing beep.

She simply brushed the crumbs from her hair and smiled, feeling smitten even by such a simple gesture.

Aunt Linney stood at the sink, shaking her head as

she looked at Paige and flung a dishtowel over her shoulder. "What does he do?"

"Uh, business."

"What kind?" Aunt Linney dug in a cupboard for a coffee mug.

"Technical business. He was an engineer, and now he has some kind of a roll-out coming up. All hush-hush."

"You don't know do you?"

"No. Not exactly," Paige said in a small voice.

Aunt Linney let out a huff in response.

"I do know I'm falling hard for him." Paige was surprised at the hint of worry in her sincere admission.

"You mean falling fast. You just met him." Linney shook her head.

Neither said anything for a minute. Linney simply traded the coffee mug with a wine glass and poured a glass of wine. A large one. She leaned against the counter and took a swallow. Paige followed her every move and waited, knowing her aunt had far more to say.

Linney let out a long slow breath. "You're on a bumpy road, kid, but I can see it's already too late to tell you to slow down." She nodded, raised her glass, and took a big swig. "Eh, he's here for now, and sometimes that's what counts." She hitched up her lips into a half smile.

Paige's worried thoughts stopped with even that slightest reassurance. She took over her aunt's clean-up efforts.

Linney put down her glass and cleared her throat. "So, Squirt, what do you have in this box that you think will fit in these cupboards?"

"Electric appliances," Paige said, feeling relaxed, without looking up from her task. "Ones I bet you don't even have. Shiny new ones."

"Oh?" Linney pried open the cardboard flaps and dug through the box. "Shiny new ones, you say. I see." She raised an object for inspection and held back her laughter.

"Yes. And if you are good, you can share it." Paige finally turned to her aunt. Her jaw dropped. Her aunt was brandishing a bright green vibrator.

"No thanks. I'm good. I don't think I'll be sharing this, uh...appliance." She set it to maximum buzz and burst out laughing.

"Give me that back." Paige yanked it from Linney's hands.

Still laughing, Linney said, "And these. Interesting choice of aprons, and it matches your eye color." She held up a very lacy, sheer bluish-gray nightie.

Michael stepped into the kitchen wide-eyed as each woman brandished the items. "I think I'm really going to like your family."

"Oh, honestly." Paige took the nightie away from Linney with a jerk, putting both the vibrator and the lingerie into the box, trying to hold back her own giggles while the other two laughed. Linney hooted the loudest.

"Nice packing, Flee," Michael said.

"Flea? Oh no. I had this whole place fumigated."

"No, Aunt Linney, he means flee as in runaway. Kind of an endearing nickname for me, isn't it?" Paige's embarrassment turned to sweetness.

Linney glared. She huffed an exhaled in exasperation. "I bet all this lovey-dovey stuff is going to become all the more intolerable as we get close to Valentine's Day. It may make me start drinking," she said and followed it with a deep swallow of her wine.

"Um, you already are. Hey, that was my wine, a gift from…"

"The Flea-catcher there, I bet. Oh, look it's called *Stop Running Away, Cabernet.* Ugh." Aunt Linney groaned.

"I thought it was tasty," Paige said, defending her wine, tipping the bottle to assess that it had only one swallow left.

"The wine is, but all of this…schmaltz." She waved her arms around them with a sneer, pulled off her apron, and hung it on a wooden peg on top of other aprons. "I think I need to go to my room and read some Stephen King to get you two out of my mind."

"Not good to keep it all bottled in there, Aunt Linney. You have a lot of mushy stuff in you, too. You should speak your mind, you know," Paige called after her. The response she got was a gesture and a less than kind one, at that. "I saw that."

"I know you did." Her aunt said something in Oneida as she started up the stairs and then called to them. "Oh, and take the back bedroom. I'm in the front. I want as much distance as possible so I can pretend it's the pipes banging not some Groundhog."

It took all of Paige's southern upbringing not to do a spit-take on her aunt's last comment.

****

"What did she say in Oneida back there?" Paige asked, stretching and twisting before leaving the kitchen.

"Glad to have us both here, and that I was to be

treated royally for helping you so much," Michael answered with a flash to his brown eyes, the amber less pronounced until they walked into the brightly lit foyer.

"No way," Paige protested. "That doesn't sound like Aunt Linney."

"Okay, she said we are welcome and not to let you wear out such an incredibly handsome man." Michael smiled and turned to his computer screen.

"Nope, try again." She poked at some of her possessions stacked in the foyer, hoping to sort out some clothing to bring to her room. The only neat box was the one of her shoe collection.

Michael came back into the foyer. "She said for me to treat you right, or she would have my balls."

"Now, that's more like my aunt."

Paige handed Michael a box of her ill-packed belongings which seemed to have clothes and toiletries. She then stacked her shoe collection over it and draped a garment bag on top. She gave up her digging efforts and grabbed a smaller garbage bag of belongings and another one with business clothes.

"And don't worry, I must take after the other side of my family. I am not big on crushing balls."

He let out a tiny gasp of commiseration and followed her lead, carrying his precarious stack up the mahogany wooden stairs.

Paige let out a huff when she reached the top landing. She stopped at the last door, grinning. "Stroking balls, that is another thing."

He let out another breath, sounding relieved or perhaps something else.

She opened the door to the room and came to an abrupt halt. Michael stood stock still behind her. A brand-new queen bed on a metal frame sat angled in the middle of the small room. A rickety dresser was in the corner with folded towels on top. Random folded sheets and a quilt were tossed onto the unmade bed, and a few hangers hung on a crooked rack in the closet. A desk with one leg missing was supported by a tall stack of books. The wallpaper was multi-layered, frayed, and peeling. The room smelled of cleaner.

"Your aunt also said one more thing. 'Bed's new, but the walls are old. Use the bed.'"

"Huh. I see what she means, but I think we should test them both out," Paige said brightly.

Michael dropped the load he was carrying with a *crash.*

****

Michael took in the room when he stepped inside. He had travelled plenty with his work and had to face many substandard hotel rooms. This was not substandard. It needed countless improvements to bring it up anywhere close to substandard.

While no cobwebs hung from the walls, the paper was peeling, revealing layers upon layers of wallpaper and paint. The only light fixture was from some indeterminant age, but mid-century came to mind, as did the fact that it dangled with a few screws loose. He knew if he hung up the garment bag, it would just slide down to the side. *If* the clothing rail held at all. He didn't dare raise the stained paper shade on the window. As exhausted as he was, deep inside, he knew he needed to rise the challenge and be strong for Paige.

He was prepared to have her run out, crying. He was prepared to have her collapse on the bed in depressed silence. He was even prepared for her to

127

throw her shoulder back and say "this will not do" and demand to be taken to a hotel as his ex would have done. He was not prepared, however, for her joy. At that, the box slid from his hands with a thud. She'd wanted to test out the bed and the walls!

He turned to face Paige, stunned. She was talking about the room being a small, perfect hideaway. He watched her take the garment bag and hang it to far side of the closet rail so it didn't slide but hugged the wall. He drank in the vision of her body, with her clothing masking her curves. She flitted, actually flitted, back to the other large suit bag and simply lay it flat in the closet.

"Don't you think?"

"Huh?" was all that came out of him.

"I said, it'll feel great to get out of these jeans and into some fresh clothes." Paige dropped her pants, panties hidden by the sweater she wore, his best cashmere sweater.

Michael closed the door with a soft click. "I agree about getting out of our clothing, but I'm not so ready to put on new ones." He pulled off his own sweater and tugged his tailored shirt free from his slacks, turning to watch Paige while he unbuttoned his shirt. She was bent over the bed, trying to stretch the worn bottom sheet over the crisp mattress, new tags and all. Her sweater rose as she struggled, showing the lace of her pink panties.

"Oh, this might not be the right size. It looks like a full sheet." Paige said reaching to the other side of the mattress.

"Let me help you," he offered, but his hands slid to her sides and under the sweater onto her smooth skin.

He nuzzled her neck, one hand gliding onto her belly.

Paige let out a soft moan and murmured, "The bed—"

He kissed her cheek and neck and whispered, "Yes, the bed first. Walls later."

"Ohh." Paige's eyes were wide when he half lifted her, turning her to her side on top of the ill-fitted sheet with a lion print. He crawled up next to her.

"That's my sweater you borrowed." His hands pushed the cashmere farther up her chest.

"Do you want it back?" Paige asked in a sugary drawl.

"I want it off," Michael said in a heady whisper. He followed it with a slow, full kiss. He loved the taste of her tongue on his, the way her gray-blue eyes glowed when they looked at him and how they fluttered closed when she sank completely into his kiss.

"Won't I be cold?" Paige teased, cupping his face, and surprising him with a deep exploring kiss.

Her eagerness excited him. It was almost impossible not to want to touch her. His hands massaged all over her back, luxuriating in the feel of her silky-smooth body. He wanted more. Much more.

"Cold? I doubt that. I can think of several ways to keep you warm." Michael helped lift the sweater off. He took in the sight of her. Since they had been thrown together during the storm, she'd been stranded and borrowed his clothing. At times, she was stark naked. She wasn't now. She wore an amazing bra panty set with lace and silken texture. Her skin was tanned. Her hair tangled but spilled over the top of folded, ocean-blue sheet. Her eyes were trusting and something else, something he hadn't seen in a long time before meeting her, something that shined. She radiated passion.

He yanked off his T shirt, wanting his skin against hers. He pulled her to him, kissing her open-mouthed as they entwined on their sides. He craved touching every inch of her.

They'd come to the room with the intention of a rest. His day started in the opulent bed and breakfast with so little sleep from a work crisis followed by a white-knuckled race to reach Paige before she took the dangerous mountain route to her aunt's. The shoveling and unloading alone would have warranted a nap. For some reason, none of that wore on him now. He was awake. He was more than awake. He was on fire.

She must have felt the same as she unbuckled his belt and slid her hand inside his slacks. She gurgled something unintelligible into his ear as her hands, her beautiful hands, stroked him. He instantly grew hard and moved to her touch along his length. His senses were on overload. He wanted to touch her, naked skin to naked skin.

He raised himself enough to completely discard his clothing, leaving two packets on the bed. Each breath he took filled his chest so deeply it was as if he were devouring the air and not just the closeness of his Paige. He inhaled her in all ways. Sight, smell, taste, and touch. He was rigid and pulsing with need for her.

He did not wait but sank back to the bed, hands cupping, molding her breasts, biting the part that dipped into the cleavage of her bra. His voice was not his own but some deep growl as he said, "I want you, Paige, every inch of you."

Her clothing had to go. He divested her of the lace bra and buried his face in her chest. Each moan of consent dripped like honey from her lips. He had to taste those again. His hands had to slide under the lace covering her very grabbable ass cheeks.

They fueled each other. Somehow a condom rolled onto his length. Their hands roved and grabbed each other.

Her panties remained on. The flimsy fabric gave way with a rip when he tried to tug her panties down. He paused only for a second and then completely tore them off, driving a deep tongued kiss into her sweet mouth. She returned it. She whimpered a hungry mewling sound and reached his back, only having skimmed over his distended cock.

It was too much. He couldn't hold back. He opened her legs and drove nearly full tilt into her, groaning. He drew back and then oh-so-deliciously in. And again. Deeper, faster. *Baseball scores. Baseball scores. Need distraction, baseball scores.* The distraction failed to slow down his thrusting frenzy. "Screw baseball."

Paige gasped, her body rocking and colliding with Michael's. In halting words drawled out in hissing syllables, she replied, "Not…ohh…the right…aah…sea-sea-season…" She held the last word in a whimpering hum as she arched against him. Paige's body thrashed to his. Her insides clenched on his shaft. Her mouth fell to an O and she cried out. All of it pushed Michael over the edge.

"*Basketball!*" Michael screamed in a long cry, followed by guttural noises as he convulsed against her, exploding, buried inside her. The incredible release felt all the more powerful with her echoing waves milking him.

He held her tightly as she clung to him. He finally

slowed and saw a lock of her hair across her face. He brushed it past her lips, and kissed her. He kissed her again and again, waiting for her to quiet, holding her.

Her eyes fluttered and then she smiled.

"Basketball? Does that have some hidden Oneida meaning?"

Heat crept across his skin. "Sure. It means, *big man cometh.*"

She laughed at that, and the long day overtook them. Her laugh faded into a dreamy smile.

He reached for a sheet and the quilt, tossing the coverings haphazardly over them. At her shiver, he curled around her, gathering her in tight. Her breathing deepened, and only when she was at the precipice of sleep, did he whisper, "*Lonoluhkwe.* Don't flee on me, Paige. I'm learning to love you."

She nestled deeper into his arms and murmured something, little more than a breath that sounded like, "Me, too."

Michael's eyes closed in contentment.

Chapter Three

Michael punched buttons on his computer and muttered under his breath, "Using up data for what? It's running way too slow."

He needed a shower. He was dressed in slacks and a sweater with his shirt and belt missing. He did, however, borrow back his thick socks that Paige had stolen. He looked less put together and felt far more at odds than his looks, especially the moment Linney entered.

"Hey, Groundhog Man. How's it going?" Linney asked.

"Could be better. Really need to get this done this weekend. Cell reception cut out, so now I have to re-run—"

He looked up to see her broadening grin and chose to ignore it. "Do you know which carrier has the strongest Wi-Fi network up here?"

"Haven't a clue." She shook her head, grinning.

He turned away and sent off an e-mail request. "Can I help you with something, Linney?"

"Well, come to think of it, yes, you can, *Tzaahneet*. Do I have that right?"

He looked at her. "Strong, industrious worker? *Tsahnit*. Close enough. And thank you for the compliment."

"Well, I was wondering, *Tsahnit*, what the hell was

wrong with *baseball* and why's *basketball* so much better?" Linney burst out laughing. She left without an answer and with a happy step straight to the kitchen.

Michael blushed again. Something he rarely did but found it happened often around these women. "Thin walls," he called after her.

"Nope. Loud man. And I don't know the word for it."

Michael called out, "*La chach-te.*"

She poked her head back in. "That ain't it, honey. But whatever you are, you are wiping out my Sagey Paigey. Dinner's in an hour or whenever it's done. Plenty of time for a shower."

"Is that a hint?"

"More like a request."

Wi-Fi or no, Michael was really liking the place.

****

"Paige?" Linney called up the stairs. "Can you come down and help, girl?"

"Sure. Coming." Paige's voice floated down into the foyer.

"And you, go up and shower."

"Yes, Ma'am." Michael pushed a few last keys and headed for the stairs.

He stopped dead in his tracks when he saw Paige hurrying down the stairs with a bounce.

Her hair was in a damp ponytail and she had on clothing, not warm clothing but layers of her own clean clothing. Clothing befitting the season but made for warmer climate. Her slightly fuzzy lamb's-wool slippers were only outdone by an even fuzzier cream, cropped sweater over her blouse and expensive jeans. She was ready for anything this evening, apart from work.

Michael caught her toward the bottom of the stairs and pulled her into a kiss before she even made it to the floor. "Mmm. You smell delicious."

Whap. Aunt Linney's wooden spoon landed her own hand, but it startled them out of the embrace and Paige into a giggle.

"It's my food that smells good." She aimed the spoon at Paige. "You to the kitchen. And you—" The wooden weapon pointed at him. "—go make yourself more handsome. And don't take all the hot water."

He dashed up the stairs two at a time.

"Did you move your car off the road?" she called up after him.

"Just as ordered." He added, "*Yo hon do.*"

"You bet I'm the boss. Well, of my house. Huh, but this isn't my real house," she mumbled. Then she called up the stairs, "But I'm the boss somewhere."

Paige called from the kitchen, "I'm stirring, but it's boiling over!"

"The kitchen," Linney amended. "I claim to be the boss of the kitchen."

****

The three set up the Formica table in kitchen for their meal. The old kitchen was large enough and so out of date it felt charmingly vintage with muted green-painted cabinets, others in varnished deep walnut with glass doors. The pegs held aprons, coats, and scarves. Dried gloves and mittens remained on the heat register while boots dried close by. Paige found placemats and stuck a candle in an empty wine bottle. Linney added a bottle of white wine labelled *I'm Out of Coffee.*

Michael, freshly showered, nodded at the bottle. "I

wish I had a housewarming gift, but it seems some Dornheim and Myers women drank it already." He found the wine glasses in the far cabinet along with a one-pound, oversized chocolate bar, which he brandished.

"That goes back." Aunt Linney pointed to the chocolate. "It's my desperation stash."

"Pretty desperate, Auntie," Paige interjected.

"Anything smaller and I would be nibbling it at. Got to have a really rough day to tap into that."

Paige set the potatoes and green beans on the table. "How long have you had it?"

Her aunt shrugged. "A few months. Working hospice care can do something to you sometimes."

Michael took the chicken from the oven and placed it on the trivet on the table. "A few months without chocolate would be a record breaker with the women in my family."

"Who said I didn't have chocolate? There's scratch brownies cooling on the stove. It's the hospice end-days when someone clutches my hand as they…" Linney stopped, took a few deep breaths, and shook her shoulders, as if that would clear away her thoughts.

She poured the wine.

"To those who are at this table and those who are no longer able to be."

They clinked and ate, quietly at first, but the conversation grew and became lighter with each bite. The chicken meal was simple, plain, yet delicious. With each sip of wine came another toast. They toasted everything from chocolate to visitors becoming friends, clean driveways, and clean *anything*. No one said, "to love," skirting the words but not the warm feelings being shared.

By the end of the meal, the conversation gravitated to Linney's days back when she lived in the old house.

"Of course, I tried not to hang out with your tag-along mom. She was a good six years younger. A bit of a bratty girly girl," she said with a wistful smile. "Your mom baked a fine pie but was a terrible cook back then. I think I was the opposite."

Michael pushed back from the table.

Paige patted her stomach.

Aunt Linney poked at the brownies with a spatula. "It looks like nothing has changed. The brownies are burnt to a crisp. Sorry." She was about to toss them out.

"Wait. I have this." Paige found a grater and scrapped off the bottom burnt part. "If we think, biscotti, they're fine. See?"

"Easier for me to take along when I leave tomorrow afternoon," Michael said.

"You're leaving tomorrow? I thought you were staying 'til Monday."

"Can't, Flee. I have important meetings early Monday, and I need to get to some reliable Wi-Fi… Oh, don't look like that. I can definitely be here by Friday or maybe even a dinner or overnight before then."

Paige sighed and let go of her look of dismay. "Okay. Just hoping."

Crunch. She bit into the brownie/biscotti. Her face screwed up, unable to hide how hard the brownie was.

"Hey, those whatevers I made might soften in some coffee," Aunt Linney said.

"Who needs coffee?" Paige crunched again, louder than any carrot bite could be, trying to smile heartily.

Her aunt shook her head. "Pot of decaf going on

for those of us who treasure our fillings. Besides, the night is still young and we had naps. This calls for game night," she declared and began to wrap the leftovers in containers for the refrigerator.

All three joined in a synchronized dinner clean up.

"So, is it cards or scrabble?" Paige asked.

"Cards."

"Scrabble."

The two answers came at once. Then Michael and her aunt traded answers.

"Scrabble."

"Cards."

They stared at each other.

"Right. Boggle it is," Paige announced.

It turned out to be difficult to play Boggle as each would crunch down hard on the dessert, breaking the other's concentration. Coffee softened the treats, but the crunch turned out to be too tempting. They turned their attention to arguing over word viability with Aunt Linney doing most of the arguing and the cheating, much to her own glee. The game changed to Hangman with the rule being to use bizarre words or phrases.

"*Calcunow* is not a word," Paige claimed.

"Hey there's calculator. Why not a *calcu-now*?" Aunt Linney rebutted, laughing at her own joke.

Michael joined in. "My turn."

His was worse.

"Paranormal distribution? Really Michael? My aunt is rubbing off on you. What the heck is that?" Paige demanded.

"This is a normal distribution." He drew a bell curve. "This is a paranormal distribution." Michael drew a ghost.

"Okay, that's it. That's the last straw," Paige announced.

Both Michael and her aunt stopped laughing and looked at Paige. She smiled and pointed to the paper.

"See? The last straw." She'd drawn a few straws and then one far to the end and pointed her pencil at it and laughed.

"That was truly awful! But not as bad as this. Why is England the wettest country? Because the queen has reigned for more than forty years."

Michael joined in. "You asked for it. The first time I used an elevator was an uplifting experience. The second time let me down."

"Did you ever screw while camping? It's f'ing in tents. Intense, get it? In tents." Aunt Linney could barely stop laughing at her own joke.

"Just like acupuncture, Auntie, it's a jab well done. But did you hear about the commodes were stolen from the police station? The police are investigating, but they have nothing to go on." Paige giggled at their groans and the paper napkins they threw at her.

"Is this better? Your calendar's days are numbered?" She laughed. "Or…I used to sell computer parts, but I lost my…drive. Even better… I was reading this book on anti-gravity, and I can't put it down."

"Make her stop," Aunt Linney begged.

Michael rose and tugged Paige from her seat.

"Wait, I have more. A man was caught stealing food items at the grocery store while he was balanced on the shoulders of two vampires. He was charged with shoplifting on two counts."

Though Michael chuckled, he said, "That's it. Say goodnight, Gracie." He took the Boggle set and Paige's arm.

"Did you know if you've seen one shopping center, you've seen the mall?" Paige made Michael groan with that as he ushered them from the room.

Paige objected. "One more. Did you know if you jump off a bridge in Paris, you're...wait for it—"

"Do we have to?" her aunt called after them.

"You're in Seine. Insane. Get it? The river. I always loved that one."

"By the way, Michael..." Aunt Linney interjected, following them toward the stairs.

"Yes?"

"Not from my side of the family."

He nodded but mumbled, "Not so sure about that." Their smiles didn't fade even after the laughter finally stopped.

Chapter Four

Paige woke earlier than Michael did. She rubbed her neck and stretched it. The bed was comfortable, but the makeshift pillows of rolled clothing and towels didn't hold up and she'd slept contorted. At one point in the night, she shifted in such a way that her head was on Michael's stomach. She tried to fluff his firm belly like a pillow, waking him momentarily with his "oof" until they shifted and returned to a spoon position, both warm under the mismatched sheets and small coverings, even though a draft blew in from the unsealed window.

As awareness crept in, she leaned up on her arm to watch him sleep. A wave of tenderness washed over her. Had it been really just a handful of nights they shared? Was she still in some sort of foggy dream of a vacation and it was all going to suddenly end? How could they be at this point, so comfortable, so relaxed…so close? Nothing at all like it was with her ex back in Atlanta, what seemed like light-years ago.

"Careful, Groundhog Man, it's easy to fall for you," she whispered, accidentally giving verbal acknowledgement to some of her deeper feelings. *Is this love?* Paige kissed his cheek gingerly before she slipped from the bed and his arms.

Robed, she tiptoed around the clutter in the hall to the bathroom. She decided to let Michael sleep as he'd had so little rest with his work emergency and all the attention he'd given her. Already he had made more sacrifices for her in the past few days than Davis had in the months of being with him in Buckhead. Make that ever with Davis.

After freshening up and still in her robe, she padded down to the kitchen and made a pot of coffee. No K-cups in this old kitchen. The coolness of the morning drew her to the oven as she leisurely made muffins, thick healthy zucchini muffins with a few chocolate chips thrown in for good measure just as her mother had shown her to do. Her hands curled around her coffee mug for warmth as she looked out to the crystalline snow drifts and snow-coated trees. The sun was starting to melt the snow from the branches.

She thought of her Aunt Linney and wished her aunt could feel what Michael and she had blossoming between them. She pulled the muffins from the oven to cool, breaking off a chocolatey corner to nibble. With a relished, "mmm," she went upstairs to change.

Seeing Michael still in bed, she was so tempted to slide under the covers again. She stood close by, let out a heady sigh, and turned toward her clothing bag.

Without warning, his arm reached out and grabbed her, pulling her to him on the bed.

"There you are, Flee."

She squealed as he rolled her onto her back.

He kissed her. He tasted of contented sleep, mixing with the sweet lingering taste of her bite of muffin. Her robe draped part-way open. Skin touched skin, encouraging the embrace and kiss to deepen.

Leaning up, his smile shined as did his rich amber-brown eyes.

He chuckled. "Any chance you can hold that thought for later?"

With that, he quickly hopped out of bed naked. She watched his firm ass dash down the hall toward the bathroom.

"Well," she said in a pretend huff to no one. She pulled herself from the bed. "And he's the one with morning breath." She shrugged, dropping the robe and began to dig through her clothing, sorting pieces before dressing in more than panties.

Michael returned, smiling broadly, holding a small face towel as a loin cloth.

Her eyebrows heightened. "Well, that doesn't hide much."

"Should I take that as a compliment?" he asked, the towel hanging on his privates as if it were a hook. A large hook on a smooth-muscled, well-formed body. He closed the door behind him.

Paige did all she could to keep from giggling.

"Take it as you wish, but take it over there." She pointed to the wall. "It's what you get for rushing off." She turned back to her task.

In a flash, he was at her side, grabbing her. "Okay, but I'm taking you with me."

He picked her up in his arms.

"Ugh. What are you doing?"

"Following your request." He carried her and pinned her to the wall where she had previously pointed. He held her there, kissing her, the towel long since fallen, but his thick erection had not. He trailed fiery kisses down her skin, nibbling her nipples to ripe, hard points. A flash of electricity shot through her. She forgot all about the disheveled room she was to call her own. She was caught between sheetrock and a hard man and lost to each fiery biting nibble he gave her.

Tingles mixed with the now familiar longing each time his hands touched her. Her body responded to him more than with anyone else. His taut muscled body— how she loved touching every inch of his toned, caramel skin. She couldn't help it.

When her breathing deepened into sighs, his lips moved to hers. His mouth devoured hers. She tasted a minty freshness mixed with hunger. He rubbed his cock against her silken panties, grinding, and brought her hands over head. Her legs opened, and then she stopped.

"Wait."

"Oh, right." Michael let go, turned, and in the small room, took three steps to the dresser, and reached for a packet.

"That's not it. Well, it is, but also this," Paige reached down and pulled off her panties, holding them up. "No more ripping panties Mr. Can't Keep It In His Pants, or in this case, hand towel."

By the time, she finished talking, Michael was back, condom applied, and this time, both his hands slipped up past her waist, and he placed her hands on his shoulders. His gaze locked onto hers, his breath coming in deep growls.

"You mentioned something about trying out the wall?"

Before she had a chance for a retort, he kissed her, pressed her to the wall, and tapped her legs apart. His own widened to accommodate the height difference. He rubbed his cock to her soft, trimmed curls on her mound. The kisses continued, her returning his.

"Don't let go," Michael said, locking his gaze.

Stunned, Paige nodded, not really knowing or caring what he meant. She held his shoulders as his hands lifted her, cupping her bottom. Her foot found the bed for purchase. He slowed, rubbing his length to her more fully, sliding back along her smooth shaved lips and then up around her clit. From this angle, she was poised on him, fire spreading up through her from her core.

No sports were murmured. He rocked, slipping past where she wanted him to enter, teasing her into a heightened need. Each kiss, each nuzzle, each stroke, she felt more than ready. She was ravenous. She tilted her hips so he could finally sink deep into her pussy. She clenched tight on him, locking him in place. She took a breath and let him lean back then drew out partly only to press down onto him as fast as she could.

Then it began. In the late morning light, she met him in a rhythm. He entered her fully, making a soft shudder ripple through her with each powerful teasingly slow thrust. He was careful to pull back from the wall enough so that his strokes could deepen. Slow, deliberate strokes. She never let go of him as she lifted and lowered herself onto him again and again.

Fire built. All else fell away, but the sound of the rhythmic thump against the wall. Their bodies collided with an increased speed and a delicious urgency. She wanted him. She needed his thickness deep in her core and sawed onto him.

Michael bit into her earlobe and whispered, "Oh Paige…" Any other words, Oneida or English were garbled with his cry of passion.

"Michael…I think I…" Her words muddled into a

held syllable. With a burning longing, Paige muffled her cry against his shoulder as she felt a dizzying flood of pleasure wash through her. She came hard. Her fingers gripped, body clenched, shaking. Lost…so lost in timeless rippling waves.

Awareness slowly returned to the Paige. His familiar kisses landed all over her face, easing her ragged breath. She no longer panted but drew in one long dreamy breath and smiled. A belated sweet gasp of passion's jolt escaped her lips and quickly vanished into a glow.

Aunt Linney's loud, sing-song shout shattered their embrace. "Paige!"

Paige refocused and cried out in the direction of the door. "I'm coming!"

"Again?" Michael guffawed, their bodies unlocking. She chuckled. Though breathless and glowing, she wasted no time in hitting him with anything within reach. It included the hand towel and her panties.

"Naw. Too cold for these. I think I need to wear a little bit more." Michael laughed again.

Paige just groaned, threw on clothing as fast as she could, and barely gave him a kiss as she flew from the room, her cheeks still flushed and her grin wide.

****

"That should do it," Paige said, shaking the dust off her hands.

She and her aunt looked up at their handiwork. At least the grandfather clock was visible and, more importantly, ticking.

Linney reached up and set the time according to her watch and carefully closed the cabinet door. The glass front had a huge crack with two types of yellowed tape holding it together. "Let's see if it keeps time then we'll try to figure out how the chime works."

"Can't believe you found it again," Paige said, following her aunt to the kitchen to wash their hands since the downstairs bathroom wasn't working. Paige moved to the side, wiping her hands on the kitchen towel.

"That clock was buried in the rubble in the corner of the dining room, facing the wall," said Aunt Linney. "I just started working on that room and only excavated a third of it. Who knows what else is there?"

Michael entered wearing expensive dark jeans and yet another impeccable sweater. The face towel that had adorned his privates earlier was now draped over his shoulder. Paige's eyes grew wide at seeing it.

"Hello, women. Mmm. Smells good in here."

Aunt Linney simply stepped forward and took the face towel from him, wiping her hands on it. Michael joined in Paige's wide-eyed stare. He nodded to Paige, and she shrugged, feeling heat rush to her cheeks.

Michael moved to the coffee pot and poured a steaming cup. "I was thinking about taking you two out to brunch."

"You could," Linney answered. "Only it's thirty minutes away. I'm hungry now. How about eggs along with Paige's muffins instead?"

"There's muffins? Sure. I'll help with the eggs." He started to pull ingredients out of the fridge while Paige turned and dug through a moving box for her favorite pan.

Aunt Linney cut a few muffins in half and put them in the toaster oven. She broke off a large piece of muffin and ate it with a loud appreciative moan. Michael was about to do the same.

"Hey, the muffins go with the eggs. Hold off, Michael," Paige pleaded.

"Don't mind if I just kickback, feet up, and watch, do you? Yuppers. Mmm, mighty fine muffins. Must be good, huh, Michael?" Aunt Linney moaned unabashedly. "Personally, I prefer muffins warm and buttery. Toasting them might only take a couple minutes. Might want to hurry with that omelet."

"Aunt Linney, stop that teasing," Paige scolded.

"Can't help it. Gotta get my kicks somehow. You don't want me to put my *wall* up or *paper* myself in?"

Both Paige and Michael looked confused.

Then Linney marched over to Paige and yanked off a piece of peeled wallpaper that had been stuck in her hair. "One way to start to remove wallpaper from the room. Not efficient, but I bet more fun."

Both Paige and Michael froze.

Aunt Linney laughed. "Watch those eggs, Groundhog Man." She re-filled her coffee mug and set the table.

They ate their meal, relishing bites, and with far less hidden secrets than assumed. Linney explained she hadn't been in the house long after first fumigating and having the small basement cleared out professionally due to water damage. She also took the front bedroom since it had the least debris and painted it a deep violet to augment light birds-eye-maple furniture.

"I actually love the room now. It's good to have a safe haven. Maybe, Paige, you could start on your room. It's cleaned but sure needs fixing up and improved furniture," Aunt Linney encouraged. "The other bedrooms are a piled-up mess. You can choose one of those as yours later. I have a plan to the de-hoarding process, but it also has to be a reasonable pace since I work on hospice cases."

"Mom thought you weren't moving fast. I think she is dead wrong. Sounds like things are flying."

Aunt Linney shrugged. "Naw. She's right. When I first walked in, I looked in a few rooms and saw a scurrying critter, food leavings, and destroyed furniture. I just turned and left. Took me a good couple glasses of wine and a friend to send me back in two weeks later."

They toasted with the last bites of muffin. "To the house and finding the treasures from what's been left behind."

As if the house agreed, the grandfather clocked chimed the noon hour. "Hey, it's on time, too." Linney smiled a lopsided smile, cheek full of muffin.

Chapter Five

"This is gross, Aunt Linney." Paige pulled the cobweb from her hand after she had tugged on the thin chain to click on the overhead light.

"Nonsense. Dirt, stone, and few cobwebs down here now. Hmm…a bit crumbly," she said, brushing her hand on the stone wall of the small basement. She found a pen in her pocket and jabbed at the wall. Then again at the plaster.

"Phew. Just the plaster between some stones. Easy fix. A few lights down here, a table, then doing laundry will be a dream."

"I thought you said this works." Paige had loaded the washing machine and tried a button.

"Sure. You just need the secret." Her aunt jiggled the dials, reset to it normal wash, and wobbled the start button. It roared to life.

Paige hid her frustration but admitted to herself that she had moments of wistful flashbacks to the posh condo she'd come from with upgraded appliances. Shiny, quiet, functioning appliances. She purchased most of the stylish expensive furniture and left it all behind, all but a few tiny pieces. She had told herself to make sure to add that to the budget list the next time her ex asked for money. The ease of her old life compared starkly to what was presented to her now, particularly with each special twist the old house required. Still, she was starting to get the same itch as her aunt to fix everything encountered.

"Bet we could jerry rig a table with something from the wood over there," Paige suggested.

Rather than replying, her aunt nodded and found a thick, three-foot long board. They stacked cinder blocks and put the board on top.

"There. Temporary folding table. Not bad."

"Works for now," Paige agreed. "It needs a plastic tablecloth. I think putting the laundry room up on the same floor as the bedrooms would be much better, though." She started up the stairs, with her aunt following.

"Sure. Depends on a bunch of things. The condition of the floors, the rooms, the pipes, the cost…" Linney groaned.

"Okay, okay. I get the picture," Paige said with home designs beginning to form in her mind.

They walked to the foyer where Michael had just ended his phone call.

"Plastic table cloth from the dollar store for now. Putting it on my list," Paige called to Linney.

"That's my girl," Aunt Linney beamed.

"Actually, she's mine," Michael said.

"Share or you don't get her," Linney teased.

"How about mine for right now at least, since I do need to go soon." Michael pulled Paige into a hug when her aunt left. "Hey, thanks for letting me take care of a few work things first."

"I'm messy," she objected to touching him.

"Hi, Messy. I'm Michael." He kissed her lips. "Mmm. Not messy there." He added a second and third kiss while she relaxed to his arms. He smiled.

"Flee, it looks like a slight change of plans. I need to go to Dallas pretty soon."

"Dallas? All the way to Dallas?" Paige objected. "But I thought you were staying right in the area and were coming around in a couple days, or trying to at least." Why was she acting this way? She hadn't meant to sound needy but had bristled at the smiling ease at which he announced his travel plans.

"Serves you right for going to a place off the grid." Michael might have been trying to elicit a smile, but she wasn't having it. Paige couldn't control it and actually pouted.

"C'mon Flee. I'll be back at least by the weekend like I said." He cupped her cheeks as she pouted.

"I know but...all the way to Dallas? I thought you were on a project."

"In Dallas part of the time. I think I need to make it to Dushore, too. Who knows what other locations?"

"Great. The shore and Dallas. Well, see you when I can." Paige pulled away and turned to her boxes still piled in the foyer for want of direction. Why was she behaving this way? She knew she needed to get a grip but couldn't get over the fact that he was traveling far from her. Was he really a rebound?

"Look, I know I said I'd try to stay over, but this is crunch week and all the more so after that computer disaster."

Paige still gave him the cold shoulder.

"All right, pouting one," he said. "I'll try to make it for a dinner or evening mid-week if it's easy driving. I'll only be forty or fifty minutes away. No promises though."

Paige stopped pretending to sort. Her eyebrows

knitted into a stumped expression. "Dallas, Texas?"

"What? No. I'm booked at an inn located in Dallas, Pennsylvania. I wish they could put me up closer to the plant, but it was easier for those flying in from out of state. I'm in the area, Paige."

"Really?"

Michael nodded and smiled. "Dushore, PA. Dallas, PA. All around the area. Not that it matters, I'll most likely be swamped. I'm still going to miss you, though."

"I'm not going to miss you one tiny, little bit." She tried to hide her smile.

"Oh?" Michael's eyebrow shot up.

Paige shook her head. "Maybe I'll miss several bits, though." She hugged him, kissed his cheek, and her hands moved lower on the softness of his sweater. "And some of those bits are quite large." One hand squeezed his firm lower cheek.

Both eyebrows shot up. He curled his arms around her. "What am I going to do with you, Flee?"

"Ahem. Nothing at the moment," Aunt Linney interjected. "You already did enough earlier. You two nearly shook the house down. Not to mention we're a half day behind, and I have work tomorrow. So, get ready and shoo."

"Yes, ma'am," Michael said.

They stepped apart, Paige with an audible huff. She watched Michael gather his small overnight satchel and computer bag and put them by the door.

"And don't come back without wine or goodies." Aunt Linney offered her hand to shake. "Safe travels, Michael Yotahala Lukas with a K."

He took her hand and then grabbed her for a hug.

She smiled widely. "Cut that out or you will make Paige jealous. And she'll get all Southern on you."

Michael turned to Paige. "You will?" he asked, moving to the porch.

She nodded with a look of fake determination. "Southern and all the other directions on you. All over you." Paige kissed him on the lips.

Aunt Linney grunted.

Paige waved off her aunt. Linney took the hint.

"Ignore her. Here's one for the road." Paige handed him a travel mug of coffee. "And here's one really for the road." She kissed him, openmouthed. It was a deep, moaning kiss.

"Bye, now. Drive safe," she said and closed the door on a stunned Michael.

Paige brushed her hands together. "There. Got all Southern on him. That should tide him over."

Knock. Knock.

Paige opened the door. "Why did you knock?"

"The doorbell doesn't work." Michael said.

Paige just groaned at the old joke.

He pressed the bell again. "No, it really doesn't work."

"I'll put it on the fix-it list," her aunt called from the living room.

Michael reached toward Paige. She closed her eyes for another kiss. Instead, he picked up his satchel and computer bag. She sighed. Just when she gave up on one last kiss and thought he was leaving, he pulled her in, holding her tightly to his broad chest.

"Soon, Flee." He kissed her again, plunging his tongue into her mouth, grinding his hips against hers, moaning until she let out a soft whimper of need. It was only then that he released her and walked to his car with bags in hand.

"Umm," was all that came to Paige's tingling lips.

"Michael, the name's Michael." He beamed. "Thanks for the amazing birthday and beyond, Amelia Paige Myers. Get some work on the house done."

"You, too. I mean, your work, not the house, and rest up," she called after him.

He nodded. "Text me if you ever get a signal. Better yet, get some Wi-Fi."

He stared at Paige and slid into his car. Something in his expression dripped sincerity. It told her he'd return. He had to.

Neither said the words lovers say. He waved before driving off, without fishtailing even once. She looked longingly after him, and it had nothing to do with how well his car hugged the road.

****

"Yup. Got all southern on him," Paige admitted breathlessly, "but then he got all Michael on me. Jury's out on who won."

Her aunt ushered Paige inside and closed the door. "You both would have given heart attacks to many of the country folk around here if they saw you. Some people around here get married before they give each other more than a shake and a nod."

"Yeah, right."

"Didn't say what was shaking or nodding."

That made Paige chuckle. "Well, now, Auntie, you still have it going on."

"Oh hush. You know it got up and went," her aunt said but smiled in return.

"Well, you're going to get it back if I have

155

anything to do with it." Paige looked at the tightly packed living room and sighed at the overwhelming task ahead. It looked like a paper storage warehouse filled with trash in between. She resigned herself to the task and clicked on a radio near the room entrance. She jiggled the old dial, turned up the music, and began to dance to the oldie.

"Get in here with your dancing self. Besides sorting, we need to tie up these newspapers to bring to the road. Recycling is tomorrow— Where you going? Big help you are." Her aunt started to measure lengths of twine.

"I am a big help. I saw an old cart in the garage. I'm getting it so we can make the trips easier. Why not make the tasks more fun?"

Linney grunted. "No, you're not getting it."

"Am, too."

"No, you're not. I am. I have boots on," Aunt Linney said, grinning. "Good idea, dirty dancer."

"Dirty?" Paige turned to see her bottom had brushed against something dark and had a thick stripe across it. "You might be right, but I think I took after you."

Linney's backside was just as bad if not worse. The offending object causing the stains went straight into the garbage.

Soon, they figured out the best rhythm. With music blaring, they bagged garbage and began tying papers into bundles. Only a few selected items went into a box to be saved for further inspection later. They stacked newspaper bundles on the cart with wobbly wheels and, from there, wheeled it to the door and put the paper stacks on the porch. Linney would later simply fill her car and trunk with recycling to place them curbside. The efficiency of the process made both Dornheim women smile. It did more than that. It helped Linney open up.

Paige had already known of Uncle Roger and the fairly recent divorce. What she didn't know was that Linney had a short, previous marriage back when Paige's mother was still in high school. Nor did Paige know of Linney's early-day travels as she called them. All of it came out as they made their way through the dusty hours of de-hoarding part of the living room.

"Sturgis? You were at Sturgis?"

"Sure." Linney took a swig of root beer. "That was with Steve. No. Bob? I forget. Don't tell your mother."

"That you went on a motorcycle with some guy to a motorcycle rally?!"

"No. That I forgot his name. She knows I went to the rally. Gotta have someone to tell so that in case things go wrong…"

"My mom was there?"

"No, Paige, Not-So-Sage. I just kept in touch with her. Can you see your mom on a cycle? Ha!"

Paige couldn't picture it either. "So, Auntie, who was your favorite?"

"My favorite what?" Linney hoisted another bundle of crumbling papers onto the cart.

"Your favorite man. No, make it your favorite love. The one." Paige must have hit a nerve. Her aunt stopped and shrugged.

"Was it Roger?" Paige asked quietly.

"Might have been apart from my youth."

Something didn't sit right. It didn't seem to be Roger. The way her aunt answered, though, Paige knew to change the subject and mood. "Well, maybe it's time you get a new favorite."

"Yeah, right." She looked at her niece. "Oh hon, I don't mean to be cynical, but look at me. Maybe my time has come and gone. You're young. Your turn to go explore, and from the looks of Oneida man, you are doing just that. Good for you." Linney pushed the full cart to the door, as if to signal an end to the conversation.

Paige would have none of it. "You're still a sexy woman under all that gruffness. Just lose the gruff."

"Ha! And several pounds. Did you know I was skinny as a rail and could eat anything back when? Sort of like you."

"Aww, thanks, Auntie. I sort of like you, too." Paige left the room to transfer the laundry before her aunt could throw anything at her.

****

The living room was cleared to actually more than just a tunnel between antique and random furniture pieces. It had some space. It had a desk. Progress.

Paige sifted through the box of appliances in the kitchen to find her favorite lamp. She and her aunt struggled to unearth a second task chair so working desks could be available both downstairs and in Paige's makeshift bedroom. Very rudimentary, all of it but functional. By the end of the day, both women felt good but filthy. Linney claimed the shower first.

Paige returned to the kitchen in search of her displaced underthings to bring up to her room when she noticed the house phone. A land line, and it was up for grabs! No issues with lack of signal with that.

After leaving a quick voice message to Michael,

Paige took the opportunity to give her mom a much-needed call. They shared stories of the weekend, at first keeping everything about Michael on a mild, mom's need-to-know basis. There was no way to explain her intense feelings for him after such a short period of time. Perhaps it was being locked away with him in an ice storm as practically strangers or how unexpectedly gallant he had been in helping her transition to where she was to live now. Paige instead deflected the conversation to the appalling state of the house and Linney's baking, which also happened to be appalling. Paige made promises to send photos, of the house, not the brownies.

"Why not?"

"I grated off the burnt parts, and we ate them. Just about all of them. They softened nicely in tea or coffee." Paige dunked the last bite in her tea, as if in demonstration. It still crunched somewhat. Then, still sitting in the warm kitchen, tea in hand, her own mixer, pans and appliances jammed in cabinets, others stacked to the side, she felt a pang, at least for the ease of her formal lifestyle.

"Mom, do you realize less than a week ago, I was working, capable, and organized? Now my things are strewn, in halls, jammed in a tiny bedroom with peeling wallpaper or on a broken desk, held up by books. I have no idea what I am doing with my life other than prepping rooms for renovation and wanting to be with Michael." She realized her error in admitting the importance of Michael to her mother. It didn't help that her fingers were toying the cloth of one of her panties.

"Before you say anything," she continued, "I know you think it's too fast, but it's like we skipped the simple dating and went to…to…well… something else. I like Michael, and just trust me, he is someone special." Before her mother could answer, she spilled more. "I feel younger around him, though. He helps out so much. I let him take care of me. Well, not at first…but oh…he's so under my skin. It's not my MO. Back in the condo, I was always the responsible one. I had to take care of everyone, including Davis's friends." She finally took a breath.

In the pause, her mother carefully answered, "I know that, honey. You still are responsible. I think you're surprisingly together, especially with what you just went through, moving out. That Davis Greer was less than mature. We both know that. This Michael sounds driven and maybe able to pull his own weight? You might have met your match. At least that's what Linney said." It had been her mother's turn to reveal too much.

Paige nearly shouted, "You talked to her about Michael?" She waved about her purple lacy panties.

"Of course, I did, sweetheart. She's my big sister and a curmudgeon, spy, horrible baker, super nurse, dear friend, slave driver—all of those things wrapped into one person. All I can say is that it's good to know Michael's staying out of the house for a few days so you can get more settled."

"Settled? I have no clue what I'm doing, just tackling sections of this dilapidated mess. Shouldn't I be out looking for a serious job?" Paige looked at the panties she held, then returned them to the lingerie pile. "Where the heck am I going to live after this?" She picked up the stack of undies and, with the phone held to her ear, began stomping up the stairs. "And don't you dare say back home with you."

"Wouldn't dream of it, actually."

"What?" She stopped mid-step. As much as Paige didn't want to return home, she suddenly felt even more uprooted by that comment.

"Oh, that didn't come out right. We welcome you home, but you need to continue out on your own and finish inventing yourself. Look, Paige, you're on a break, a detour for a bit. Consider it a vacation from work when you're doing other things."

Paige nodded in a mumbled agreement, continuing up the stairs.

"You'll adjust there, and my sis will adjust to you. It's not a forever place for you but make your home while you two are making it habitable. Carve out a space there first. You didn't need me to tell you any of that, I bet."

"No, I guess not, Mom." Paige took in the look of her meager dilapidated bedroom. "I guess I can find a department store and maybe fix up my temporary room a notch above mere functioning. It really is a squatter-packed mess in most rooms here. I'll send pics when I get to a Wi-Fi spot."

"No rush. And Paige, it's really not just about that house. Your aunt really was scarred by Roger, you know. In the short time you've been there, it sounds like you got her to laugh. I think she needs you more than she lets on."

"I hear you."

"One more thing, honey, remember to buy a mop with the scrubber on it and those bigger work gloves. Wouldn't hurt if you bought a few new buckets and a solid wallpaper scrapper."

"Thanks, Mom, for not babying me."

"Babying? I'm just helping. Remember to floss and—"

"Eat my vegetables. Right. Love you. Grown Up Paige signing off."

Paige hung up with a bright smile just in time to hear her aunt scream from the hall, "Shower's yours!"

Paige found her aunt's things accidentally left behind in the bathroom. It included underthings surprisingly lacier than expected and a leopard print bra. "More secrets, eh, Auntie?" She knocked on her aunt's room. She opened the door, and Paige gasped. The room was stunning in a deep violet with light blonde furniture and an iron rail bed frame painted a buttery off-white. Different but charming. "Wow. Looks great!"

"Thanks. I kind of like my hair up in a bun, too."

"I meant the room."

Her aunt grinned. "I know you did, but I gotta get those compliments when I can. Planning on keeping those or can I have them back?"

Paige looked down and quickly handed the clothing to her grinning aunt. "Phone's yours. Mom's free."

"I'll call her some other time. I work in the morning, so it's reading time for me. By the way, thanks for coming to help, Paigey. G'night." She closed the door before Paige said another word. She got the hint and then some. Maybe she wasn't so different from her aunt, after all. Not as brusque perhaps, but she loved her private time, too, especially reading.

After a shower, Paige padded her way down the cluttered hallway to what was now her room. She looked at the disheveled mess and felt a pang. Strangely, it was for Michael and not for her old life.

Reaching for her lamp, she noticed Michael had left the Boogle set open on top of her dresser. He spelled out letters in the box top "U R SPECIAL TO ME."

She pulled out her cell and texted, *"So are you, Groundhog Man. Thank you for the note."*

The signal was not strong enough to send. Somehow, she thought he knew. Michael was under her skin and close to her heart. Special didn't come close to covering it. Did he feel the same as she did? He must. She knew they both felt a powerful draw to each other, one that needed to continue. What that draw was, they dare not say. Not so soon.

When she turned in, Paige inhaled the scent of the towel and folded sheets that served as her pillow. They smelled slightly of Michael. She slept alone but didn't feel it at all. In the haze of near sleep, she sent a wish for her aunt to be open to feeling the same way again.

Chapter Six

Just as the ice and snowstorm seemed to lock everyone in one place, the melting of the snow sent everyone out in all directions. Her Aunt Linney had a new hospice care assignment starting up and drove to her appointment with the family. Paige had unpacked and organized further in her room, tucking items away, knowing she'd work on the walls first and couldn't have everything spread out.

She needed to shop. Not the kind of shopping done in Buckhead where style and name brand were coveted at any price, especially on sale. A usable winter coat was a necessity and several other items, all practical. She assessed what was necessary to fix up her room and thought to also include the dining room, which apart from the grandfather clock, had not been attacked. She would claim that to do.

Her list grew from cleaning supplies, to include spackle, wall patch, brushes, and paints, in addition to the mop her mother mentioned. She wasn't sure what supplies her aunt had. Armed with credit cards, some money in the bank and more of a "buy it and return it if not needed" mentality, she left the farmhouse with determination, not waiting for her aunt's return.

"I took several wrong turns, but I ended up in Scranton," Paige said when she'd later called home from her cell, thankful to reach her aunt.

"That's the only way people end up in Scranton— by accident. What's up?"

"I'm in the bedding department. Is the bed a queen size in the room I'm using?" Paige got a confirmation and reviewed home improvement purchases. When asked, she detailed the contents of her department store shopping cart to include a couple pillows, the rest of the cleaning supplies, and a winter coat. "Do you need anything else while I'm here, Aunt Linney?"

"Sure, a couple things."

"Can you text it? Oh, right, you don't like to text. Hold on getting paper."

"No need, Squirt. I trust you on the cleaning stuff. Grab some work coveralls."

Paige pulled out a paper list anyway. "What size?"

"Whatever you wear. And boots—make that waterproof work boots. You'll need 'em."

"That it?"

"No. Some kind of snacks for munching as a reward. Whatever you like."

"Got it. De-hoard rewards. What else?" Paige had her pen poised.

"Just a big thank you, kid." Her aunt hung up.

Paige's purchases were far less lavish than her shopping sprees had been in Buckhead. Not that she missed it. At least not yet. What she did miss was the internet. Her homing instincts sent her to a coffee shop, replete with acoustic guitar music, overpriced coffee, and excellent Wi-Fi. The shop even came with a handsome bearded barista with green eyes who smiled warmly and seemed to drink in more than coffee as he looked at her. She smiled back quickly, deflecting any flirting she'd next expect. She was careful to thank him quickly, but her drawl seemed to have an effect on him.

She took off her new puffy white coat and sank into a chair far from view of the counter. She also easily sank into her competent office mentality, with her laptop open, paying bills, transferring addresses. Texts pinged in on her phone. She flew through them and sent several to friends. After the first one, Paige set the rest of Michael's aside. His texts were to be treasured.

She noted her ex's texts and emails had changed from pleas for her return to money requests. This time, Paige made sure to include his parents and her mother on her responding email to him. She wasn't Davis' puppet anymore. She explained in the email to her ex that she had paid her part of the rent through the whole month, though she had already moved out. As to the furniture, which she loved, he had a choice to keep it all. She'd transferred the final payments to his name. If he kept it, she was owed at least one half the value, receipts attached. Should he sell it, she was to get her portion which was three quarters of the value. Very detailed, professional, and precise. The fog of live-in boyfriend/girlfriend had lifted. Without her blinders on, she realized how much he'd been leaning on her and not the other way around.

"No more, Davis Martin Greer. No more. Take that!" she said to her computer. She sent the email with a flourish and took a big swallow of her coffee.

While her business acumen was in full force, she gave forwarding information to her previous employer and requested a letter of recommendation, which had been mentioned to her when they laid her off. After all, had she not accepted the promotion, she might still be employed and had been one of their best workers.

Professional and calm.

She sat back for a moment on that thought. She'd felt her efficient self all day. She'd speed-shopped. Her car was packed with cost-effective purchases. She would tackle the important Wi-Fi issue for the house next. She pulled up a list of providers.

Paige stopped. The word Wi-Fi reminded her of Michael. Her mind went from sharp business mode to something far more languid. She couldn't help herself and instead began reading the saved texts from Michael:

"I'm here at the Inn, safe but far from sound. Flee, you are on my mind. How is it that I miss you already?"

"While my program was compiling, I reviewed the best Wi-Fi for you. In case it helps, here's the break-down for the top three…"

The text was long and detailed. It saved Paige research time. She was amazed at how thoughtful her Groundhog Man was. He didn't gush. He helped. Again.

She read the next two texts.

"Why did I send that text instead of telling you about how I wish I could nibble my way down your chest and stomach? I know why. If I stop to think about you, my body betrays me and I'm in public."

"I want you, Paige."

Her eyes popped open at the last one. Heat rose to her cheeks. Okay, he gushed, too. He gushed very well.

She began to type a text.

"I miss you, too, Groundhog Man. I miss hearing your voice whisper to me. I miss touching your—"

She nearly jumped out of her skin when a cat

brushed her legs. She'd accidentally sent the incomplete text.

"Oh, you sweet thang." Paige picked up the cat and petted him, calming down. A text pinged in:

"Touching my what, Flee?"

She laughed and sent further texts to Michael.

"Face? Other parts?"

"All of you?"

"I'm in a coffee shop. Not sure if it was the cat or your texts that startled me most. I'm petting the cat, and my mind is racing. Just thinking about you gives me butterflies."

She quickly sent two more texts:

"No. Make that more than butterflies. I get a whole menagerie of fluttery, crawling things."

"Ignore that. It didn't come out right."

Michael's response was fast.

"I'll say. I was going to suggest taking a shower."

"Cute. Thanks for the Wi-Fi list, Michael. It really helped. Thoughtful present by the way."

"In that case, Happy Early Valentine's Day. Saves me buying you waxy chocolate."

Paige quickly responded.

"What about flowers?"

He just sent an emoji of roses and a note that he had to rush to another meeting. She sighed as she had been one button away from calling him.

Paige was assessing Wi-Fi options for the farmhouse when two last texts pinged in.

"Jealous of the cat, btw. Jealous of anyone who gets to spend time with you, naked or otherwise."

"Strike that. Save the naked just for me, Paige. xox"

Paige drank the last of her coffee, with her heart racing at heat of his text. She mouthed the words she texted back to Michael.

"I want to be naked just for you, too."

"Whoa, all right." Came the blushing words of the bearded barista who was clearing off her cup right then. "I'm ready, you Southern Sweetie." He dropped everything on the table to next her and came at her, arms open.

Paige's cheeks were instantly heated. "I meant him." She pointed to her cell near the cat with one hand and blocking him with her other hand.

"Mr. Cat?" The barista paused as if he were considering it. He shrugged. "Okay. I could go for that, too." With a wide grin, he came at Paige again.

She made a full football block. "No. No. I meant my text. Nothing against you or cats." Her phone rang. "I have to take this."

"Gotcha. No touching the cat, only you." The barista left her tableside, dishes in hand, and motioned he was going to the counter, smiling and nodding his head as he did so.

Paige rolled her eyes. "Hello, Aunt Linney. What's up?"

All she said was, "Get home soon. Bring mousetraps. Kind ones if they got 'em."

"Did you see a mouse?"

"Only in the garage. The house was taken care of by pest control first thing, but still…"

"Oh no. Do you think they're hiding in the debris?" Paige shivered at the thought. "Let's just shovel out the whole dang bunch."

"We can't, Paige. There's good stuff in there, too,

like jewelry. I found a couple hundred dollars stashed in an envelope, not to mention all the family heirlooms. Too bad it's not summer where we can sort outside." Then she heard something crash, followed by her aunt swearing and hanging up.

She held the cat and said in a sugary tone, "Looks like we could use one of you. Do you have a kitty friend who can come stay at the farm?" It just meowed when she put the cat down. In no time, she had arranged a Wi-Fi company to come to the farmhouse later in the week and packed up to leave the shop.

Before stepping through the door, the barista was at her side. He handed Paige a pet adoption flyer from the bulletin board. "Meow, you sweet thing. Call me when you want me. My number is on it. Never did it with a furry before, but I'm in." He opened the door for her, *accidentally* brushing against her.

She stepped out, a bit dazed, mumbling to herself. "Furry? Sweet thing? Oh no… He thinks I want to…in a cat suit? Or is it with a cat?"

Paige cringed at either prospect and made a concerted effort to note the coffee shop location. She would make sure to avoid the place.

The barista waved, most likely thinking her perusal of the shop was a look of interest.

Chapter Seven

Paige unloaded her purchases into the farmhouse, loving her new white winter coat even though it was a no name generic. It was warm and reasonably cute with a hood. She loved her drivable gloves with matching hat and scarf. Even the new, crisp sheets on sale and the shiny packaged cleaning supplies she liked. Mouse traps she did not.

Mousetraps were something new to her. She certainly never set one up. Though the grizzled old man had showed her how, twice, a trap nearly snapped on her finger. She bought humane traps as her aunt had requested, but the man in the hardware store made her buy a packet of six of the real ones with the promise she could return them. The humane ones were far more complex. She flinched as she set up each trap.

Her renovation learning curve continued as she began scrapping her bedroom walls. Flecks of deteriorated wallpaper stuck on her skin. Her aunt was right. Again. Work clothes did help. She would eventually learn to put a scarf over her hair. For now, she was in denim overalls, flannel shirt, and an oversized T shirt that read "*Bad outfit day*."

"Nice flannel," was all her aunt said over a meal when she saw it. Her aunt was in a sweatshirt that read, "*Strong is the New Skinny*."

"It was Davis'. I seemed have taken some of his

clothes from the dryer before I left. He never did the laundry. Bet I left him some of my panties and sweat pants, too. I figure it's a trade. Care for a jersey or two? One's his favorite game day shirt."

"All the better. I'll take it. C'mon let's get back to work."

Paige grew tired of scraping wallpaper, so she worked downstairs, sorting inch by inch, foot by foot of the dining room debris, saving very little of her findings. She'd turned up the music and sang with it as she whittled away at the space.

Linney screamed. Paige hopped over waste bags, rushed to the stairs, and saw her aunt lurch out of one of the bedrooms, slamming the door. It was one of three rooms upstairs that had garbage mixed in with antiques, practically to the ceiling and limited walkways through them.

"Are you okay?" Paige called up.

"Not really. Let's just say, new meaning to skeletons in the closet." Linney flew down the stairs with a bread box size plastic bag in her hands and rushed outside to the garbage. Paige approached her aunt gently after she returned and was scrubbing her hands.

"Why don't you work with me for a bit in the dining room? I set up a mousetrap in the corner already, so we should be safe. Not to mention, if I'm not mistaken, there's a bunch of clocks under there. Let's get all archeology together and excavate." Paige smiled and Z snapped her fingers.

Her aunt turned, hands on hips; her disgruntled expression changing to a smile. She must have been unnerved since no retort came.

They dug. Paige opened aged and sometimes mildewed folders, tossing most of it into yet another large garbage bag. Every now and then, there was a folder or an unbroken paperweight or trinket to save.

"What about this?" Paige asked.

Her aunt smiled, lovingly handled the piece of sculpture a five-year-old made, and threw it out, telling Paige the history of the item some sibling had made.

"Are you sure Uncle Bob wouldn't want that?"

Aunt Linney gave the best eye-roll shake of the head any Dornheim woman could give. "What do you think?"

"I think I am getting garbage guilt."

The stained holiday cutouts she held in her hands were yanked away by Linney and tossed into the garbage with a growl. Paige got the picture and stepped up her game, pausing less.

"This looks important. A house blueprint from 1980. Where do you have the other renovation documents, Aunt Linney?"

"Um, well…"

"You do have some? I gave you my own receipts."

"Those are on the kitchen counter."

Paige returned with them. After a discussion over restoration expectations and budget, Linney stomped up the stairs and returned with an empty expandable folder, a few files, and a box filled with crumpled papers.

"Have at it sometime. I do enough reports with work. All I know is we need to clean this out and hopefully ferret out things to sell to help pay for the bigger projects. Then we can sell the house unless a family member buys it at cost."

"Okay." Paige took it all in. She told herself to look at the situation as a professional work project, and she would take it on. She put the blueprint in the box and set them aside with the other necessary paperwork.

Linney's posture looked much more relaxed. She gave her aunt a hug.

"Cut that out and keep sorting, Squirt." But Linney smiled.

Paige reached into something gooey and threw that handful out with a shudder. After a few more handfuls of less foul material, she unearthed something else. She felt her stress lift. "Wait. Look, a music box. It's a filthy one, but maybe it can be saved."

Her aunt pulled it from her hands. She stepped away with it.

"Are we keeping that one?" Paige called after her aunt, knowing that the answer was yes.

Paige shrugged and went back to work. She pulled out an eagle statute. It was broken and sharp and went straight to the garbage bag without guilt. Unfortunately, it seemed to have been serving a purpose, namely keeping a mountain of papers, party hats, and waste from avalanching, so avalanche they did. Under it was a box. Not a corrugated box but one that looked special.

She knew she should deal with the paper mess first, but the aged box called to her. She opened it. It had letters, stacks of bundled letters with yellowed stamps and flourished writing. Some were addressed to Ida, her grandmother. Some to Amelia. Amelia? That was Paige's first name. Most had postal dates on the letters from the 1950's, some even older.

"Hey, Aunt Linney. I found a bunch of letters. Want to read some?"

"No way. Toss 'em," Linney called from the other room.

"You sure?" She called back.

"Yup."

"Can I keep them?" Paige asked.

"Yeah, but read 'em on your own time. Keep working, slave."

"What about you?" Paige put the box of letters in the foyer.

"Big boss prerogative. I'm trying to get this music box to work."

"Cheater." Paige knew what to do. She turned up the music and went back sorting and singing. She did, however, hear a loud objection from the kitchen. She hoped it was just a groan, but it did sound very much like swearing.

****

The next day was the same—scrape wallpaper until fingers were raw then trade with mind- numbing sorting. Paige had brought the letters she'd found up to her room, or rather the hall outside her room. She'd been too tired to read them. *Maybe tonight*, she told herself, scraping away on the wall, piece by piece. The man in the home improvement store said it would be a "cake walk" with warm water, unless of course the wall was not made of sheet rock.

"Of course, it's not sheet rock. Why would this stupid wall be sheet rock?"

Scrape. Scrape, gouge, scrape.

"Why make anything easy?"

She finally tossed down the tools and stretched. Not even her yoga stretches helped. She had already called Michael once today for a fast, whispered moment. Time for the dining room. But she walked right by it to the kitchen. Lunch.

"No wonder I'm a grouch," Paige said to no one. She had skipped lunch while her aunt was off on her hospice job. She washed her hands haphazardly and wasn't in the mood to make anything. The bag of cookies called to her as did the open bottle of wine.

"To the good life, wherever it may be." She took a deep swallow and chased it with three cookies from the package her aunt had left out.

"Did you know your doorbell doesn't work?"

Paige nearly choked. She tried to swallow but couldn't, so she squirrelled the cookies in her cheek. "Who the hell are you?" Her drawl along with the cookies made her question come out a mumbled mess.

"Hey, there. You must be Linney?"

Paige shook her head.

"Whoops. Must be the wrong house."

The man in the plumber gear carrying tools turned to go. Paige tried to call after him but couldn't so she downed the wine first.

She gasped. "Wait…sorry. I'm Paige."

"Don't be. Your parents wouldn't like that." The middle-aged man laughed at his own joke. "Plumber, comedian—same thing. Good for the pipes. So, what seems to be the problem?"

Paige wanted to say "your jokes" but held back and instead directed him to the downstairs powder room and the vague instructions her aunt left for him.

He smiled and opened the door. His smile disappeared. "Whoa. That's terrible."

"Really?" Paige objected. "We cleaned it as best as we could, carrying buckets in so you wouldn't have to work in whatever mildewy mess was in there."

"Not what I meant. Orange walls. That wallpaper, it's…what? Neon with flocking? I think you might have more work in here than I do."

"Not so bad if there's sheet rock under there." She left him to the room. Was it the wine talking or was she starting to sound like a DIY channel?

The hours wore on. Paige made it through part of the dining room enough to unearth a charming old rocker that could use a new cushion. She added "cushion" to a list posted on the wall for later hunting or purchase. A song came on she liked, so she cranked up the music and danced, forgetting the plumber.

He stepped from the bathroom, nodding with the music, which he said his niece liked. Paige made note he didn't mention a wife. She also made note of his graying-brown hair and his okay physique. Her matchmaking wheels spun. Unfortunately, they spun while he was explaining something of needing a different set of tools and what part of the faucet could be saved for the new cabinet. He said something of the new toilet Linney purchased needed some kind of bendable something and he would be back tomorrow if that was okay.

Paige just smiled and nodded pleasantly, completely missing most of what he'd said.

Her words spilled out nervously, "Could you make it later afternoon? I'm sure you'd want to meet up with Linney. I mean be with my aunt. See her and show her your bendable bits. Whatever."

The plumber looked nonplused and packed up to leave. He turned to Paige. "Cute accent, Miss, but I don't catch half of what you say. Hope your aunt will be here tomorrow. I have some interesting piping to show her."

It was all Paige could do not to burst out laughing.

****

"Okay, Aunt Linney, the crusts are ready and rolled out. I'm putting them in the fridge. All you have to do is make your best filling." She had worked out a perfect scenario of her aunt meeting and falling for the plumber. She had to set her plan into action.

"Why am I doing this?" Linney grumbled.

"Because you said you did pie fillings the best out of desserts."

"But why again are we making pies?"

"We talked about this." Paige sighed. "Because it is good hospitality to be able to offer guests, such as myself, something to eat or drink."

Linney looked at Paige as if she were nuts. "You live here now. Well, as much as I do."

Paige's southern came out full force. "Guests. Other guests. People who come to help. Anybody." She was practically shouting now. "It's nice."

"Okay, okay. You don't have to get huffy. I'll throw something together tomorrow. And no, I won't burn it. Okay?"

Paige exhaled. Her smile could not even begin to hide the frustration she had at trying to help her aunt get back out there. Before she returned to do one last chunk of the dining room, she added, "Oh, Aunt Linney, could you wear something nice tomorrow?"

"I always dress well for my clients."

Paige wasn't having it.

Her aunt continued, "Okay, okay. Matching sweater and no holes hidden in it."

Paige smiled. It was a start. A start on a very, very tall order. Operation *"Linney Meets the Plumber"* all set for the next day.

****

Paige complained to her mother briefly while her aunt was on a hospice shift. "I'm trying my hardest for Aunt Linney to step up even a fraction. It is so frustrating to make her come out of her *I could care less about men because of Roger* cocoon. She's fighting me all the way."

"Somehow, I can relate, darlin'. If you recall a certain tomboy…"

"Oh, Mom, don't start that again."

"Of course not, dear. But out of all your friends, who exactly doesn't go that extra mile? Not that you need to. You have to remember Linney was a hot hellion in her day. A real looker. Give her—"

Paige cut her off when she heard the garage door. "Gotta fly. Hot hellion just pulled up."

"Remember patience, Pai—"

But Paige had already hung up.

"What are you doing wearing those?" she asked when Linney came downstairs a few minutes later.

Her aunt gave her a look. "What we've been doing the last several days. Sorting and de-hoarding this mess." She stuffed her hair in half-done bun, tugged her dirty, stained sweatshirt, and asked sarcastically, "What do you think I was doing?"

"I mean I thought you would say *hi* to the plumber in your work attire."

Her aunt just rolled her eyes and went to the kitchen after something dinged. She came out carrying a hammer and started back up the stairs. It was only then that Paige noticed her shirt read, *"Feel safe at night, sleep with a nurse."*

"Aunt Linney, come back down. You have to visit with the plumber. He had bendy pipe questions that I never listened to." Paige nearly shouted over the sound of an electric screwdriver.

Her aunt turned around with a sigh.

"Plus, he's got great hair even if it's graying," Paige shouted. "He's about the right age for you, and he even has a nice ass." The last part she said after the noise had stopped.

"Hey, there. Heard that." The plumber stepped from the bathroom. When had he arrived? "Sound travels in here, doesn't it?" He shook hands with Linney and turned to Paige, "Thanks for the comment on my butt. Flattering especially with that accent of yours. Just to let you know, I'm married with three kids though."

Paige gasped. She saw their shared conspiratorial looks and half-stifled snickers at her gaffe. It was all Aunt Linney could do from choking back her chuckles.

Paige just flounced. "Well, before I go back to my endless tasks and you to your bendable pipes, do you happened to have any brothers who aren't married with three kids?"

"Sure."

"That's wonderful, isn't it, Aunt Linney? Please follow me to the kitchen." She continued talking to the plumber as they walked. "My aunt is single if you didn't know. Is your brother her type?"

Paige handed him a hot mug of coffee.

"Might not be. He's married with *four* kids."

That got a laugh from Linney that echoed from the

foyer.

"Thanks for the coffee, Miss."

"You're welcome. Please think harder on those single men and you might get some pie."

"There's pie?"

"Why sure there is. They're cooling. My aunt made it. She's cute and great at baking, just in case you know someone who wanted to know."

At that moment, her Aunt swore and entered. Her hair half out of the bun/pony tail, with a profound amount of dirt on her face and shirt.

"Damn vacuum cleaner bag burst." The only part of her shirt visible now was, "*sleep with a nurse.*"

Paige stepped in front of her aunt and began to usher the plumber out.

"She cleans up well, and think pie, okay?"

"She'd be plumber putty in some guy's hands I'm sure. Stop by when you're done cleaning up well." He continued to chuckle heading to the foyer.

"What the heck is that?" Her aunt glared at Paige.

"A doorbell," the plumber said.

"I thought it was broken," Paige said, quickly leaving the kitchen and her grousing aunt.

"I fixed it for you earlier. Forgot to test it. Works great now. It needed a battery and had a loose wire. Something common around here," he said and laughed his way into the bathroom.

"Not funny plumber man," her aunt said, following him. "And here's your O ring you left behind. How will anyone use the necessary without it?"

"Thanks, and I promise to look for someone for you."

Linney just grumbled in response. Her aunt

returned to Paige and shook her head. "What the hell was this match-making thing about?"

"What? It's called networking."

The doorbell rang.

Linney ignored it and continued to glare at Paige. "No, it's called pimping."

The doorbell rang again and then a knock echoed.

"I'm my own pimp thank you very much." At the last sentence, her aunt had yanked open the door.

A roundish man with a goatee stood smiling nervously before them with a clipboard in hand.

"Do you want something?" Aunt Linney snapped.

"Not sure…but I'm here for the Wi-Fi."

With Linney on the doorstep and the man looking up at her, he was eyelevel with her ample, albeit, stained shirt demanding others sleep with a nurse. He clearly looked flustered.

"Oh, you want Paige. She's a millennial."

"Okay then." The Wi-Fi man stepped in, tapping off the last of the snow from his boots.

"Where do you need to set up?" Paige asked.

His eyes trailed after Linney, so much so that he leaned around Paige and ignored her question.

"I said where do you need to set up?" she repeated.

"Wherever that interesting woman needs to do her pimp thing," he responded.

"What? Oh, she was just joking with me. It's my aunt. My single Aunt Linney. How are you with pies? She bakes you know." Paige escorted him to an alcove of the living room, ideal for any router. Partly because it was central to the house, partly because it was one of the few spaces that had been cleared out.

"You first," Paige later said to the Wi-Fi man after

unlocking the attic door.

He had a flashlight and seemed fearless as he walked up the creaky stairs heading to the attic. "Not bad up here. You're safe."

"I wasn't worried," Paige said, trying to cover the goosebumps on her arms. The bulb swayed after the Wi-Fi Man pulled the chain. The light flashed onto the thickly dusty pieces of furniture.

"Good space up here. Headroom even. Floor boards are old oak. Not bad. Think about fixing it up."

"Along with everything else. It's actually one of the only places that hasn't been hoarded to the rafters." Paige took it in. The small cracked window looked out to the front yard, the two side ones to the meadow. The windows gave muted light through the papers covering them. Most of the flooring was in place, though the insulation looked old. More to add to the list.

She and Wi-Fi Man negotiated where to cut in for the dish needed for Wi-Fi reception. He went down the stairs for the ladder he'd left in the upper hall. Paige began poking at the drawers of a hutch and moved to the dresser, sliding most of the drawers open to reveal empty vintage linings. One drawer wouldn't budge.

"Let me help. I have gloves." He gave it a jiggle and a tug, and the drawer opened a bit. He reached in and pulled it all the way open. "Here's the culprit." He pulled out two small tied stacks of letters and handed them to her. Far newer letters than the ones she had previously found. She took the letters and left Wi-Fi Man to his work, thanking him and encouraging him to have a slice of pie when he was done.

****

Paige danced a happy cha-cha-cha step. Her aunt

joined her, holding Paige's hips and kicking out to the sides. They sang.

"We have lots of Wi-Fi." *Kick!*

"And the toilet flushes." *Kick!*

"We have lots of Wi-Fi." *Kick!* The song continued like a conga to the kitchen with the plumber and Wi-Fi Man following just shaking their heads.

Coffees were poured for all. Paige ended up with tea since the pot ran out. Pies were sliced and plated. One was apple cranberry with caramel. The other mixed berry. Linney and the Wi-Fi man sat at one end of the table. With beaming smiles, all four dug in nearly at the same moment. Smiles completely disappeared on two of them.

Paige swallowed hard.

The plumber reached for a napkin.

The Wi-Fi Man just said, "Mmm. What is that? Salted caramel? Kind of savory, but I like salt."

Linney just nodded and ate a second and third bite. Paige stared in disbelief. The plumber shrugged in near horror. It was salt with a hint of apple flavor. She bit into the berry slice. Her cheeks puckered.

Wi-Fi Man's smile widened. "Woo wee. That berry pie has a pucker. Not too sweet."

"I skipped the sugar in it." Linney said. "Better that way."

Wi-Fi Man seemed to agree, chomping through it.

"Yup, not too sweet, all right," the plumber agreed. "Great crust though. Could use some ice cream."

Paige was already on it. She and the plumber scooped big portions while the other two waved it away, grabbing for seconds on the pie. And then it happened.

"Delicious pie, Linney. I'd like to pay you back and take you out," the Wi-Fi Man said.

"Well, I don't even know your name," her aunt rebuffed.

He pointed to his uniform. It said George. "I'm George."

"My first husband's middle name was George. Didn't stick with him, it turns out. So, I better not."

"Just one date. I can change my name to Cedric if you like it better. It's my middle name."

"I guess George will do. I work an odd schedule with hospice care," Linney said and stopped talking.

George let her. The other two just stared, clinging to their mugs, ice cream melting over the bitterly tangy pie slices.

"Hmmm. Okay. Lunch. Nothing fancy," Linney said flatly.

"I know a great diner," both George and Linney said at the same moment. They both stopped.

Linney eyed him suspiciously. "You first, where's yours?"

He told her.

She just nodded and ate a bite of pie. She looked him up and down. "Deal, George. It's a deal."

They set up a time for Sunday.

Paige walked the plumber out of the kitchen. "What happened back there? Did the salt get to their heads?"

"Naw. Good plumbing does it every time. Can't believe the same person made the crust that did those fillings."

"Yup, pretty hard to believe, isn't it?" Paige looked away, guiltily.

The plumber smiled a knowing smile and gave her the bill along with instructions of which pipes to wrap in the basement. They discussed the cost-effective placement of another bathroom at some future date. He also gave her his card.

"Remember to call me before you turn on the outdoor shower in the summer," he said "You two don't look like you have change to spare, and I wouldn't want to see a flood."

Paige smiled and nodded. *There's an outdoor shower?*

"Thank you again," she said, really meaning the words.

"You're welcome, and you're doing a good job trying to fix things up, including this old eyesore of a place. Call if you need help." He seemed to mean it, too.

He smiled and left. It was then that Paige noticed his bill. He had reduced his charges. Still pricey but reduced. She and Aunt Linney were inching toward being part of the community.

Meanwhile, her aunt was in the kitchen inching toward something very different. She was becoming closer to dating a middle-aged, balding man. Thankfully, something showed promise even if it wasn't Paige's skills in a speedy renovation.

Chapter Eight

The next day, nobody came, apart from one man to pick up ornately carved chairs Linney had sold to him.

"Dust catchers," she'd called them, but the price collected paid for the plumber's bill.

The rest of the day was just the two women. Linney wasn't at the hospice job. First task was the stubborn wallpaper in Paige's current room. Linney produced a magic tool with spikes, borrowed from a fellow nurse, and scratched the paper layers in swirls.

"We need the window open for this part." Her aunt informed her.

Paige removed the paper covering the window. She screamed when she saw the bones of a tiny critter trapped between the storm window and the inner one. Her heart raced. A warm sunbeam spilled in through the window, calming her shivers. "I need to put curtains on the list of things needed."

"Make it ear plugs for me. My ears are ringing from your scream," her aunt said with one finger plugged in her ear and wiggling. "I found lots of cloth in a bin downstairs. For now, look through that before buying something new."

Paige nodded while Linney took care of the window.

Paige filled a bucket of hot water as she had before. Only this time, they put in a chemical adhesive remover. They applied it and waited. They started peeling and scraping. Pieces actually came off. Tiny shreds but faster than before. Linney sat, bundled on the floor working on a corner near the open window.

"So, how's your hospice case?" Paige asked.

Her aunt inhaled and exhaled slowly. "Something's not right with this one. Seems to be declining much faster. They told the family a good two months." She shook her head. "Lucky to get two weeks. Hard when that happens. Makes it hard to soften the blow."

Paige stood up and put her hands on her aunt's shoulder. Linney patted her hand. Paige massaged Linney's neck and upper back.

Though she grumbled about it, Linney moaned into the touch. "Keep working girl."

Paige moved back to her spot, scrapping off layer after layer of wallpaper. Her aunt asked her about the lay-off she had and complimented her on pursuing the recommendation. They spoke of Paige's career, related fields, and possible positions in the area, even if it was temporary.

Then the conversation drifted to Michael. Paige stopped and stared off dreamily.

"Oh, for Pete's sake. No, make it my sake. Go ahead, call the man. Otherwise, I won't get any work out of you."

Paige took the portable landline phone from her aunt. She beamed and whispered a breathy hello to Michael, followed by, "I'm stripping."

"Oh, brother." Her aunt rose, stole the phone, and put it on speaker. "She's stripping wallpaper, and I'm here, too."

"Michael, help!" Paige shouted. "My aunt is

asphyxiating me."

"No, I'm not. The window's open."

"Isn't it about twenty degrees out there?" came Michael's rich voice.

"Puts hair on the chest," Linney said. "Well, mine at least. Plucked a stray hair the other day."

"TMI Auntie." Paige stole back the phone. "We're working with chemicals to get the wallpaper down." She clicked the phone off of speaker. "When are you coming?"

"Seems like anytime you touch me."

Paige's blush was all that was needed for her aunt to let out a huge groan.

"That wasn't me. That was her. I mean, I didn't make a sound like that. Well, I do but not this time."

Her aunt rolled her eyes and turned to her task.

Michael chuckled. "Paige?"

"Yes?"

"I can't stay long. Hold on."

The pause felt like an eternity. Why did she get so school-girlish with him? What did he mean he couldn't stay long?

Aunt Linney looked over at her and smiled a cheesy grin before shaking her head and returning to the chemical peel-scrape technique. Each moment on hold made her heart race and her mind spiral. Was this handsome, incredible business man just easing into a brush-off? Why did her mind go there? No matter what, she needed to put up a brave front, didn't she?

Just as she nearly reached a crescendo of panic, he returned to the call. "Sorry, Flee. I'm in the middle of things here."

"Of course. Understandable. I guess I should let

you get back to work."

His voice became muffled as if he were cupping the phone. "I love hearing your voice, Paige. I miss you, and I'll try to be over tomorrow night."

"Oh me, too, Michael…I mean I miss you, too, not that I'm coming over." She whapped her hand to her forehead several times for sounding so idiotic. She heard another mocking snicker from her aunt.

Michael's warm laugh eased her. He let out a long audible breath. Her mind reeled in a different direction, one where her pulse quickened. He wrapped up the call with his repeated assurance that he would be there the next evening and through the weekend.

"Bye, Michael. I-I…" Her words faltered. "I'll see you," she said in a dreamy whisper and hung up. Silence hung in the air.

"Well, now, you didn't say it," Linney pointed out.

"Say what?" Paige straightened her posture and scraped off wallpaper. "Oh, that. Oh, Aunt Linney, it feels so right. He is coming back, isn't he? I love the rush when he holds me or how my heart races when he's here." Paige smashed the sponge onto the wall, the same spot where Michael had pressed to the wall and taken her days before. She rubbed it and rubbed it.

Her aunt shook her head and rolled her eyes. "Seriously? I think the cleaning fumes are getting to you."

"Huh?" Paige shook herself from the reverie. She moved her hand from the spot and scrubbed hard all around, scraping where needed. "It's more than the fumes. It's the…the…"

"*Nuwak.*"

"New wak, old wak, whatever that is, I agree."

Paige paused. "Wait, what is that?"

"Lust."

Paige thought and shook her head. "More than lust, don't you think?"

"Only time will tell."

Paige frowned.

Her aunt sighed. "Yes, more than lust. He looks at you with something way better than lust. He looks like he cares for you."

"He does, doesn't he?" Paige scraped with long smooth strokes. "He's a good man. I never said that before with such conviction about someone I was seeing. There's something in him that appreciates my achievements, not just my curves. Chemistry and… Oh Aunt Linney, could he be—"

"I know where you're going. Hope so. Don't rush it, Squirt…but he could be. Lord knows you deserve it."

"We all do." Paige inhaled with a deep sated breath. She coughed.

"Told you the fumes were getting to you. Go dump that bucket. Hot water'll do the rest. Let's get this done before we take a lunch break."

The adhesive remover worked on walls, separating the paper, but had the opposite effect on them. Though one was twice the age of the other, in the hard-working chemical haze of the past few days, the two women became closer than they had in all the years before. They both knew it, but neither said it.

****

Aching from the scraping, Paige stretched and balanced in yoga poses in the kitchen while Linney whipped together a lunch. They talked, teased and laughed.

Linney tried to bend into one or two of the moves with Paige but groaned. "Paige, sorry, but I think fat women don't do yoga. I feel like a certain doughboy, or girl in my case. Good title for a book though."

Paige disagreed and helped her aunt stretch more, holding her in a pose. They ate and talked about the letters written to Grandma Ida and Great Aunt Amelia that Paige had skimmed.

"I thought they would be all love letters. Most were about crops or apples or weather. Amelia's letters were a bust. I'm named after her, but the only thing I know is that she was pined after."

"Pining's good."

"Yes, but no details at all. Who knows what they looked like? He could have been skinny as a rail or have thighs the size of tree trunks."

"Worse if hers were the huge thighs."

They both laughed but Paige stopped long enough to assess her own thighs and shook her head.

"Don't be disappointed. People were repressed back then. Lots of babies, though, so something must have been going on." Linney bit into a piece of non-sugared berry pie.

Paige followed suit except her pie had sugar sprinkled liberally over it. "I almost gave up on the letters until I came across one from Grandpa Benny."

"Oh?"

"He wrote to Grandma Ida about how he was clearing stones from some blazing hot field. He described how he watched her coming to him with a thermos of water. He said he drank the whole thing, but it didn't quench him. He said he couldn't do what he wanted to with her with her family in the distance or something like that. I do remember this part. He said, 'When I ask you this time, will you say yes?'"

Both women sighed and sipped from their mugs. Paige's was coffee, Linney's wine.

"Oh, there was another letter from Grandma Ida I liked." Paige set down her mug. "Something like she had to love him with a name like Dornheim, and that he had to do it right and not in a letter if she were to become Ida Fetzer Dornheim."

Both women laughed.

"I remember Grandma Ida." Paige started on the dishes. "But what was Grandpa like? All I remember of him was a sort of glassy-eyed Alzheimer's stare."

Linney sighed. "It wasn't all love and hugs growing up. At least not to me, being the oldest. I had to care for the others. Every family was that way to make ends meet back then, especially in farming areas. Oldest took care of youngest. Pop was religious, sort of more like congregational, his way or the highway. I kinda wonder if he picked it up from Uncle Fredrick. There was a force, the drunkard. Not big on people of any color, Native American included, the idiot. He was cuckoo for Cocoa-puffs. Old reference. I always hated it when he came over, always drunk.

"Did my Mom like him?"

"Uncle Fredrick? She didn't know him. My Dad? Sure, he was all smiles for your mom. She was his baby girl. He had it easier by the time she was a teen. Good crops and lots of help. Oh, stop giving me puppy dog eyes. I had way more fun than your mom ever had. She never even sat on a Harley let alone poured whiskey in a bar in the Arizona desert. So, quit." Linney smiled.

Paige followed her with a bucket filled with the

chemical bottle and tools needed for the downstairs bathroom.

"Okay. Just one more. Who's Samuel and Marilyn?

Linney stopped short and tightened her eyes. "Where did you hear those names?"

"Letters. I didn't get a chance to read them."

The fierce expression from her aunt hit her like a Mack truck. *Linney.* Her aunt's name wasn't from Linda. It was from Marilyn.

"Oh. I just realized *you* are Marilyn. They're your letters, aren't they?" A wave of panic washed over Paige. "I'm so sorry. I had no idea. I'll get them. I honestly didn't open them. Please forgive me."

Her aunt just shook her head. "Nah. It's okay. Just all this talk of Uncle Fredrick the Spiteful somehow twisted it. I'll tell you. It's time I told someone. Your mom doesn't even really know."

Paige stopped in her tracks. Her aunt, her quirky, generous aunt trusted her and needed her. She felt a rush of compassion and warmth mixed with fear at what her aunt might say.

"C'mon Squirt. We need to get this sickeningly awful wallpaper down. I'll tell you as we go. Who puts tangerine flock wallpaper in the powder room? Oh, right, my own mom who thought it would be cheerful, years and years ago."

As they worked, her aunt told of Samuel. She spoke of his deep chocolate skin and it being a time when multi-racial romance happened in cities but was not heard of in rural places. And how, in a farm community, people stayed with *their own kind*, which meant Episcopals didn't mix with Lutherans even, let alone other intermixing.

"Oh, Paige, he was a muscular dream. I remember it like yesterday. Skin dark, smooth, and hairless. Smile so bright when I approached him. He was a good swimmer. So there goes another stereotype."

"*Nuwak?*"

"Big time and caring. He was my first love. I would have married him had things worked out differently. Our family wasn't big on him nor his on me. He left for college and took my heart with him. I broke up with John George because he was prejudiced."

"The Wi-Fi guy? I thought—" Paige swirled the scratching tool over the flocked paper.

"No. He's George Cedric. Not him. Who knows about him? I meant my first husband back when I was far younger than you are now. I married him because I was expected to. We both hated every minute. My divorce sent me traveling." She poured the strong scented de-glue chemical. "I met men along the way. Roger, you know. Tom, he wasn't bad or Big Emo. He was good at—" Redness spread to her cheeks as she applied the chemical. "Where was I?"

"Um, I thought you were telling me about Samuel, but I can roll with it."

"Right. Samuel. Man, was he a hunk."

Linney drank wine. In the enclosed space, the chemical fumes were strong. The draw fan barely helped.

Paige worked closer to the open the door. "Do you need a break?"

"Naw. Just started." Linney's words slurred a bit. They both sponged on the chemical. "Do you know we once did it right there in the creek?" She pointed to an east facing wall. "A mile thataway. We were kissing and swimming in our underwear. That rope swing was a blast, all the splashing." She waved her arm for effect. "Did I say underwear? No bra even. You have to try it. So freeing."

Linney's arms were waving still. Paige stopped scraping and stared, completely drawn in. The chemical needed more time and so did the story.

"Samuel wasn't ashamed of his body. He taught me to appreciate my own form. Not that I didn't look as good as you do, kiddo. I was the package just like you."

"Now I know you need some water. Come with me." Paige gave her a hand up.

Her aunt complied and kept talking as she followed, "I swung so high and flew off that rope. And when I was climbing up that muddy bank, he just turned me around and kissed me and pressed me into the mud…"

Paige poured water into a glass while her aunt continued, "And then, oh, that was the first time. Mud all over me, squishing against him."

Her aunt motioned while Paige plunked ice in the glass one at a time.

"D'you know, it didn't hurt. It was heaven, Paige. I rode him for hours. Soft mud, hot air, water lapping. The memory's so real."

Paige had poured her aunt a huge glass of water, but drank it all herself. Both women stared into the void, thinking about the story.

Paige snapped out of her trance and gave her aunt water, pouring herself another. She raised her glass to her aunt. "Here's to mud in your eye."

****

After Linney's stirring tales and much more water,

she and Paige returned to wallpaper stripping in the powder room. The fumes had slightly disseminated. Peeled pieces lay in twisted piles on the powder room floor. Lower layers peeled back with a struggle.

"Why didn't you look for Samuel?" Paige asked.

"I dunno. Figured it would have happened. He could have found me."

"Really? Think about it. Marilyn Dornheim. But you are now Linney Smith. Hmm. Nearly the same."

"I tried once on Facebook. Too many Samuel Jackson's. Not to mention Samuel L. It wasn't him by the way."

"Do you have any lead? Any reunion?"

"Hmm. Someone said he had gone out west. Maybe Utah or Colorado?"

"Okay, that helps. Anything else?"

"Are you trying to fix me up?"

"No. I'm trying to get you to reconnect so you can move on." Her aunt sneered when she'd said that. "Okay, okay. But wouldn't it be cool to talk to him?"

"He did have such a dreamy voice. He would whisper my name in my ear. Do you know what that's like? It felt like my clothes would fall off me." She ripped off a big chunk of wallpaper.

Paige nodded and ripped. "Flea."

"Yes, I know Michael calls you that."

"No. Flea or tick, or some dead thing stuck inside this wallpaper. Eww."

They both laughed.

"Seriously, Aunt Linney…"

"Just, please call me Linney at this point."

"Okay, Linney at this point." That got another glare. "Okay, Linney. Did Samuel have a middle name?"

"Sure."

"And it was…"

"Shh…I'm thinking." She scraped and ripped off wallpaper for another minute and stopped. "Reuben!"

"Please tell me that is his name and you aren't hungry."

"It is his name, but I'm also getting hungry. Wish pizza got delivered out this way."

The third miracle of the day happened. The first was removing wallpaper from Paige's room. Second was stripping the powder room walls. The third came with getting a pizza delivered. It was only lukewarm but delicious. The chemical fumes mixed with the pizza scent and permeated the house. Though the temperature dipped far below freezing, the women opened the windows, and ate pizza, all in a happy haze.

Then Paige did something even more amazing. She found a phone number for a Samuel Reuben Jackson…in Colorado.

****

It wasn't that it was late. It was that they were exhausted. Paige let Linney shower first again, thinking it might be sobering. By the time Paige toweled her hair and walked to the stairs to head to the kitchen for tea, she heard her aunt's voice through her open bedroom door and dashed downstairs. Uncharacteristic though it was, she quietly picked up the kitchen extension and was rewarded for her eavesdropping.

"Hello?" came a deep voice.

"Is this Samuel? Samuel Reuben Jackson?" her aunt asked.

"Yes." The man's smoky voice hung on the word.

Her aunt let out a puff of breath and went silent.

"Look, if you're calling me," he said, "and you don't even have your script down, there's no way I'm buying whatever you're selling, so maybe we should cut this call short and you should go on to the next one on your list."

"No, wait, please. I'm not selling anything. I wanted to speak with you," Linney said.

"Who is this?" the voice rumbled.

"I…I waited so long to talk to you, and now I don't know what to say."

"Who is this?" the voice asked softer this time.

"Sam?"

"Your voice sounds familiar."

"It's me."

"Marilyn?"

Paige nearly gasped into the extension at his recognition of her aunt's voice.

"Yes."

"Pennsylvania Marilyn? Pennsylvania Marylin who's supposed to be dead?"

"Pennsylvania Marilyn who is very much alive, and for a multitude of complicated reasons I'm back in Pennsylvania right now. And no one calls me Marilyn anymore, not since…well, for a long time."

Silence.

"Is it really you, Samuel?"

"Yes. So, what are they calling you now?"

"Linney. Linney Smith actually. I married a Smith, and then I divorced the Smith, among other things. What about you?"

"Name's the same as you can tell. Married and divorced. Never really stuck… This is so unbelievable

Marilyn. My Marilyn. Any chance we can do this on video chat?"

"I'm not sure I'm ready for that yet. I'm barely used to the thought it's you and I'm hearing your voice again." She had a softness to her voice. "Besides, I don't look like I did in high school."

"Does anybody? I, for one, am bald and a bit rounder." They both said rounder at the same time, then gave a nervous laugh.

Paige didn't mean to, but she couldn't help herself as she listened on the extension, thankful that her grandma had a home with old school phones with old fashioned portable extensions. Her toes wiggled at the laugh the two had just shared. The two past lovers got more and more comfortable as the call went on.

He spoke of the shade of an oak tree down by some stone fence and how he lifted her up on the wall. "Do you remember how you got me so worked up kissing that I just pushed your underwear aside and…"

"I remember like it was yesterday. Sometimes, I wonder if only it could have been different. I would have loved to have stayed with you. Then…"

"College happened. Life happened for us both, Marilyn. Oops, Linney."

"Please call me Marilyn. Seems right somehow. I miss your voice. Remember how we used to sneak into the closet to talk? You in yours, and me in mine. Hey, this closet right here as a matter of fact."

A door creaked open.

"Only there is no chord being stretched on this wireless phone." She sighed. "I came back to help my mom in the end. Both my parents died. The house fell apart even before probate and the squatters. I'm renovating it now with my niece's help. You wouldn't believe it, but she found your letters this week."

"Oh, those. Not much of writer back then. Or now for that matter."

"I wish I could have found you sooner."

"I did look for you, too, Marilyn," Samuel said with a murmured sigh.

"Actually, you're my early Valentine present from my detective of a niece."

Paige inhaled, hoping they didn't hear her. She really did need to hang up but was addicted to eavesdropping.

"Are you still there, Sam?"

"Yes. Just lighting up something."

"You smoke now?"

"Only the good stuff, but I prefer it in cookies."

"Where do you live now? The phone number says some kind of Colorado number, but it could be anywhere."

"It is Colorado. I have an idea. How about this? I'll look you up in Facebook, and you look me up?"

They did just that. They scrolled through each other's photos and told stories. Neither had kids but had nieces and nephews. He had pets.

Paige hung up the extension quietly. Step one done. Make that two. Old flame and possible new flame with Wi-Fi man. The rest was up to her aunt.

Paige's room was chilly, though the window had been long since closed. She added an extra blanket and draped Michael's shirt over her new pillow. It still had the vaguest scent of him or at least so her mind told her as she curled up clutching it. He would be back in her arms tomorrow.

In her exhaustion, she didn't see his text until the next morning.

"Coming back to you is like wanting to rush back home. It should have been sooner. Sleep well, my sweet Flee."

Chapter Nine

Paige's aunt slept in and then rushed to her hospice care work. Paige just slept in. Excavating much of the trash in the dining room had revealed valuable items to sort through. She did this with an easier pace, cleaning off an entire collection of tins, which she lovingly stacked in the foyer. It almost looked like a brick wall of antique tins, most likely a few carrying some value.

The nearly twenty clocks were placed on or around the dining room table for detailed cleaning, further assessment, or repair. She probably should have worked longer but didn't. Having Wi-Fi was like a dream and far too tempting with music and direct access to accounts. Emails were easy to send. She stopped short of getting caught up in social media, since she was still incognito from her ex and his whole fraternity Buckhead crew.

Paige rose and stretched, deciding to cook something. She began to marinate a defrosted roast. She peeled and cut root vegetables, singing as she went. Meal prepped. Though Michael would probably ask her to dinner, she wanted him to have a home cooked meal.

That gave her pause. Did they really skip dating and go straight to homebodies? She looked down at her baggy clothing. Not just homebodies but a frumpy homebody?

"I'm too young to play frumpy housewifey. Forget

it," Paige scolded the innocent roast before putting it in the oven.

Yoga clothing called to her. She slipped into her formfitting things, expecting them to be tight with the calories she'd been consuming. Surprisingly, when she looked in the nearly unserviceable mirror propped in the hallway, her yoga outfit looked like it fit. That brightened her smile, even if the mirror was foggy and most likely misleading.

She brought her mat to the foyer, appreciating the airiness the tall ceilings afforded. With soft Indie music, she moved through her yoga positions. It would be another hour before Michael arrived. Or so she thought.

She was wrong. Almost through her routine, Paige bent into a wide-angle fold, hands to the floor, bottom to the door. She felt a sudden cold breeze on her upturned cheeks and looked between her legs. "Michael?"

"I knocked." He grinned and dropped his bags, arms open. "I see you are very ready for me."

She should have been miffed. She wasn't even apprehensive or ready with a return quip. All she felt was happiness unfurl at the sight of him. She straightened and ran, ponytail bouncing, into his arms, and nearly bowled him over as she hugged him.

"Love what you've done, Flee."

"The place. Yes, huge progress."

"No, Flee, your outfit and that flexibility."

"Are you going to kiss me, make lecherous comments, or what?" Paige demanded.

"How about all three, especially the *or what* part?"

Michael made good on his promise. He pulled her body against his, wrapping her in his arms, his coat open and enfolding her. He kissed her with a reacquainting flit of tenderness. The sweet kiss of greeting was only momentary.

Paige's breathing deepened. In an instant, he had her turned, back pressed to the door and making her gasp in no time. Cupping her ass cheeks, he lifted her. Never releasing her from his hungry kisses, her legs wrapped around him. He ground his hardening cock against the thin fabric of her yoga pants. Unfortunately, her leg slid on his coat, bringing her to her feet.

His laugh resonated in the foyer.

"Not sure you can tell I missed you, Flee." Michael's pants bulge was more than evident.

"Hadn't noticed," she lied breathlessly.

"I have something for you."

Her eyebrows shot up. She avoided saying, "I can tell" and instead tugged him up toward the stairs and bedroom. "Aunt Linney's at work."

"Oh?" He threw his coat on to the worn newel cap in haste and lifted his travel bags, leaving the music and yoga mat behind. His light brown eyes never left sight of her, not even glancing to any of the house changes around him.

By the time they reached her hovel of a bedroom, she tossed off her exercise bra and ripped clothing from him, the door to the bedroom left open. His shoes and pants flew off. His tie was stuck. He just yanked it overhead, flinging it somewhere out the door and over the handrail. They fell to the bed, Paige on her back, he on top.

His deep voice growled, "No need to rush."

Paige felt the exact opposite. She silenced him, mirroring his deep, hungry-tongued kisses. His large, warm hands touched, exploring every inch of her naked upper body. His kisses left trails of goosebumps. He tugged on a nipple and let it snap, sucking it, sending shockwaves of longing through her.

His hand alternated from gentle, gliding strokes to rubbing her yoga pants so firmly that the seam sank into her folds, eliciting a whimpering moan. He bit her neck and trailed up to her lips. The next fiery kiss tasted of Michael and slight musky salt from her own skin. Her legs pulled him, grinding against him through her pants. He tore the packet so hard it sent the condom flying.

Her laugh flooded over his moans as he rose to dig for another in his clothing. She took that moment to tug off her pants and panties, leaning back, breathing so heavily that her breasts rose and fell with each breath. He rolled on a bright red condom. She eyed him and giggled again. He stood before her, his amber eyes set to hunger, melting her smile into a smolder. He crawled over her.

There was no mature, sweet, lovemaking. There was only a raw fire. Positioning her legs wide apart, he drove deep into her. Rocking back, he then sank in again, the mushroom head of his cock driving all the way in. He ground into her.

Paige's breathless, silent cry locked her mouth to an open O as she felt the fullness of his cock buried in her pussy. The pounding rhythm increased the frenzy. She clenched him and bucked against his body. Limber from her yoga, her rush of sensation amplified. She whimpered, trying to hold back from exploding too quickly, but the pulsing crush of his broad chest against her with each filling stroke nearly drove her wild.

Her eyes popped open when he knelt back on his

heels, taking her with him, lifting her upright to near sitting. With each stroke, he arched and lifted his pelvis as he thrust into her, groaning a deep animal sound.

"P-p-please come!" She heard herself scream.

Colliding with each stoke, they did exactly that, gazes locked through the spasms. They clung to each other, Paige open-mouthed, breathless. Finally, with a gulp of air, her body unclenched. They unlocked and collapsed onto the bed on their backs. Both speechless. Both gasping.

"That was…" Michael panted, rubbing his side.

"Incredible." She grinned, kissing his face.

"Painful…ow…my side…stitch."

Both snickered. She massaged his side, kneading out the knot to his squawking groans.

"Too much stress. I need more exercise," he confessed.

"I think it's our exercise that got you this way," she teased.

He nodded. "A warm up next time. That, or greet me in your work clothing instead."

"You think that would help?"

He shrugged. "It might slow us down. One extra layer of clothing." He chuckled, drew her closer, and threw the covers over them.

"Would love a few minute's rest, sweet Flee." Michael barely had his eyes closed when he fell asleep.

It was only later that she learned he'd started at five a.m. just to get to her sooner.

By the time he came to the kitchen, the roast and vegetables were done. The food had been plated and the simple table beautifully set for two, complete with a candle. As requested, Paige was in her work clothing—

jeans and a sweatshirt that read, *"Warning Explicit Content."*

"Like what you see, handsome Yotahala Lukas?"

"Thank you, Amelia Paige, *tewakwelyákhwaˀ.*" He had his hand on his heart, his eyes showing he was taking it all in.

"I hope you just said you're hungry. Because I am. Not to mention thirsty." She chugged water again.

Before touching his food, he reached for her hand. "I don't just like what I see. I love it."

Their eyes met, and Paige diverted the stare first. The warmth of his hand holding hers shot through her. Time stood still. Had he just almost said he loved her? She couldn't even think the word, let alone feel it, could she? Wasn't it too soon, and who knew if he was even staying around? Maybe it was just afterglow talking.

The adrenaline rush ended with a deep inhale and the scent of food, kicking her back to her senses. Still, his words lingered in her mind.

He pulled back his hand, breaking the stillness of the moment. "Nice sweatshirt, too, although the warning is just a bit late."

****

After dinner, and perhaps inspired by the burst of released energy for Paige and the nap for Michael, the two began to research the clocks she had unearthed. The first idea had been to unload them all at an antique shop or two. When they looked up the value of a Howard Miller Emporia clock, at well over ten thousand, they saw the error of that method.

"No, put it over to the right. Yes. Right there, Paige said. "Got it. These pics should work with the chimes video. What did we call this one?"

"It was a German Hermle Black Forest Mantle clock, working chime, all original parts," Michael said. "I think we said it was going to the antique dealer website. The next one is nearly the same but has dings and scratches, so it's going on eBay, flat rate shipping or free pick up."

"Okay, set up that one, label it number… yes…number 14." Paige said looking between her notes and the computer screen. "Just needed to make sure I have the right file…okay, ready."

Paige had explained to Michael, she'd only skimmed a few of the bills and was going to set up the books the following week for the house restoration. She suspected funds were far more limited than the costs, maybe even by half and preferred not to deal with loans. The clocks were one way to recoup costs.

Together, Michael and Paige started to get a better handle on the clocks, researching them, deciding which was for quick sale, which needed repairs, and which were the treasures. Some of the clocks they thought were valuable—an ornate cuckoo clock—weren't and others far more valuable. They'd worked so well together, it was almost like a game.

"And these are just the clocks. Who knows what else you find, Paige?"

"But some have to go to the family or stay with the house. That grandfather clock for one. Might be lucky to be worth a few hundred with the warping, repairs, and chips, but it belongs here, cracked glass and all."

Michael looked at it. "Maybe. I wonder if we could have someone cut a replacement glass. Look, it just has rudimentary latches holding it in place."

"I do not," Linney came in, knocking snow off her

boots onto the pad near the front door. "My latches are well formed."

Paige helped her off with her coat, hanging it on the makeshift broken coat tree she'd recently set up with the help of duct tape. She hugged her aunt warmly.

Her aunt smiled but said, "Quit."

"Aww, Auntie, are your latches all grouchy and hungry?"

"Leave my latches out of this, and what are you and handsome doing? Or should I not ask?"

"Each other." Paige said quickly at the same time as Michael said, "clocks."

He threw Paige a fake stern look and came to greet Linney, holding out a hand. She grabbed him into a hug.

"Sure, him you hug. Me, you shoo," Paige protested.

"Part of the work incentive program. So's this." She shook a bag and headed to the kitchen.

Over some cocoa and a late-night dinner for Linney, they caught up on each other's news, including an "attaboy" and "attagirl" for the sale method of Grandpa Benny's clock collection. They learned of Michael's work in vague terms, since he was not at liberty to divulge details, including his company's name. The house progress was discussed as was the decline of Linney's hospice person. Even the weather and predictions of impending storm were talked about over the surprise cookies Linney had brought—a gift from the family for agreeing to take on double shift through the next night.

What they did not share was how Michael's tie ended up on the foyer chandelier. The fixture was damaged and not ornate enough to be considered a true chandelier. With the tie hanging high overhead, the house was a cross between tumbledown country and frat house. The light was not on the immediate to-do list. Getting the tie off just might be.

****

"But I have to get one more thing, Paige. I'll be back soon. The glass took far longer than I thought," Michael said through her cellphone. He had gone out to pick up window glass for the grandfather clock. Because it wasn't deemed valuable but sentimental, especially since it already had repairs, replacing the glass made it appealing. It wasn't the highest priority, though.

"I think you are just trying to avoid the fun of digging through gunk," Paige said then screamed. She had pulled open a drawer to a dresser-like piece of furniture tilted over some boxes behind the hutch. It has an old rodent nest in it.

"Sounds like real fun. Maybe I need to run even more errands?"

Paige heard a car door slam. "Chicken."

"Okay, but I thought of going for a nice meal out tonight."

Paige's skeevies made her move to another location. "Now I know you are avoiding this house. Or is it me? Were you going to dinner on your own tonight?"

"Of course not."

"Good."

"How about I go try to pick up a woman in a gay bar? Oh, right I did that, and go figure she wasn't even gay. You're not, are you?"

"Not in the least gay or happy even, since I'm stuck working on my own. Please get home soon."

He chuckled, agreed, and hung up.

Paige stared at the fireplace a couple hours later. It was behind the mountain of books and had a teetering stack of antique, framed pictures on the mantle. With another storm due, she thought a fireplace might be useful.

Linney came from the kitchen and stood next to her. "What are we doing?"

"Looking."

Her aunt held her coffee and looked with her. "Why?"

"I was wondering if this thing worked and why it was hidden, and if we needed another heat source, would burn this house down?"

"It works fine. I had it cleaned before we piled stuff near it. I'm heading to work soon and have to stay overnight. How about you quickly pick five books from the heap, and I will do the same. The rest of the books, let's pack up, and I'll bring them to the hospice center. Then you can see to the fireplace. It's not the prettiest, but you're right, it would be nice to have it in the cold. Okay, ready, set, get your books."

Paige was amazed at how easily her aunt turned de-cluttering into a game when she was in the mood. A doable fast game.

She asked about Samuel and got a shrug with a smile. She then asked about George and was told her diner-date for tomorrow still worked with her schedule. All of it cryptic, but all of it on track for her aunt to have a happy Valentine's Day.

The doorbell rang, followed by Michael letting

himself in and calling out, "Hey, the doorbell works. I have something for you. An early Valentine gift."

Both women ran to the foyer with Linney front and center. Michael stood holding a cat. A skinny, scrawny cat. A white-footed calico with a white stripe down its face and a red bow. It twitched, jumped from his arms, and ran into the kitchen.

"A cat?" Paige said with a smile.

"A cat," Linney said with a snarl. "I do not want yet another thing to take care of. No fur. No beasts. What good's a cat, anyway?"

Michael started to object, "The gift was for—"

"Valentine's. I know," Linney groused.

Paige knew it had been meant for her. She kissed Michael on the cheek and whispered, "Shh," and nodded toward Linney.

"Here kitty, kitty. Here, you mangy mouth to feed." Linney followed it into the dining room. All three gasped. The cat was eating something. Something possibly with a tail.

"Good girl. Good boy. Good whatever," Linney said. She stood close to the cat. "Look it's winking at me."

She picked it up and gushed at it in baby talk, "What a good wittle, winky-dinky you are." The cat twitched, then relaxed and purred. She petted it and put it down.

Michael and Paige stood in stunned silence.

"Valentine gift accepted." Linney added a word that sounded like "yo yanny."

Michael leaned his head to translate for Paige, "It's good."

"I'll say," Paige whispered. "A mouser."

"You two take good care of Winky there. I need to rush off to work." Linney grabbed cookies, keys, her purse and turned back, remembering the box of books to donate. "Bye, now. Good luck with the fireplace."

After she left they heard her swearing outside, sending expletives about the snow coming down.

"What just happened?" Paige asked.

"I think she stole your Valentine present."

"And how did you think of getting me a cat in the first place, let alone that one?" Paige asked as Winky came out of hiding, stopped, stared at them, and then flew up the stairs.

Michael struggled. "I saw the pet adoption sheet you had in your room, called the place, and asked them to show me a few mousers. This one was the thinnest and kind of needful. I figured it would mouse hunt the best."

From the foyer, they saw the cat bolt along the upstairs hall in one direction, freeze, and bolt again the other way, running full tilt straight into furniture.

"And did you think to ask about mental issues?"

"It's male. What kind of problems could it have?"

Winky yowled and flew down the stairs. It chased something...a small metal Ben Wa ball, which he'd pushed.

"Yours?" Michael asked.

Paige shook her head. "Glad to say it's Linney's."

Michael, thankfully, didn't ask if she meant the ball or the cat.

By that late afternoon, Michael and Paige had set up a make shift box with kitty litter in the basement. The kitty litter came from the supply used for traction, instead of salt, on icy driveways. Winky didn't seem to mind and had already tested out the box. They also found an old, flat cushion, shook out the dust, covered it and made a bed for Winky in Linney's room. Winky would have nothing to do with it until they put the second Ben Wa ball on it. He purred at that. Only Winky knew the whereabouts of the first ball, and he wasn't saying.

"He fits right in, don't you think?" Michael asked cheerfully as the cat passed by.

Paige twitched and winked back, imitating the cat. Then she nodded and laughed.

She held the large glass panel in place while Michael worked on the grandfather clock. She'd finished telling Michael about Linney's old flame and the possible new one.

Out of the corner of her eye, Paige caught something small scurry by. It took all her strength not to let go of the glass. Winky zoomed out of nowhere, caught the something, and trotted off.

"The men are coming out of the woodwork, but so are the mice," Michael said, adjusting the final piece.

She couldn't have said it any better if she tried.

"Look," Paige pointed inside a corner of the main part of the grandfather clock. She saw a tiny carving etched into the wood.

They made out "I+B" scratched inside an etching of a heart. Ida and Benny. Unfortunately, right next to it was a chewed hole. Michael was right about one thing. A mouser of some sort was needed, even with some quirks.

Winky came close to them, then shook and twitched his head before settling down to watch them. Quirks didn't even cover it.

Chapter Ten

Though Paige sometimes claimed she wasn't very romantic at heart, she looked forward to the promised candlelit dinner more than she ever had before. No dust, no work clothes, no chiming clocks, no cat, and no fumes. An escape from renovation to relaxation, and not just that, the outing was with Michael. White linen, candlelight, music—all of that with amber-eyed, deep-voiced Michael.

She thought all those things when she showered to get ready, encouraging her hands to linger slowly over her body. She shook out of the moment. She had to hurry. He was buff, and she needed to do just that— buff. No time for a full mani-pedi. This is where her Carolina upbringing stepped in.

She sped through her primping process, coating her toenails right over the previous color to a shiny Valentine Red. Her fingernails were buffed, trimmed, and clear coated. She even dared a swash of make-up and dashed to the bedroom, cased on her sheerest pantyhose and her LBD, the one with a crimson accent. A touch of jewelry and Paige was ready.

Michael stood at the bottom of the stairs, straightened his cuffs, and looked up to see her. He froze, wide-eyed. Carrying her exquisite red shoes in one hand, slim pocket book in the other, she bounced down the stairs, earrings sparking as they caught the light.

Michael said nothing but beamed. Suited, as he had been so many times since they'd met, he never had seen her in cocktail attire. "You look…"

"Like I am going to freeze," Paige finished his sentence as she glanced out the window. The snow was already on the ground. She handed him her shoes and bag and slipped on the only boots she had, her waterproof work boots. She threw on her coat and flung her scarf around her neck.

"I'm really looking forward to going out with you." Paige said, without fully acknowledging the look of amazement in his eyes.

"Oh Paige." Though one hand held her shoes and the other gripped the wine bag, he found a way to embrace her, sweet, long, and tender. "You're stunning."

"Yeah, yeah. Sure, sure. You have to say that or something like it. Honestly, I don't see it," Paige said, standing bundled before him. She thought she looked like she'd forgotten her pants under the white puffy coat.

"My cute, adorable, sexy Flee. One of these days you might even realize you're beautiful." He shook his head. "Bet you'll just say it's what's underneath that counts."

"My coat?" she teased.

He shook his head no.

"Under my dress? Actually, I have on black lacy things."

Michael's breath caught. "I meant your warmth and light heart. But, hold on, black lacy things? Care to stay in and head back upstairs?"

"You do realize you are talking to a hungry woman in a coat who will go all Southern on you again."

"Please do."

"Food now, handsome. Tablecloth, candlelight, music, the works. I'm not going to wear those spikey heels for nothing."

"You're not wearing them, Flee."

"I will be Groundhog Man."

She took her shoes and pocket book from him and tried to flounce out the door. It was more like a childlike stomp. Outside, she tipped her head back and caught snowflakes on her tongue. "Amazing, isn't it?"

"Yes."

When she looked, his heated gaze was directed at her and not the softly blowing snow.

****

A powdery snow began to swirl, making visibility lower and the mountain roads slow going. Paige snuggled into the plush seat of Michael's rental.

"I think you'll like the Italian restaurant I found," he said, his hand brushing against her upper thigh but soon had to return to the steering wheel on the slick roads.

If you keep that up, I would be happy in a snowbank, Paige thought, but all she said was, "I'm sure it's going to be lovely."

They came to a T intersection with a red light and stopped to turn into town. Two boys were holding sign boards in the cold, taking turns calling out to their car.

"Potluck. It's for charity. Mrs. Tilzner and also for our uniforms," one boy said.

"She's a nice teacher and has some cancer thing. The food's good," the second boy chimed.

"Yeah. My mom made the meatballs and helped out."

"Just down that way a quarter mile." The boy pointed the opposite direction from town. "They decorated with candles and everything."

Michael looked at Paige.

She smiled and nodded quickly.

He turned the car and headed toward the potluck dinner. "I said I'd take you for a candlelit dinner, Amelia Paige Myers. You heard the boy. They have candles and everything."

"Cheapskate."

"Nu-uh. I brought wine." Michael teased.

She knew both were clearly pleased with their choice. The quiet dinner could wait.

The car lot was filling up. Paige insisted on walking from the car and quickly slipped into her shoes once inside when he left to hang up the coats. She straightened her hem and turned to see stares in her direction. Most people were in jeans, some in slacks or simple wool dresses. Michael was at her side, getting equal stares but from the women. He beamed back.

The venue was a gym with the entrance doors blocked by registration tables, manned by a row of middle-aged women. Most attendees were bringing in food items and paying the minimal ten-dollar fee a head, less for children.

"We didn't bring anything, but I have wine," Michael explained pulling out his wallet.

"Let me see." The gray-haired woman eyed the bottles and simply took the white. Michael smiled. "Okay, you can pay half."

"It's for charity, right?" Michael asked. She

nodded in response. "Well then, we should pay our fair share."

"Okay, but it'll cost you, twenty a head, double if you want full treatment."

"Full treatment it is." He handed over the money, Paige held to his arm for warmth as the wind whipped from the door every time someone opened it.

The registration woman put the remaining bottle of wine in a paper bag, "Keep it like that. Regulations." Then the woman dinged a bell repeatedly and called out, "Big spenders."

All eyes turned to them. Again. Out of nowhere came a high school girl, smiling with an abundance of braces. She escorted them into the gym.

Michael entered with his arm around Paige, her heels conspicuously clicking on the floor. She was thankful to cling to him with all the attention they were getting. The girl had asked them to go through the food line and indicated their table dead center of the gym where she put a sign saying "Reserved" and wrote a question mark where it indicated a name.

Dish after dish lined one wall of the gym. Just like the people in the room, the food came in all shapes, sizes, colors, and even ages, some more recognizable than the next. The people near them loaded their plates with astonishing speed and volume, cutting around them. A few smiled her way. She smiled back, still nervous from the conspicuous attention her outfit garnered.

Michael was not. He spoke with ease as he piled two plates high, one with salads and sides having gotten advice from women near him. The smell of the warm food inspired Paige to follow suit, and her plate filled.

It was only when they sat at their assigned table that Paige noticed it had a real table cloth littered with red confetti hearts and a small tea light.

"Not bad, Mr. Groundhog," she said, smiling warmly, pushing back a soft curl. Once seated, she felt far more comfortable. That and the table was tight. Michael was close. The room quickly filled with people. The noise level began to increase.

"Mmm. This dumpling, whatever, is actually tasty." Paige swallowed happily, candlelight shining a glow on her colorful filled plate.

"Lucky for us, the registration lady left us the screw top wine. Actually, this is the nicer bottle. Care for some wine, Flee?" Michael spoke over the din.

"Yes, please. I really need it. Did you notice the stares?"

"What'd they say?" shouted an exceptionally short octogenarian with trifocal glasses and a dentured-smile. She sat at an adjacent table with two other blue-haired women, all huddled close to each other. She stuffed a finger in her ear and adjusted her hearing aid with a piercing whistle.

One woman was taller than the others with a long neck and a football helmet of hair dyed jet black. She answered first. "He found some fleas in the wine."

"Then she said if you have to pee, go upstairs," said the one with a large nose and a profound number of wrinkles.

"Oh," said the first smiling and nodding her head. She looked like an elderly fairy in thick glasses. "He must not need to go. He's just staring at her pretty face. They make a lovely couple, don't they?"

The wrinkled one just sneered, and the tall one

announced that she liked the softer food better. She scraped some of her food onto the wrinkled one's plate. The music pumped on, quieting many conversations. It was actually a lovely mix of recorded classical music. The elderly fairy woman swung her feet to the music and nodded her head in time to it.

Paige raised her wine glass. "To a night on the town."

"And the whole town in our night," Michael added. They laughed, drank, and ate. "I promised you atmosphere, just not what kind."

"Well, personally I like it all. Apart from this pink stuff."

He tasted from her plate. "Has your aunt's baking written all over it."

They both cringed and nodded their heads.

"Got to hand it to you, Groundhog Man, you keep taking me to the most memorable places."

The elderly fairy was smiling at Paige and did a happy finger wave, then giggled at being noticed. Paige waved back and raised her wine glass to her. Michael saw the exchange and joined in, toasting the elderly trio.

"To your—" His words were lost by the loudspeaker.

"Hello, folks. Thanks for coming out in the snow. Knew you would. We're hearty folks and all the more so with that food, eh? I want to thank the organizers and all of you for the fine food."

There was applause.

"Except Millie's pink ambrosia."

Many laughed.

"Settle down now. You know she makes it for

Leroy. You here, Leroy? There he is. Course, he is. Charitable man."

"Has to be!" someone chimed in.

More laughter.

"Anyway, we have a long way to go to reach our goals. Let's all dig in and buy those fifty/fifties. We all know Mrs. Tilzner and her fine contributions." A smattering of applause. "That's right, let's give her a hand."

She stood weakly and waved to solid applause and cheers.

"Then there's the Cougar uniforms, and if there's enough, something for the girl's uniforms, too. Valentine's Day is just around the corner. Maybe you'll win and get something extra. Be generous if you can."

At that, students descended with tickets in hand. A small teenage boy approached their table. His voice cracked as he asked, "Any chance you'll buy some?"

"Sure. How many do you think we should buy?" Michael tried to encourage the boy's eye contact, but he only shrugged. He looked like he was going to crumble, staring at the ground.

Paige asked him kindly, "Are you one of the Cougars?"

He shook his head no.

"Do you know Mrs. Tilzner?"

He nodded. "She's real cool."

"I see. How about if we take a bunch of tickets then."

The boy looked up. She smiled at him.

"Here you go." Michael gave him a hundred-dollar bill.

The boy energetically pulled off stack after ten-stack of red tickets. Michael draped them over Paige as if it were fine jewelry, leaned in, and kissed her. The boy ran off screaming that he sold all of his.

"Care to make a dash for it?" Michael asked her as they finished what they wanted of their meal. He rose to clear their plates.

"And skip dessert not to mention all the loot we could win?" She motioned her head to the ladies.

Michael nodded in understanding and handed the elderly ladies some of the tickets and took plates from two of them. The wrinkled one groused, not allowing him to help. She stood and thumped her walker behind Michael to the dish drop off.

"Where are they going?" the little fairy woman shouted but was ignored by the other.

Paige leaned in and answered, "Clearing dishes. They'll be back soon."

"Ohh," her lips held the word in delight. With eyes big as saucers, she asked, "Are you from Alabama?"

"No. Carolina. Originally my family's from around here."

"Around where?" the tall one repeated with a sneer.

"Underwear?" The little fairy woman played with her hearing aid again.

"Yup. Pinching me again," the tall one said.

They both nodded together. Paige just smiled at the odd turn of comments.

Michael returned, carrying a tray of dessert plates. He put two on their table and three for the old ladies who smiled at that "nice young man." The wrinkled one just shrugged and traded plates while the tall one looked away.

Paige and Michael ate mystery desserts, drank their wine poured from the paper bag and enjoyed the swirl of the remaining floor show of people. He leaned in, hand to Paige's cheek, and pulled her to a sweet kiss. The lights flickered.

"Impressive. You did that?" she asked pointing to the lights.

He shook his head. "I did this though." He slid his hand under the table cloth and onto her thigh.

Her breath hitched. "Is that offer to make a dash still good?"

Before he could answer, the announcer came on. "Okay folks. Time for what you have been waiting for."

"Looks like he agrees. Let's go." Michael said.

"Shh, son, the numbers," the old fairy woman smiled, clinging to the tickets he'd given them.

The atmosphere became palpable with excitement. Numbers were called out for two door prizes first. Cheers surrounded the tables of winners. The large prize was next. Paige followed along, staring at her own tickets as the number was called.

"You won!" Paige cried out to Michael.

It was as if the whole room groaned in one sound followed by comments.

"Figures some stranger gets it."

"Outsider always does."

Michael was called up to the front with the winning ticket. Murmurs and sneers continued to follow him.

"Heard he bought five hundred tickets."

"Just getting his money back."

Michael just held his shoulders strong and walked with a steady pace up to the man with the microphone.

"Ticket's good," the announcer confirmed. More

groans.

"I'd like to give it back." Michael said, his voice carrying into the microphone.

"How much?"

"All of it. If I do, will you reach your goals and get them their uniforms?"

"For the boys," one girl called out. Some boys cheered.

Michael comfortably spoke into the microphone, "Who's the coach for the girl's team?"

"I am," a strong woman's voice called out.

"No promises, but I can see if my company will sponsor them. I'm Michael Yotahala Lukas. See me afterward, so I can get your information."

The girls cheered.

"And," Michael continued. "I might be visiting the area, but Paige, here, is not a stranger." All eyes turned to Paige. "It's her big night out. She's working real hard to restore the Dornheim place. Do you know it?"

Murmurs buzzed around the room.

"Real dump now."

"Eye sore."

"It is, but it won't be. Amelia Paige Myers may sound like she's from the South, but it's her grandparents place. She and her aunt, Linney Dornheim Smith, are pouring all they have, their time, their savings, and hard work into that place every day. You know what that can be like."

Murmurs of agreement followed.

"So, if you have any goods or services," he said slowly for emphasis, "for a reasonable price or want to buy something from the home, please leave a card. Paige would surely appreciate it."

Paige sat staring at Michael. Embarrassment readily gave way to gratefulness when others approached her. Soon, music came back on and the crowd shifted and mingled. Card after business card dropped onto her table as people started to filter out. Some mentioned what they did "porches." Or what they needed "walnut hutch" and even wrote it on the card or a slip of paper. Some just gave their humble thanks or a blessing. Paige wrote on the backs of some of the cards or papers and accepted their thanks. Michael was tugged over to the Tilzner family before he could return to help.

"Bet he gave the money back just to show off to her," the tall woman said, pointing to Paige.

"Bet he did it just to get in her pants," the wrinkled one snarled.

"Yes, I love a good dance," the tall one responded.

"I love young love," the little octogenarian said. She pushed up her trifocals, beamed, and added with glee, "Oh look! Cookies!"

Mrs. Tilzner's grandchildren had moved around to the all remaining tables handing out carefully decorated, heart-shaped cookies, each in its own plastic bag. Two little girls came to Paige, and one handed her a cookie.

The little one didn't speak but just clutched Paige in a hug and said, "Fank you, nice lady."

No amount of control could stop the soft tears from rolling down Paige's cheek. Michael caught her eye from across the room and looked at her quizzically. She just smiled and bit her lip. She mouthed the three little words but wasn't sure he saw it.

When the old ladies wobbled away, escorted by the

nursing aides, the littlest one said, "Ida. That was her name. Ida Dornheim. Big heart."

Paige could have sworn the others said, "Big breasts."

"What about nests?"

Chapter Eleven

"Mmm mmm, I wish time would stop." Paige said with a languid sigh.

"I think it just did. That wind-up clock finally stopped ticking."

Michael and Paige were curled up on the ancient, sheet-covered loveseat. Throw pillows made it somewhat comfortable. His suit jacket was off and she was half draped on him, her LBD riding up.

She wiggled her toes toward the small fire. Nuzzling her cheek against his face, she turned and kissed him. He softly returned the kiss. Both were still too full and sedentary to move. Totally relaxed. He rubbed his full stomach.

"How'd you know to do what you did back there?" she asked. "It's good you did what you did, when you did it, because I bet it's needed more than I thought."

"Not English, Flee." His stomach rumbled.

She leaned up a bit. "The budget, the bills, the project costs—all red. How did you know?"

"I didn't, Paige. Renovating a place always costs more than expected. You need help from professionals, and those costs really add up." He smiled and brushed back her hair. "Truth is, I didn't know what I was doing. It just all came out. I wanted them to see you as I do."

"A woman with a drawl in a cocktail dress?"

229

"No. A woman who is trying to conquer a mountain with a broom. Make that several mountains." His stomach made a strange gurgle. "All I did was tell them you needed their services. It'll still cost you, but at least you might get their support and maybe even the townie rate."

She nodded, turning a bit so she could rub his stomach. "It's well…it's like a whole community just gave their approval of some sort."

Winky inched around the corner and rubbed the leg of the loveseat. Paige sighed, stretching in place, eyes locked to the embers of the fire. "And the food wasn't that bad either."

"I don't know about that." Michael lurched up, groaning, and ran to the powder room.

Winky jumped up and took Michael's place on the warm love seat. He circled the spot, pushing against Paige, and purred.

"Hey, you're not so bad, little fella, are you?"

He licked his paw and rolled against her more. She would think the exact opposite later when she saw the amount of fur he left on her little black dress. It became a little fur dress instead.

****

Romance came in many forms. A bad stomach wasn't one of them. Their night of love making never followed. For Michael, it was a night of uncomfortable sleep and bathroom trips. Paige had found him the antacids and rushed out in the morning to bring back seltzer, ginger ale, and a drink with electrolytes, not knowing his remedy of choice. Her brothers used all three at different times, including a horrible recipe for hangovers involving things that made her flinch at the thought of it.

Michael was of no use in the de-hoarding process that day. She chose to tackle some paperwork, so she could keep him company. It was already early afternoon when they sat at the kitchen table while he sipped seltzer.

"Did you have the brown meatball?" he asked.

"Yes." She taped business cards given to her onto a stained poster board she'd found. One section was for things people wanted to buy. The other cards were placed into categories of help offered.

"Okay, that wasn't it. What about the spinach soufflé and potatoes?"

"Nope. Wait. I had scalloped potatoes. What soufflé?"

"Must be the culprit." Michael moaned and popped another antacid.

"Sure. It couldn't possibly be the amount you ate," she said.

Michael burped and grinned sheepishly.

Linney entered the kitchen at that moment followed by Winky. She'd just returned from her job. "What's all this?"

Paige began to tell her of their evening, the business cards, and how she was going to hang it in the hallway for easy use.

Her aunt cut her off, "No. This. You two sitting here," Linney said. "He's burping and popping antacid while you are surrounded by…accounting? How long have you two been together?"

Linney plated some leftovers and put them in the microwave. Michael looked green again.

"I thought you were heading out with George,"

Paige said, continuing her task.

"That's later. A girl's gotta eat." She shoveled in a large bite of green zucchini. Michael flew from the room. "Is he sick?"

Paige nodded and finished telling her about the potluck and all that happened while Linney ate.

"You never go for the spinach soufflé around here. Mrs. Teeter sometimes makes it with the old eggs. Makes you sick every time unless you have an iron stomach."

"Thanks for the heads up. I'll remember it next time." Paige said looking up from the file system she had been setting up.

Linney finished eating and pulled Paige away from the papers, hoping to make a dent in one of the rooms upstairs before napping.

They left Michael to his own devices and a piece of very dry toast. By the time Paige came down for something to drink an hour or two later, he had the expansion file nearly filled with sorted renovation papers and bills.

"Wow. We should get you sick more often," Paige said.

"Don't you dare. I'm just now feeling better."

"Well enough to…" She motioned upstairs.

Michael looked iffy. Winky dashed by chasing the Ben Wa ball. He caught it and rolled over on top of it, rubbing his back, and momentarily curling up.

"Maybe well enough even to do what he's doing," Michael said.

Winky turned over and rolled his belly back and forth on the ball and then hissed at it.

"Strike that. I have no idea what he's doing."

Paige didn't either. She shrugged, "Not my cat. And thankfully not my toy either for that matter."

She failed to mention she had her own toys, but that would have to wait for a more energetic, playful time.

They headed upstairs hand in hand. As enjoyable as cuddling was, it wasn't like the torrid moments they preferred or had shared many times before. It was relaxing and sweet, filled with soft touches and massages as they curled up in bed. Paige spoke of her disbelief of how short a time they'd actually been together. Michael pointed out that they'd been together more hours than most people several months into their relationship.

She knew in her heart that wasn't it. It was much more than being locked away together a set number of hours in a bed and breakfast. They matched. They relished the other's company. They flourished together and their bodies craved the other's touch.

But somewhere deep inside, she knew to temper the relationship so it built and didn't flame out. The loving way his hands rubbed her back said what he felt the same. And when she turned toward him, softly stroking the line of his handsome face, she knew her eyes poured out the same meaning.

Neither spoke of love, but the words hung nearly palpable between them.

****

At the door early that evening, soft kisses became the promise of things to come. Maybe because their lazy snuggling left them with a sweet longing instead of bright afterglow, Michael's leaving that day was all the more wrenching to Paige and from his actions, to

Michael also. Valentine's Day was only two days away. He'd promised to return even if were only a short time on February 14th. Still, the parting felt more like a tearing apart than just a quick "see you soon."

A kiss. Another touch. A smile. Some unnecessary comment. Another kiss. He stood at the door, bags at his feet, unable to let go of her.

"Oh, for Heaven's sake!" Aunt Linney grumbled. "You, get your things, tell her you love her, and leave. And you, Squirt, stop moping. Blast your loud music when I go and get a move on. We can't start putting this place together until we finish clearing it out. Now step out of my way. I have a diner dinner date with George. I'm not even getting free Wi-Fi out of it, so he better be a helluva lot more fun than you two were today."

"I was sick," Michael protested.

"You're both sick, all googly-eyed. Move your butt. A hungry woman needs to go." With that, Linney left.

It took a beat, but both laughed.

"You heard the woman. Go." Paige kissed him with a happy *mwwwahhh* sound and shooed him away, smiling.

"Love ya. See you soon," Michael said hastily and picked up his things. He didn't turn around, but Paige heard his breath catch just a bit.

"Well, that wasn't so bad, was it?" she asked herself.

The cat answered with a yowl from the far corner of the living room.

"Critic."

****

Paige managed to fill several garbage bags from

234

one of the spare upstairs bedroom. The master bedroom had a larger possibility of hiding treasures, but she wanted an easier space to clear. She did so, as much as she could as fast as she could. Even though the music blared, her ears were on alert for Linney's return. Her aunt called it a date, and she wanted to be there at the ready for support.

No Linney—yet.

Paige tired of lifting the garbage bags that needed to go all the way out to the street for pick up. By the third one, she'd devised a cardboard sled for the stairs so she could just slide it down. It worked even to bring some of the bags out over the snow covering the driveway.

Her mind was on Linney's lateness, ranging from elation that she was out on a date to worry over her being out too long. She stomped off the snow ready to hang up her coat when she noticed the last and largest bag upstairs.

With an exasperated sigh, she brought the soggy cardboard back up. Paige applied the same slide-the-bag-down-the-stairs routine but with the wet cardboard and sharp heaviness of the contents, the bag ripped completely open, spewing the contents from nearly the top step all the way down.

It was right then that Linney stepped into the foyer.

"Do you know how late you are?" Paige called down the stairs.

"Not late enough by the looks of it. I can come back when you're done."

"Ha. Ha. The bag ripped."

"I see that. I think I will have to table your title of Sagey-Paigey."

"Not funny. Do you know how worried I was? You didn't have your cell phone." Paige started to stuff the mess into a new bag, jamming in the pieces.

"Sure, I did. I just turned it off." Linney left and came back with another garbage bag and wearing an apron over her clothing that said, *"Everyone has their price. Mine is chocolate."*

They both bent to the task.

"So, are you going to tell me?" Paige asked.

"Tell you what?" Her aunt started from the bottom and worked fast.

"About your date. Your diner date you called it." Paige worked her way down from the top.

"What about it?" Linney picked up pieces.

"How'd it go?" Paige picked up pieces.

"Fine I guess." More pieces.

"Fine as in, oh, he's cute and fun and I want another date. Or fine as in he can take a hike before I see him again?"

"Fine as in fine."

Paige huffed. She jammed in three items. "Look, I am just trying to help you out. It seems I've dated more than you have since Roger. I'm trying to be a good niece and friend here and help set you up."

"I…" *Stuff.* "don't…" *Stuff, stuff.* "need…" *Jam.* "your help!"

"Everybody needs help." They both grabbed for the last chunks.

"I don't. Never did. Never will."

Paige's heart twisted with the pang of hurt.

"Oh Paige, not what I meant at all. I meant with dating and whether or not I do it again. How about this? Think of him as out of the picture then it won't bother you."

Paige was still upset but nodded.

"C'mere Squirt. I didn't mean it about the help thing. I just meant about fixing me up. I need your help, here. Boy, do I. We all need it of each other, in some way or another. And some of us more than others. Let's walk this to the curb. Okay? We can even do something corny like wish on stars like you used to love doing as a kid."

Paige forced a smile. She wasn't upset about what Linney had said about helping each other. Whether she acknowledged it or not, everyone needed a sounding board when it came to relationships. She knew her aunt just wanted her to stop prying. She was upset about George maybe being out of the picture.

That meant it was one guy down and only one guy to go for *Project Fix Aunt Linney's Broken Heart*. A project that had a Valentine's Day due date and that was only one and half days away.

Chapter Twelve

"Oh no!" The chocolate was gone—Linney's emergency stash chocolate saved for bad news. That meant something happened with her hospice patient. Paige wasn't ever told any details of the cases. It was private, but she did see how much each patient meant to her aunt.

It just can't be happening. A patient couldn't have died. Not on Valentine's Day. She'd worked so hard to make the day special for her broken-hearted aunt and now this.

Paige was frantic. Until she was half-way through eating it, she didn't even notice she ate a second heart-shaped brownie she'd made for Linney and Michael. They were lightly frosted, soft, and had the perfect number of nuts. She'd been putting away ingredients when she noticed Linney's missing chocolate bar. She steeled herself for the necessary call to her aunt.

"Aunt Linney, hello. It's Paige," she said, drawl thick and serious.

"I can see that on my caller ID. What's up?"

"Well…is everything all right? I mean with you…and…"

"Paige, I told you I'm not talking about dating, especially at work."

"No, no. Is everything okay at work? Okay, I'll just say it. Your chocolate is gone, your emergency stash."

"Hell no. You ate it?"

"What? No."

"You made it sound like somebody died," Linney said over the phone.

"Well, that's what I thought. The bar is gone from the kitchen."

"Oh, I know that."

Paige was stumped. "Well, where is it?"

"In a tin."

"In a tin? So, nobody, you know…expired?"

"Nope." Linney's voice softened. "Alive and as well as can be expected."

Paige let out an audible sigh of relief. She moved to throw out her napkin and saw a dozen roses in the garbage.

"Wait, what's this? Red roses?"

"Oh, those came, and I figured they were from Roger, so I threw them out. Hate Valentine Day's anyway."

"What if they were mine? From Michael? Or someone else?"

"Sheesh, didn't think of that. Clean 'em up, would you?"

"Oh sure. I've got nothing better to do than wash roses. Before you go, do you have plans for the night?"

"Other than VD avoidance? Nope. Might just hang out tonight. Bye."

Paige stood in front of a sink, trying to wash coffee grounds, old tuna, and vegetable peelings off the roses. It turned out to be a delicate process.

Her thoughts wandered to Linney. Did she need company tonight?

Her mother chose to call at that moment to wish

her a Happy Valentine's Day and asked Paige to be on the lookout for some roses for both her favorite women and that it had a funny card. Paige assured her mother she would do just that as she continued to wash the buds.

"Are you sure you're okay, Paige? You sound funny."

"Yes. I'm fine. Linney's fine. Michael's recovered, and the cat is strange."

"What cat? Michael's recovered from what?"

"Happy Valentine's Day Mom. Gotta run, bye." Paige hastened off the phone, feeling guilty about the roses her mother had lovingly sent. She managed to save most of them, though the buds looked a little worse for the wear and had a slight, non-rose, almost tuna odor. The broken ones, she just floated in a small bowl on the table next to the brownies. It looked charming actually with the scarf tablecloth she set up.

The doorbell rang. Paige hurried, nearly tripping over the cat as it leapt out of nowhere in front of her. The cat turned, hissed, and hovered in the corner, staring at the doorbell. The cat was proving more inexplicable, giving her pause before opening the door.

"Happy Valentine's Day," Paige chirped.

"Whatever. Sign here." The rushed flower delivery person handed her a dozen red roses.

"They're beautiful," Paige drawled. The delivery person grunted and drove off without even looking up. In fact, she wasn't even sure of the gender, just hurried.

The card was soggy. It had a picture of a bulldog on the front and read "Happy Valentine's day Beayotch!" The signature was blurred. It didn't even have a name it was addressed to. "Okie dokie, Mom.

What exactly have you been drinking?"

Still holding the new vase of flowers, the doorbell rang again. Before she could open the door, the cat ran across her path, hissed, and hid. She looked about, half hoping for a hidden camera. Paige opened the door to a flower delivery service. A different flower delivery service. She stepped outside.

"Hey…" Came the voice under a hat, long hair, and beard. He held the syllable far too long. "Happy V Day. You live here, right?" He had a mellow California way about him.

"Yes."

"Cool, cool. Needs just a little fixing up, don't you think?"

"We're working on it. Can I help you?"

"Oh right. Have some flowers for you." He held out a huge vase filled with beautiful mixed flowers and waited, no instructions, the clipboard tucked under his arm.

Paige took matters into her own hands and handed him the first vase of flowers, took the clipboard, signed it, and took both vases back. The cat yowled, and the door slammed shut behind her. She turned to enter the house, but with her hands were full, she couldn't open the closed door. "The door?"

The mellow delivery man of indiscriminate age just stared and nodded at her. "Yeah. Not sure. Don't need to replace all of it. Just a board or two, some wood putty, filler, and stain."

She sighed, handed him back one set of flowers, opened the door, and took the flowers back. "Oh, the card?"

"Right. Here's my card if you want help on the

house." She showed him her hands were full so he stuck it into one of the vases of flowers.

"I meant the card with the flowers."

"Right, well, there's this thing with that."

Paige waited. And waited. "And the thing is…"

"I love old houses. You can expand the porch this way." He stepped up to what was left of the porch with broken rails and slanted roof. Then he stepped away staring up at the roof line.

"The card. For the flowers, you were giving me one." Paige used every last bit of her upbringing to not scream at him.

"Right. Sorry. I'm filling in for someone. I really do woodworking. You see, I have all these cards." He stuffed the clipboard back under his arm, pulled out a stack of a dozen cards, and fanned them in front of her. "Pick one."

"Any chance you could pick it for me? Maybe one with this address or our names?"

"What names?"

"Linney, Paige, oh, it could also be Flee or Marilyn. Or even Smith or Myers."

"Hmmm. I have *My Sweet Love, Pookie, Sweetpea,* and even *Honeypot*, but I don't see any of those."

"Really?"

He nodded.

"Okay, then pick one, and I'll pretend it's the right one."

"Cool. Here you go." He tucked it into the roses. "Just so you know, I might mess up on helping out with flowers, but I don't with woodwork. It's my thing, Linney Paige Flee Marilyn Smith Myers, whichever one you are."

Paige looked at him. A man of indeterminate age, lots of facial hair, and a selective memory. She chose to just smile and let it all ride. "Got it. Call you for woodwork. Not too costly, are you?"

"Naw. If the house has good bones and the people have a good spirit, I don't cost much at all. I do it for the art."

Paige saw a genuine smile with some intelligence to it. "What was your name?"

"John Bailey Kernstonberg, no relation."

Paige had no idea who he meant and was beginning to doubt he was related to anybody in the area or even on the planet. "Thanks John."

"Just call me Bailey."

"All right, Bailey. Happy Valentine's Day."

This time, she made it all the way into the house and put the flowers down, one on some boxes, the other on the table near the entrance. She almost tossed out his card but decided to put his with the other business cards and wrote *loves woodwork* and *odd* on it, circling the word Bailey. She came back and circled the word *odd*, too.

The random card he chose for her read, "I should have told you this before. I love you, Valentine."

The breath knocked out of her lungs. She stood, stock still and stared at nothing. Winky joined her and, for the first time, brushed against her leg. He smelled vaguely of tuna and roses.

"Could it have really come from Michael?"

The cat just purred his answer.

****

Paige broke from her reverie when her cell rang.

"Happy Valentine's Day, Flee!"

"Oh, Michael the flowers—"

"Might be…" *Static.* "…so, I will…" *Static.*

She stared at her phone and sent a text to no reply. The Wi-Fi worked but the cell reception remained flakey at best. The day was not going as planned. As for the evening, she wasn't sure what it would hold, let alone with whom. She desperately loved the holiday and fate seemed to be against her. Rather than despair, she turned to tea and a snack to get her going.

Paige stepped into the kitchen. The vase of roses was spilled over, the buds trampled, in broken bits in a puddle on the floor. Winky sat up on the table, directly on top of the frosted brownies, and was leaning over eating the roses. He turned, meowed sweetly, and ran into the basement. She simply left the kitchen as it was and locked the basement door on him.

There was only so much weirdness she could handle, especially on Valentine's Day. Every spot she saw in the house was makeshift. She craved clean. She craved normal. She craved an office job and work, moving tasks from inbox to done. It was close to crisis point for her.

Instead of working on de-hoarding, she made an executive decision and gave herself the afternoon off. She wanted to look for a real position with a paycheck and benefits. Never before did she feel so pleasurably certain doing a job search and comfortable in sending out her cover letter and resume. At least, she told herself, working on the computer was a relaxed, clean activity. She hid away, job searching, ignoring worries over her aunt and the dilapidated farmhouse. She sent out job application and queries, without even keeping pristine track.

Still slightly numb but ready for the task, Paige returned to the kitchen. She took pictures of the roses on the ground, the cat bitten petals, and of the brownies, smashed with cat fur coating them. Evidence. For what, she didn't know. All of the smashed roses and ruined brownies were thrown away and the kitchen cleaned. She put out a few brownies from the refrigerator. At least, they were heart-shaped. Then she put them back in, thinking the better of leaving them out.

Winky was, perhaps, a direct cause of her vicissitude. She knew exactly how to get back at him. She opened the cellar door.

"Here, kitty, kitty. Here, Winky. Bath time." She would not let him have the upper hand. That and his fur was matted with frosting.

Paige filled the upstairs bathroom sink with warm sudsy water, expecting a battle. Winky not only didn't scratch her but let her wash him. "Who are you, Winky?"

He even stretched as she poured warm water over him to rinse. The fluffy towel she'd wrap him in for drying was a whole other issue. He yowled at that, claws out.

"Fine. How about the blow dryer?" She set it on low and kept moving it so his skin wouldn't overheat. She put back on the red bow. He actually looked…well, less scrawny. She carried him into Linney's room where he rolled the Ben Wa ball onto his cushion and curled up around it.

"I'm bathing now. Please do not destroy the house or get filthy. I need this."

The cat looked at her with a cross between distain and belittlement and twitched. His face looked calmer after that.

When it came to her bath, it was bubble-filled, scented, and so long she had to add hot water, twice. Her empty stomach made her finally budge from the tub. The oddness of the day seemed to wash down the drain. It was Valentine's Day. She got flowers, probably. The cat was clean, for now. She would be seeing her dreamy Michael, maybe. And Linney had started to date, sort of. Nothing at all was firmly set, but that fact alone made Paige finally feel normal again.

****

"I figured it out!" Linney called up the stairs when she returned.

Paige had been primping and found her red thigh high stockings and a crimson scarf that she tied into a bow tie. She wasn't finished dressing. In fact, she was practically naked.

"Did you hear me? I figured it out."

"Okay, okay. Coming." Not seeing her robe at hand, she grabbed her coat, zipped it up and bounced down the stairs.

"The roses were from your Mom. Wow, they cleaned up perfectly in fact—"

"In fact, that was the second set of roses. Let me show you the first set." Paige found her phone and showed photos of the flowers she washed. Then the next photos taken after the cat destroyed the roses, followed by the cat having a bath. Her aunt laughed and picked up Winky who'd come to her side.

"What a naughty-waughty, widdle Winky dinky." Linney coddled the cat as all three made their way to the kitchen and poured tea.

"So, one set from Mom, one set from—"

"Michael. Most likely the mixed flowers, so I put them in my bedroom for safekeeping."

"The destroyed set might be from Samuel. I put in a voice message to him. Waiting for a return call." Linney pulled out her cell and saw a flashing icon. "Maybe I missed his call." Linney pressed a button, and Paige leaned closer. Linney moved away and whispered, "It's him," as if he could hear through the message. Her shoulders slumped. "Not Samuel."

"But you just said it was him."

"I meant the message, not the flowers. He told me Happy Valentine's Day and that he was busy but come on out to Colorado some time for a visit." Linney looked concerned.

Paige was more than concerned. She was dejected. All her matchmaking wasn't panning out. She did well with Chloe from college and even helped out hopeless Brian. Her own aunt? A big fail.

"This calls for chocolate," Paige said and pulled the brownies from the refrigerator. "Happy Valentine's Day, Auntie, I mean Linney. Will you be mine?"

Her aunt took a big bite. "Your what?"

"Valentine?"

"Michael's job it seems. These are cold," she grumbled.

"Oh Linney, I know you are sad about Samuel, but someone will come along—"

"Huh? Sad. No. I'll visit him some time. It was good to reconnect. You were right about that. Freeing and good memories. But Paige, he has his life, and I have mine. Besides, he does pot." Linney shrugged. "Not for me. Gives me a headache." Linney bit into a second brownie. "Me, I like chocolate and wine.

Speaking of which…"

She pulled out a small box of chocolates hidden under a bag of chips on top of the fridge. "Happy VD, Squirt."

Paige's face lit up, and she threw her arms around Linney. "You do love love!"

"Yeah, yeah. Don't get all sappy on me. I know you and your mom read all those romance things, so I thought I'd go along. Besides, I wasn't sure if Yotahala boy was going to come through or if he was—"

"Nuts!" Paige had already opened the box and was eating one.

"That, too. Gimme those." Linney laughed and dug in. They sat and soon playing cards came out and were shuffled.

"Gin!" Paige landed the needed seven of clubs. She threw down her cards and brushed a brownie crumb from her coat, not having bothered to finish getting dressed.

"I let you win." Linney chuckled.

"No way. Confess. I took you down."

The doorbell interrupted any confession.

"Please tell me it isn't any more flowers," Paige said.

Linney followed her to the door. The cat flew in front of them. This time, Linney hissed at the cat. He cut off mid yowl.

"Gotta show 'em who's boss," Linney said, sticking out her chin.

"Yeah, right. Like that helped." Paige guffawed, but it did. The cat sat by Linney as the doorbell rang again. Paige opened the door.

A teenage boy with a profound number of pimples

and a huge smile said, "Have something for you. Sign here."

Linney took the box, and Paige signed.

"Is there a card?" Paige asked.

"Yes," the boy said and accepted the tip Linney gave with thanks. Her aunt shut the door, with a few snowflakes drifting in on the breeze.

Paige grabbed the card before Linney could. She read aloud, "Surprise! Happy Valentine's Day, you furry lover!" She didn't read out the rest. *Call when you need some petting!*

Her eyes grew wide as she remembered the mishap with barista man who tried to pick her up at the coffee shop. Linney didn't seem to notice. Paige opened the box, which held some cat toys, including a tiger-striped leather piece. Her cheeks went way past warm to a red-hot at seeing the thing, her imagination taking a turn, a deep turn, knowing it was most likely an adult toy.

"Well, Paige. These adoption places are going to all lengths. I can see it, though. Winky was an unusual case. Weren't you my sweet dinky doo? You smell good, the way your sissy, Paige, fixed you up though." Linney wandered off to the loveseat with the cat.

"I am not his sissy," Paige called after them. She headed to the stairs to get dressed but was stopped by the doorbell again. She hesitated but was impressed that Winky ignored it.

She opened the door asking, "Did you forget something?"

"Yes. I need to do this." And with that, Michael swept Paige into his arms and kissed her. They paused, staring at each other, and then beamed. Paige threw her arms around him and hugged him tightly.

"Is it just us?" Michael asked.

Paige broke the hug and shook her head, motioning to the living room. "Linney's in there playing with the cat. She called it off with Samuel, too. Sort of. I'm not sure we can leave her like this."

Michael nodded in acceptance. He caught sight of the flowers. "Red roses?"

Paige cut him off. "We think those are the ones from my mom."

Linney laughed heartily from the living room.

"Nice. Too bad my flowers weren't delivered. They said there was a mix up with a fill in driver."

"I think I got them, Michael. They're beautiful. The cards might even have been yours."

Linney walked past the foyer, talking on her cell, only nodding in greeting to Michael, "I'm with you. Let's protest this commercial holiday."

"See what I mean? She's just broken-hearted," Paige said and sat on the stairs, deflated. Her white coat rode up enough to accentuate the red fishnets she wore. Michael gently sat next to her. His eyes widened when he looked toward her legs.

Linney re-entered, coat on and bottle in hand.

"Uh-huh. Right. That'll work. I'm okay with Cheetos but way prefer the salmon. I sure could use those hot tub jets, too. How about I bring a bottle of Pinot Noir? I'm with you. Who cares if it's supposed to be a white wine? Hold on." Linney looked at Paige and Michael.

"Ta ta, you two. I'm hitting George's hot tub in protest of the holiday." She walked to the door. "Oh, and don't wait up or worry, okay? Bye."

Michael stood. He almost ran to the coat rack,

pulling off his snow dusted scarf and coat. "Did you hear her?"

"Yes, she is protesting the holiday."

Michael stepped toward her with a kind-hearted smile. He offered her his hand, pulling her from the steps.

"Flee, my sweet, caring one. Think about it. Your aunt, who refused to date, is going to a hot tub with a man, carrying only a bottle of wine, and told us not to wait up."

It sank in. It all sank in. Paige's heart pounded in her chest.

"Oh Michael, you're right. She might not like the holiday, but she's back in circulation." She threw her arms around him again.

"Boy, is she back in circulation." He pulled back enough from the hug to look into her eyes. "It also means we have the house to ourselves." He tilted up her chin and kissed her, his lips still cold from outside. "Mmm, you taste of chocolate."

Paige didn't respond but continued the kiss, inhaling the smell of snow and pines that he exuded. The mix was breathless. She finally broke from their languid embrace and stepped back. "I almost forgot. I have my valentine present for you."

She stood with her back to the stairs and slowly inched the zipper of her coat down. All the way down. Taking a modeling pose, she held the coat wide open to reveal nothing but the thigh high fishnets and the red bow around her neck. "All for you."

In that moment, the door flew open. Linney came in. "Nah. I'll pass. You two go ahead though. Forgot the brownies."

Paige slapped her coat shut and stood in shocked silence. Michael, try as he might, couldn't stop laughing. With the plate of brownies in hand, Linney came back through.

"Turns out she takes after me," she said to Michael as she pointed to Paige, "I was worried she would be like her mom, all proper without enough spunk. But no, she has *atunhétsla*, spirit, this one." Linney opened the door and added, "All you need to make it work is three little words."

"I love you?" Michael and Paige said in unison, realization at what was said, startling both of them.

"Maybe. But I was thinking, *take your vitamins*. You need to keep up your energy." Linney left the house laughing.

No sooner had she closed the door than she popped her head back in. "You need to see this."

"See what?" Paige zipped up her coat and stuffed her feet into her boots.

"Paige, wait." Michael caught her. His mouth moved and finally words spilled out. "If you would have gotten the right flowers and card, it would have said, *Should have told you this before. I love you, Valentine.*"

Paige said the last words in unison with him. She did have the right card! She had the right man, too!

He gathered her in his arms. Her lip quivered. He stopped it with a tender kiss.

She finally whispered, "I did get the right card. I love you, too, Michael. I even thought of making a huge sign but thought you might find it too hokey."

"Really?" Michael released her and threw back on his coat. "Come with me."

They stepped onto the broken stoop of a porch and stomped over snow drifts to look out onto the meadow. The moon was hidden behind clouds, but there, in the dim light among the animal tracks, were two red hearts spray painted in the snow. The words, "I love you, Flu!" were spelled out.

They both laughed.

"It's supposed to read, Flee. I love you, Flee. I think those are deer tracks across it."

They stood there looking at the scene, grinning for the longest time. One or the other would chuckle, but they held tight to each other, looking out at the vista together.

Only much later, when they were curled in each other's arms after making love in Paige's room, did Michael admit, "Paige I think—"

"You're hungry?" Paige asked, grinning.

He nodded with a smile.

"You need vitamins?" she teased.

"Definitely. And to say I think I fell for you the first day we met."

"Me, too." She smiled looking into his delicious amber eyes.

They mumbled of getting up but instead, ignored their hunger and fell asleep, entwined.

****

If someone came to the door, no one would be the wiser that they'd made love, except that one of her fishnet hose dangled next to his tie on the foyer light fixture. The other stocking was under the contented Winky on his make-shift bed next to the Ben Wa ball.

Everything was far from normal, but it was wonderful. In fact, it was ever so happily perfect.

Ginny B. Nescott

Paige's Lucky Charm:
A St. Patrick's Day Romance

Chapter One

Amelia Paige Myers blushed reading the text she'd sent late the previous night to Michael, her handsome crush. He'd moved well past crush to love interest. Pulsing hot love interest. He was dark-haired, lean but muscled with a part-Native American physique, and smooth warm-toned skin. His face showed an inner calmness with amber brown eyes that could flash to a smolder in a heartbeat.

She shook her head clear of the thought of him and tossed her cell phone onto her bed covered with a new fluffy quilt. It was the only "new" in her cramped makeshift bedroom, in the far corner of a creaky old Pennsylvania farmhouse stuffed to the hilt with her grandparents' possessions. They had passed away and with them the secrets of where treasures were stashed in each of the hoarded rooms, leaving Paige and her aunt to whittle down the mess. She didn't mind it, or at least, told herself so.

The wallpaper in her room had been removed and the closet rod straightened to hold her well-appointed work attire from her previous life. The light fixture still hung precariously, and her work desk was missing a leg and stood only with the help of a stack of books. She eyed one erotic title but dared not pull it free, since it would tilt the desk and dislodge her laptop and files.

She'd given up plenty to be here—a gorgeous

Buckhead apartment, a job in a sleek Atlanta office building, and a boyfriend the size of a linebacker but with the seeming brains of an avocado.

Paige pulled her hair into a ponytail and tucked in a sheer designer blouse into her tailored black pants. She stepped around stacked boxes and furniture in the hall and stared into a vintage mirror. Between spots, the mirror reflected back a cute, shapely blonde twenty-something in an outfit far too expensive for an interview for a temporary day job. She shook her head, bobbing her ponytail, and returned to her closet. Off came her blouse, replaced with a cotton one and a simple blazer. She grabbed her phone, bounced down the stairs into the kitchen, and made one last mark on the calendar system she had just devised. Her aunt would surely notice it.

She tugged on her boots and zipped into her puffy white coat, ready to make her way on the snow-covered roads to her interview. As she opened the kitchen door, a scrawny mouser-cat jumped in front of her.

"Oh no you don't, Winky. No cat fur before an interview," she said, hearing her own words resonate with a distinctive Carolina drawl.

Winky yowled. Paige lovingly picked him up and shooed him toward his toy. "Quiet now. Linney had a late-night shift at hospice."

Winky turned, stretched, and sat down, licking his paw.

"Hey, maybe you're learning." Paige smiled brightly and pulled the door closed behind her to the sound of a crash. She sighed before stepping back inside. "Then again, maybe not."

****

An hour or two later, Linney Dornheim Smith stretched, bleary-eyed, and looked at the kitchen cabinet door in front of her. She couldn't miss it. Two printed calendar pages. Behind the door were coffee mugs, and below it the filled coffee pot. Hot, beautiful, delicious coffee. She poured some in a mug, spooned in sugar, and reached into the fridge for milk. Mindlessly, she poured the milk in, drank a large swallow and waited for the creamy deliciousness to present her with some level of consciousness. She nearly spit it out. She looked down and saw that her niece had changed her whole milk to fat free. She cursed but only her cat heard her.

"First no cream, now whole milk turning into thin watery, blue, fat-free milk. Not even one percent? No way. Paige!" She screamed at the top of her lungs. She coughed. Middle age was not for the weak. She called again but heard no answer. She leaned in and looked at the calendar. This orderly, invasive thing in her place of solace, the kitchen. The place of carbs and calories. The place that was turning more orderly and healthier by the minute. Not if she could help it.

She opened the freezer and spooned some ice cream into a fresh cup of coffee, microwaving it enough to melt. "Mmm mmm...much better!"

Linney was short for Marilyn. She was short for many things. She was short-haired, short-fused, and short on appreciation for men; at least in the last year and a half. Linney was also short on funds, something that didn't matter much in her previous fifty-two years. She'd make do sometimes and splurged others. She had lived a packed, adventurous life and seen much of the U.S. on the back of a motorcycle. That was all disassembled by a gut-wrenching divorce from her ex after catching him in bed with another woman. A thinner, younger model of herself, for which she gave her darling Roger a fat lip and a fatter stack of fast divorce papers. Alimony was not happening though, since it turned out she was more of the bread winner.

Linney was through with that relationship and claimed not to be ready for another. Lately, she gave her all as a hospice care nurse. And that was her "day" job. The continued clearing out of the hoarded mess that was once her parents' house took all her extra time, not to mention funds she didn't have. The renovations hadn't even started yet. She would be hell-bent to avoid taking a loan even if it were from the family.

Linney had a secret weapon and that was her spitfire of a niece. It was Paige who put up the calendar. It was Paige who circled March 17th, the day before a work crew came to tear down some walls and put up some new ones. Most of the upstairs needed to be cleared of debris, treasures, belongings, and furniture by then. Paige had arranged the pending permits. She also had someone make sure the structural integrity of the hundred-year-old Pennsylvania farmhouse could withstand the proposed changes in the drafted plans.

Paige was a twenty-six-year-old, southern-drawling, dirty blonde made even dirtier from the de-hoarding projects she did and work clothes she frequently wore. She'd turned in her southern living to help with the inherited family homestead. She did more than that. She took charge without knowing she had done so.

Her niece not only took charge of the renovations but stepped up to help Linney on the path of dating again. Linney had dug in her heels and doubled down on the sarcasm, but Paige, sweet, sexy Paige, proved far tougher inside than Linney ever expected. Paige was determined to get Linney exercising, no matter how many times she was told that "fat women don't do yoga" or that "cleaning is exercise." Worse than that, Paige got them both eating healthy. Well, most of the time.

Paige was going to be the death of her. Or so Linney would tell the cat. But in her heart, she knew that her adorable niece was just what she needed to get her life back on track. Something she didn't really want to tell Paige but suspected she knew.

"Will you look at that? Pencil marks on each date. Dots on some dates. X marks on others. Things to do. Sell the hutch by this date. Ship those clocks by that. She thinks we're going to have the furniture out and down the stairs within three weeks. Ha! We can't even see the furniture in the fourth bedroom from the mess in there. Winky, I think we need to toss Paige out with the recycling."

****

"Heard that. Why not with the trash?" Paige entered the kitchen door, smiling and shaking off the snow. She removed her cherished coat to hang on a peg. Her boots kicked off with a loud thud. They were not as loved but kept her feet warmer and drier than her Valentinos or Guccis did. The bitter cold made her almost forget about those. Almost.

Her aunt stood glaring at the calendar when Paige leaned in to give her a peck as she passed in search of a mug. Her drawl thickened with emphasis, "Did you hear me, oh Barely Awake One? I asked why you wouldn't put me out with the trash instead of the recycling."

"Recycling is much more orderly, which fits this retentive MO you have going. Besides, there's still some life in you, Squirt."

Paige smiled. "Are you whining about that calendar? It's not any busier than we've been. Just in writing to keep us coordinated." She poured herself something to drink and reached in for a homemade tofu-carrot breakfast bar, drawing Winky's favor away from her aunt. Paige broke off a tiny piece for the cat. Winky chewed on it and spit it out, his eye twitching before he ran from the room.

"See? Even that cat won't eat your tofu this and your blue-water-milk that."

"Hey, it's yummier than your overly-salted, salty caramel apple pie. Not to mention, it's good for you." She poured the fat free milk into her own steaming cup of coffee and tried to hide her expression of distaste.

"Ha! See? Too far. Listen Paige, you have to compromise on some things. A little give and take…"

"This coming from a woman who has a completed bedroom and isn't living in a broom closet like I am."

"At least your broom closet comes with a hot guy in it sometimes."

"Yours could, too."

"What? Teddy bear George? Not hardly. Besides, when I do see him, I'd rather escape to his place. He has a hot tub—a working hot tub and no debris."

"Point taken. So, about George…"

Linney's squinted glare shut down further inquiry.

Paige had tried previously to garner more information about George, who her aunt "wasn't dating but just seeing and sharing comforting moments." Paige had no luck. Linney was reasonably happier, forcing Paige to let go of the topic each time.

"Which comes to the next thing—I think we need—" Paige started but was cut off by her aunt.

"No, no, no. No more to-dos. Didn't anyone ever hear of just doing what you want to? Work is work, but the rebuilding and renovating of a house back into a home is more of a, well, an art installation. It needs to be done with feeling and randomness."

Paige already had heard how calendars, charts, reports, and permits annoyed Linney. Her aunt had enough reports as a hospice nurse. Patients always came first, and their overwrought, worn out families next. Reports came last. Paige saw the farmhouse as their patient of a different sort, one they could actually bring back to health. Skilled helpers were needed soon, and with them came scheduling and permits even if Linney didn't like it.

Fine. She could do the paperwork, but she did need her aunt to help. She let out a sigh and smiled. "I was just saying we needed to find colored pens. I thought you could write up the hours you're expected at work since your hospice schedule rotates. I'll put my hours up in another color."

Linney stopped mid-dunk of her health bar. "What hours? You have a job?"

Paige grinned. "Just came from an interview. Don't want to jinx it, but it looks like it."

Linney glared back. "Can't you hold off on a job outside this house for a while? How will you find time for projects, Michael, and the cat?"

"Winky? He's yours. Michael works, and so do I.

Besides, after the work crew starts, I'll just be underfoot. The job is temporary for a couple months maybe, and we need the money."

"You're selling everything we find. All those antique clocks, not to mention the hutch."

"Everything we don't need and the family doesn't want, you mean. A third hutch? We need the capital way more."

"We need whole milk."

Paige looked at Linney and relented. "I'll get one percent milk next time."

"Two percent, lighten up on the schedule crud, and part-time it at most for now, and you might have a deal." Linney mumbled something vaguely like "pushy woman."

Paige ignored her, adding, "I didn't know we were negotiating what I do."

"Sure. All of it's up for negotiation. Lucky I'm not ordering you about. You are in my kitchen, after all." Linney grabbed the pencil and wrote in things like, "night off" or "Squirt does it" or "due date for better jokes." She started to draw funny faces on the days that had already passed.

"Do I need to get you some crayons?"

"Sounds good, but I like modeling clay better."

"It's called dirt and comes with the garden next month," Paige crossed off one of the items to do on the calendar.

"Next month? Try a few months. Remember, you live in the north now. There's still snow out there—a good standing eight inches."

The kitchen door flew open.

"Standing eight inches? You peeked, but why

thank you," Michael said as he entered, grinning widely.

"Michael!" Paige flew into his open arms and held to his muscled form made all the larger with his tailored overcoat. "I thought you were coming tonight," Paige blurted out happily.

There was a slight pause. Linney groaned. "Please no jokes about how you come every night. I'm eating."

"Of course not, Linney," Michael said with a hint of a smirk.

Paige gave him a peck on the cheek. He was still in his overcoat. The snow coated his shoulders and dusted a sparkle to his dark hair. Michael had a warmth and presence, and a slight color to his skin from his heritage, making his smile all the brighter. Normally a focused, hardworking man at thirty-one, he was instantly lighter near her. That and impassioned.

"Although..." He grinned and added some words in Oneida that sounded like, "Wa day se nee o." *Wate²sh∧ni·yó* roughly translated to "good chance," an expression she had learned.

That earned another groan from Linney. "Here. Let me pour you some coffee..." By the time his outer coat was off, under Paige's suspicious eye, Linney handed him the coffee with the blue milk in it. "Tell me what you think of the milk."

Michael cringed but drank the whole thing down. "Thin. I prefer cream, but still refreshing? No matter. Just the boost I needed for whatever's in store," Michael said to Linney but was looking straight at Paige, gaze locking. "I'm on a longer lunch break."

Paige felt his eyes undressing her.

Linney was washing out her mug and hadn't

noticed. "See? Cream. Even Michael wants something more."

Both Michael and Paige's eyes grew wide. "Is that true, Michael?"

"Sometimes, especially now." His voice deepened.

"Well, I may have to rectify that." Paige took his hand.

He squeezed it and stoked his thumb deep into the crease of her palm. The touch sent shivers into her.

"Oh sure, you give him what he wants, but all I get is fat free milk," Linney said, back turned to them, washing the remaining dishes.

Paige stifled her giggle, ineffectually.

Linney stopped, turned to see Paige and Michael, realization of what she'd said spreading across her face. She shook her head. "Sheesh, Winky, pretty soon those two will rub off on me."

The cat ignored her completely and rolled on his catnip toy, talking in his own blissful language.

Paige and Michael followed suit, slipping into their own world. Though it had been artic outside, Michael's touch was not. His warm hand brushed Paige's cheek, and his lips skimmed over hers. She kissed him with a sweet heat and heard his breath hitch.

His amber brown eyes locked onto hers. He tugged on her hand, eyebrow raised. She took the hint and moved to the kitchen door.

"That's right. You two go off and do what you want. I'm doing the same," Linney called out.

"You are? Good for you," Paige answered, heading to the foyer.

"Wait, what?" Linney appeared dishtowel in hand looking flustered. "Well, not quite the same. I'm going to take a break. I'm going to go sort in the sunroom before my shift. How's that for rebel? It's not even on the schedule."

"You go, girl. Rebel up, Auntie." Paige giggled as she flew up the stairs with Michael.

Chapter Two

Paige had entered Michael's life unexpectedly less than a month back. It seemed a lifetime. She was bright, resourceful, and so beautiful. Something about her grabbed hold of his heart and didn't let go. He was five years older, had never considered dating younger, but he met his match with her. They fell for each other intensely. For now, they lived in the same area, but only for now. It was a sizable obstacle to overcome but not this day. With a long lunch and some seclusion, they had other matters at hand, especially with her libidinous invitation.

Like magnets, both felt a pulse-pounding visceral reaction whenever they were close. A look, a touch, a breathy whisper from Paige could send his blood surging. This was no exception; it was far worse.

They flew up the stairs together, Paige tugging him to a side bedroom. They rushed in, and he slammed the door closed, clicking the lock. His breath caught at seeing Paige's intoxicating longing. He pinned her to the closed bedroom door. His voice came out a ragged growl instead of words, causing her face to beautifully flush.

Finally, he could kiss her in private. He did so with abandon. He held her and kissed her savagely, open mouthed, and so intense he heard a whimper escape from her lips. He pulled back, breathing in a desperate

267

rhythm, looking to her gray-blue eyes for an invitation as he removed his suit jacket and carelessly threw it on the floor without regard to the cost of the expensive material.

Paige did more than invite his lips back with a gentle kiss, she returned it with one of her own ravaging fierce kisses, nails digging into his shirt. He pushed her short blazer off her shoulders. His hands were all over her. Fire flared. His mouth was on her neck, biting at her skin, tasting slightly of the warmth of the baking she'd done.

She moaned in little gasps, swallowing hard. "I...I had no idea showing you another cleaned out room would have this effect."

He leaned back and looked into her eyes. His small chuckle broke the spell of the urgency of the moment. "Flee. Your text. That's what did it."

He let her go from the door to glance at the bedroom. It had a twin-sized mattress leaning against a wall and nothing else but an antique mirrored vanity. She picked up the jackets and hung them on the door knob, moving with languid strides toward the deep-set window.

Between dreamy breaths, she pulled off her slacks and said, "The view—"

"Is amazing." Michael's shirt and pants were gone in a flash. He drank in the sight of her, partly undressed, not the snowy, tree-filled view through the window. He lifted her onto the recessed window sill and reached to her lower belly as his body opened her legs. The cold of the window was evident when his other hand pressed to the old glass panes to pull her close. His mouth was on hers again, fervor renewed. He drew back from the kiss, tugging at her lower lip.

"Tell me what you wrote, Paige," he urged in a whisper as he nibbled her earlobe, nuzzling his cheek to her rosy flush. He tugged open the small buttons of her blouse.

"Um…I…I said that I had missed you and that… Oh," she moaned.

He stopped her moan with an aching needful kiss to her lips again, eating them voraciously.

"Don't let me interrupt…" He chuckled, his voice low, knowing it was mesmerizing to her. His lips traveled down her neck while he unhooked her bra.

"I…found my hands traveling on my body." Paige stopped as his warm hands reached under her loosened bra, cupping her firm welcoming breasts. His thumbs brushed her nipples.

He stopped moving and kissing. "What else Flee? Tell me and don't stop."

Her eyes widened. He drank in the lust shining in them.

"Your eyes are bright amber, Michael. I see the snow reflecting on them."

He raised an eyebrow. "That's not what you wrote, is it?"

She shook her head. He resumed his salacious kisses, traveling ever closer to the dip of her cleavage. Knowing the reaction he was having on her, he egged her on. "Please continue."

"I…texted you last night that my hands cupped my breasts and tugged at my nipples. I wished they were your hands."

Michael looked at her, slowly sliding his hands up under her shirt and over her shoulders, removing her blouse. Then he slid her bra off. He bent and kissed her, biting little bites from her shoulder toward her nipples. He kneaded her flesh as he sank to his knees. He paused, giving her an assessing stare. "Stopping again?"

"No, no…I was distracted."

"Like I was all morning thinking about that text?" He grinned, savoring the feel of her against his hand.

She closed her eyes. "I said my hands were gliding on my honey soft…oh." She let out a sweet moan and leaned farther back on the deep window sill only to lurch forward when the window touched her back. "I wanted to feel your hot breath on me, all over me."

Michael did just that. He tugged her nipples to a ripe hardness. He licked under her breasts and mouthed her skin, lower ever lower. His hands roved over her legs and stopped. He arched an eyebrow.

Paige quickly continued, "I think I texted of having you massage and bite my inner thigh and how I wanted to feel your finger inside of me like my own finger did."

She blushed red at the admission. He liked that. In fact, he loved it. He rubbed his hands on her inner thighs and interspersed it with trailing fingers teasing her lower lips. He suddenly bit at her mound through her panties and was rewarded with a small squeal. He pushed her panties to the side, trapping the light green lace in the crease of her thigh. He lowered his mouth to her, and he sucked at her sensitive spot, once.

"Where did you slide you finger, Paige?"

"Inside me," she said in a whispered pant.

"Tell me, exactly, Paige. Use the words…" he urged, his mouth and fingers so close but not at the exact place. She wriggled.

"In me. In my pussy. My tight, needy pussy…"

Michael eased his middle finger inside her slit, sliding it deeper and deeper, slowly, agonizingly slowly to build her molten need.

"Please…" she sputtered. "Please touch me, finger me, have me. Oh Michael!" Her voice turned urgent and lust-filled.

He did as asked. His finger sank in and moved faster, twisting, pumping into her with a second one added while he lapped up and around her clit. He sucked hard until she moaned a whimper, then licked and blew a cool jet on her. His fingers jammed in and out while he watched her exposed flesh. He bit at her pussy lips, then licked to soothe his bites. His thumb rolled around her clit, and he ground his fingers in deeply, then halted all movement.

"N-n-no. Don't stop. Right, my text…I said more…Kissing. Filling…something. Please."

He smiled, licked and nibbled more. A finger found her bottom and brushed over it. Her body shuddered against him.

"I want you in me," she whimpered.

"Soon. But first, I want you, now, like this. Come for me, Paige." He looked at her, fingers driving in, curling, and then buried his face again, efforts re-doubled.

"I wanted t-t-to wait for you-oo-oo." Paige screamed, holding the last syllable, one hand pressed to the window frame, the fingers of her other hand gripping in his hair as her body shook in rankled spasms against him.

He stopped only when he heard her finally take a

deep breath. Untangling her fingers from his hair, he stood and kissed her mouth, letting Paige taste her own honeyed essence. Her eyes popped open, telling him she might have been new to the sensation. He rubbed his knit boxers against her, attempting to milk another wave of orgasm from her, against him.

"It's far from over, Flee." He used his pet name for her as he ran fingers through his hair, pushing it back into place.

"What about…" Paige muttered.

Michael grinned. "Lunch? I just had mine," he teased.

Her jaw dropped, and she tapped him. "Jerk!"

"No. Didn't have jerk chicken. I had a sandwich, actually."

She huffed.

"C'mere." He wrapped her in his arms. "And you?" he asked, brushing her hair back.

"Just a snack, but I could have more."

Michael motioned to himself. "Well, I'm right here if you want me. Groundhog Man at your service in all respects of the word."

That earned another groan from her. It also earned further playful swats, but he'd backed up, loving that he could razz her. The playfulness grew. She came at him, and he dodged. He jumped, moving behind the twin mattress. She knocked it to the floor. He picked her up, slung her over his shoulder, and squeezed her bottom cheeks.

"Hey, put me down."

He smacked her ass.

She kicked when he twirled her and threatened to toss her down, only to place her gently on the mattress.

"Did the text really bother you?"

He knelt next to her. "What do you think?"

His hardness was evident through the close-fitting knit boxers. He pulled off his undershirt, patting his smooth chest, knowing she was watching his muscles flex. He reached over to the door and his jacket, his crotch brushing over her face. She grabbed his hips and kissed him through his boxers. With a moan, he pulled the string of condoms out of his pocket but didn't immediately back up, kneeling close to her.

Not wishing to force the point, he rolled, landing on his back and pulled Paige to him, kissing her again. She broke the kiss and locked eyes with him. His hands joined hers in pulling off his shorts. His cock sprang to life, having been trapped too long.

"Your text drove me wild, Flee. I did all I could to rush here to be with you-oo-oo…" Like Paige, he cried out holding the last syllable in a song. His words turned to a groan when her mouth covered his tip. He ached for more of the tantalizing warmth her silken tongue gave him. He rocked his hips to her movement.

She stopped and grinned. "Tell me more. What did you want?"

He smiled, his hand playing with her long blonde hair. "Flee, you sure you are okay with this?"

She nodded.

In a murmur, he said, "I want your tongue and red lips on my cock. I want you to lick me."

Her response was to lick all the way up his erection, sliding it part-way into her warm mouth. She pumped it tightly. He guided her through the movements, to show her how he enjoyed it most. Shivers of delight rocked into him. She pulled from him and tilted her head, slid her lips back and forth on his length, then sucked his cockhead, again, eliciting his moan at her mind-bending attention.

She stopped once more and looked at him, repositioning herself in a kneeling position between his legs. She kneaded her breasts instead of touching him. "You stopped talking," she goaded.

He didn't need much encouragement. He growled. "I want your mouth on my hard cock and your hands on my balls. I want to suck me until I can't stand it, and then I want to bury myself in your hot, wet pussy."

Paige's eyes widened in seeming surprise at his guttural words. They widened the way they did when she seared with arousal and raw sexuality. She leaned down and sucked one ball then the other and took his dick part way into her mouth. She pulled back, only to lick all the way to the top of his shaft, then take him back into her mouth. Her movements continued and quickened, making his blood pump red-hot. He was iron-hard and on the edge.

He ripped open the condom packet. She drew her mouth off him, but her hands remained. On her next downward stroke, his hands joined hers. Following where her sweet lips had been, he unfurled the condom and sheathed his throbbing cock.

He needed her. He wanted to plant himself all the way deep into her tight, wet folds. His moans grew until he shifted to lay on his side, pulling her down. He whispered her name as he opened her legs and slid his cockhead back and forth along her slit, before sinking into her pussy. "Paige…"

"Oh Michael," she cried with a quiver to her voice, sending thrills into him.

They fell into an inarticulate groaning rhythm, so slowly at first. Then, with a grind of his hips, he pulled back and drove into her with a force, indicating the beginning of the frantic pulse of a hungry, ravaging pounding. Her kisses and bites matched his. He drove his cock in and out, angling it differently with a craving to fill and refill each crevice. His hips rocked both of them until they were past the point of lust and completely lost.

Michael thrust deeply with a wanton need to be completely linked inside Paige with each stroke. He pulled her arching body up to his and kissed her, smothering her moans. Her body shuddered, and she whimpered.

He could not hold back any longer. He slammed the hard slab of his body against her and came with bellowing growl from deep within. Her own orgasm followed, with a breathless O until it found a voice.

"Paige, Paige, Paige, I love you." His voice came as a gasp at the end of his mind-wrenching pinnacle. Since the words had spilled weeks before, they came so readily from his lips in a hushed whisper of a mantra at times like this. It was all so easy with her. Her delicious body yielded and responded to his almost instantly. He could never get enough of being with her.

They slowed. He kissed her all over her face, and she his, until both collapsed. He rolled off her. Forgetting the smallness of the mattress, he landed on the floor. She laughed, flushed of face, and scooted over so he could join her on the twin mattress.

He laughed, too, and kissed her forehead, scooping her back into his arms. How he loved holding her. "Anything you want to say to me?"

Paige's face lit up. "I'll text you."

Michael flew into laughter and followed it with tickles until she gave up and said, "Okay, okay. I like groundhog for lunch?"

More tickles.

"Time out. Time out, or I'll have to pee."

He didn't stop until she giggled her way into squealing. He loved to hear her laugh.

"Okay. Okay." Paige took a deep breath and dreamily added, "I love you. I want to stay here with you all afternoon." She kissed him sweetly.

Afternoon? The moment broke with a reminder from the clock. He looked at his watch and swore. He jumped up and gathered his clothing. He began to dress, regretting the feel of cloth on his skin so soon after they were curled into each other.

Still naked, she stood, flushed and glowing, and helped him, fixing his tie while he tucked in his shirt. As she pulled the knot up to straighten it, she leaned in and kissed him again. "Michael, I guess I don't want to say those words too often. I'm afraid to wear them thin. You must know that by now."

He did. He pulled her to him. They stood together, he dressed in his suit, her naked. "Never too much with you, Paige. I love you."

He meant it. Looking at her this way tugged at some other awareness deep inside. His job in the area would soon come to a close. Then what?

He shook clear of the thought. No further words were said. One kiss, one look, and he rushed out the bedroom door. It was only at the bottom of the stairs that he called up to her, "Best lunch ever, Paige."

Aunt Linney stepped from the living room,

seemingly oblivious to what had transpired between them. "Don't let it get around we serve good lunch around here. I don't want to be feeding any strays."

Michael blinked, burst out laughing, and waved as he hurried to the door, overcoat only half on.

He could hear Linney call up the stairs, "Hey, Paige, do you have any leftovers? I'm hungry, too."

That earned chuckles as he drove along the ice-slickened mountain roads back to work.

Chapter Three

Michael and Paige met as often as they could through the rest of February. Each moment in each other's arms solidified their feelings. Each house project done together became less like work and more like some challenging puzzle they playfully completed together. He encouraged her to take a moment to relish completing a task as they both hastened to the next, with Michael sometimes feeling the angst of her overly-large renovation plans, though he rarely said so.

Both were driven and stayed on their own tasks when they were apart so that the free time together could be all the longer. Some of it was spent in the bedroom or lingering with a plate of dinner in front of the mantle-less fireplace, since that, too, had fallen. Better were the times they spent skin to skin, curled up in each other, which they did with frequency. Surprisingly coordinated, as a couple, Michael and Paige were on a clear path.

The renovation plans were anything but. The calendar sheets in the kitchen were filled with markings and arrows. The February calendar page had been left up in March, since many of the projects were still undone. Some of the March items Paige thought could be put off were already complete. Scratchy notes were scribbled and blurred on the posted pages, showing everything was in flux. The calendar system, which was meant as an organizational tool, turned into a reminder that the renovation project was not going as planned. It was off in all sorts of tangents.

Paige drank her morning coffee, with two percent milk, looking out at freshly fallen snow. March. The window showed two shoveled tracks barely good enough so that a car could get in and out without fully clearing the long, curved driveway. It was a short cut that afforded her a moment for coffee and reflection as she warmed herself.

She sighed. Most of the important items on the calendar were still not done, along with finding funds for upcoming costs without hitting credit cards again. The calendar had the harshest and most persistent reminder—March 17th.

The cat hopped up on the cushion on top of boxes of Paige's summer gear, which had landed in the kitchen for want of space. It was warm near the heat register and gave Winky a view of the outdoors, though he seemed to intently watch her instead. She gave him a quick pet and returned the calendar, yanking down the pages, feeling anxious by the circled date. It had nothing to do with the house renovation or St. Patrick's Day. It was the day Michael's roll out project was to be done, and with it, his excuse to stay with her.

Maybe her aunt was right in objecting to the calendar pages.

Paige finished her coffee and posted a piece of paper where the calendar had been that read, "Clear something. Clean something. Organize something."

She picked up the cat. Sensing her need, Winky actually let her hold him and purred his consent.

"How can I do it? I want to stay here to finish this

all. I have a temporary café job and a call back for a real career position. I didn't mean to look for that, but it seemed to come my way. I'm bright and capable enough, aren't I? I want this to keep going. But, oh Winky…" A tear rolled down her cheek. "Michael. I know he'll have to go back to his corporate headquarters and…and…" She refused to give voice to the word *leave*.

"Long distance lovers? Does that work? I hate commuting, Winky. I need to finish the house, at least. How can I leave here otherwise? He keeps telling me it will all work out, but how? My heart will shatter without him. Did you know that?" She looked out at the pristine snow drifts, letting the tears fall.

Linney made a slumped appearance in robe and slippers with a yawn and mumbled, "Morning." She poured coffee and added milk, not even noticing that Paige acquiesced into buying two percent. "Calendar?"

"Gone. Too confusing."

Her aunt nodded and mumbled something else without gloating at the calendar removal. She just looked at the sheet and added the word "laugh." She paused and wrote in, "Be happy you have another day." That took Paige's attention away from her worried thoughts about the future. Something was not right with her aunt.

She took a deep breath and brushed away her few tears. "Are you okay, Linney?"

Linney tipped her head and stared out the window. "Shoveled enough. Thanks."

"Linney, what's wrong?"

"Huh? Oh. Hospice." Linney sat down heavily. "Too soon like I thought. Not to mention we're short-staffed since a nurse is out for a family emergency. Three coming to an end most likely at the same time. I have to stay there a few days and nights in a row now. I don't feel comfortable not being available to each of them. The families need a familiar face even if it is just mine. So hard sometimes. One is only in his forties." Linney swallowed a gulp of coffee. "You okay here by yourself for a bit?"

"Of course." Filled with empathy, Paige rose and handed the unusually mellow Winky to her aunt. She hugged her aunt tightly where she sat. Then she pulled out eggs, veggies, and toast. "How can I help?"

"Reach me if I email or text you."

Paige stopped. She was surprised by the request since she never saw her aunt ever text. She just nodded.

"Can you talk to the woodwork candidates?" Linney flattened the crumpled March calendar sheet. "Three guys coming today."

"Sure. I took a waitress shift tomorrow though." Paige stared off, ignoring the ingredients before her.

"Good. Glad it works out. And Paige?"

"Uh huh?"

"I like my eggs cooked and bread toasted, Squirt." Linney smiled, motioning to the untouched ingredients.

Shaking free of their shared melancholy, Paige smiled, washed her hands, and began to cook. Linney put down the cat and started to do a yoga stretch on her own as Paige had tried to teach her. That was new.

"Jokes. We need to stick to a program of chocolate and jokes. We can make it, kiddo. All of it. Work. The house, too. You'll figure out this Michael thing. It's meant to be, trust me on that."

Paige turned to the cat. "You ratted me out to Ms.

Eavesdropper here, didn't you?" The cat just twitched and ran from the room. "Scaredy cat!"

"Nope. I figured it out on my own. Bright me. Unfortunately, I'm also a hungry woman. Feed me, Squirt," Linney said, bending to another pose.

"Bossy pants. Hey, you're looking a tad bit skinnier, Auntie."

"Stop staring at my beauteous body and think about what food you might pack me to take to work."

"Yes, ma'am." Paige had no idea where Linney hid her oversized chocolate bar for sorrow repair, but she did know where the cookies she froze were. As soon as breakfast was prepared, Paige packed those, along with a sandwich or two, carrots, fruit, and a note of support.

Winky zoomed by one direction, rolling his favorite ball. Then he ran back the other direction while they ate. They had hidden the embarrassing Ben Wa balls the cat coveted as a play toy and replaced it with a lighter, neon green one intended for cats. Unfortunately, the ball bounced unevenly, driving Winky crazy. He ran in a circle, chasing the ball. It reminded Paige that things go in a big circle.

Focus on helping the next person. Things will work out. The hospice needed Linney, Linney needed her, and she could lean on Michael. And perhaps, just perhaps she needed to be a bit more upbeat for them all. Linney could use that bolster so she could help others.

"It goes in a big circle like, Winky," Paige blurted out of nowhere.

Linney nodded.

Winky stopped running in the circle and walked straight into a wall. He shook it off and dashed away.

"Maybe not exactly like Winky," Paige corrected

herself.

"I don't know about that. Feels like I bash into walls head first many times. Here's to walls, Winky, and shaking it off."

Linney and Paige toasted with their toast. Paige even put out the jelly for her aunt. And, to her surprise, her aunt didn't even use it. But Paige did.

****

"What do you mean you don't want to come here to look at the mantle?"

The man on the phone explained something about hearing Bailey might be interested and to call him for work on sheet rock instead.

"Bailey? Who's Bailey?" Paige moved to her poster of business cards and notes. "Oh, you mean the flower delivery guy who likes to do woodwork? That Bailey? I didn't even call him."

The man on the phone answered, "Well, you or your house made an impression on him." He continued refuting Paige. "Rumor has it Bailey will be arriving close to dinner time."

He hung up with an assurance he wanted work and he'd show up for the sheet rock work and maybe even the porch building crew when the weather cleared, just not something Bailey could do since he was the best.

After they hung up, Paige realized he'd said something about a crew. "What crew?" she asked the cat. "Did you schedule work on the porches?"

Winky meowed.

It was almost as if the community took it upon themselves to act as the general contractor. Definitely not like Atlanta. Paige decided to roll with it.

Bailey or no, she'd already met with one

reasonable man, Bob. He was bald and nodded a lot but had references. He measured, nodded more, took notes, and said he would email an estimate for a list of work, broken down by projects. She liked that. It showed Bob had a sense of business acumen.

She looked at her ugly non-destructible watch hidden under the sleeve of her work clothes. She had time to clean out and sort a few more drawers of the master bedroom before the next appointment.

The next potential worker was slumped shouldered, fairly young, and quirky. He said he was available in a couple weeks and could do it "cheap" to each project Paige mentioned. He also sniffled whenever the cat came into the room but claimed he could "take a whole pile of allergy medicine" and not to worry since it didn't make him too drowsy to work. He started sneezing. She made note and, after he left, wrote, "No power tools, best outside, needs supervision," next to his name on her laptop.

She hadn't heard from Michael all day and sent him a quick text about checking out woodworkers. His text came right back.

"My wood works fine, especially near you, Flee."

"I'd like to test that out. Linney is scheduled at the hospice around the clock for a couple days."

"I'll try to come by tonight if that's okay?"

Paige sent him smiles in response but heard nothing further, knowing it meant he was in another meeting.

An apple was only enough to hold off her hunger while she made dinner. She decided on lasagna. More cheese laden than normal, but she'd add extra veggies along with the meat for good measure. She planned to drop some of the casserole off at the hospice center before her work the next day.

The smell of the sauce filled the kitchen. She snitched pieces of mozzarella while she cooked, music adding to the warm ambience. Onions cooked, spinach wilted, and the ground meat sizzled. All the components came together in two trays, which she put into the oven but didn't turn on. She needed to run a quick errand and didn't trust the old oven to be on while she was gone.

****

Paige returned, juggling two small grocery bags in hand as she opened the door to the kitchen.

"Let me help." A pleasant, bearded man took the groceries from her.

"Thanks," Paige answered with a smile. She followed it with a scream. "What are you doing in here?" she asked, panting for air.

"Oh right, right. I'm inside. You expected me outside. Cold out there though." The man smiled widely with calm, indiscriminate-colored eyes under long, indiscriminate brown hair. He started to unload the groceries, nonplussed.

Paige stared wide-eyed at the bearded, hairy man. "Bailey, right?"

"Hey, you remembered my name, Bailey. Cool. Not John or Mr. Kernstonberg or John Bailey Kernstonberg. Just Bailey. And you're Linney Paige Flee Marilyn Smith Myers."

"Huh? Oh! All the possible names I gave you for the Valentine flower tags."

Paige became less threatened and more confused by having this particular stranger in her kitchen. Maybe it was his overly mellow *meant to be here* friendly demeanor. He had struck her as *harmless but off* when he had visited before as a substitute floral delivery person and completely mixed up all the flower orders. He was odd then. Now he was…

Her thoughts froze as she watched him put away the grocery items in exactly the places she would put each item.

"How could I forget? You live in a house that just cries to be restored, Linney Paige—"

Paige held up her hand. "Only half those names are mine. The others are my aunt's. We can sort that out another time. Paige. I go by Paige," she corrected. "And more importantly, I live in a house that was locked." She emphasized the last word as she eyed the long haired, bearded man suspiciously.

"Oh, about that. I fixed the strike plate for the bolt so it sets in properly. A lock's not a lock unless it works," he said matter-of-factly, opening the oven and checking the pans of lasagna. He turned the dial lower on the oven. "Smelling good already, Linney Paige Flee, er, I mean Bi-Paige. Salad fixings you bought look good, too."

"Bi-Paige? No, Bailey. It's Paige. Not Bi-Paige. What am I doing?"

"Uh oh. You're confused. Well, hmm, maybe you're just hungry. Seems you need some food, but the lasagna isn't heated through yet. How about taking off your coat and…"

Before Bailey finished addressing her rhetorical question, Paige had taken off her coat and boots, stuffed her feet into slippers, and left the kitchen for the restroom.

He walked after her and stood in the foyer. "We already think alike. Get comfortable and take a tour, then eat."

Staring in the mirror, she could see her cheeks weren't just rosy from the cold outside. They were red from frustration at having an unexpected someone simply pop in. Not even warm water splashed on her cheeks changed their hue. She switched to cold water. She hoped to wake herself up. The cold water brought her to her senses, which told her nothing was making sense. She addressed her reflection, "Roll with it."

When she stepped from the restroom, she was refreshed in some ways, others, not so much.

Bailey was bent sideways looking up the stairwell. Then he turned the other way. The cat came and did the same, mirroring him.

"Uh, excuse me?" she asked. "Did you finish the tour of the living room?"

"What? No, of course not. Wouldn't do it without you around. I was taught that would be impolite."

Paige had no words.

Bailey beamed as he entered the living room. Unlike other rooms, it was livable and less overstuffed. His hands moved along the frame of the bay window. He seemed to almost dance as he touched the wood, running his hands firmly against surfaces. "Dark mahogany, on this shelf, too." He sighed.

"Hate to interrupt your…whatever you're doing, but it's the mantle we need to attend to. It looked so flimsy that I took it down. Definitely not original. I was thinking about painting the brick, but it's crumbling, and I think if we can afford it—"

"A stone façade would be perfect," they both said

together.

Bailey smiled, the corners of his eyes crinkling into lines. He was older than she originally thought.

Paige was baffled. She gathered herself and continued, "I know you're here for the woodwork, and I have no way of doing the stone first since I have to clear out upstairs for the scheduled work. We have so many other... Where are you going?"

He had rushed to the sunroom off the living room and said things like perfect, bead board, and restore some parts, make others new and livable. He looked at Paige. "Any objection to bead board sunroom ceiling? That pulls in a bit of your southern. Caught as much from your accent. Walls are too flimsy. It should be more of a screened in porch so that means..." He ran back through the foyer to the dining room and felt along the back wall. "Perfect. How about a door leading to a wood-paneled study here? You know, the one you need. It shouldn't be upstairs. Makes the structure work better, too, I bet."

She remembered there was a question over whether or not a closet could be placed instead of the mudroom. Dang, if he wasn't right about a study.

"Good Wi-Fi and view back here, I bet. And then the back porch can lead to the outdoor shower or maybe it should be from the sunroom? Can you show me the blue prints you have approved?"

"Sure...but...hey, wait. We don't have money to do all this. Make that not even most of it."

He looked straight at her, speaking intently, "You can't afford not to."

That hit a chord inside her. Before she could stop herself, she went to her laptop in the living room and pulled up the scanned blue prints showing the intended work upstairs and projected later work.

He pointed at the laptop screen. "See? This room shouldn't be a mudroom. It should be a study. No change to the foot print. The mudroom can be the back covered porch, and just put up a deck extending to the shower. That way no new permits are needed. Plus, you get more closet space. Built-ins would fit."

"Money, Bailey. More money is needed. I'm not able to do the work, and we can't afford to hire it all out."

"You don't have to. It will all work out."

She threw her hands up in exasperation. Her phone pinged. She excused herself leaving Bailey to stare at the plans on her laptop. The text was from Bob, the woodworker she had planned to hire. He pulled from the job without explanation. She would have to call him later, otherwise she would be stuck with Bailey. That thought sent her into calling the contractor now. He didn't answer. She texted him, asking why he wasn't interested and if it was just that he needed a different time frame.

He answered, "Hire Bailey. He's the best."

At that, Paige stomped back to Bailey in the living room. "What magic hold do you have? Nobody else wants the job. They all say to hire you if you want it."

He just shrugged. "I like woodworking and carpentry. Hey, who's this?" He was looking at photos of her aunt on her laptop. He was so calm and kindly inquisitive that it disarmed her as he helped himself to her computer.

"It's my aunt, Linney. People used to know her as Marilyn." She leaned over him and pulled up some more photos, some of Michael also, which further lulled her into acceptance that a near stranger was insinuating his way in.

"A looker, eh?"

The photo was one that included Michael and Linney so Paige readily agreed with Bailey. Winky brushed against her so she picked him up, but he leapt out of her arms and directly onto Bailey's lap.

"Hey, fella." Bailey smiled, showing off his wrinkles again under all the hair and beard.

"May I ask your age?" she asked.

"Sure." He stared at a photo of Linney making a face and gave no further answer.

"Okay… What's your age?" Paige hid her annoyance by placing her hand on his shoulder to get a better look at the photo.

"Oh. Right. I'm fifty-four. But…hey, now, too old for you," he said with a grimace.

"What? Not for me. I mean I wasn't asking for me." She pulled back her hand.

"Cool, cool. Better. Didn't want to get all rejecty on you." He relaxed as did the cat.

"Oh, like the others I called for estimates?"

"Right. They weren't rejecting you or you them. They can come. I can teach Bob. Can't have Calvin near cats though. Only for porch help later."

"You're planning on doing the porches, too?"

"Might. All of it waits to be seen. Smells like lasagna's ready." With that, Bailey lifted the cat from his lap and quickly moved to the kitchen. He was drying his washed hands by the time she entered. He removed both lasagnas from the oven and put them on the stove top. To her astonishment, he pulled out a plate and served himself a small piece, without so much as being offered. He took a forkful, blowing on it, and ate it standing in the middle of the kitchen.

"Uh, help yourself," Paige said, amazed at his boldness.

"Will do." Bailey smiled and took a second small bite. He nodded with a pleased expression, returned to the pan, and put another heaping helping or two onto his plate. He placed it on the table and spooned a small portion for Paige on another plate. He motioned for her to sit. She did, still stunned into silence.

He ate two more bites, giving a moan of appreciation. "Mmm-mmm. Okay. I'll work here." Bailey announced.

"What?" Confusion rang in her mind and voice.

"You can really cook, so I'll do the job." He scooped up a large bite.

"We haven't talked price or projects or time tables or anything. What if we don't agree on salary for the projects?"

He said nothing but nodded and looked away, waving at his half-open mouth to cool it. She poured him a glass of water, which he gratefully took.

"It's so good, I didn't want to even wait for a salad." He swallowed another grateful bite. "Paige, here's the offer. You pay for supplies and what you can. Just keep the food coming and we'll all get along fine."

Paige was too dazed to answer. Hunger pulled her from her contemplation as she, too, bit into the warm goodness. It was delicious.

He smiled. "Good, huh?"

She moaned in agreement. After a few bites, she regained her sense. "The work is costly. Even the wood."

"You have trees. Saw a fallen birch I can use for something."

Paige wasn't convinced.

His expression remained calm and reassuring. "Renovating a house into a home is about art. You have to do it with feeling and warmth, not numbers and projects. It isn't a business exactly. It'll be fine."

She stared. She'd heard almost the same "renovation is art" from Linney. Maybe it was the delicious carbs in front of her. Maybe it was his mellow attitude. Without seeing his work or references, she knew Bailey had just become a temporary part of their lives. "Okay. You're hired. Or maybe we're hired by you?"

He raised his fork in a quick toast of acceptance and nodded. "So, tell me about your aunt."

To her continued surprise, she did. The two were laughing with her tapping his arm by the time Michael stepped in.

"Michael!" She leapt from her seat, still grinning.

"Am I missing something?" Michael asked, unmoving.

Bailey answered, "Yes, you sure are, man. Great lasagna, your lover, here, made it. Come join."

Both Paige's and Michael's eyebrows shot up. Michael had stopped pulling off his overcoat.

"Oh right, right. She didn't say as much, but the flowers you sent and the way she looked at the photos of you on her laptop told me you two were something." Bailey pointed to Michael and Paige with his fork before taking another bite.

Paige sheepishly brushed off the snow from

Michael and hung his coat, whispering, "It's Bailey. Tell you later."

Bailey continued both eating and talking. "Paige, here, can cook. Smart one. Need to get her to relax about deadlines and worrying over money though."

"Ha!" Michael cut a piece of lasagna and then a second piece before sitting. "I've been trying to get her to do that. Sometimes, it's difficult to switch from work to home, just like I used to tell Susan before…"

He was met with stone stares and turned to his food.

Bailey broke the silence. "Paige tells me how sweet Linney is."

Michael let out another, "Ha!"

"Hey, now. She is. Sometimes. Well, when she's not sarcastic. She's good to those families in hospice." Paige told more than she probably should have to the stranger who was becoming warmer in her eyes. Less indiscriminate.

A horn honked. Bailey rose. "Gotta roll. It's my ride. Sorry to leave you with the dishes. I'll start next week sometime."

"When? What is your price? What supplies do you need?" Paige saw his expression dimming. "Right. Those are the things that will work out, right? Just roll with it?"

"Exactly." Bailey shifted the collar of his coat and opened the kitchen door. "She's all yours, man. Mellow her worries out. Looking forward to meeting this Linney Marilyn person next time. See ya."

With that, Michael and Paige were alone at the dinner table. Almost. Winky yowled his need for dinner, too.

Chapter Four

"Oooo, that feels good. To the left. Right there. Ohh, perfect." Paige had won the flip of the cards and got the first massage. With the house to themselves and the kitchen cleared, she opted for a foot massage in front of the fireplace. The fireplace still functioned though the crumbled mantle leaned against the side of the bricks.

Michael had pulled the twin mattress down to the living room, sliding it in front of the loveseat. They had finished their perfect hideaway with pillows, blankets, and fresh sheets draped over the loveseat and mattress. The softly falling snow added to the cabin feel of the night.

Still clothed, Paige wiggled her toes, leaning back dreamily, lounging on the mattress, her head and arms falling to the cushion of the sofa. She stretched, languishing in the divine feel of Michael's hands. He had his laptop charging and soft jazz playing. She moaned as he massaged each needful spot perfectly.

"Baby-blue toenails, Flee?"

"Sure, I pick it by the name. It was called *Can't Find My Czechbook* as in the country not the bank thing. At the time, I was missing my checkbook. Do you like it? It matches my panties. I think."

"Maybe we need to make sure." Michael moaned in a deep tone as his hand moved to massage higher on under the cuff of her pants. He leaned forward and slowly unzipped them. "Besides, it's warm in here."

He kissed her. Paige pulled him to her, kissing him, massaging his shoulders, hands gliding on his expensive, thin sweater. It came off as did her pants. Firelight coated her legs and his arms a golden hue.

He reached past her to a glass of ice water. The ice cubes sparkled in the firelight. The warmth of the glowing flames made water droplets condense on the glass. Michael pushed up her sweater and dragged the cold wet glass down her skin agonizingly slowly. Her breath caught.

"You said your toenail polish matched your panties. Those panties are a deeper azure. Tsk. Fibber. What should we do about that?"

"Stay the whole night and make sure my nighty gives you the right shade of blue-ue-ue," Paige moaned as Michael nibbled the trail down her stomach where the water droplets had landed.

"Can't stay the night, but you were saying something about giving?" He pushed up her bra over her chest, freeing her nipples to his touch. His lips tugged her there. "I want to be a gentleman and take all you offer."

For her response, she dragged her nails up his back through his undershirt and pulled it over his head.

"I have an early meeting, but I would love to iron out this nighty-panty-nail polish issue with you now. Something has to give."

What gave was Paige's sweater and bra, leaving her breasts naked. The way she leaned back, sitting in front of the loveseat, made her body arch and her nipples become little points that cast a shadow in the glow of the firelight.

Michael's chest broadened with each deep breath as he gazed at her with a glow to his amber eyes. He whispered something in Oneida and followed it with the word, "beautiful." He drank from the water. His hands moved where he stared, cupping, molding her breast. His cold lips followed. He bit one nipple while the other was treated to an ice cube.

Soft panting gasps escaped her. The treatment moved to the other breast. Ice melted in a rivulet down her skin, goosebumps chased after each cold drop. His warm hand slid into her panties, cupping her. Then he slid an icy finger along her slit. Her whimpered cry was lost in his deep plunging kiss. She held to him, any part she could reach.

The remaining clothing was torn away. And there, in front of the fire, they fell naked onto the mattress, scissored together. His condom sheathed cock rubbed against her clit.

He whispered, "Trust me?"

She nodded. Her eyes grew wide in the firelight as he pressed an ice cube to her excited clit the same moment he thrust within her. She gave voice to the rush of feelings that collided deep, so deep within her. Stinging cold, heat from the fireplace, hardness held fully within her, and a crying, lustful need. Her insides squeezed on him, locking him there. She was on the edge, the timeless edge. He let go of the ice, touching her face to angle her head and bring her lips to his greedy mouth.

Paige broke the kiss when he bucked so fast her whole body jiggled. Even her cry was more of a machine gun groan. Her eyes popped open, and with toes curled, her inner walls clenched, and she was lost again. This time, she exploded into a thousand pieces and held tight to his strong muscular body.

Skin to smooth skin, he ground powerfully into her and wrapped his rippled arms until he heard her breath turn to a cry of passion. Her voice echoed as her body, flushed in release, shook again. His moans told her he was almost at the same juncture.

Without warning, an awareness of her twisted leg came to her. She suddenly shifted, trying to stretch a sharply pinched nerve. She grabbed at her leg, "Charlie horse."

Michael pulled from her with ragged breaths. She bent over the covered loveseat, stretching out her leg as he rubbed it.

With the pinched nerve relieved, his eyes drank in her exposed bottom. His hands trailed all over her, massaged along her slit, and even brushed her sensitive rosebud. Paige was on the edge again.

He knelt behind her, entering her wetness in one stroke, growling of how he wanted to fill her in all ways one day. She could only gasp out her consent. Arching, she reached back to him, gripping any part of him she could hold. His strong forearm moved around her. He thrust into her deeply, slowly, making her savor each stroke. She twisted enough to kiss him.

He filled her again and again, his muscular thighs brushing against her, his pelvis meeting her warm cheeks. The rhythm changed and sped up.

"Michael, please," was all she could say from the precipice.

It was all he needed. He bucked hard, all the way into her tender pussy, holding her to him as he jarred in and out with a fiery, fast hunger. In her half awareness, he reached for the ice and held it to her nipple when he drove all the way up into her. He pulled almost out and thrust back in, sawing quickly and followed with a grinding twist.

Both cried out, both exploded, Paige open-mouthed and arched against him. He held her, eventually calming her, slowing her. Each kissed and touched what they could reach. They collapsed to the mattress, cover tugged over them. Both murmured unheard words of pleasures. They entwined and slept, exhaustion stealing words of unspoken love.

****

Paige shivered and opened an eye. Winky twitched near her head. She looked around. She was huddled in Michael's arms, the fire long since died past embers. The early light of morning was brighter than normal as it reflected on the newly fallen snow.

"Michael." She shook him. He moaned and pulled her in tighter. "Michael, morning, I think."

"Huh?"

Winky stepped closer and leaned over his face and meowed loudly.

"What the…" Michael rolled Paige aside and threw off the blanket. His expression was harsh. "Morning? What time is it? I said I couldn't stay over. Janet needs me to get her in the morning."

Paige grimaced as she rose. She shivered and covered herself with the blanket. "Hey, I have work, too. Might be just a temporary waitress job in a café, but it's work."

"It's not the same, and you know it."

"No, Michael, I actually don't know it. I know you

have a professional position, but I have no idea of the details of what you really do and, apart from hearing the name, Janice, who you do it with."

"Janet," Michael corrected as he began to dress in his crumpled business attire.

"Janet, Marsha, Cindy, the whole Brady Bunch for all I care. Not my fault. This—" Paige pointed between the two of them. "—was a mistake." Her drawl ratcheted up with the increased apprehension at his undeserved rudeness.

"How can you say that?"

"What? I need coffee. It was an accident we fell asleep. Not us. We aren't the *mistake*…are we?"

Michael found his watch. He dashed to the powder room without answering. His silence cut into her leaving her a lot of thoughts to unpack. Coffee. She needed coffee.

Paige wrapped the throw blanket around her like a bath towel and stomped to the kitchen to start the coffee. She still had time to make her shift. Winky followed her. She poured out his food and petted him. "Thanks for waking us, Winky. We have plenty of time I bet."

She knew she was wrong when she looked out. The snow tracks she'd shoveled were covered with new snow, far too thick to drive through. More shoveling was needed, and not just tracks. She stepped into action and called the French cafe, saying she needed to shovel out, but she would be coming for the shift. They thanked her, relieved to have the help, and told her to drive safely.

Paige swallowed the first of her coffee when Michael entered. He barely looked at her. With that greeting, she nearly sneered and did all she could not to gruffly hand him his coffee. "Milk's in the fridge. Not sure if we are out of your preferred cream. Whatever we have I'm sure it will help *lighten* things up."

He grunted, not even taking the bait to ease the tension. She re-wrapped the blanket and snuggled into it, still naked underneath. He looked out the kitchen window and swore, seeing the snow. She let him have his thoughts, most likely about the botch from staying over.

"You know, Michael—"

His cell phone rang. He immediately turned away and answered.

"Janet, hello. Good morning." Instantly, Michael's face and demeanor brightened. "Yes, the snow is something. About that. It looks like some shoveling is needed before I can travel anywhere… Uh huh… Bad by you, too?" He burst out laughing and moved to the hall without looking back at Paige.

She choked down her coffee and left to get ready to shovel, his voice echoing, "Uh huh… sure… Any video meeting format works for me. Maybe later we can still meet over the finalized…"

****

Paige came back down calmer and bundled up. Michael's voice echoed on the video chat. He had set up in the living room, tacking a sheet up on the wall behind him, presumably to give him a solid work-appropriate backdrop.

She approached him out of view. She knew she was interrupting his ever so important meeting but hoped for an "I'm sorry" or at least an adoring smile from him before she stepped outside to do her share of shoveling.

Instead, his smile disappeared when she entered. He distractedly waved her off and then laughed at whatever this Janet person said.

Paige shoveled. She was hot and had long since opened her coat. She wasn't used to this treatment from Michael. Her emotions rolled from anger to hurt to being confused. It was uncharacteristic of him. They both had accidentally fallen asleep.

She shoveled, pushing the light snow to the side, thankful it was powdery and not wet. She kept shoveling and thinking.

Hurt. She was becoming hurt. She remembered shoveling with Michael before and how it was all a light playful game. Davis wasn't like that. The ex she'd left behind in Atlanta wasn't playful, except when he was rutting with his football buddies. Davis was large, buff, and nothing like smooth Michael. Michael elicited such passion from her.

But what happened this morning? Who the hell is this Janice, Janet, Michael-stealer?

Her cell phone pinged a message. She grabbed for it, hoping it was Michael. Maybe he had realized how gruff he was with her. Instead, it was her mother. She peeled off one warm mitten and texted back that she was shoveling before her temporary work shift and would catch her later. Of course, it pinged again with more questions from her mother, which she would answer *later*.

She finished shoveling and knocked snow from her boots when she entered the kitchen. Hanging her coat on a peg, she then settled down for quick but much-needed snack and a second cup of coffee. She could hear Michael's jovial voice carry muddled words through the house.

After eating a jam-slathered toast slice and swallowing her coffee, she rationalized the morning as just getting up on the wrong side of the bed or in their case the wrong bed and the wrong room. She needed a shower, but first she would look in on Michael.

With a soft step, she entered the living room, smiling and waving at him. He seemed to smile back at her. Paige mouthed and motioned that she finished shoveling.

Michael nodded and said aloud, "Thanks, you're the best."

Paige beamed until he finished his sentence, "Janet." That knocked the wind out of her. Her lip quivered. He looked at her with concern but was called back into the video meeting.

She flew up the stairs and stood in the hot shower far longer than needed. Tears rolled. "Focus, Paige, focus. Linney needs you. The house needs you. You can overcome this. He's just being a jerk. But why?"

She dressed in traditional wait-staff attire, black slacks and white blouse. Her hair was ponytailed. She might not earn much, but every bit helped, and the new job got her out of the house with people her own age. She would get back on her career track after this, especially if she got called back on the initial interview she'd had last week in corporate product sales. She knew not to overreact about Michael. Not now. *Do what needs doing then worry about him later.*

When she came down the stairs, she found him waiting for her.

"I was just going to find you. I can help shovel

now that my meeting is done."

"I already finished." Paige moved to the kitchen.

Michael followed saying, "I told you I would help."

"When?"

"Maybe you didn't hear me. Like you didn't listen last night when I asked if you had an alarm set."

Her southern drawl came out in full force. "When the heck did you do that? When we were sleeping in front of the fireplace? Or maybe you are confusing me with your Janice."

"Janet."

"Janet, right. I have to remember that name. Maybe I will use it more. Maybe when I want to see you smile instead of sneer at me."

Michael's shoulders dropped, and he sighed. "Don't get upset."

"Don't get upset? Are you kidding me? After the repeated cold-shouldered and rude behavior I got from you all morning? Do you know how cheap it makes me feel after what we did last night?" In her overwrought state, her voice quieted with the last sentence. She drew in a breath, hoping for composure, but banged things as she readied the lasagna to take to Linney.

"Are you eating all that?" Michael tried to joke.

Paige glared at him.

"C'mon Paige. Sorry, but I did have this important meeting. Janet saved the day by talking them into a video session because of the snow."

Paige gnashed her teeth. "Ooooh Janet, Janet, Janet. Who the hell is Janet anyway?"

"Someone I work with back in the home office. I messed up coming out here last night, and she—"

"Saved the day," Paige said in a mocking tone. "Sorry, you messed up by seeing me. Sorry, I got in your way by having incredible sex. Sorry, we enjoy being together. Well, I hope you enjoy your time with your precious Janet when you go running back to her in a couple weeks. If you don't mind, I have to drive my car without snow tires to my simple, temporary *waitress* job so I can pay for a house I will never live in and keep feeding a boyfriend who can't stop gloating about a woman back home."

"Paige, don't be like that."

"Like what?" As hard as she tried, her tears fell. "Don't be hurt by someone I love who treated me horribly all the while praising another woman?"

Michael's face showed how her words affected him. His expression turned to embarrassment then remorse. He tried to reach for her.

She pulled back and turned away. He inched closer slowly and held her. She cried. Hard.

"Paige, I'm sorry. You're right. I was an ass. Please forgive me. This was a crucial meeting on my two-month project. The next few days are especially vital. J—well, she's my fellow employee who came into town for a couple days to assist. We work together."

He tilted her chin and kissed her tear stained lips. "You're not in competition with her. There isn't a competition at all. And if there were, you already won. Just sorry the prize is me."

Paige took in what he said. She sniffed and hugged him with great relief.

"I thought I lost the whole deal," he said, brushing away her tear.

"You nearly did," Paige mumbled through her sniffles.

Michael squared himself and inhaled at her serious twist of meaning. Then he sat on the kitchen chair and pulled her onto his lap, holding her. "Flee, listen to me. We will go through far worse than this together. But that's the point. Together. You have to know I care about you even when I'm not on my best behavior. We will figure out what happens at the close of my project. We have to, because…well…because I love you."

Paige nodded. This time she flung her arms around him and whispered, "I love you, too. Hate Janet, but love you."

"It's a start." Michael let out a laugh. He brushed back a stray lock from her face, cupping her cheeks in his warm hands, and kissed her tenderly. He handed his car keys to her. "Here. Trade cars for the day, and no accidents. It's a rental."

"I think I should stick with fishtailing in my car instead of not being insured."

"You'd be insured. I added an extra person for five dollars a day. Just in case. Don't make me come after you and get those five dollars back though."

After another kiss, Paige rose from his lap, threw on her coat, and grabbed her parcels and his keys. "Wouldn't dream of it." She left and then popped her head back in the door. "Oh, I fed the cat but not you, so help yourself. Text me if need me."

Before she drove away, Michael had already texted her. "I need you, Flee. I want you in my life."

Paige texted back. "More than Janet?"

His answer was, "Hands down."

Paige laughed at that, thinking of all the places her

hands were down and hoped Janet had never been there before and, more importantly, wouldn't be there in the future.

Chapter Five

Paige drove the curving mountain roads in the unfamiliar but easy-handling, larger car. The plushness of the vehicle made her temporarily wonder, more specifically, what Michael did in his corporation since he'd moved up from Senior Engineer. Though safer than driving in her car, the roads still were dangerous with ice patches and uneven plowing. She waited until a red light to push a few buttons to turn on the music system and activate the Bluetooth, another luxury missing from her own car.

No sooner had she done that, an announcement interrupted with an incoming call from her mother. "Mom, I need to call you later. I'm heading to my temp waitressing job. The roads are not completely clear."

"Then why are you picking up the phone?"

"It's Michael's Bluetooth system. Let me call you back or get me tonight since I have to also bring some dinner to Linney."

"Where's Linney?"

"Mom."

"Right. Bye, dear. Be safe, and Dad knows about your Atlanta job and where you are."

"Wait? What?"

But Paige's mother had already hung up. Her mom had kept the layoff and her leaving Atlanta from her father for fear he would demand she come home to

Carolina. She was determined not to backpedal and run home to her parents. Paige felt more and more entrenched in the renovation project, and if she admitted it, to Michael. When he was in front of her, it was hard to think of anything else.

Now, even apart, Michael crept into her thoughts constantly. Her thoughts wandered to his light brown eyes and broad chest when she drove around a curve. A squirrel startled her out of the daydream. Heart racing, she swerved, narrowly missing the squirrel and slammed on her brakes over an ice patch. The car took over with a *tap, tap, tap* to the brakes until she regained control.

"Phew. Nearly owed him five dollars," she said to herself, switching to quieter music as she came closer to town.

The Bluetooth cut in again. Before anybody spoke, Paige said, "Look, Mom, I told you the roads are snowy and icy. I'm on the Bluetooth. I'll catch up with Dad later."

The answer came, only it wasn't from her mother's voice. It was a man's southern voice, and not even her father's. It was her ex. Davis Greer. "It's not your Mom, Paige, and you don't have Bluetooth in your car. Snow and ice? Where the heck are you? I have been looking all over for you. I know you're not at Jessica's. And now I know you're definitely not at your parent's."

Paige's mind raced. No words came.

"C'mon Paige," Davis said more softly in his creamy drawl. "I just want to meet with you. Talk to you. Stop hidin', please."

She finally spoke. "I'm not hiding. I'm trying my best to move on." His voice still held something in her heart. Not the passion she felt with Michael but more like the warmth of a long-standing friendship. She felt the words slip from her lips, "I hope you're okay."

"No. I'm not. I miss you. My parents thought I should've fought harder for you. The condo is empty especially since Chrissy left."

"Chrissy left? You mean she moved in and then left?"

"Only for a little while. She took—"

Paige punched the *end call* button. *Another woman had already moved in with him?* He didn't hear any of what she said after, the kindest of which was, "baby" "idiot" and "good riddance." Somehow hearing his voice changed from a spark of rekindled friendship to a sense of permanency to their break up. She finally felt at ease with his being out of her life. More than that, she felt good about it.

Strangely relaxed, she pulled into a parking spot near the shop. She grabbed her belongings and stepped out of the car. Her boot hit ice, but she didn't fall since she was still holding onto the car door. The winter was trying it's best to take a toll on her.

She chuckled to herself. Michael. First the brakes, now the ice patch. Even when he wasn't there, he seemed to be looking out for her. Something she wasn't used to at all. But something she was afraid she might get very used to. *Don't be ridiculous. I can care for myself.*

The problem was that she also cared for Michael, more than she would let herself admit.

****

"More coffee?" Paige smiled. The pink polka dot apron she wore added to the ambience of the adorable

French café, which was surprisingly crowded with the mid-day lunch patrons even in the snowy weather.

The man nodded, and she poured and cleared off the next table in a quick swoop. The breads were all homemade by two chefs claiming French names, though they were not. The soups were hot and lush. The glass case had delicacy after delicacy lined up, as would a European shop. It was a comfortable daytime waitress position for her to cover while someone was out on maternity leave. She had enjoyed waiting tables back in college. Best of all, this position had two other fellow employees, both young and quick to laugh.

The aroma in the room was divine, and the tidy decor of the sweet café was a delightful getaway for Paige. Checked floor, café music, chocolate truffles, and smiling patrons rounded out the lovely setting until a patron whispered to Paige's co-worker that the restroom desperately needed attending.

One owner/chef looked to the wait staff and said, "No maid service today because of the snow. One of you handle it, please."

"Where's the cleaning supplies and gloves? I'll do it," Paige cheerfully volunteered.

"Really?" Lucy replied. "I owe you a drink then."

"Yeah. Right. We get a cup or two of coffee free."

"No. I meant when we go out. Come with us sometime soon, Amelia Paige."

"Sure. I'll take you up on that Lucy-cakes." The shop owner made Paige a cute name badge but took her first and middle name from the application instead of just Paige. She didn't mind. In the café, she was called "Amelia" as much as "Paige" to her newfound friends.

In minutes, the restroom was replenished and

shined. Table service and the cash register kept Paige busy. Lucy and Paige fussed over a little five-year-old girl in thick glasses who was celebrating a birthday. They added a pink doily and a candle for girl's pink cupcake. They sang to her and later danced with her to a song she liked. An extra pastry even found a way onto her plate. Before the owner could even think of objecting, they said it was from Andre, only to hear the other call out, "and one from Pierre." Added cookies went to the girl's grandma's plate. The tip more than covered the cost of the extra goodies. Her shift came to a close before she even knew it.

"Can't wait to see you all again," she said hanging up her apron in the back.

Paige left with some tip money in hand and a cup of carrot soup, along with traded cell numbers from Lucy and Beth and promises for a girl's night out. At one point, it almost felt to Paige that she should be doing the paying for being there. Almost.

****

Paige keyed up her cell after she slid into Michael's rental car. She had several messages from Davis—of course—and her father—gulp—which she answered with a quick, "I love you, Dad. I'm doing well. Trust me. Talk soon." She also texted Michael that she was leaving work to stop by Linney's hospice.

She followed directions to the hospice center and parked near a snowbank. She touched herself up in the car mirror before walking up to the main building of the center. With a lasagna and a bag of goodies in hand, she approached the reception desk. Her heels clicked in the somber spotless building. The mood so much more reflective than the pleasant café she'd come from.

Linney didn't come down to meet her. Instead, Paige received a text, more gibberish than English, but it gave her a general idea where to find Linney. She was met in the hall kitchen by a red-eyed Linney.

No words were needed for Paige to hug her aunt tightly. "I'm sorry, Auntie."

"This? Oh, this is just allergies," her aunt lied. Linney was rarely allergic to anything. "So, what do you have for me? Tofu on dry bran?"

"Hardly. How about a pan of homemade lasagna and news that a man named Bailey has agreed to do our woodworking at a fraction of the cost?"

"How much?"

"Materials, which might include our own fallen trees, and food, plus what we can pay."

"Hmm. Sounds so good it could be a scam," Linney said, inspecting the lasagna before putting a quarter of it into the oven to warm and the rest to the fridge.

"Thought so, too. He grew on me. He's a different sort and sees renovation and woodworking as an art form." That got Linney's attention. "And boy, can that man eat, even though he's fit. This is the second tray. Oh, and this is for you or one of the families." Paige handed over a bag.

"What is it?"

"Brownie mix with fixings. Just needs a bit of water and stirring before throwing it in the oven. It might be a good distraction for someone."

"That's really thoughtful, Squirt. Honest." Linney looked off.

"Time for a quick cup of tea with me, Auntie?"

Her aunt nodded.

Paige found cups and the bags while Linney stretched. The water was already hot. The tea plain. She added honey to both cups.

A raspy voice cut into the quiet, "Linney, could I ask you— Oh, is this the sweet little niece you mentioned?" An older woman approached, neatly encased in a Chanel suit from some thirty years earlier.

Linney nodded and took her untouched tea and simply handed it to the woman. "Tea?"

"Why, thank you, honey." The old lady held the Styrofoam cup as if it were a treasure.

"Honey? That's what's in it," Linney said, putting on a brave smile, holding up the honey bear.

The old woman gave a small laugh. "I hope you know how special your aunt is, sweetie. She has got to be the kindest soul I ever met. Come sit with me when you can, Linney. I have a question." Her smile shifted her wrinkles upward on her face before she limped away.

Paige looked at her aunt, perhaps in a new light.

"What? So, they don't see me like you do at home. Trying to keep up a brave, pleasant front. Hey, I'm not that bad of an actress, you know," Linney said pouring a replacement cup of tea.

"Really? Ever been on stage?"

"No, but I feel like I'm auditioning every day. Aww. Don't look at me like that. I'm holding up fine. Go, Squirt. And thanks for the grub."

Paige started to leave. She came back and gave Linney another hug to which her aunt just said, "Git." But her eyes weren't red anymore, and she was smiling.

****

"Look, Davis, I told you, snowy roads. It's getting

313

dark even. Take a hike and not toward me. Stop calling. Stop texting. Move on, big guy."

"But Paige, I can come to you if I just knew—"

Click.

Paige had it with her ex. She inhaled and refocused on the sharp curve of the mountain road. Though it wasn't quite dinner yet, the winter sun near setting, the tree-lined roads were already shadowed in darkness, hiding ice patches. She put on top '40 radio. The Bluetooth rang in again.

"I thought I told you not to talk to me anymore, Davis."

"And if it's not Davis?" Michael's voice came on.

"Michael? Yay. Michael. Hello. I can talk but only a bit. Distracting on these roads."

"I can tell. Davis, hmmm?"

"Oh, now don't you start getting jealous on me. That's my job," Paige said, making light of their earlier tiff.

"Wouldn't dream of it. When are you coming back? I wanted a few minutes with you before leaving this lovely dilapidated home."

"Dilapidated? How about pre-renovated? Anyway, I'll be home in a few. Ta-ta," Paige said cheerfully.

"Ta-ta? Who says ta-ta anymore?"

"Toodles?"

"Worse, Paige." Then Michael added a, "Cheerio."

"Tally ho," she responded.

"That isn't even a greeting."

"It isn't?"

"No. It's not," Michael said with mirth in his deep voice.

"How's this?" Paige honked the horn as she pulled

into the driveway.

"Paige?" Michael said into the phone.

She honked again and clicked off the phone, grinning. Michael must have taken the hint because he greeted her at the door. She rushed into his arms and kissed him, snow trailing on the foyer floor.

He lengthened the kiss and murmured her name. "Much better greeting."

"Really? I was thinking of improving on it." She unloaded her belongings in a heap while he tugged off her coat, and in record time, she was kissing him deeply.

He reached for the coat stand and hung her coat a good foot away from it, letting it fall to the floor. He didn't notice. He was busy moving her up against the wall, kissing her with a devouring haste.

Their clothed bodies pressed together, each rubbing to the other. Something so readily tugged deep inside Paige, sending her reeling. His lips found her neck, her hands sank into his hair, both flushed in the heat of desperate kisses.

His cell rang, breaking the spell. He pulled from her panting breaths, grabbed his briefcase, coat, and bent to get his keys from the snowy puddle on the floor. "I have to go, Flee. Dinner meeting."

She just stood, stupefied looking at him. "Uh huh."

He had his hand on the doorknob and turned one last time to Paige, kissing her sweetly on the forehead. "What you do to me." He shook his head clear. "I owe you one," he flashed a knowing smile and left.

Paige just looked at the door after it closed. It took a minute or two for her to surface enough from her hungered stupor to move.

Winky brushed by her leg.

"That man can kiss, can't he?"

Winky just licked at the tipped over the remnants of the soup from the cup on the floor and didn't say.

Chapter Six

Things have been known to hit the fan. This time it literally did. After Michael rushed off, Paige decided to work a couple hours on the over-full master bedroom. Apart from the hallway temporarily stacked with furniture pieces, it was one of the last rooms upstairs needing to be cleared. It was also the largest and had been packed nearly to the ceiling.

She'd been at it for several minutes when a colorful object near the top of the five-foot mound of clutter in one corner caught her eye. She climbed up and extracted what looked like a green vase from the rubble. Stepping back, her foot caught, making her lurch. The vase flew from her hands, smashing directly on top of a fan. Glass shards exploded all over.

Paige swore and said to no one, "Sure hope that wasn't valuable."

Thankful she had on her thick overalls, gloves, and long sleeves, she bagged the vase pieces and the broken fan in no time. She saw glints of the green glass under a tall-boy dresser. She held the flash light to it and went all the way onto her belly to reach it with a hair brush since the broom couldn't angle under it.

The flashlight also revealed something taped to the bottom of the old, care-worn dresser. She tugged at it and pulled out an envelope. *Porch* was scrawled on the front of it. Inside was foil, and in that, a wad of cash.

She handled it again, hoping for more information then pocketed it in her overalls and dove back onto her belly. Another envelope. *House*. It didn't have the foil but seemed to have a few more bills than the last.

Most corners of the dresser legs had wooden support underneath. One corner looked different. When she squeezed her arm back under the dresser near the back leg, something felt irregular. This time, she pulled and brought out a small box. She tried to open it, but it was glued shut so she decided to save it for later. She pocketed the box and made sure no other items were under the dresser. The mountain of debris near it prevented opening any of the drawers.

Her decluttering of this area moved from slow and meandering to something much more urgent. She laid waste the mess before her, bagging most of it for garbage, all in the effort to unearth the dresser drawers. In the end, she filled several garbage bags before being rewarded with working space. Moth eaten clothing pieces came out of the first drawer, which she immediately threw away. She screamed as a mouse carcass came out of the second overstuffed drawer.

"Winky, get in here!" No cat in sight.

Paige yanked out the drawer and dumped the contents into the open garbage bag. She tugged at the paper lining so she could throw that out as well. More money floated down, a few bills having been chewed. She continued the process, finding something under each drawer lining. Not silver linings but green ones. Cash green. The pockets of her overalls looked like she was practicing the art of nut collecting, with envelopes and cash stuffed wherever she could fit it.

When the entire tall bedroom dresser was cleared

of scraps and the perplexing cash, Winky appeared, meowing at the garbage bags. He twitched and pawed relentlessly at one bag.

"Is something in there? Better not be another mouse. Don't rip it open. Here." She hoped for another prize as she opened the bag back up. Winky jumped in, pulled out an empty grease-stained envelop. "Big help you were."

Winky meowed in response and turned his back to her with his tail twitching.

Though far from finished, Paige was calling it quits. The room looked more spacious and she had her pockets filled with envelopes and cash. As she put the last drawer back into the dresser, she saw a faded date carefully etched inside the corner with a carpenter stamp.

She stepped back and stared at the dresser. It seemed old, antique old. "Whatcha think, Winky? With some care, it could look good again."

The cat meowed, barely turning to look from atop the remaining debris mountain.

Paige was undaunted. She rubbed off some darkened lacquer from the marking. The wood was a deep rich color. Valuable or no, it had charm. She hurried to the bathroom and came back with a damp washcloth. She took another swipe at the date stamp, this time with Winky right next to her. It looked like 1820 something or maybe 1920. She secretly hoped the dresser wasn't so valuable it needed to be sold but just old enough that she could keep it.

Paige exhumed her cell phone from an overstuffed pocket and took photos of the dresser and the date marking, having to shoo Winky away twice while she tried to accomplish the task. "Big help you are. Git, you silly cat."

Whether affronted or for once following a request, Winky twitched and darted from the room, screeching down the stairs.

"Sorry, you beast," she called after him, scrolling through the blurred pictures. "This one's not half bad," she said, staring at a photo of the cat not the date stamp. Winky was growing on her more than she'd admit.

A while later, Paige unloaded the cash and findings, dumping them all on the dining room table. Winky returned, inspected them, and left her once again to do the sorting alone. More than one envelope said *House* or *Mad Money*. The saddest one was the one marked *Vacation*. The paper of the envelope was yellowed. A trip never taken.

She took a photo of that and then some of the whole stash. She couldn't help but call Linney. To her surprise, her aunt answered. They talked about the findings, and she texted Linney a few pictures.

"Holy cow. Is that a ring box in the photo, Paige?"

"Have no idea. It's glued up and gross."

"Wash it or get a knife. Your Grandma said something about giving me a Courage Ring when I first became a nurse. I never got it since she said she misplaced it. Maybe I should pass it on to you."

"No way. It's yours if that's what's in the box." Paige paused. "Hey Linney, finding all the stashed cash, feels…well…odd, doesn't it? Didn't Grandma and Grandpa have a bank account?"

"Sure, they did. They just didn't trust 'em, I guess. Not to mention, we misjudged how bad my mom got after my dad passed. The hoard mess tells it all. She had so many illnesses that the Alzheimer's wasn't noticed until the very end. My brother didn't quite believe it. Your own mom thought it was just the medicine. When I got to the house, I realized too much was blamed on the squatters. Much of it must have been your grandma, too. That's why we're treasure hunting, and you seemed to have hit some of the jackpot. Dresser linings? That's impressive. I only found one envelop in a cookie tin when I had cleaned out the kitchen."

Linney paused. "Guess that explains why there was hardly any money in the bank. I originally thought it was just because of the medical bills." Another pause. "We're past probate and the contents are fully the family's possession. How much did you find?"

"Who knows, Aunt Linney? Several grand I hope. I'll add it up. Actually, I'll do a spreadsheet of envelops, too. We'll definitely be able to pay for some of the carpentry with this. Grandma Ida seemed to have intended for porch to be re-done, too. It's sweet in a way that we get to honor her and do the work she wanted done with those funds."

Her aunt agreed and added, "You're a lucky charm."

"Not too lucky. I broke a vase," Paige confessed.

"Don't worry about it. Probably not worth anything unless it was green."

"Er, um…"

"That's it. I'll dock it from your pay."

"I'm getting paid?"

"Sure. It's the same as the cost of you living in that luxurious house, so it's a wash. Most likely at least. Who knows?"

"Gee thanks."

"No problem, Squirt. I gotta run."

"Me, too. I want to finish this and clean up from all this money. It's literally dirty money." They hung up before Paige could ask how the hospice cases were going. Then again, Linney would have shared if she could have. Perhaps this little bit of good news might have given her something to think about.

Though tired, Paige quickly counted and organized the newly found cash from her grandmother. She set up home improvement spread sheets on her laptop and marked the new folder *Ida's Gifts*. Her heebie-jeebies from the discovery waned. Work crew for the retrofitting of upstairs rooms were to be paid from the sale of the antique clocks she had completed with Michael's help. Now, Bailey and the woodwork crew would have some funds. They might just be able to make the renovation happen after all.

Paige stretched. Before turning in for the night, she looked at her email and saw a note from a company about a real job. It requested an afternoon phone interview in two days. Her heart raced, but she calmed herself before replying. She saw a second email from the company with "urgent" marked in the subject. Her heart sank. She inhaled and read the note. Her heart raced again. The phone interview was cancelled but would she be available to meet at the company Friday morning instead? It was a last-minute interview opening, and they wanted to extend the invitation, rather than wait for the next hiring cycle.

"Yes. Yes. Yes!"

Winky looked up at her, staring nonplussed, licking a paw.

"You could be a little more excited for me. An

interview is awesome, isn't it?"

He rose, twitched, then yowled.

Paige wasn't sure if that was Winky's attempt at support but didn't care. An interview for a real corporate position again. She wasn't sure who the lucky charm was, but luck was on her side today. Her fingers quickly clicked her happy email response before she showered and collapsed in bed.

****

Paige's waitressing shift at the café was a blur the next day. The French café was packed and busy. Still, she managed to share the good news about landing the interview to excited cheers from her co-workers, Lucy and Beth. The owners groused but smiled once she agreed to work more hours in the upcoming weeks should she get the job.

"I don't know, Amelia Bean. I'd wear your hair up for the interview," Lucy said, wiping a table.

Beth collected plates on the table next to her. "Wear it down and to the side, Paige."

Patrons chimed in with opinions. A tally was taken. She was to wear her hair up for the interview. She was sent home with supportive hugs from co-workers and two muffins by way of well-wishing from the owners. She was also asked to save the following Tuesday or Wednesday for ladies' night out.

After settling in at home, Paige bit into a muffin from the café with an audible, "Mmm." She checked her phone again but there was no response from Michael from her texts. She didn't dare mention the interview to her mother until something was far more certain. Even mention of the found stacks of cash would have to wait in case she slipped out the interview news.

She flipped through the mail, took a carelessly large muffin bite, and filled her cheeks like a squirrel. She nearly choked when the door unexpectedly opened.

"Mimmy more mere!" Paige reached for her drink, trying to swallow as she did.

Linney looked ashen and put her things down, smile finally appearing, "Not English, Squirt, or Oneida for that matter." She patted Paige's shoulder, reached past her, and broke off a huge bite. "Cinnamon Muppin. Mot bad."

The water helped as Paige could clearly say, "Linney, you're here!'

Linney swallowed hard. "Looks like it. I have been working around the clock. They sent me home, asking me to get some...fresh air." Her voice caught.

"Did young Mr. Swenson..."

Linney just nodded and turned away. It was clear she took his passing hard. Paige knew better than to ask more at the moment. She brought Linney a hot tea with milk and sugar. She also placed the second muffin in front of her. Even Winky came out of nowhere, brushing Linney's leg.

"Do you want chocolate?"

Linney shook her head no. "They said fresh air. So, that's what I'm going to do. Care for a walk in the snow?'"

Paige's feet were tired from her double waitress shift, but she didn't hesitate to say, "You bet. Where to?"

Linney looked up from the tea. "Campfire Cove. You'll need some warm things."

"On it."

****

324

Both women were bundled. The sun glistened on the drifted snow so brightly that the sunglasses Paige wore only partly cut the glare until they reached trees. The path wove into a grove of hemlocks and pines—dense, but not so dense as to block out the sun or make the ground dry. Snow was everywhere. A bird flew off a tree limb, making the branch bounce and shake snow onto them. Paige beamed. Linney's ashen face pinked in the soft chill of the breeze.

Their demeanor was quiet, Paige in the amazement of the scenery. Linney's face showed she was still locked in whatever difficulties had been faced in hospice. They walked farther. Paige looked over at her aunt and gave her a sideways gentle push. Nothing. She did it again, so that her aunt ever so slightly brushed a tree sending snow onto her.

Her aunt guffawed and then squinted. "That's it, Squirt." She bent and made a snowball. "I'm counting to five."

Paige started to move as quickly as she could in her heavy boots. She stomped toward cover as running was not an option. Her aunt must have known it.

"One, two, three, five!"

Splat! Paige was hit on her back. She turned. "Whatever happened to four?"

"Okay, you asked for it. Four more coming your way."

Paige lunged behind a thick pine tree, making her own snowballs, and flinging them in Linney's direction.

"Missed me, Squirt!"

Paige peeked out and ducked back. A snow ball flew past her. Linney stood close to a tree thickly coated with snow. This time Paige took aim. Before

Linney could wind up her own throw, Paige threw her snowball, not at her aunt but at the trunk above her.

Twaackk! The snowball hit the tree, hard. Snow dropped all over Linney.

"Ahh," Linney cried out while Paige laughed. Then she yipped as Linney came at her. One thing Paige hadn't counted on was Linney's long strong legs. In no time, she tackled Paige, stuffing snow onto her and inside her hood. Paige did the same but she was no match.

"Uncle, uncle!"

"Nope. Aunt, aunt," Linney corrected.

"I give. You win. You win!"

Linney finally stopped and flopped onto her back.

Both women, hair partly matted with snow, looked up, watching their cold breath make frosty swirling wisps in the air. Paige pulled off her wet mitten. Her hand was red from the cold, but she managed to take a snow-covered selfie with Linney, or so she hoped, sun glare blinding as her sunglasses were lost in the snow.

Paige finally stood and yanked her aunt up. They brushed snow off each other, smiling. Paige could tell that her face was chilled as red as Linney's. "So, where's this cove?"

Linney pointed. "Just past that ridge. You've been there in summer, Squirt, but you might have been too little to remember."

"Still am smaller, you bully." Paige tried to flick snow from her recovered sunglasses. The streaks reflected prisms of colors when she put them on.

"Aww, quit yer bitchin' and move your itty-bitty self," Linney said, only she was the one huffing a bit as they came to an incline before the dip down to the cove.

In summer, it was much easier to reach, but the snow drifts made the going slower for them both.

As they passed through the stand of dogwoods and white birches, the view opened to a small clearing below. Soft white pines stood in a half circle, their hanging branches weighted with snow. Maples flanked the far side. The star of the show was a large catalpa tree, bark showing the bumps of age. Under a high branch was a fire pit with benches made from fallen logs. One spruce looked out of place set against the birches.

Paige looked around. "I think I remember this."

Linney cleared a spot on a log and sat down. "Thought you might. You made us plant that spruce tree. Man, has it grown."

Paige sat close to Linney. "I think I remember. It was a sapling I found. I wanted it protected and warm so it wouldn't get sick like Grandpa." The tree had been planted shortly before Linney's father had died, making the hike to the cove all the more relevant.

They sat quietly, lost in the memory, wet from the snow fight, but warm enough in the shielded cove. "Do you miss him?"

"Grandpa or Mr. Swenson?"

"I meant Grandpa, but sure, Mr. Swenson, too."

"Of course, to both. Maybe your grandma even more. Especially now, finding out about those envelops yesterday. Makes me think about her." Linney looked away, her lip quivering slightly. She inhaled and stopped. Then she turned to Paige, suddenly smiling. "Toward the end, she told me she and my dad did it outside and that's how they got me."

"Here?" Paige jumped up.

"Naw. She also said my dad carved their initials in a tree where they did it. No initials around here. So, you're safe."

Paige sat back down.

"Although I did it right where you're sitting," Linney said, chuckling.

Paige wasn't sure if Linney was pulling her leg but didn't want to find out. "Eww, TMI, Auntie."

"Well maybe not right where you were sitting…"

"Still TMI," Paige said, walking the way they came.

Linney followed. "Maybe it was over there…"

Paige stomped through the snow. "You take the cake, Auntie."

"Nope. Never did it with cake." Linney kept taunting and laughing as they walked back. Paige pretended to mind more than she did. Her aunt was smiling and exercising, not pounding down chocolate and crying over someone's passing where she worked. A first. The banter continued until the farmhouse came in sight. By then, Paige had spilled the beans about the interview, thinking her aunt might object since the home repairs would be secondary to a career position.

"Wrong, Squirt. Means if you get the job you might stick around longer. Who else can I tease if it's not you?"

Paige took in a quick cold breath. The last comment set her matchmaking wheels spinning. Who else could her aunt tease? George? The mailman? The woodworker coming next week or someone from the construction crew? All of them were plausible choices. It seemed Paige had one more job to keep on her list, and that was to fix up her aunt.

They pulled off coats in the warmth of the kitchen. Snow plopped out of the leg of Paige's outer pants, adding to the fray of discarded items, most of which had landed on a towel. Their toes were wet, cold, and turning red. Linney claimed the shower first. Paige let her and haphazardly prepped dinner, throwing something into the oven, shivering as she did.

Once she was in her room, Paige began to strip off the remainder of her cold, wet things to the serenade of Linney's off-key and very loud singing as it floated down the hall from the open bathroom door. Paige's cell rang and she pressed the speaker button. She could barely hear over Linney's sharp crescendos.

"Michael!" Just hearing his voice ratcheted up her happiness.

"What the hell is that noise?" Michael asked on the phone.

"That's me taking a lump of snow out of my bra."

"Huh? I meant the wailing." Michael paused. "But snow out of your bra? How'd it get in there?"

"Linney."

"She put snow in your bra or is she making that noise?"

"Both."

Michael honked.

"Some response."

"No. It was a doe. A deer."

"A female deer? Was it followed by a ray, a drop of golden sun?"

"No, Flee. Don't do it. Don't break into song on me."

It was already too late. "Flee, a name, I call myself."

"Fa, a long, long way to drive," Michael sang back in a deep, surprisingly melodic voice. He added in a spoken voice, "Which I am doing and I don't want to run off the road."

Paige giggled and sighed. "Okay, Michael with the yummy voice, I'll hang up. Just as well since Linney might be done and I need to go sink myself in a bath." Her voice took on a heady deeper tone as she continued, "A slow, long, luxurious bubble bath. One of those where I get to slide a loofa all over my naked body. So warm that it can only be outdone by dinner as it simmers in the oven."

"Oh stop, Flee. You're killing me." Michael's voice was low and breathy.

"About the bath or the dinner?"

"You'll have to wait and see." He hung up. He wasn't expected until the next day.

Paige thought it was the dinner that had him fired up. She was hoping he would prove her wrong. Very wrong.

****

Paige let the water run, filling the claw foot tub with bubbles. She put a tall glass of water and book on a stool close at hand. She washed her face and brushed her teeth, setting her phone aside to play on a very bluesy station. She was ready. More than ready. She took off her fluffy white robe and hung it on the door hook next to the remnants of Linney's under things. She stretched, clipped up her hair, and turned to step into the tub.

Whoosh! The bathroom door opened, followed by a knock. Linney stepped in, leaving the door wide open. Winky stole in behind her.

"Linney!" Paige tried to cover herself.

"What? Don't let me stop you." Linney turned to face Paige standing naked holding a washcloth over her left breast. Linney was in a rose-pink robe with leopard print collar and belt. She grabbed her underthings. "Oh. Right. You like privacy sometimes. C'mon Winky."

Winky stepped down from the stool, having drunk some of Paige's water before tipping it over.

"Winky!"

"Well, don't call him back if you want him to stay out, Shy Naked Girl," Linney called from the hallway, having left open the door.

Paige shut it. It didn't have a lock. At least one that worked. She let that thought go and stretched again, readying herself. She filled a paper cup with water, turning up the music. She slid into nirvana of a bath, immediately relaxing to the luxurious feeling, moaning a soft coo of appreciation for all things pampering. Music, bubbles, scents, and warmth all coalesced. Perfection as she wallowed in the bath for some minutes. Perfection short lived.

The door flew open again.

"Linney," she screamed, holding the last syllable.

"Guess again. It's Michael," he said in his deep resonating voice, hiding very little of his lust and anything else.

"Michael?" Paige sat up in the bath.

He dropped his briefs, tossing them aside, grinning. "In the flesh."

Her breath caught as it did every time she gazed at his toned body and smooth caramel skin. In that same moment, the door flew open again.

"What do you need?" Linney asked from the open

door.

"It's Michael."

Michael grabbed for anything, holding the now empty water glass partly obscuring his privates.

"I can see that," Linney said, grinning wide-eyed.

"I thought he was you," Paige said, hiding under the bubbles.

"I think you need glasses, Paigey girl." Linney snickered and hesitated before leaving. "Good seeing you, Michael...all of you."

"I'd say the same thing, Linney, but your robe is closed," Michael barbed back through the closed door. Winky meowed. He lifted the cat and put him out the door as Linney returned to pick him up.

"Oh, my wittle Winky," Linney cooed. "Did that big handsome man scare you? And I mean big, don't I. What a show off."

"I heard that," called Paige through the door.

"No, you didn't." Then Linney loudly added something in Oneida, sounding like "lanigatay, lowlaynowanna."

"I heard that," Michael called and quietly added, "Thank you."

"What did she say?"

"She said to share the bath nicely."

"She did not," Paige objected, noticing Michael's grin and reddened face. She leaned forward to pour in more hot water. Michael took the opportunity to slide in behind her, pulling her back to him.

"Her syntax was all wrong, but..." Michael's voice trailed off when Paige wriggled back between his legs, rubbing her hands on his thighs.

"Go on," she urged.

"That's exactly what I was thinking." Michael's arm reached around her breast, the other tipped her head so he could kiss her.

They both sighed in appreciation. She touched his face. As the kiss deepened so did their moans. Water covered their warm silken flesh. Michael slid her nipple between his fingers, clasping it there, tugging it to full length. Her whimper was lost in the kiss.

His other hand found hers and, interlocking fingers, sank it into the water and along her skin. He lowered their hands between her legs. Her eyes popped open, fluttering as he explored her more fully, taking her fingers with him. Her breath deepened and then became tiny gasps of need. He stroked her inner folds, pressing her fingers inward until one sank into her pussy. His larger hand guided the strokes, pulling free only to reach for a condom. Her hands stayed petting her folds while he rolled on a condom. He brushed a stray hair matted to her neck and kissed her there, nibbling his way briefly to her lips and back to her earlobe.

"Oh, Paige I want you." The deep growl of his whispered words echoed in the Leonard Cohen's song pouring from her phone.

With those words, they submerged into their dream of silken pleasure. He lifted her back onto him, wriggling to enter, slowly so slowly until they were locked together. Legs open over his, his arms holding her tight as their languid movements made delicious soft waves in the water. The warmth of the citrus floral bubbles kissed her skin.

Paige's head fell back onto Michael's shoulder, twisting enough for a brief kiss, only to close her eyes and let everything wash over her. His muscled body pulsed and rose in long strokes. She ground down onto him, twisting him to every fold of her pussy. Rising and falling, the once unhurried movement grew into a hungry, insistent sawing onto his thick hard length. Her need bubbled deep within her. A shudder of release flew through her, clenching her onto his thickness buried all the way inside her. Crying out, she felt his body go rigid and join her orgasm. Nina Simone's sultry notes covered their cries. He held her tight in his arms.

Michael pulled out with a sigh. Paige slid, turning and clinging to him in her own afterglow. He held her, kissing her forehead, cheeks, lips, anything. He just kept kissing her. She loved that about him and cuddled tighter.

She inhaled deeply and exhaled slowly. "So, are you going to tell me what Linney said?"

"Roughly, handsome man carrying a big pack."

With that, they laughed and shared whispered stories until the water grew cold. Later, they dined on an overcooked dinner with her bantering aunt. They all slept soundly. Michael joined Paige in her unfinished room, which, thankfully, now had a lock on the door.

Chapter Seven

Paige stretched with her light yoga routine early the next morning. She was carefully arched, belly upward, and parallel to the ceiling in the table top position when Michael snuck up and kissed her. Distracted, she lost her balance and collapsed, sitting hard on the floor.

"Hey!"

"Sorry Flee, have to run." He grinned, biting down on a piece of toast and holding it in his mouth while he stuffed his arms into his coat.

"Wish me luck at least," she said, rubbing her bottom.

"Muck at meast. Muyyy." He flew out the door, toast in mouth, computer bag in hand.

She realized she had forgotten to tell him about the interview. It didn't matter. She could always tell him later. She only had enough time for a few more yoga positions and a quick shower before she'd have to leave for the company interview.

Dressed in her most formal and expensive business attire, she petted Winky and washed her hands. "Stay back you fuzz maker. This is an incredible opportunity, and I don't want to blow it by having cat hair all over me."

With that admonishment, Winky did the opposite and brushed up against her.

"Ha! I was ready for you." Paige waved her lint brush at the cat as Linney enter the kitchen.

Linney squinted her eyes and woke enough to defend herself with a nearby potholder. "Too early for this, Squirt. Just came down for a sip, and I'm back upstairs."

Paige momentarily inspected her aunt. She seemed more than marginally better than the day before, especially with more color in her brightly patterned robe and slippers.

She gave her aunt a quick peck on the cheek. "Well, I'm off."

"Always knew you were. Where to again?"

"Corporate land for the real live interview I mentioned. I'm excited. Gotta run."

"Good luck Squirt, and don't forget your weapon. Seems you still have some Winky fur on you."

Beaming, Paige took the lint brush and dashed out the door in professional attire with papers in hand. She looked the part except for the oversized puffy coat and her silly, peppy giggle. With a wave of the lint brush, she was off.

****

Paige's bubbled enthusiasm for the interview came to a halt as she entered the room. It wasn't the expected small office one on one with HR or a supervisor but, surprisingly, a whole group of people in a conference room. She inhaled deeply, glued on a smile, and let her inner positive mantra of *you got this* roll in her mind. With shoulders squared, she marched in, focusing on titles and names as best she could when introductions were made.

Questions flew. It seemed each manager or director

had her resume in front of them and took turns asking. Her background was established. Her answers short and concise.

"Since the recent layoff, any further employment or endeavors?"

"I'm in the beginning stages of helping a dear relative renovate and restore an old farm house into a home." Paige also mentioned her temporary fill in position at the café to keep busy, though neither was her career.

They nodded. The practiced neutral expressions still showed interest.

Without looking up, the woman who'd been introduced as coming from corporate asked, with a sternness in her voice, why Paige thought she'd been let go.

Paige would normally have flinched, but for some reason, she remained calm. "I worked hard in my Atlanta position and did quite well as my recommendations show. In fact, so much so, that I had been recently promoted. Had I not been, I would still be there since they only let go of all employees at that supervisory level. Frankly, I loved the work. In a way, the layoff brought me into a whole new part of the country and set of experiences for which I am grateful. It expanded my life skills."

They probed what she learned to which she responded, "I like new places and new experiences more than I expected. I also found out all-wheel drive and tires with traction are very desirable in winter."

Murmurs followed that response.

When asked what she liked in the area, Paige described her new home's potential and how it came with an aunt who couldn't bake and a mouser cat who ran into walls. Paige found herself also speaking of the charm of the snow-bound area, including the friendly people at the Valentine potluck for charity, the donut shops named after Indian spices, and how the area is a blend of cultures new to her. She mentally thought of the gay nightclub when she first landed in the area during the icy snow storm.

Most of the group of managers and executives were nodding in agreement to her descriptions. The out of town executive did not. "Hard to believe, Ms. Myers, that you would trade in the luxury and social life of Atlanta for what you describe as a drafty hovel in the middle of nowhere. How do we know if we hire you, you won't just leave soon after?"

Paige looked her in the eye. "If I may be so bold as to be candid, you don't know that about any applicant, do you? I can only say it seems I'm no Miss Atlanta Buckhead. With honesty, I am surprised at my admission. I will tell you this. I came here in the dead of winter without a thick coat, to a home that was little more than a hoarded mess. Just yesterday, I hiked in the snow for the first time. It was breathtaking. If I can fall in love with the area and the people here in this weather, I can only imagine how beautiful it is around here in the summer, especially when we finish the home renovation. I'm here for the long haul."

And there, in that interview, Paige had not only found her inner voice, she found an answer. Her own admission in a small but important moment. If she were to be hired for this position, she knew she would want to stay even if Michael left. Something inside her was not ready to leave, regardless. Not yet. If commuting was in her or Michael's future, so be it.

One older, balding manager broke the silence of the room. "It is gorgeous in the mountains around here in the spring and summer, but, shh—our secret."

The Sales Director asked, "So, do you pitch?"

Paige looked at a loss as to what to say and her expression had to show it. "Products?"

"Baseball," he answered, adding, "we have mixed company leagues around here."

She smiled in relief at not having to do an impromptu product pitch. "I can pitch a bit, and I'm not too bad at slugging. I grew up with older brothers and a field down the street. Out of practice though. I can also cook and remove wallpaper, should that become needed."

The interview continued on friendly terms. To Paige, that meant either they were very interested in her or that they had no interest and were filling the time. The next question made her think it was the prior.

"Do you have any trouble traveling out of state for initial training?"

She quickly answered, "No," then thought further about it. "Pardon. Actually, I have a work crew starting the week of March twentieth and would prefer to be here the beginning of the week if possible."

"Noted," answered the female executive firmly. Nods and smiles came from others. "That seems to wrap it up here. Please go with Mrs. Armseldale and to conclude the missed phone portion of the interview in person. It includes more particulars of the work site and benefit details. Thank you, Amelia—Paige, I mean."

Handshakes and thank yous quickly followed as she was ushered out.

After she stepped from the room, Paige heard the words "spunky," "could be go getter," "forthright," and maybe even something about fitting. She thought the job possibility was looking better and better and could hardly wait to share this with others, including Lucy and Beth at the Café, where she was headed.

****

Exhausted from a long day and her waitress shift, Paige opted for simple meal of fast chili with lots of cut corners. Linney was home but due back to hospice the next morning, and Michael wasn't expected until late that night. *Netflix and Chill* was decided as the best solution, only now the chill being really to actually chill.

With wooly socks and sweat clothing, Linney and Paige ate on the loveseat, watching a movie streaming onto her laptop. They huddled close over bowls of chili and far too many chips and too few carrots to crunch on, both agreeing a real TV would be good but neither wanting to commit yet to the expense.

Michael entered the scene after his business dinner, squeezing in next to Paige on the other side, only catching the last few minutes of the movie.

Linney left them to the old sofa, with Paige telling Michael of her day. He nodded as she spoke and was soon fast asleep, snoring. She had no idea if he even heard any of it.

"C'mon, Groundhog Man. I think you'll be more comfortable sleeping and snoring in my bed."

"With you?"

"The sleeping part, sure. I'll leave the snoring up to you...and please don't tell me otherwise."

"Wouldn't dream of it."

****

They slept like logs on Paige's queen-size bed under thick covers. Winky's midnight yowl woke them only to return to sleep. They stirred at Michael's phone alarm, and his mumbled words, "false alarm" when he rose only to return and pull Paige in tighter. The quilt slid off. Paige tried to cover herself with his pajama bottom until Michael reached for the quilt and pulled it back over them. They slept, each waking only momentary. Snow lightly fell, just enough to christen the ground white again.

When Paige finally rose, she nearly punched Michael with her stretch. For that, he woke, pulling her in. She balked at kissing him with her "onion-chili breath" and tried to leave the bed only to be tackled and tickled.

"No-o-o. Stop. Uncle. Yatze. Anything. I need to pee."

He stopped tickling only when she promised to return immediately. She did, after freshening up, and found him snoring, holding both pillows. Dressing quickly in her favorite sweater—the blue one she borrowed from him—she made her way to the kitchen for coffee. A note from Linney said she would be returning late Monday or Tuesday from hospice.

"Yes! We have the house to ourselves!"

Winky fed off of her excitement and dashed off, returning with a cat toy, some sort of matted zebra-striped, fuzzy ball. It was disgusting, but they learned to limit Winky's access to catnip toys since his twitching increased exponentially. It was either that or the questionable Ben Wa ball. Winky dropped the fuzzy ball near Paige.

She picked up Winky and, in a baby tone, told him, "By *we,* I meant Michael and I, you jealous, little, scruffy thing." She petted and scratched his chin before letting him go.

"Caught you. You're conspiring with the enemy." Michael stepped in, wearing his PJ bottoms, scratching his belly as he reached for the coffee. "Knew you liked that crazy cat."

"Never said I didn't. Just said he was mentally unstable."

Proving her point, Winky dashed by one way, and then the other, several times in row before running into a wall.

"Point taken," Michael said, sitting happily and heavily at the kitchen table.

Paige pushed the note toward him, drinking the last of her cup. "We have the house to ourselves, and it's the weekend."

He swallowed heavily, grimaced at the bite of homemade breakfast bar he took, and said, "In that case, Flee, you are wearing way too much clothing."

"Not if I'm working on the house."

Michael finished his coffee and slowly said, "I want to work on you. House later. Dinner out and maybe even something else is in order." His eyes locked on hers, "But first, you."

He held out his hand. Paige swallowed hard. And it wasn't on a sip of coffee.

****

Paige was worried, and she was sure her expression matched it.

"Downhill skiing?" Paige asked in alarm as he brought in skis. "This is the errand you did while I finished clearing more of the sunporch?"

"I helped you, didn't I?" Michael had unloaded a few kitchen pantry essentials and was now bringing in ski apparel. "Besides it's not downhill. It's cross country. The snow is perfect around here, and the slopes are gentle enough. We can take it easy. Think of it as sliding. Besides, you gave me the idea with you and Linney hiking around the property." Paige handled one of the rented skis as he continued, "Anybody can do it. It's fun to try new things."

Her life was filled with "new things" since she left the South a little over a month ago, which she pointed out in a drawl enhanced list. New home, new climate, new projects, interviews, and even work. She failed to include some of the new intimate sexual positions and new places she'd tried with him since he became part of her life. A very yummy part.

He hugged her where she stood. "Okay, Flee. You don't have to do it. I can go it alone tomorrow."

"Tomorrow? I thought you meant now." Paige blushed and whispered, "You sort of wore me out a bit earlier, and I thought maybe we could—"

"Have a repeat?"

"Yes. But I was thinking dinner first."

"Smart woman, but then you're learning from the best of them."

"Ugh. For that remark, you're taking me out to dinner."

"With pleasure, Flee." He pushed back her hair, tipped up her chin, and kissed her forehead. "Candlelight." He kissed her cheek. "Tablecloth." He kissed her other cheek. "Wine." He kissed her lips with what started out as a tender kiss.

Paige relaxed to the kiss, returning with her own ardent one. She looked up at him, dreamily when he pulled back from the embrace.

"If you don't stop looking at me that way, we'll never make it out to dinner, let alone upstairs."

She didn't erase her expression, not one bit, and it seemed fine for both of them.

By the time they surfaced from their frenzy, their stomachs were growling and the last reservations had been taken at the fine restaurants within driving distance. She came down the stairs in casual clothing and started to pull items from the pantry.

"No, Paige. I said I was taking you out, and I still am."

"I really don't want to wait and hope to get seated somewhere," she protested. It wasn't the first time they missed going out for a "real" dinner. In fact, they hadn't yet. Michael's kind expression reassured her as he held out her coat. She slipped her arms into the sleeves. "Okay, but you promised candlelight, tablecloths, and wine."

They stepped out the door. "Right, the wine..." Michael returned with a bottle tucked into a carrier bag. "Let's go. I know just the place."

****

The diner booth had laminate tabletops. Michael had placed handkerchiefs on it by way of a tablecloth, along with a rolling video of candlelight from his phone. Their small paper cups of wine were hidden behind tall, dark-colored glasses of water.

"One loaded Saturday Night Special, medium, and one Exposed Thanksgiving Special, strings attached, extra cran," the gray-haired waitress happily called out to the cook.

He took her hand across the table after placing their burger and turkey sandwich orders. "Hope it meets your approval. The food's great and fast, and with you, there's even some ambience."

Paige looked around. Leftover Valentine decorations hung in one corner, some paper Easter eggs in another, and a shiny green shamrock cutout was taped to the cash register. The salt and pepper shakers matched, and the ketchup bottle was full. Things were clean.

"It's perfect," Paige cooed. "Tablecloth, candlelight and"—she raised her paper cup of contraband liquid—"wine, just as you promised."

They toasted. The wine was humble but delicious.

"My turn to impress you." Paige brought out her phone and pulled up a site with bad puns of the day. "Time for tasteful entertainment," she said wiggling her eyebrows. "Here's one. How much does a hipster weigh? An Instagram." That brought an immediate groan from Michael. She continued with more, including, "Did you know they're trying out glass caskets. Not sure how the public will receive it. It remains to be seen."

Soon, she not only had Michael laughing, but the old couple in the table diagonal to theirs chimed in with "One more."

"Okay, you asked for it," Paige warned. "I used to be addicted to the hokey pokey, but I turned myself around."

Michael covered his face and shook his head.

The old man chuckled. "You're killing me."

"Don't say that too loud, Herbert. You'll insult

Rocko. He might overcook your meatloaf next time," the waitress teased the other couple. "Here you go, you two. Saturday Night and Exposed Thanksgiving Specials. Eat up and restore your lovey-dovey energy." She grinned with a half-cocked smile, walking away with a swing to her hips and a squishing noise to her shoes. "Cute ones, ain't they, Gladys?"

The old couple nodded with a smile.

Michael was right. His burger was cooked exactly right and sloppy with delicious toppings. She stole his fries, and he her lightly cooked string beans. The open-faced turkey sandwich had freshly roasted turkey meat and even stuffing and sweet potatoes, all of which Michael helped her with. They spoke between bites. She mentioned interviewing but didn't want to jinx it by telling him too many details. He spoke of a phase of his project working well. It was only when the topic hit his project completion did the conversation grow more serious and smiles die away.

Michael refilled her wine. "It looks like next week I might have to fly out of state, too."

"But I thought you'd be here at least until St. Patrick's Day."

"Yes, but I have other facets to my work."

Paige's fork lowered.

Michael reached out to her. "I told you I can't say much until the changes that are going to—"

"Be released on the seventeenth," they both said in unison.

"I'm trying my best to work out something that makes it easier for us to be together. Trust me a little while longer, okay, Flee?"

Paige nodded and with a deep breath, smiled at

him.

They returned to their meals and soon began to trade bites again. They toasted the evening with sips of wine from their paper cups. He rose to use restroom and pay the bill. Her thoughts changed to worry as she watched him walk away. She was more than falling for him. She already fell. Hard.

The waitress came by the table, clearing the plates. "Mmm mmm. That guy is so handsome. If I were only thirty years younger, I'd steal your fiancé from you."

"We're not engaged. I'm not even sure if he's staying around or if I am for that matter."

"Oh honey, he's staying. Trust me. I don't see that look often. He's keeping you no matter how much either of you run apart. My advice? Don't run." The waitress looked up and saw Michael standing by the cash register. "Coming honey. I'll ring you two love birds up. And I wouldn't mind it if you accidentally left what's in that wine bottle you've been hiding."

He did, along with a big tip and an appreciative smile, then helped Paige with her coat, keeping his arm around her.

"C'mon back, you two. We have green pancake special St. Patty's weekend that can't be beat."

"Sounds good," Michael said.

Paige didn't hear even the slightest note of irony in his voice. It made her smile knowing they were trying to make it work. That, and having a sated belly and a handsome man holding her.

She stopped in the parking lot, reached up, and kissed him in full view of the diner. The folks inside noticed. She could tell by the applause and how Michael was taking a bow.

Chapter Eight

Paige's look was anything but confident as she stared at the skis the next day. Earlier, she'd explained that she had never been skiing or snowboarding, apart from water skiing twice. Even then, she enjoyed bouncing on a tugged inflatable more. But with renewed encouragements from Michael, she found herself agreeing, if not excited, about cross-country skiing. Soon she was layered in clothes and comfortably bundled. With an extra pair of the socks, the used boots he had rented for her seemed to fit.

"You owe me big time if I fall on my butt," Paige said as Michael helped click her boots into the skis in the driveway.

"I owe you just for being a good sport," Michael said. "As for falling, consider it all part of the learning."

Paige sighed at that and rubbed her bottom in sympathy of what was to come.

Once she became comfortable with some basic moves he showed her, they headed out. With only passing clouds, the day felt warmer than it was. Paige proved to be a fast learner, especially on the level ground. Michael set tracks for her to follow, though she did fall several times until she got the hang of gripping her poles and cutting back and forth on even mild downslopes.

Soon, Paige could appreciate the landscape more

than mechanics of each stroke on the skis. The snow was a crystalline powder. They took a winding route, hoping to head toward a creek about a mile from the home, far from the cove she'd hiked to with Linney. They skied, sliding along deer tracks into a pine forest, branches laden thick with snow. The hemlock and pines looked like they had been covered with thick white frosting, frosting that glistened with sugar.

Paige stopped, her breathing heavy and visible as she exhaled.

Michael noticed and expertly crossed one ski and turned back to her. "Are you okay?"

She nodded. "Listen."

He did. The heavy snow drifts and trees brought a blanket of quiet. He never asked what she heard. Instinctively, he knew. It was a quiet of a magnitude only nature could make.

The scene was particularly breathtaking where she'd stopped, even better than the tree groves she and Linney had hiked through. He moved closer to her and left his poles standing in the snow. He held her softly, and kissed her. The kiss, like the snow, was cool to the touch and so tender and gentle that it landed like a whisper. A breeze blew, nipping their cheeks as they turned to see the swirl of glistening snow.

"So, beautiful," was all she could whisper.

"Couldn't agree more," Michael said, looking straight at her.

She took in the compliment, then brushed it off with a grin, rolling her eyes and pushing off on her skis. "Ruined it."

Michael stood flummoxed. He struggled to dislodge his poles before catching up to her. He gave a laugh. "And how did I ruin it?"

"Too schmaltzy movie moment," Paige teasingly drawled, turning toward him. "Next, we'll have some bunny hopping out—" She stopped and her jaw dropped. A rush of wonder flooded her. A deer stood frozen still not twenty feet off to the side of Michael.

He followed her gaze, looking over his shoulder. He smiled and said what sounded like, "Oska noon too." *Oskanu·tú*. "Deer."

The deer startled, leapt up, and sprung out of view.

With a smooth turn, Michael circled back to Paige. "I think that tops the schmaltzy, huh?"

She nodded, beaming. "Wonderfully schmaltzy. Just wish I had a picture of it." She thought he was coming in for another kiss but only straightened her pole grip. With a toothy grin, he pushed off straight downhill on the next slope, tucking into a fast run, teasingly leaving her wanting.

"Show off!" Paige called down the hill.

Michael waited at the bottom, taking a few pictures of her. She had the forest setting behind her as she attempted to zig-zag toward the bottom, bobbling on the turns. Her skis crossed on one turn, and she nearly fell. She looked up and saw he'd thankfully missed that photo op. He was fussing with his phone and setting up a selfie.

Here goes. She pushed off down the last bit of the slope, trying to get into his photo. She hit a stick, teetered on one ski with the other foot in the air, poles out, right before taking a big fall.

Michael laughed but soon was at her side, helping her up, brushing off the snow, making sure she was okay. Embarrassment was the only major injury.

He clipped her boot back onto the ski. "Now who ruined it?"

"Ruined what?" She asked.

"My perfect picture." Michael pulled his cellphone out of his pocket. "See?"

"Erase that."

"No way." Michael pushed off, leaving Paige to chasing him. She couldn't catch him and rested against her poles. In the quiet, she noticed the doe tucked in the woods again. She tried to flag him down, but the action just made the doe prance away. She found Michael waiting for her around a bend.

"You missed it. I saw a…"

"Deer." Both said at the same time, and Michael added, "Oska noon too."

"Oska noon too, Groundhog Man." Paige blew a kiss and pushed forward.

"Syntax is wrong," he called, following her.

"Lots of taxes are wrong." She laughed.

They continued, and on flatter parts where they were tandem, they talked to each other. They found an old road and skied on it for a while before veering off. Soon the sun lowered and hinted at painting some ridges in pink early twilight. The farmhouse had been gone from their sight for well over an hour or two. The creek, which Paige had pointed toward never came into sight either. Nor any road at this point.

Paige stopped. "Not for anything, Michael, but, where are we?" The concern she felt spread through her, making her breath quicken. She became more aware of the aches in her body.

"Aren't we heading to the creek? You said it was a mile east. Come to think of it, we should have passed it long ago."

"I said I thought it was. Are we lost?"

"Might be, but we can figure it out."

"What?" Her voice was so loud that two birds flapped out of a tree in alarm. "We're lost? I'm gettin' cold an' thirsty, not to mention my thighs are throbbing." She added, "Don't you dare make a joke about throbbing thighs."

He almost bit his lip to keep from smiling. He did, however, stare at her thighs. He winked. "We'll figure it out. Wait here." He pushed up a steep slope to the side. He had to herringbone-walk his skis up the hill but made it to the top and over it.

Paige paced in place by sliding her skis back and forth. She continued to complain to herself, more drawl than ever, "Skiing, he says. Cross-country is easy. So-o good for exercise, he says. Safer than downhill, he says. My butt hurts, and I'm probably going to die out here an' serve as a frozen dinner for the wolves."

"Woo!" Michael's normally deep voice came out as a cry reverberating over the landscape.

It didn't sound happy. She loudly answered the call, "Michael. I'm coming. Don't let the wolves get you."

She pushed hard, huffing but fell forward, the slope too much for her.

He came over the crest. "What are you doing? I thought I asked you to wait. Aww, Flee, I'm coming." He reached her and helped her up, shaking his head.

"I thought something got you."

He smiled, holding her. He said a word in Oneida. "Nothing to worry about. Honest. I think I know the way back to the farmhouse. This hill and the one after is too steep though, especially if your thighs are throbbing." His smile inched up on one side. "I saw a flatter route around the hills heading into those woods. Long haul but we can do it. And as for being thirsty…" He took some fresh snow and bit it. "Want some? Eat it slowly."

The roundabout route brought them within sound of a tinkling creek, but they decided against following it since it meandered farther out of the way. They skied through a bumpy pass in the woods and nearly out of it and headed toward a gap where a large maple tree had fallen. Paige leaned against the wide trunk to catch her breath.

"This tree is still solid, very little rot. Look how tall it is. Bet it was hit by lightning." Michael said, poking at the trunk more.

Paige bit into another fistful of snow. "Could you take some pictures of it? I want to tell Bailey about it. He was looking for wood from our property. Why not use a tree that's already down?"

While Michael took pictures, she put down her poles, popped free of her bindings, and unzipped her coat. She stretched. He caught that with his phone camera, too.

Pocketing his phone, he moved to her, smoothing back her hair with his ungloved hand. She looked into his eyes. Though they were in the woods, the sun filtered through, shining on his face, making his eyes a lighter honeyed brown. Amber eyes and caramel skin. Her heart raced. He moved closer, tossing off his other ski glove, tilted her chin, and kissed her.

"How do you do it, Michael?" she murmured.

"Do what? Kiss? Let me show you." He grinned.

Cupping her face, he kissed her, tenderly. He kissed her again and again, each time moving closer, each time, lingering longer.

She smiled, breathless, willing herself to speak. "I meant, how do you make me melt just with a look or a touch?"

In a heady deeper whisper, he answered, "I think the feeling is more than mutual."

He leaned in, pressing her tighter to him, and kissed her, drawing her lips to his. His mouth skimmed her neck and moved to her earlobe. She grew so warm, instinctively, she unzipped her hoodie and he, his coat. His tongue trailed down her neck, and his hands slid inside her coat to her thin tank top.

A soft cooing moan came from deep inside her. A moan that he reacted to. Even in ski boots, he deftly shifted slightly, sliding her back toward the fallen base of the tree trunk. He nibbled and mouthed his way down Paige's softly dipping cleavage. Her pulse quickened and her eyes closed. She gripped his muscled back under his opened coat. His kisses returned up her neck and then he devoured her lips, tonguing her deeply. He pressed her body against the wide tree trunk, grinding his hips against hers. Tendrils of fire and hunger shot through her. Even through layers of clothing, she could feel his hardness moving against her.

"Oh Michael, I want you," came out of her as a breathless declaration of everything pulsing within her.

He stopped long enough to look into her eyes then returned to his hungered frenzy of kisses. His lips moved lower, and he bit a love mark on her shoulder, making her pant puffs of air. Her eyes opened. And there, over his bent shoulder on the dimmer side of nearby oak, she saw the initials carved into a tree. I + B carved into a heart.

Her mind reeled and finally she broke from the lust-filled frenzy. "Ida and Ben."

"What?" Michael continued to kiss her.

Paige took a deep breath and swallowed. "Michael, the initials on the tree. Ida and Ben. My grandparents. I think this is where Linney was conceived."

Michael's face read like a book. He took several deep breaths, stepped back from Paige, and squared his shoulders. "Right. No protection. Well, other than your obtrusive grandparents butting in." He smiled as he regained composure, moving farther away. "Even from the grave your family…"

She didn't let him finish the sentence and plunked a snowball against his back. Her pent-up energy had to go somewhere fast. With quick reflexes, he threw one at her shoulder before she had her coat zipped. She came at him, tripping on the poles, and fell lightly onto her knees. "Oww!"

Michael was there almost as she fell, holding her arm to lift her, only to have her yank him down, and stuff snow on him. "I had older brothers, remember?"

"And I have bribery photos in my coat, remember?"

She flung more snow on him, laughing.

He retaliated with a tickle instead. "Truce. C'mon. We need to get back before dark." He gave her another kiss, a sweet one this time. He got them both on their feet and brushed off some of the snow. "I guess I had that coming."

"You almost had me coming." She blushed

crimson at the words that accidentally spilled out.

"Hadn't noticed," he lied, grinning widely.

She zipped up and clicked into her bindings.

He picked up his gloves and readied both of them for the trip back to the farmhouse. "Maybe we'll have to claim a tree of our own one day." It was his turn to have color flush his cheeks, the implication of what he said dawning on them both.

Soon, Michael had them back on a footpath trail to the clearing. They traveled partly in silence as the sunset began to coat the lawn in a colorful splash of reflected twilight hues. They could see the welcoming image of the dilapidated home in the distance and pushed to make it back. Paige stopped twice to catch her breath up the slight incline.

"I don't know about you, but how about ordering pizza for dinner?" Michael asked.

"Did you say pizza? Now I know you want to seduce me. Yes!" Paige said, finally collapsing on the broken front porch, unsuccessfully working her bindings with her cold fingers. Michael came to her aid, removing her skis and standing the sets next to his car. "You know it takes at least thirty minutes to be delivered. How about cookies and milk for an appetizer?"

"Now who's seducing who, Flee?"

Paige had yanked off her boots outside. She saw her reflection in a window. She was completely disheveled, with a flushed face and her hair a tumbled mess from her hat. Even her grin was sloppy. "Can't be me. I'm a mess."

"Sure, it can. They say a way to a man's heart is through his stomach." His coat was unzipped, and he lifted his shirt to reveal a toned mid-section. "Have at it."

"Oh brother." She turned and entered the kitchen, calling behind her. "Keep your shirt on. Make that your shirt and shorts on, at least until we have a proper meal of cookies and pizza."

"You sure you don't want an improper meal?" Michael asked as he closed the door behind them, shedding his snow-filled clothing in a careless heap. He stretched, wearing only his underthings.

Paige's eyes popped open, but she waved him off, grabbing for the cookies. "Dial first, cookies and milk second."

"I can't wait for third," and he didn't have long to wait. The pizza was delivered warm but eaten cold. Very cold and ravenously.

Chapter Nine

Monday morning came bright and early. For many. Not for Paige. Michael was up and gone, leaving a note by her coffee mug, that he loved the weekend, that the ski clothes were washed and in the dryer and that he'd try to be back Tuesday after work. He signed it with "xox your GH Man." When she finally, slowly, achingly made her way to the kitchen, she saw the note and hugged it. Her legs, arms, and most of the rest of her were all stiff and sore from skiing, making stairs a trial. He made it possible for her to avoid doing laundry down in the basement.

She poured herself a full steaming mug of coffee and sat with a sigh. She re-read the note and kissed it. "Thank you, Michael." Her foot hit something. She turned her head to read a crumbled reminder note on the floor near the table, which read, "Buy Condoms."

Winky popped up out of nowhere onto her lap. She petted him. "Hey fella. How are you? Do you think that note's meant for me? Doesn't matter. Condoms aren't needed until Tuesday, are they, Winky? We're keeping them in business though."

The cat tilted his head, and his eye twitched. He leapt from her lap and pawed at the note, playing with it until he decided to dash off carrying it. She made no move to chase him. Instead, she finished her coffee, waiting for the painkiller to sink in before tackling any project.

She stretched when she rose from the table. Remembering that Bailey, the woodworker, might be arriving later that day, she opted to finish clearing the sunroom. She hoped he could use it for his carpentry equipment. Linney had done most of the work, but as with most of the house, it wasn't complete. The sun warmed the unheated room somewhat. Still, she wore her thick layers and gloves while sorting. The storm door was cracked open so she could toss items directly outside into a large rolling garbage can.

Soon, she was lulled into the rhythm of sorting things into "trash," "maybe," "recycle," and "keep but clean" piles. Making double-use of her time, she called home. As she listened to her mother, who seemed to have more than something to say, she threw in many uh huh's, yes's, and no's. The uh huh's were winning.

"No, Mom, I didn't need to hide the chocolate from Linney. Honest. We took a hike in the snow—oww… Hold on, Mom." Paige put the phone on speaker and rubbed her shoulder as she had lifted a particularly heavy chunk of broken statute to throw out the door, sending it crashing into the trash can.

"Are you okay? What happened?"

"I'm fine. Just my muscles hurt. I'm sore from Michael." That brought a gasp from her mother and a quick attempt at correction from Paige. "Not what I meant. We had a busy weekend and even went skiing."

"Skiing?"

"Cross-country, but we went farther than we planned," Paige said aloud and under her breath, "way farther." She even made herself blush at that, thinking each time she had been *with* Michael recently. The bath, the sofa, in bed, nearly the snowy tree outside, the bed again… As she mentally counted, the words slipped out, "Oh my heavens."

"What is it?"

"Sorry distracted counting. Maybe I should focus more on my project."

"All right dear. Father's proud of you, too. He told Davis as much. I'll hang up."

"Hold on." Paige nearly screamed in the phone. She took a calming breath. "Mom, is Dad talking to my ex-boyfriend still?" She didn't want to say his name.

"Well, honey, Davis does call here every now and then. Your father said he was proud you were back to multi-tasking and even had a temporary job while you were interviewing. That's when Davis said he should take a trip somewhere north to find you."

She clunked her gloved hand against her forehead. "Please, Mom, tell me Dad didn't give away where I was."

"Of course not, honey. Besides, Pennsylvania is a big state. Don't you worry, and remember to call us when you hear about the interview. Good luck, sweetheart, and Paige?"

"Yes?"

"Take it easy with your, ahem…exercise?" Her mother hung up laughing.

****

As the day wore on, Paige could move better, not quite to her fast-paced perky ways but with increased energy. With the laundry folded and bathrooms scrubbed, she turned to cooking. They were low on groceries, but she found a large sack of potatoes and leeks.

"Okay, Linney, potato soup it is," she said to no one as she nibbled at some fruit and prepped the meal.

With the radio blasting, soon the pot was filled and brought to a simmer. While she was at it, she threw together a couple of crust-less quiches, using left over veggies and some large sweet onions. "That, with a salad, should hold us off for a few days. Right, Winky?"

"Not sure. I'm feeling pretty peckish today," a male voice sounded next to her. It came from a tall, bearded, bushy-haired man with a quirky smile and bright eyes.

Paige jumped. "Bailey? You startled me. Don't you ever knock? And how'd you get in here?" She opened the kitchen door to assure the lock still held, which it did.

He just looked about the kitchen, assessing the wood cabinets. She waited for his answer.

"Oh, it's not rhetorical. You want me to say something. What's the question?" He lifted the pot lid and inhaled, smiling.

"How did you get in?"

"Sunroom, of course. Unlocked for me, I figured. Hey, it looks like you cleaned it out for me. Thanks, Amelia, Paige, Flee…"

"Bailey, we talked about that. I'm just Paige."

"Right, right. Okay, Just Paige. Ha, ha, ha. Just joking. Okay, Paige," he said emphasizing her name with pride. "I didn't see you around so I went ahead and set up some saws, carvers, and other tools and stuff in the sunroom. Also, put a couple boards in the foyer to settle. Better to work with it once it is room temperature."

"Bailey, I'd like it if you rang the doorbell." Paige quickly added, "That is, the next time you enter, okay?

"Sure thing. Hey, do you have bay leaves? Love bay leaves in my potato soup."

"That's after I emulsify it. Come to think of it, I'm not sure. The spice cabinet is up—" Paige didn't need to finish her sentence. He was already digging for the bay leaves, placing the container on the counter with a grin.

"Your apple looks really good, and dinner's a ways off, so, um…"

She handed him a washed apple. "Are you always this hungry?"

"It comes in spurts. Oh, I got more wood to carry in. Can I use the front door?"

"Sure."

As they ate their apples, she told him about the large fallen maple tree, promising some photos and they talked about types of wood on the property. His face lit up as he described some of the projects he intended to do. They sounded costly. Not only in terms of materials but in terms of food, since she saw he had devoured his apple in record time.

"Help yourself," she said and handed him a second apple. "I'll be upstairs de-hoarding more if you need me."

At this point, she really hoped he was as good as others claimed him to be and not just at eating.

Only a few minutes later, the doorbell rang. Paige dropped what she was sorting. With her pinned hair bobbing, she hurried down the stairs as best as her sore legs allowed so soon after the skiing adventure. She wasn't sure if someone was due to collect the spare china cabinet.

"Oh, it's you, Bailey."

"You guessed right." He smiled, stacked some boards against a wall and left.

Winky stared from the corner, looking skittish. Paige returned to her work, groaning up the stairs, legs aching.

The doorbell rang again. Paige made it down the stairs, again. Bailey nodded to her, smiling as he dropped more wood.

"Are you going to bring another load of wood in?"

He shook his head, petted the cat, and left. Winky purred before rushing off. She returned upstairs to sort more rubble, rubbing her thighs as she went. She was handling an odd glass statute, trying to determine if it was worth keeping when the doorbell rang again.

"Oh, for Pete's…" She threw the statute into the trash and stomped down the stairs this time, ignoring her aching muscles. "I thought you weren't bringing in any more wood."

"I didn't. It's the stucco mix for the stones for the fireplace."

Paige was a riddle of emotions. Bailey was driving her nuts in the short time he was around, but it also seemed he was going to help tackle more projects and tricky ones at that, like re-facing the crumbling fireplace. "Oh, I…uh…never mind. And thanks."

She turned to head back up and stopped. "Bailey, do you need help?"

"Nope. That's it for now. I have some facing stones for the fireplace on order at the home improvement center to look at. You'll need to choose which you like better. They're both good materials and low cost. Also not too heavy, so no pressure on your old floors—" He cut himself off. "Hey, during dinner, maybe we can put together some mantle ideas. Saves time for me."

"You mean to eat and draw plans?"

"Not what I was thinking, but okay. I didn't want to have to build a couple mantles and see which one you like better."

"Did you do that before?"

"Yup, but they liked them both so they made an electric fireplace in the master bedroom with the second mantle. I could do that for you, too."

"One's plenty, and we can check out mantle images on the internet, too." She turned and started up the steps again. She stopped. "Just checking. Are you sure there isn't anything else you need before I go upstairs?"

"How about a taste of the soup?"

"Not finished, but sure, help yourself."

"And some coffee."

"Fine."

"Maybe a—"

"Help yourself to anything in the kitchen that isn't earmarked for dinner." She made her way upstairs before he asked for anything else. As she reached the landing, she heard a crash and commotion.

"Winky!" she cried, but the cat sat licking a paw right in front of her. It took a moment to register that the crash came from the kitchen and not the cat. Back down the stairs she went, thighs throbbing from the effort.

Her aunt was there, looking flustered, with Bailey on his knees in front of her, picking up cans and wrapped food items, happily muttering. Aunt Linney was bent over, trying to stop him.

"It's okay. I have it. Oh! Did I hit you?" She ineffectually ended up dropping most of the produce in her hands, right on top of Bailey. She stood dumbfounded, holding a plastic bag with wrapped fish inside.

Paige watched the scene unfold in a stupor.

Bailey grinned, looking up from the floor. "My fault entirely. I think I surprised you. Oh, hey, Paige, look who walked in. She didn't use the doorbell, though."

Paige wasn't sure where to go with that comment so she opted for an introduction. "Linney meet Bailey, the woodwork expert I told you about. Bailey, this is—"

"The vision from your computer pictures." He stood, holding an array of squash. "Marilyn Linney Dornheim Smith. Way better in person, don't you think? A pleasure." His smile was bright, set against his full brown-auburn beard and long rich brown hair. He was very fit, and close to Linney's age.

The look on Linney's face told Paige she was making an assessment of Bailey and it was far past favorable. The more Paige looked at her aunt, the more she saw a woman who was taken in, maybe even smitten. In fact, she was blushing-school-girl-meets-rock-star gone.

"Yes, I do, too. No, I mean a pleasure that is." Linney held out a hand to shake.

He moved to take her hand and said, "Squash." He turned to put down the squash.

Linney's hand remained out. She must have noticed that she was holding a bag with wrapped fresh fish and said, "Trout."

He simply reached for her hand and, instead of shaking it, raised it to his lips, plastic fish bag swinging as he kissed the back of her hand.

Linney stared at him.

"Oh, right. Right. The kiss is too much." Bailey changed tactics and hugged her, holding longer with an extra squeeze that crossed the line from friendly to wanting to be very friendly. "Paige said I could help myself to anything in the kitchen that wasn't earmarked for dinner. Are you earmarked for dinner?" Bailey asked with sincerity, looking straight at Linney.

Paige choked out a cough. She expected Linney to take him down with a quip for such a blatant advance.

Instead Linney smiled and, with a stammer, said, "Uh…you might be *fishing* for trouble there, but we'll see, Bailey."

He chuckled and took the fish from her hands.

Paige silently mouthed to Linney from behind Bailey, "What the hell?"

Linney just shrugged and mouthed, "I don't know. He's cute."

Paige did an eyeroll with a half audible groan. Their silent conversation came to a close as he turned to put a couple items into the pantry. He looked straight at Linney, staring an extra beat before he helped her remove her coat, standing just a shade too close.

Paige couldn't watch any more of the train wreck happening right before her eyes. "Ahem," she said, with a fake throat-clearing. She pushed past Bailey to attend the soup and turn the oven on. "The rest of the groceries aren't going to put themselves away," she said, spewing her mother's words before she could stop herself.

They both snapped to. Linney excusing herself to "freshen up," a term she never used. Paige dove into cooking for escape. The evening was a blur.

Linney came out of her haze. Bailey remained odd. Winky twitched. Somehow the simple meal grew larger with the fish included and a salad added. Paige perfected the creamy potato soup to her liking, which, thankfully, matched Bailey's. Woodwork was discussed as well as generally terms of Linney's hospice care.

The food was devoured. Bailey took the lion's share, leaving only a fraction for lunch the next day. With the kitchen tidied, ideas for the mantle were explored. Paige brought her laptop to the table and mantle images were viewed for added clarification. Finally, playing cards came out. Bailey was a quick learner of the simple games and an agreeable, jovial player, much to Paige's pleasant surprise. But Linney fell back to her laughing, cheating ways when they played BS.

Apparently, some things don't change even when newly smitten.

****

"Time for me to go," Bailey announced out of the blue. He stood, patted his belly, but instead of heading out the kitchen door at the close of the evening, he turned and walked into the hallway.

"Go?" Linney said sadly.

"Go where?" Paige said, perplexed.

Bailey looked straight at Linney, "To bed."

Paige had never seen her aunt blush, yet tonight she couldn't seem to stop. Paige interceded, "Okie, dokie. Let's see if I can phrase this correctly. Where is your bed?"

"Mine's at home, but while I am here, I think the living room is as good as any. Looks like you have a twin mattress already on the floor. Unless…I did see a room upstairs at the end of the hall."

"That's my room," both Linney and Paige said in unison.

"Mine's the unfinished one," Paige clarified.

"I like the one with the cat bed better."

Linney actually raised her hand, "That's mine."

He nodded and smiled, picking up Winky as he stared at Linney. Paige looked from Linney back to Bailey and back again, unsure how she felt about whatever was going on between them.

"Bailey, I think I speak for us both, don't I, Linney, when I say it's fine for you to stay a day or two *in the living room.*"

They continued to stare, and now he was doing something like wiggling his eyebrows and making Linney chuckle.

"Okay. That's it. I hate to break up this staring contest, but I am going to. I'm exhausted and have cross-country skier legs and butt. I need sleep. Bailey, please use the downstairs restroom unless you need to shower. That's upstairs, but remember to knock and wait. Linney will get you blankets, sheets, pillows, and whatnots, won't you, Linney?"

"I like whatnots," Bailey said as he returned to staring at Linney.

"Me, too. And look, the cat likes you, Bailey. Winky's not even twitching," Linney noted.

Winky turned to Paige, his closer eye twitched while the other one was still. Minor improvement, but it did make him seem even more deranged.

Linney and Bailey stood motionless.

"Hello people," Paige chimed in. "Bathroom and bedtime. Everybody shoo."

They scattered. Winky was the first to obey and flew down the basement to his litter box. He yowled with a higher pitch than normal. It was Paige's turn to twitch as she clomped up the stairs. Most likely, Winky caught a mouse. Either that or he was complaining. In any case, she was surprised to think that he was the quickest to follow orders.

She collapsed on her bed and texted Michael a few times. "Help, Bailey's here."

"The drink? Save some for me," Michael texted back.

"Not the liquor, the woodworker. And Linney has it in for him…as in a crush."

Michael texted back quickly. "Uh oh. I know what a Dornheim woman can do to a man."

"You don't know the half of it. Goodnight handsome Ground Hog Man. Zonking out."

"It's going to be a while before I sleep. You have me wondering what the other half is that I don't know about you. Sweet dreams, Flee. Love you."

Paige fell asleep, hugging her pillow and murmuring her response to Michael, which he couldn't hear. "Love you, too."

Chapter Ten

Dashing. Paige and Linney were dashing very early the next morning. Linney needed to get to work in the hospice, and Paige had a double shift at the café. They dressed in a hurry and were scurrying in the kitchen. It came to a halt when Bailey entered in a slow lope, smiling widely in his soft thin suede coat.

Had he trimmed his beard? Paige did a double take.

Linney just stared at Bailey, even when he stole some toast and left to assess the fallen tree for wood potential.

Paige gulped the last of her coffee and pulled on her coat, looking for her toast. "Earth to Linney. I said, what happened to my toast?"

"Toast?"

"Yes, the thick nine grain toast you said you'd replace after stealing my first two slices?"

Linney pointed to the kitchen door and said dreamily, "Bailey."

Paige huffed, stole back a piece from Linney's plate, and threw another into the toaster. "Gotta run, Auntie, and you better snap out of this or you'll be late."

"He's more handsome than I thought."

"Focus, Auntie. People need you." Paige stuffed another bite of toast in her mouth and headed out the door.

"People need breakfast first."

"Check the toaster. Ta-ta, Auntie," Paige said, voice muffled with the warm thick slice.

"Toast thief."

"Takes one to know one."

Paige nearly made it out of the driveway before slamming on her brakes and fishtailing on an ice patch, having to stop since Bailey stood in the middle of the driveway. She lowered her window. "Bailey?"

"Uh huh. You have a Cypress behind the Norway Spruce."

"So, we do. Care to move? I need to get to work."

He walked up to her window and smiled. "Your car doesn't have the right tires for winter. You might fishtail if you slam on the brakes."

"Thanks for the advice. Have to run. Good luck on the projects inside." Paige added under her breath, "Which I hope you complete soon."

"Okay. Drive safely in your dangerous car."

"Thanks for the well-wishing," Paige said with sarcasm.

"Anytime. Anytime." Bailey smiled his clueless smile.

In her rearview mirror, Paige saw Bailey stomp off in the snow with amazing speed. "That man is a riddle. Thankfully, one I don't have to solve."

****

Paige returned home from her exhausting but fun shift at the café. Lucy had been there, and then Sally came for the second shift. The position not only gave Paige an opportunity to meet some of the locals, but she was truly enjoying working with a staff her own age.

She learned how Lucy took a break to travel Europe with her cousin before finishing her degree. Pieces of their backgrounds had been shared in snippets between working tables. Paige had happily promised to meet up for Girls Night Out the following night to learn more about these fun, new friends. Later, details were texted back and forth among the friends, choosing the location and who was sharing rides with whom. She drove home without fishtailing once on the salted roads.

Paige barely had time to put down her belongings and say hello to Linney and Bailey in the kitchen when Michael entered from the hallway. He was freshly showered. The image of Michael in low hung sweat pants, no shirt, and a towel around his neck distracted Paige from anyone else in the kitchen.

"Michael!" Paige beamed and rushed to him, requisite waitress ponytail bouncing.

"Hello, Paige, and oh hellooo, Michael." Linney's eyebrows shot up at his near naked attire as she sat before a half-eaten plate of food.

"Michael? Oh right, right. Paige's lover," Bailey said, mouth full with food tucked into his cheek as he rose to shake hands. "How's it going, man?"

"Great, fine, uh, Bailey, isn't it?" Michael gave a glancing kiss to the bewildered Paige. "I'm starved. I brought some take out from a certain Indian place Paige and I had gone to."

"Yeah, thanks for that, bro."

"You ate it?"

"Sure did. Good stuff."

"All of it? That was meant to be our dinner," Michael said with a look of confusion and deflation mixed with starvation.

"Oops. Just finished a plate or two. Might want to bring more next time."

Michael had texted Paige earlier not to worry about making dinner since he was bringing some. His expression turned to fuming, and he said something in Oneida under his breath.

Paige took action and stole a bite from Linney's plate. "It was delicious, Michael. Thank you so much." She knew better than to add, "It's the thought that counts," to a hungry man.

"We have homemade potato soup still, don't we?" Paige asked Linney and Bailey. They mumbled agreement between bites. She opened the refrigerator. Her tension lessened when she saw the contents. "How about I also whip up chicken sate with veggies? I found some organic peanut butter in here."

"Sounds great," Bailey eagerly replied.

"You already ate, and it happened to be our dinner," Michael retorted.

"Just thought you would like an opinion."

Paige huffed quietly in response, choosing not to give a snarky answer as her Southern upbringing told her to refrain.

After several mouthfuls of soup and the promise of the rest of dinner cooking in a pan, Michael and Paige became far more relaxed at the small kitchen table. If this had happened to her ex-boyfriend, he would have blown a gasket.

"So, Bailey, are you temporarily living here?" Michael asked.

All three answered at the same time.

"I am."

"He is," Linney dreamily replied.

"He is," Paige said, trying her best to curtail her exasperation.

"He is?" came another voice a half a beat later.

"George!" Paige and Michael said in unison, followed by Bailey saying "George?" with curiosity. Linney just turned beat red and choked. George stepped in with tools in hand.

"Busy house," Bailey added happily.

Linney gulped water.

Paige interceded, "George is our Wi-Fi Man. George, meet Bailey who's our Woodwork Man. You know Michael already, I believe."

The men all shook hands. Winky screeched by and ran into the other room followed by a crash. Linney flew out of the room amid the handshakes.

"And that was Winky, our newer member to the crew, that Linney went to help. Good mouser. Odd cat," Paige explained.

"I'll say," Michael murmured. The pan on the stove sputtered.

Paige rose and put on her best southern smile. "George is here to move the router or add a new one, right? Bailey's here to work on the mantle and about a thousand other special carpentry projects. Michael why don't you take them to living room."

"But dinner—"

"Will be ready real soon. Especially with Linney's help. Any chance you can send her in here?"

Michael proved to be a quick read of Paige's intention, especially with the sizing up looks George and Bailey exchanged. He walked between them. "Well, let's see what we have going on."

Linney snuck into the kitchen. "Winky just

knocked over some of Bailey's tools. Smart cat. Thanks for your part of the save, too, Squirt."

"You owe me one," Paige said, stirring the dinner faster than needed.

"One? You mean one of the men? Okay. You can have Michael. I'm keeping both the other two for comparison."

"Keeping two? Dangerous, Auntie," Paige said, handing the stirring spoon to Linney while she made the sauce for the sate dish.

"It's my middle name."

"No, it's not. You're barely back into dating, and suddenly you're playing with fire. Not to mention, you can't get involved with an employee let alone an odd one who seems to want to move in."

"Sure, I can. Watch."

"That's not good business," Paige quipped back.

"It's not business. Renovation is art."

Paige stared.

"Okay, okay, Squirt. Point taken."

"I just don't want to see you get hurt." Paige took over and poured the sauce onto the chicken. "Besides what about George?"

"I don't think he wants a romantic relationship with Bailey." Linney laughed.

"Aunt Linney, you know you're playing havoc with my brains."

"It's my job. Keeps you on your toes, Squirt." Linney opened the wine Michael brought.

Paige tapped the cooking spoon and plated two dinners. "Dinner!" She heard several sets of feet. "For Michael and I," she added and heard one "yes" followed by two moans.

"Wine for everyone, compliments from Michael," Linney added.

That earned only one moan. All four kitchen chairs were taken with Bailey leaning on the cabinet licking the spoon. Michael's dinner vanished in record time. They all toasted to the house's renovation.

George rose to leave soon after, handing Paige the bill. Linney took the bill, smiled, and stuffed it into George's breast pocket. "Try making it smaller."

He whispered something to Linney that made her laugh and escort him outside. Bailey lingered in the kitchen, acted casual, washing a dish or two, but leaned to get a peek out the window. He stared straight at Linney when she stepped back inside. "You seeing George?"

"Might be."

"Sleeping with him?" Both Paige and Michael looked aghast at Bailey.

"Might be." Now, they looked aghast at Linney. She never flinched.

Bailey didn't blink an eye. "Would you like to go with me?"

"Maybe."

Paige and Michael turned to Linney, then back to Bailey. At those last words, they looked at each other with questioning expressions at what was happening.

"Not asking the next question about sleeping with me. I know you will if I please you the right way. And that means I need to win you over, Marilyn Linney Dornheim Smith. I plan on doing just that—with my craft in wood."

Paige nearly choked.

Linney blushed, took her wine glass in hand,

grinned, and said, "To your wood."

Paige couldn't suppress her laugh any longer. She raised her own glass. "To everyone's wood."

Michael said something that sounded a lot like, "Wakaleeyo."

Bailey repeated it and added, "Amen to good wood."

They all toasted and laughed in agreement, though Paige's felt her face flush beet.

****

The cat yowled in the middle of the night, waking Paige and Michael. She sat up in bed but didn't hear a further crash so she let Michael tug her back into position, spooning around her. His hands softly stroked against the cotton shirt she wore, his briefs warm against her pantied bottom. She murmured something about wanting him but exhaustion won over, forcing her eyes to drift closed and for her to slip back to sleep.

In the haze of half awareness, she woke again, this time to the feel of skin on skin as their legs entwined. In her dream, to her urgings, Michael had removed the impediments of clothing and slowly slid his shaft between her legs. Soft moans filled the air. She spoke of her longing as her breathing deepened when she touched him. A rocking, lingering pulse grew. There, in the middle of the night, in a languid haze of a dream, they clung to each other through a small shudder of her release.

Hours later, Paige awoke, panties fully on, the dream only a foggy notion. She yawned and stretched at length, feeling sated and well rested.

Michael was already partly dressed in his pants and unbuttoned shirt, with his fresh tie dangling. "Did I wake you, sleepy head?"

"I'm not sure. Did you…I mean, earlier…did we?"

Michael shrugged and smiled. "Not sure what you are saying, Flee, but I have to get ready."

He left to shave. She lolled in bed.

"Yoga," Paige finally said aloud, as if to tell her body what to expect next.

She freshened up, pulled her hair in a knot in front of the mirror, and hopped down the stairs to lay her yoga mat down in what was left of the foyer. Wood piles and supplies cramped her space but the airiness of the ceiling still added comfort. The circle saw buzzing echoed in from the sunroom, breaking her meditation. She retaliated by putting her music on louder and moving through her yoga positions.

"Mind if I watch?" Michael asked, holding a plate of breakfast.

Paige looked between her legs, bottom high raised. She nodded and then broke the pose, standing and reaching her hands to the ceiling, palms pressed together, one foot propped on the other knee. "Not at all."

He took a seat on the stairs.

"Want to join?"

Michael pointed to his food, but Bailey, who'd just entered, said, "Sure." He stood next to her, attempting to hold the pose and said, "Wait."

He shook out his arms, wiggled, and then twisted his hair out of the way. He looked different without the mass of hair. Different but unusual as he'd chosen a knob like hers. She did her best to ignore Michael's reactions.

Bailey swayed. Paige moved to the Firefly pose,

legs arched over arms. He tried and fell back.

"How about doing something easy?" Paige offered.

"Sure. I like easy," Bailey said.

"Bet you do," Michael mumbled. Paige glared at him. "Er, I said 'gotta chew.'"

Paige moved into the Bow pose, sitting and pulling her legs in a raised V.

Bailey could match that. "Wowza. I really feel that in my thighs."

"Me, too. It means you're doing it right."

Before Michael could offer a comeback, she glared again. He held up his palm and changed the subject. "So, are you taking a shift today?"

"Nope. Working on the house." Paige twisted to a half hand stand, half shoulder stand, toes pointed to the ceiling.

"Oh, Fallen Angel pose. Cool. Cool," interjected Bailey who, instead, rose to a downward dog, butt facing Michael. "Looks real cool, doesn't it?"

"Paige's? Yes. Yours is a bit—"

"Sloppy, I know." He rose and groaned. "Gotta get back to work."

Paige knelt on all fours and lifted one leg up. Her opposite arm reached back toward it.

"Oh hell, Paige, if you keep this up, I won't be able to hold off until dinner to see you again."

"You'll have to do better than that." She switched legs and arms. "It's Girls' Night Out like I mentioned. We'll have to wait until tomorrow."

Michael said something in Oneida but didn't translate. "Right. Well, I have to fly out of town tomorrow, early Thursday morning. I forgot to tell you."

Paige broke her pose and looked at him. "Do you need me to cancel?"

"Course not. Go have fun with your new friends. I can't stay overnight anyway. I'll be back as soon as I can, Flee, but it'll be at least a few days." He rose and kissed her forehead. He shook his head. His amber eyes seemed to flash. "Just wish we had more than half-asleep sex last night."

"I knew it!" Paige threw her neck towel at him. He dodged it.

"Missed me," Michael said from the hall heading to the kitchen.

"I already do," she called after him. She returned to sitting twisted stretch.

Two minutes later, Michael came back, full business attire, and pulled her to her feet. "For that thought, you get a full goodbye kiss."

They held each other and kissed so deeply that she felt that surge inside her again. "Mmm mmm. Are you sure it's not a *hello* kiss? Or I-figured-out-what's-going-on-after-the-seventeenth kiss?"

Michael pushed back a stray lock of hair. "Patience, Paige. I'm working on it. This business trip is part of it." He held her face. "Aloha is the best I can do." He kissed her again, this time long, slow, and deep. He smiled. "From the look on your face, Flee, I think Aloha isn't bad at all."

She grinned a dopey grin and sighed as he left then sat back on the mat. Yoga seemed done for the day. Winky came and sat by her. She petted him. "There he goes again. I do love that man, but each time he leaves, it makes me wonder what happens when his project comes to a close on the seventeenth. Besides St.

Patrick's Day partying, I mean. That's what? Ten days? What about Michael and me? Does he get transferred far off? Do you know, Winky?"

Winky purred and rubbed himself against her. Then he dashed off.

"Never get advice from a cat, if you ask me," Bailey said softly.

"Well, no one asked you," she said without looking at him. Her voice was curt without meaning to be. She rose and began to fold her mat. "Sorry."

He looked concerned, but the knob hairdo took away from it. "It's all right." He poked at the supplies and smiled. "Just saying, dogs are better at advice." He picked up the heavy wood and easily heaved it over his shoulder. "Besides, you and Michael, you're a love thing. The seventeenth is a date. Love things win over dates. Love is love."

Paige stood still, trying to parse his advice. The only thing she got out of it was that she needed coffee before even attempting to work on the house. That, and Bailey might be more caring than she first thought.

Chapter Eleven

Tap! Tap! Chug! The group of Paige's new girlfriends let out a collective puff of air after the strong alcohol shots, followed by the near obligatory "whoa" or choking sound and then a guzzle of water. Girls' Night Out started with half price appetizers and four-dollar mini-cocktails. The seven women squeezed into the bar's corner booth, which made sharing snacks easier. Not many items were ordered though, with Lucy, Paige, and Beth eating more than Sally and the rest.

With very little in their stomachs, they toasted to their new friend with the funny accent, Amelia Paige. She shared her interview success and learned of the other women's degrees and jobs, apart from part-time at the café. They even had a struggling musician amongst them—Kyra.

Soon the day of de-hoarding the house slipped far out of Paige's mind. It started as a pleasant, easy going night, made light with interspersed laughter. Then, somehow the discussion went from best place to buy shoes to most romantic places for dinner and slid downhill from there. Lights got dimmer; the music louder. It all went haywire when the bartender rang a bell and said it was Buckshot Time as he stared right at the women. One dollar a shot for all single women, and their table had many admirers it seemed. Even though

Paige had tipped the bartender to make their drinks light, the number of freebies added up.

Shots came around again and again, six glasses at a time. Drinking games started with lamest name for pet. Sally won for her mother's new bird named Cheepers Creepers so she didn't have to drink, but the others did. *Tap! Tap! Chug!* Worst excuse for being stood up. Patty won that with, "Taking the dog to the groomers, and he didn't even have a dog!" *Tap! Tap! Chug!* Most embarrassing high school moment. Lucy's first period wearing bright white pants won hands down. *Tap! Tap! Chug!*

"Oh no! Whatcha do? Go home?" Paige asked with a slur to her words.

"Naw. I had art class next so I grabbed different paints and *accidentally* threw them on me. There was no way I was going to let John Hornswoggle see me like that."

"What ever happened to that football hunk?" Beth asked.

One of the other girls said his "Horns were cut off. Now he's just a woggle."

Somehow that proved to be riotously funny. Sally and two others then needed to dash to the bathroom. They ended up flirting with men at the bar afterwards and came back to the table with two male interlopers who were shooed away with a few phone numbers but not before they brought more shots.

"I have a good one," Beth offered up, slurring a bit, but seemingly a little less drunk than others. Her question proved otherwise. "How about the most unusual place you made out?" Beth put air quotes around "made out," which was more than a loose term for "had sex."

A glass elevator ride in Pittsburgh won, although, from the look on the Kyra's red face, Paige suspected others may have done far worse. Kissing on skis in the woods wasn't even a contender. *Tap! Tap! Chug!*

The trick to the shots, Lucy and Paige learned, was to slosh with the taps so that less of the watered-down alcohol made it into their mouths. The others didn't seem to learn that trick.

"What about you, Paige?"

"Yeah, got one you'd win?"

"Shh. Paige's turn to choose."

"What's she choosing?"

"Next one."

"It's a shot."

"No-oo a question."

"What question?"

"Shh, listen. I love her accent. Don'tchew?"

Lucy finally chimed in, "Go ahead, Paige, lay it on them."

"Is shum-one gettin' laid?" Patty asked.

"Shh. Paige."

"Okay, to Paige getting laid," Patty said and drank her shot.

Paige almost drank to that herself. Instead, she rose from her end seat at the booth, wobbled, and with the thickest drawl she could muster said, "Biggest baby you ever dated or lived with. Howsss that, ma'am?"

All the women spoke at once, offering things like spider removal or when their guy had a cold. Beth's ex from a few months back kept surfacing. They all knew him and began conceding to Beth. Paige continued to counter with Davis Martin Greer who she left behind in

Buckhead. It seemed a stalemate.

"Photos ladies," Kyra spoke out. Beth's photo was of a light-haired big guy at a frat party long after closing time, covered with chips. He had what looked like a penis drawn on his forehead.

"No fair, Beth. That was college."

"Okay, how about this? That was a month before I left him." It was a picture of the same guy almost in the same collapsed pose with Cheetos all over him, minus the drawing. "Top that."

"I don't have pictures of his dirty laundry… Well, this one." Davis was in a picture with his football buddies, arm in arm, blond-haired, big-smiled, and completely muddy.

"You left that behind? Are you nuts? He looks like a sweety that needs loving," Beth countered grabbing Paige's phone. Others murmured consent. Paige could have sworn someone said, "I'd do him." She turned to see who said it.

"I mean I'd date him," Sally blushed and corrected herself.

"I'd date and do him," Beth offered.

"Davis is all yours, girls, except he's in Atlanta."

Lucy chimed in, "Looks like Beth's the winner." She added as she raised the shot glass, "There's only one thing I can say, women. Plane tickets to Atlanta." *Tap! Tap! Chug!*

Beth stared at the picture on Paige's phone. "Seriously, Davis is cute, Paige. So, where's a picture of this Michael you've been going on about?"

Paige's eyes nearly crossed at the last shot, which seemed stronger than the others. She shook it off and took back her phone. To her surprise, she didn't have many photos of Michael, and she couldn't show a couple of the ones she did have. She found one taken on Valentine's Day in his suit.

"Whoa."

"Yummm...handsome."

"Older."

"Yeah, but older is bigger," Paige offered.

"Don't you mean wiser?" Lucy asked.

"Sure, that's ssswhat I meant." Paige giggled at her faux pas. She spoke of how Michael was more than the looks and was the whole package.

"Well, he sounds like a keeper," Lucy said.

Paige's thoughts went darker, and she answered, "Hopefully, if he wants me."

That brought a hush until the bartender walked over carrying the final six shots.

Without noticing the bartender behind her, Sally called out, "Littlest package on a guy."

The bartender spilled two of the drinks as he put them down. Patty fell into hysterics, and all of them joined in the laughter. Amy just blushed as the bartender's arm swept near hers.

A man was about to approach their table but was waved off by the bartender, "You don't want to go there now, bud, trust me."

That brought new laughter, followed by, "I'm definitely going to win that one with Dougie. Remember him?"

"How can I forget? I dated him before you."

Paige kept quiet through the topic.

Lucy noticed. "You don't have any complaints in that department, do you?"

"Absolutely not," Paige said and raised her shot

glass, chugging to renewed laughter.

The bartender returned with two replaced shots and attempted to clear the table.

"Let me help you," Kyra said.

There was an exchange of eye contact between them. The table fell to a momentary hush.

"Closing time soon, ladies." He placed the bill in the middle of the table. "Everybody have rides?" the bartender asked but was looking straight at Kyra.

She smiled at him.

Before Kyra could answer, Sally interjected, "We'll work it out."

The bartender nodded. With his tray loaded with empty glasses, he gave a quick wink and a whisper to Kyra as he left.

"We will?" Lucy asked. "It might be time to go, but look at Patty."

They all did. Patty looked like she was about to drop right into her napkin.

"Not so good. Since she was designated driver," Beth said.

"No-oo way yay hoo-say. Ho sazes? Hoziers? Nope." Clunk went Patty's head.

"Beth, it was your turn," Sally said while Lucy clicked onto her texts.

"But…I…uh oh. It was?" Beth asked.

Kyra nodded to Beth, "I thought so."

"I thought it was Patty," Lucy added.

"Looks like we screwed up this time," Sally said. "Okay let's see." She turned around. "My brother's friend is still over there. Bet I can talk him into driving me, Patty, and Amy home." Patty looked up, grinned, and dropped her head onto Sally. Sally pushed her off.

"Kyra looks like she's covered. You three live the other direction. Why don't you get an Uber?"

Lucy looked concerned. Beth became animated, "My ex—remember?"

She went on about Uber drivers while Lucy leaned over in a whisper to explain to Paige in slurred words about Beth's ex being one of the only Uber drivers around here at night. He once ended up taking Beth and her date home. Something about swearing and trees.

Paige lost track and started texting and calling. Linney wasn't to be found. Michael. She called Michael.

Of course, he came through and would drive them but didn't sound like himself.

She downed one last shot without remembering to tap at all.

****

Michael took a long swallow of coffee and squinted at the late-night glare of on-coming cars. Lucy and Beth had been dropped off. Paige was next.

Paige was flushed hot and dopily grinning, trying to make a coherent thought. "What a night, huh?"

"A thrill a minute," Michael said and mumbled, "Especially since I have to sleep and get to the airport before dawn."

She didn't seem to register his remark. "Well, I for one haven't been so whoo-hoo drunk like this sssin a while. Have you? Actually, wait, wait. I got drunk the weekend I firssst met you-oo. Well it wazz juzz me, but *your* wine. Sheesh. Never used to. Go north, get buzzzzzed." She giggled.

He said nothing so she continued, "Well, the others are gone. So, uh...it's just me and you." She poked him.

Michael's jaw was tight and his expression stern. He took another swallow of coffee.

Paige puffed her cheeks and blew out a breath. It reeked of alcohol. She knew she was in trouble, but her brains didn't have control yet. Her mouth did. "So. Are you going ta ask me ta move away with you or are you leaving me in the cold? Hahaha, cold. Actually, I'm warm now."

She tugged off her coat, making Michael lean to avoid her fist. He also avoided answering her.

Confusion took hold. "Do you know, I can't remember if I told you."

"Told me, what?" he asked.

"Huh? Oh, Michael, I love you." Paige beamed. "I will even give up my new job for you, and you…" She poked him again. "You don't even know that, do you? Training would start out of state thatta way." She pointed out the car window.

"Job? The waitress position?"

She wiggled her finger. "Na, na, na. Not the Frenchy café. That's temporarararry. Temporarr…ily." She concentrated and corrected herself. "That's just for now. The career job I mentioned. 'Member? Well, don't think I told you, but I was given it today. Offer details comin' soon. I can get going again. Money, reeesponsibility, 'n' meetings, just like you. But I'd give it all up so I can go with you, but nopey. Michael didn't ask me. 'Bout a week away, and he's zooop takin' off. Not even asking me to commute."

"What job?"

"A good one." Paige paused to think. "I could take the job an' lose my heart, but I will get a ring. My grandma's courage ring if I behave and let you go."

"What job, Paige?"

"Monitor and Ventures, in m-m-marketing and product-y placement."

"Here? In this area? The large company?"

"Yupers. Landed the big ca-hoona. Part of the celebrating." Paige looked ahead and tried to focus more clearly.

Michael was steel-eyed as he drove. He finally spoke. "You can't take the job."

"I can't?" Paige turned to look at him, dumbfounded, then she smiled. "Oh, right, you want me to follow you."

"No, that's not it."

"What's not it? You don't want me?"

"No…I mean, yes. Stay, but just not with that position."

Even drunk, she could tell he was angry. She was confused. Did he want her or no? All that came out was, "Huh?"

"Look, let's talk when you're sober."

"No, no, Michael. I might be drunk as a skunk, but I'm so-sobering up fast." She swallowed back a hiccup. "I'm not stupid." Her words still slurred but grew clearer. "You just told me not to take a job but that you didn't want me to follow you either. You want me to stay here but not get a career? Well, that's…that's f'ed up. What century are you?"

"Not what I meant." Michael started to mumble in Oneida.

Paige looked at him and began to mumble in a form of Pig Latin she knew as a child. He gave her a sideways glare. "What? If you can go all Groundhog on me, I can go all Pig Latin on you."

"Calm down."

"I am calm!"

"No. You're not."

"Maybe. But I'm making way, way more sense drunk than you are sober. Michael, it's me. A drunk me, but me. What are we doing after your project ends?"

"I can't tell you until I hear back. And that'll be after this trip to fix an urgent engineering issue. Then we'll have all the options. And there's a real solid one. How long until you have to respond?" Michael asked, pulling into her driveway.

"To what?"

"The job offer."

"I...I don't know. It's Wednesday." Paige counted on her fingers. "I get the details sent to me tomorrow. Bet they want an answer by Friday or maybe Monday. Why?"

"Haggle with them if you need to. Come up with a point of discussion. Stall." He parked the car near the front door. "But give me more time."

Paige stared at him. He looked stern and tired, but mostly he looked immovable. Her lip quivered. "Time? That's all I've been giving you. That and my heart, but it just doesn't seem to be enough." She whipped open the car door before he came to help her. After two steps, she tripped on some ice, slipped, and hit her knee hard on the ground.

"Flee, wait." Michael rushed to help her up.

"No. No more waiting." She pulled back from his guiding arm, nearly fell again, and dragged her treasured white coat in the muddied snow.

She hurried straight to Linney who stood by the

door. Concern was thick in Linney's voice. "I just came home myself. We got her from here. Thanks, Michael."

Michael's eyes filled with unfallen tears, and he nodded. He stood staring up at her.

Linney turned away, helping Paige. Just inside the open door, Linney asked, "What the hell happened to you?"

She clung to her aunt's arms. "I fell in love. It hurts."

"Always does, Squirt. Always does." Linney closed the door.

****

"Do you remember the rest?" Linney put hot coffee in front of Paige, sunshine streaming in the kitchen window.

Paige's night had been a rough one. "Nope. Not really." She sipped at the coffee, hangover in full force. "Something about not taking the job. Maybe he dreams of me being at home only? Sure, one day I'll settle down with kids, but I have more to give. Much more to save. I'm not ready for housewifery. Ouch! What are you doing?"

Linney had bent and pushed up Paige's leggings to poke at her swollen knee. "Sorry. Here." She put Paige's leg up on a nearby box and found some frozen peas. "Put this on your knee, Squirt."

Paige did as she was told, warming her hand on the coffee mug after handling the cold pack. "All that kept playing in my head in the car was how he didn't ask me to go with him. He didn't once ask me to move in with him or commute. He was the one always saying it would work out and then..." She looked up at Linney and her jaw dropped. "Oh, my god. Is he breaking up with me?" She moved the ice from her knee to her head.

Linney turned from the stove and shook her head but still had a look of concern.

"Why does this feel so wrong?"

"Your knee?"

Paige shook her head. "No, Michael. It wasn't so confusing or didn't hurt anything like this with Davis. And that was bad enough to send me packing. This is so different."

"That's because Davis was an immature blockhead in Buckhead and not for you."

"I want Michael."

"Then get him."

"He has to get me."

Linney let out a breath. She sat, looking straight at Paige. "Don't play games with this one. He's older than his years. I think there is some missing piece to this. Talk to him." She slid Paige's phone to her.

Paige let Linney's words sink in. She picked up the phone and called Michael. No answer. She texted him, saying the words aloud as she did, "Your hungover drunk skunk wants to talk." She put the phone down and stared at it. No answer. She drank her coffee while Linney plated a small breakfast.

"Might be bad reception. Try again later, Squirt, and try to eat."

Paige nibbled at the eggs and opted for the dry toast. Linney rose to bring them both glasses of water. As she did, Paige picked up her phone again and quickly texted, "Michael, at least let's talk."

Without an immediate response, she followed it with another. "Not sure what to think." Her lip quivered.

Linney took Paige's phone away.

"Hey there, Dornheim women," Bailey said, smiling at Linney. He poured himself a cup of coffee and opened the refrigerator.

"I have it," Linney said. "The milk that is." There went her blush, doubled down as Bailey's hand touched hers when she handed him the milk. Paige looked away. Once she'd had an ardent desire for her aunt to start dating again, now, with her world spinning in confusion, she didn't want to think about it.

"Paige, here, is licking her wounds from last night," Linney offered.

Bailey chugged most of his coffee and bent down on his knee to look closely at Paige's injury. His hands were surprisingly gentle, and his gaze very focused.

Linney asked, "Whatcha think, Doc?"

He stopped inspecting. "How did you know I had my doctorate?"

Paige and Linney looked at each other. Paige asked, "You do? In what?"

"Medicine." Bailey crooked up a grin. "Naw. Just pulling your leg. In Philosophy and a Masters in Art."

"You're kidding right?" Paige asked with a little too much surprise to her voice.

"Nope."

Linney's phone rang so all she gave Bailey was a thumbs up and a smile. "Uh huh. Sure. Trade shifts and work today? Hold on." Linney looked straight at Bailey who returned her thumbs up. Paige just stared at the interplay.

Linney continued on the phone, "No problem…uh huh… Be there within the hour." She hung up and took a big swallow. "No use staying here and watching you mope, Paigey kins. Got to dash. So, Doctor Bailey, what are your findings?"

Bailey gently prodded Paige's knee. He seemed focused as he felt her knee, twisting it slightly with the demeanor of a physician, and said, "In my opinion, her knee is scraped and quite bruised. No sprains or breaks." He stood. "If it swells much worse, take it easy. We don't want to exacerbate a hidden stress fracture. Doubt that you have one, though. For now, intermittent ice and leg up every so often. If it feels sore, peppermint oil to the temples or painkiller if you prefer. Let's see how you do." With a placid expression on his face, Bailey held out a hand to Paige to help her to stand.

Linney beamed.

Paige just looked bewildered. She stood, flinched, and rubbed her knee after she pulled her hand from Bailey's.

"Squirt, are you going to be okay if I go in?" Linney knew to hand Paige a painkiller, which she took with the last of her water.

"I can keep an eye on our Squirt," Bailey offered.

"Since when did I become Squirt to both of you?"

"Since Linney's leaving me in charge."

Linney put a hand on his arm. Bailey turned to her, dark eyes locking on her light ones.

Paige interjected, "Wasn't there supposed to be dashing?

Linney nodded. "He is. And I need to be." His grin slid into a full smile. Linney let out a soft moan under breath and left to get ready.

Bailey stood, looking after her. "She likes me,

Squirt."

"Paige. Name's Paige."

"Nope. Today you are Squirt."

"Fine. Then you will be Doc. So, what's up, Doc?"

"Ouch. Now I think *I* need a painkiller." Bailey smiled.

"Ha, ha," Paige said sarcastically but nearly cracked a smile.

"C'mon, Squirt. I'll take a break from the crown molding in the living room."

"I thought that looked done except by the fireplace." Paige cleared the dishes.

Bailey helped. "No way. Needs a second set."

"I thought it was beautiful."

Bailey beamed at the compliment. "I cut the curves in the wood myself. It'll be even better with the next layer. I was holding off anyway for stone work on the fireplace. You need to choose the stones after your shift tomorrow."

"What shift?"

"Right, right. Linney accepted for you tomorrow morning."

Paige dried her hands. "Anything else you two have lined up for me?"

"Sure," Bailey answered.

"And that is…"

"A surprise. March, Squirt. We're finishing the upstairs master bedroom clean out."

"We are?"

"You bet. You can sort some of that jumble while sitting down if you need to. We're done here so move it."

"Sheesh. Some comfort you are."

"Not meant to be. I'm a distraction."

Paige made a face at him but couldn't help smile after. She pulled out her phone, but he took it away. "Hey!"

"Sorry, no phoning on the job." They walked to the stairs. "I'm getting some boxes and bags. You head up but hold the rail."

She started up the steps, slowly. Earlier in the week, the soreness of the climb was the result of skiing. Now, it was the hard spill she took running away from Michael. Some luck she was having. She called down to Bailey, "What about computers? I need to see the details of my job offer."

Bailey easily caught up with her. "You can check when you have a break at lunch."

"Slave driver," Paige said and stopped after reaching the hallway.

He flew past her, put the boxes down, and bumped into Linney when he turned, his hand hitting her breast.

"Oh," they both said in unison, followed by "Sorry" in unison.

"No, my fault," Bailey said.

Linney disagreed.

Paige's eyes rolled, and she noticed neither moved. She faked a cough, saying, "Late."

"I need to go," Linney said but barely moved.

"Bye, dear." Bailey kissed her cheek, and his gaze followed her all the way down the stairs. "You gotta love those curves."

Paige hoped he was talking about her aunt but wasn't sure if he was speaking of the spindles of the banister where his eyes lingered after Linney had gone.

****

The day was spent in a flurry of activity, partly to hide Paige's aches, both physical and of the heart. Hoarded piles diminished faster than ever before. Bailey was speedy with removal of bags, making many trips up and down the stairs. The small room next to Linney's, barely big enough for twin bunks, had been emptied. Much of the desired spare furniture was wedged into the room. To Paige's delight, even the hall was mostly cleared.

During a late lunch, with Bailey close at hand, Paige reviewed her offer details. "It's great. What a solid offer!" She spoke without a breath, listing one thing after another about the position. She was flushed with excitement.

"That's good, right?"

"It's great."

"In that case, wow, congratulations," Bailey said, nodding and left the room.

Winky stared at her.

"How can he understand some things implicitly and other things be so clueless about?"

Winky twitched then ran head long into a shadow on the wall.

"And look who I was talking to." She smiled and shook her head. "I only hope I can take the position."

Her pride swelled as she re-read the offer. She had received it on her own, without guidance from her parents or college. She did, however, follow Michael's suggestion, when she sent her email reply. She wrote that she would be delighted to accept the offer, but that she had some questions before final commitment.

A quick reply from HR came saying that was understandable and she would have those answers mostly likely by the time she was due in for drug testing early next week. The email had ended with, "Glad to have you on board." All of it was moving ahead smoothly. All except Michael.

By evening, Paige sat in the master bedroom, nearly cleared, apart from furniture pieces. She stared at the tall dresser as Bailey joined her.

"She's a beauty," he offered.

"I like it, but is it too expensive to keep? I wanted to paint it and maybe keep it," Paige said. "That is, if I stick around here."

He seemed to reflect on her pensiveness. He quietly moved to the dresser and ran his hands over it, assessing the date stamp, the marquetry, the fluting, burls, and footing, offering several hmms and comments during his careful inspection. "It's a nice piece all right. I think it can be buffed and the original finish kept for a better price."

She let out a saddened sigh.

He looked at her and spoke again, "But…the drawer bottoms need to be re-done, the legs should have better feet or bracing. See how it can wobble? And well, I think I agree with you. Keep it and love it. Not worth the money you could get for it."

Happiness swelled inside her. "Really? I'm able to keep Grandma Ida's and Grandpa Ben's dresser? The lucky one I found the stashed money in? You're right. The dresser just needs some love." She stood quickly, flinching when she put pressure on her knee. It didn't stop her from grabbing Bailey and hugging him. "Thank you."

"Gosh." It was his turn to blush.

****

Bailey stirred for a snack. Winky came out of nowhere and brushed against him. He bent to pick up the cat and petted him until the twitching died down.

"How are you doing, Winky? Looks like our Squirt is hurting. Oh, but you should have seen how happy keeping that impressive dresser made her. You can't put a price on it even if it's well over three thousand dollars. Right, fella?"

Winky meowed and jumped from his arms.

Bailey raised his glass of milk in salute to his furry friend.

Chapter Twelve

Paige stared at her phone in bed that night. Still no text from Michael. She texted him as if he were still reading hers, each message a few minutes apart.

"I did as you asked, Michael. I stalled the company on the offer."

"You said we would have challenges, but we would face them together."

"Still no answer? Say anything, please."

"Who's Fleeing now?"

A few soft tears landed on her pillow. There had to be a reason he's out of reach. A reason other than the obvious one, that she blew it with the best relationship she had.

A knock came at her door, startling her.

"Paige, it's me." Linney entered, still in her work clothes, followed by Winky. "You and Bailey did amazing work today. Kudos. Now, hand me your cell, Squirt."

"You've got to be kidding me. I'm not a child."

Linney held out her hand.

Paige resisted. "I use it for an alarm."

Linney's hand was still out and her foot tapped. "I'll wake you. C'mon. Quit pining. Michael will come around. It could be crappy cell reception for all you know. You need sleep. We all do."

Reluctantly, she handed over the phone. "I'm

telling Mom on you, Aunt Linney."

"Very mature. Go ahead. She's the one who asked me to do this."

"My parents know? You called my parents?"

"For your information, she called me out of the blue. I hate to tell you this, but parents know. They always know."

Winky added a yowl and left.

"It's a prison here."

"A prison where the guards love you."

"That's kind of sick, Auntie."

"You're right but it's late. I'll come up with a better one tomorrow."

Linney's footsteps could be heard down the hall. Paige's head hit the pillow again. The pillow in a prison she was fighting to stay in. A hovel of a prison that felt very much like a home when Michael was there or she knew he would return. She hugged her pillow and looked out through the window. The shade was up part way.

That night, like she had when she was a little girl, Paige wished on a star. With fervor, she wished for her love to come back to stay this St. Patrick's Day.

****

Paige wasn't the most chipper at the French café the next morning. At least her knee wasn't too swollen or throbbing anymore.

"Hey, what's up with you? Trouble with your lover in paradise?" Pierre chided her from the kitchen.

Her lip wavered, but she put on a brave smile for the patrons. Lucy noticed, smiling warmly at her friend and shushed the cook. He returned with an expression so weird, even Paige had to laugh.

The packed tables, lively French music, and routine gave Paige little time to sulk. She did, however, tell Lucy a short version of her fight with Michael and his following silence act. Before Paige left, Lucy held her in a hug and handed her a small bakery bag. "You'll pull through. You got this girl, right?"

"What? A muffin?" Beth asked as she just arrived.

"No, not the muffin. She's going to make it work out with Michael," Lucy corrected.

"Something's up with Michael? Then you need a bit of—"

"Faith," called out the cook.

"—chocolate," Beth finished. She pulled out two small chocolate pastries from the cabinet. "Here complements of the café."

"No, they're not," called the cook. Lucy shooed Paige out, hanging her apron for her.

Paige could hear the argument continue.

"Yes, they are."

"You girls are costing me."

"We're helping you. Look at your waist Pierre."

"Bah…" Something followed in fake French. Then she heard the familiar peals of laughter.

Paige had been reluctant to leave the house that morning, and now she was reluctant to leave the parking lot at the café after her shift. She mindlessly ate one of the pastries in her car as she pulled up her texts on the phone. Still none from Michael. One plea, though, to call her aunt on the house phone, which she did.

"Hey, what's up?" came Bailey's greeting.

"Um, Bailey? It's Paige. Do you always answer the phone like that?"

403

"Nope," Bailey said followed by long silence.

"Bailey?"

"Yes?"

"I was told to call."

"Oh, right, right."

Paige smacked the phone to her head, took a breath, and continued to listen as Bailey explained what he needed her to review in the home improvement store, including the choice of stone façades for the fireplace, along with foyer chandelier possibilities at antique store.

"Doesn't Linney want to do this?"

She heard "Hell no" in the background before Bailey responded. "Linney thinks you would do a better job of it. I've narrowed down the choices."

Paige soon had her marching orders, which included to stop looking at her phone. "How could I know to call you if I didn't look at my phone?"

Bailey complimented her on the logic. He then added a hint about a take-out Asian Fusion place he particularly loved, just in case she was hungry.

"Not particularly," Paige answered, luxuriating on a bite of the muffin.

Linney came to the phone. "Squirt, he means to bring home dinner. Aim for the healthy options and bring lots. Double what you think. It seems he wants to be paid mainly in food."

Paige mumbled with her mouth full of muffin. "He eats so much."

Linney whispered the rest. "Maybe, but I would like to keep him happy. He's doing incredible things here." Linney clicked off.

"I bet." Paige wondered what exactly those two

were doing alone. Together. Suddenly, she was in a hurry to get through the errands, in case they were intended to stall her.

****

Paige was efficient if nothing else. She chose the soft-tone river stone for the fireplace. She took pictures of her first and second options of the chandeliers and another at a second lighting store. Now that she had a signal, she texted the photos to both her mother and Linney who agreed with Paige's favorite.

If other texts were sent and received away from the farmhouse, Michael must have gotten his. Then, why didn't he answer?

She shoved the thought out of her mind. She had to. Something was off, but it would remain that way until she heard from him. She didn't dare admit there was a possibility she wouldn't hear from him.

She perused the menu at the front desk of Tiki Chow and quickly placed a large but not terribly expensive order. "No msg, and oh, also a quart of brown rice, please."

A male voice came from behind the screen separating the dining room. "Paige?" A bearded man's head popped into view. "I thought it was you, Kitten. I'd recognize that sweet accent anywhere. Don't you look adorable in your bouncy, playful ponytail."

It was the barista from the coffee house a few weeks back. The one who not only hit on her but thought she was into pets in some unimaginable way. Before she could respond, he waved for another hot tea.

"Come sit with me."

"I can't stay. Paul, wasn't it? I'm just picking up take out for my aunt."

A very short and very un-shy Asian woman rushed over and, pulled out a chair. "You sit. Sit. I bring you tea. You talk with nice, handsome man. He's a good customer." Paige found herself sitting, knees nearly touching Paul's, with a hot tea placed in front of her. "Besides, you put in big, big order. It take time. Take twenty-five minutes."

Paige relented.

"So, what's up, Kitten? How's that stray cat you adopted working out?" Paul neatly ate his food, motioning dishes to her who waved them off. He had light eyes, a big smile, and a tight trimmed beard. If she were interested in other men, he would have possibilities, but her world seemed to center on Michael.

"Our cat? He's...well...different. My aunt seems to have claimed him and named him Winky. He's a little less scrawny, well not as skinny at least, but he still runs into walls. Thanks for all the toys you sent me. I mean the cat. It was for the cat, right?"

"Your choice who it's for. Especially the feather one."

Paige's eyes grew wide at the last remark.

He laughed to ease the tension. "Kidding. But it was the least I could do. Glad somebody took Twitcher."

"Winky," Paige corrected him.

"Winky. So, what's his favorite toy?" Paul ate at a steady pace, beard spotless.

"The chewies are scattered around the house. He hides them, but I think his favorite is still the set of Ben Wa balls he sleeps with."

Paul choked and reached for his tea, which he'd

already swallowed dry. The waitress was at his side in an instant, refilling his cup. "First, you're a furry, and now your cat is into kink?"

"No! No, not at all. Not to either. I mean the cat does like Ben Wa balls, but they're my aunt's. The tickler you got him ended up in my room, but I didn't…"

He stared at her.

"This is so not coming out right." She sighed and leaned in, whispering. "Look, I'm not into furry. I'm not even sure what that means. Besides, I have a boyfriend. At least I think I do."

He chewed thoughtfully. "Is your boyfriend the dude who bought Winkers?"

She nodded without correcting him. "Wait. How do you know?"

"I was there. Oh, maybe you don't know. I'm a barista, sure, but I also work at the shelter and a vet's office. I decided to go back for my degree in Veterinary Medicine."

"Bet you'd be good at it."

"Grew up with animals all my life. I have a sense when it comes to animals and some people, too." He smiled and took a few more bites.

Paige stared off, drifting to thoughts of Michael.

"What's going on, Kitten? Ever since we brought up your boyfriend, you've been acting deflated."

She gave a weak smile.

"C'mon, you can tell me. You know I want you, but not like this. What happened?"

She tried to stop, but she spilled an abbreviated story in record time. He listened intently, eating all the while.

"Hmm." He took a swallow of water. "Did you ever try e-mail? You kept saying he didn't text you and that he's traveling. What if he lost his phone or didn't bring his charger? Try one more time but email instead."

Her heart lifted instantly. She looked up and eyes widened. "Why didn't I think of that?"

She yanked out her phone and clicked to emails. Without meaning to, she read her email aloud as she wrote it, "Why won't you answer my texts? I want to work this out. Please reply or call me, Groundhog Man." She added *XXOOXX* to the end of it.

"Ah ha!" Paul grinned. "I knew you were a furry!"

"I'm not. Michael's Groundhog Man because his birthday—"

"Big order is ready!" announced the small Asian woman.

Paige was flummoxed and rose to follow the woman to the front desk. "I have to go." She gave him a quick hug. "But thank you, Paul."

"Wait, can we at least stay in touch? You can tell me more about you and groundhogs. Or maybe you have some friends who aren't attached?"

She gave in. "I might. Here. Give me your phone." She keyed in her contact info. "I do have a few new girlfriends. Maybe you can meet us for St. Patty's Day?"

He quickly agreed.

She picked up the bags of take out. "And Paul, the furry thing. Not so much, okay?"

"I know purr-fectly well what you mean." He winked.

She had an immediate shiver of regret for giving

out her contact information.

The owner leaned in as she walked Paige to the door. "He jokes. This month furry jokes. Last month it was all fruit jokes. He's bright, maybe gets bored. Needs a girl. You fix him up, okay?"

"I'll try." Paige had no idea why she should but knew she just might do that.

"Good, good. Here's special fortune cookies. Green for Irish Patrick Day. Hope you come back soon."

With that, was ushered out.

****

Paige flew into the kitchen. "Hi everybody!" she called out and put the Tiki Chow take out on the table.

"Paige, honey, I have news—"

She kissed her aunt and flew past her. "Save it please. My cell phone's out of batteries. I need to check my emails." She turned and almost bumped into Bailey.

"I smell some awesome—"

"In kitchen. Can't talk. I need to go up to my laptop." She hurried up the stairs as fast as her knee allowed, still wearing her coat. She opened the door to her room. To her nearly empty room. No laptop. No desk. No bed. All missing.

"What the…" She stared, then returned to the hall to find Linney and Bailey.

"That's the news, Squirt. We moved your room."

"If you recall, the room you were in is going to be the closet off the master bathroom," Bailey added.

Linney continued for him, "So, we went ahead and set you up in the room with the view down to the orchard."

Paige raced ahead of them. She ran to the tiny, tiny

room next to Linney's but opened the door to find even more stray pieces of stacked furniture and a note marked "keepers." She stared, dumbfounded.

"Not there, Squirt."

"Oh." Paige did an about-face and passed the bathroom and opened the next door. The room was the same one she and Michael had been in once when it had been empty, save for the twin mattress. A memorable room with the deep window ledge and charming view. It also now had a queen bed, a small vanity, a wardrobe, and a huge beautiful dresser. Her grandparent's lucky dresser.

"How? When? Who?" Paige flung open dresser drawers. The drawers opened smoothly. The tall dresser had gorgeous wood bottoms. Her clothing would fit with so much room to spare. Extra drawers and nooks. It looked refurbished, sanded, and refinished, with only a hint of varnish. The rich wood grained showed with burls and patterning. She stood, mouth open.

"Say something. It's not painted like you mentioned but we can," Linney encouraged.

Paige found her voice. "No. No, I love it. I love you. Both of you. It's perfect. Is it mine?"

They nodded.

She hugged and kissed them. Both of them. For a fleeting moment, her aunt looked like she did when Paige was little and Bailey looked like a proud parent.

Bailey blushed and started reviewing the steps he took to refurbish it. Paige just kept touching it and playing with the drawers. More than once, he mentioned how strong Linney was and what a help she was fixing the dresser. Linney smiled with pink to her cheeks.

Paige finally turned to the vanity near the window. It seemed to be serving as a desk with her laptop and desk items on it. The books that had been supporting the makeshift desk were in a box on the floor.

"We didn't get around to moving your things or figuring out a real desk," Linney said.

Paige barely heard. She was beaming.

"There's lots of spare furniture we can toy with or make a brand-new desk all together," Bailey said.

Linney added, "That's for another day. We ran out of time."

"And steam. I'm starved," Bailey finished Linney's thought and stepped to the hall with her.

"You can play with it all later. Coming Squirt?" Linney asked, barely waiting for an answer.

"Be right there. I have to check something." She plugged in her phone and opened up her laptop. There on her laptop was the email she so long awaited. She looked out the window of her new room to the darkened sky. For all the hurrying, she was nervous to open the email from Michael.

"I thought my message reached you. I'm out of the country, working nearly around the clock on a retrofit to a damaged plant. Sorry no texts—or time. More later. Love, Michael"

For now, that was all she needed. That and some of the delicious food she had smelled all the way home.

Chapter Thirteen

Paige woke early the next day. She had to. The sun streamed in from the curtainless window. The night before she'd grabbed much of her things in hurried trips from the old room but only put them haphazardly into the new room. Right on top of a stack of clothes were her coveralls and work clothing, a reminder of what was needed for the day. Reluctantly she rose.

When she made her way to the kitchen, she found the coffee was already made and Bailey was leveling some food with Linney.

"You're up early for a weekend," Paige said. All she heard in response were mouthfuls of mumbles.

A truck pulled up the driveway. Suddenly, both Linney and Bailey dropped their plates in the sink and downed the last of their coffees. They threw on winter coats and gloves and dashed outside with Linney asking for sandwiches to be made.

Voices spoke over each other.

"You're here early."

"This is going to be fun."

"You have the chainsaw?"

"Hey Adam, this is Linney."

"She's a beauty."

The last comment got Paige's attention. She looked out the window. She couldn't tell if "beauty" meant the truck, Linney, or something else. Linney and others were unchaining an all-terrain vehicle.

"Remember, Bailey, you got it just for today. It's a weekend, so I should have charged double."

"You did. You promised two days," Bailey said, grinning." Maybe your son can help me with some of the larger logs later in the day, and we'll call it even." They shook hands and unloaded the truck.

Linney came in. "Pokey with the food, Squirt. Let me help you." In no time, sandwiches were made and a thermos filled. "We're going to cut and drag some fallen trees for wood for the house projects. Can't wait."

Paige looked out the window. The truck was gone. Bailey was loading the ATV with chains, tools, gas cans, and gadgets.

Linney continued, "You might want to fix up your room while we're gone and maybe wash the walls. We can push your dresser against the wall when you're done. Supplies are in the master bedroom. See you, Squirt."

Paige finally took her second sip of coffee. She had never seen her aunt this way but suspected, from her stories, it wasn't uncommon in her youth. She cleaned the kitchen disarray and sat down for a bite of muffin. All she found was the empty bag. She settled on the peanut butter sandwich accidentally left behind. It was the kind of morning where a book beckoned to be read. Even Winky was resting. She thought better of it, downed her coffee, and headed up to her assigned task.

Soon, she had music blaring from her laptop, clothing tucked away, and the furniture draped to prevent damage. She discovered that the walls needed more than washing. They needed a fresh coat of paint.

Searching the garage for stored paints, she found the fresh can of off-white base coat she'd bought and mixed a splash of Linney's violet paint into it. She added a touch of some older charcoal paint. She smiled a mad-scientist smile at the result. It made an off-white-gray with a slight mauve hint.

Her technique of rolling paint was far from perfect, but it got the job done. She occasionally looked out the window she'd opened to let out the fumes. Laughter spilled in through the window. Linney was driving the ATV, hauling a huge trunk of a tree, with Bailey helping her steer. Winky pushed open the door and hopped on the window sill.

"Shoo. You'll get paint all over you." Paige lovingly picked him up and petted him as they looked out at the scene below. "Aunt Linney seems happy with Bailey doesn't she? Not the same as George. Hmm. Hope they know what they're doing. I sure hope it doesn't get messy around here, do you?"

Winky meowed, jumped from Paige's arms, and left the room. It was only later that she saw a large swatch of paint on his left side, which exactly matched the paint smear on her coveralls.

****

Paige awoke at twilight. Winky sat atop of her plastic-draped bed, meowing at her face. She was sprawled, half-sitting on the floor, with her face and arm draped up onto the bed. Her cheek that the imprint of crumpled plastic.

"What? Huh?" She brushed back hair from her face, unfortunately with a paint brush. Though most of the paint was dried on the brush, it left a good swatch. She stood slowly, stretched, and put the ruined brush in a water can to ineffectually soak. The walls of her new room were painted, but the trim was only half-done.

"What time is it, Winky? Oh no! The chicken might be burnt." She heard the sound of a truck horn and did what she thought was hurrying down the stairs, but for all her painting aches and aggravated knee injury, it was more of a quick hobble.

Linney and Bailey entered the kitchen the same time as Paige. All three spoke at once.

"Eww. Smells like paint."

"Bleck. Smells like diesel."

"Mmm, smells like chicken." Bailey smiled and opened the oven.

Both women spoke at once again.

"What the hell did you get on you, Squirt?"

"What is that crud on you, Auntie?"

"Who cares? Wash hands, let's eat. It looks done." Bailey won.

Paige elevated her leg as they ate, per Doc Bailey's request. They shared stories of the day, often not waiting for the other to finish.

"Two matching chunks of the tree trunk are going to be end tables," Linney said with excitement.

Bailey continued for her, "I think we have some solid cherry wood for table tops. Maybe a console table or a small one for the foyer. It doesn't look like it'll cut right for the mantle. Might want to use that tree you and Michael found for that."

Paige spoke of the email she got from Michael and how she came up with the wall color choice.

Linney removed a burnt piece of potato skin. "One thing, Paige. Where are you going to sleep?"

"My room? Why?"

"The fumes?"

"Oops. I guess I didn't think of that. I was just so excited."

The new room was closed off, window opened. Bailey brought the twin mattress to the floor of her old room. Together, the three re-analyzed the blueprints of the upstairs renovation and comparing it to the space now that it was mainly cleared. Slight adjustments were discussed and the poster of things to sell or buy was revised. The words curtains and sewing came up. The words "tack up a blanket temporarily" were received with much more enthusiasm. They closed the evening by taking turns fumigating themselves in welcomed hot showers.

No mention was given as to where Bailey was to sleep, nor was it asked, although with the twin mattress taken, the creaky sofa became a far less than desirable option. Paige's original room in the farmhouse was even more austere with her belongings gone and the twin mattress placed directly on the floor. She still had her phone and laptop for company. Before bed, she received promises of painting trim help from Linney in exchange for fireplace masonry work the next day. Weekend or no, it seemed all three of them were on house duty the next day.

Though Paige had a catnap earlier, she was bone-tired. It was still early but felt like the middle of the night. She was happily surprised to find Michael emailed her minutes before. Her Michael. Soon, she and Michael found a rhythm typing short emails back and forth. He typed emails from the hotel lobby, which turned out to be the only place he could send personal messages.

Paige's next email to him read, "When you said Cali, I thought you meant California. I thought it was just a cute name for the state not a city in Columbia. Just like when you said Dallas I thought it was Texas not PA. I'm still not clear though. Why can't you text again?"

Her question must have come off as more direct than intended. He told of using a borrowed Quad Band GSM work phone due to signal issues and international data difficulties. He added, "A plant was damaged by a storm. I was called in as part of the emergency team to fix it. We were to retrofit the plant next year anyway, so we're trying to complete both tasks at once, saving time, money, and jobs. We're working incredibly long hours."

Michael immediately followed it with another e-mail. "Paige, I'm so sorry. I hated leaving you upset and unsteady, especially finding out you didn't know where I was traveling. I should be back in the U.S. in Ohio in a few days. It'll be easier to talk then, even if I might not make it back your way until close to the project end date. We might be apart, but I do love you."

If that wasn't enough, he closed with, "Please give me another chance."

Her heart raced. Hunched over her laptop, she wrote as quickly as she could.

"Just one? You have a million chances, but I'm supposed to play it cool and say, perhaps. So, I'll say perhaps. Perhaps I love you, too. Perhaps I felt my world shatter when I thought I lost you. Perhaps the whole conversation was a blur. Perhaps I'm incredibly proud of you. Perhaps I'm thankful you are safe and can't wait to be with you again. Perhaps I can't stop thinking about your chest in the firelight."

Michael's email response came quickly. "No perhaps from my side. I definitely can't stop thinking about your chest in the firelight."

A second response followed, "I feel at home when I am with you, Paige."

Paige stared at that email. Another one came in.

"I need to go. Call you stateside as soon as I can. Until then, I send you love and my salacious thoughts. XOX, Michael"

The words "at home when I'm with you" stuck with her. It stuck when she painted the next day or when all three worked on the stone façade of the home's fireplace. Sometimes, she found his words profound or endearing. It had a relieving sense of permanence. Other times, she wondered if he meant she was just part of the furniture. She brushed that doubt aside. Feeling at home, whatever way he'd meant it, was a powerful thought.

All the more so when Bailey, Linney, and Paige collapsed on the rickety old sofa that night, squeezed together, staring at the fireplace and their day's handiwork. The metal lattice screwed to the old bricks had only been half covered with stonework.

"Beautiful," Paige said. The others just nodded and smiled. Home, to Paige, seemed a wonderful place.

Chapter Fourteen

"Your chances are being used up," Paige said on her cell phone after she arrived home from a double shift at the café three days later. She'd already had shifts both previous days along with a visit to Monitor and Ventures for drug screening and paperwork details.

"You said I had a million chances," Michael protested.

She heard a car door slam. He was talking on his cell in Ohio.

"Not real math, I meant in *lover-math* terms. Michael, why aren't you here? Get your buns back to PA. You already missed Pie Day on March fourteenth as it is." She nibbled at some grapes but pushed it aside for pie, proving susceptible to her own suggestion. Their conversation had started a few minutes earlier, but she hadn't had much time to discuss all the home improvements nor the confirmation of her wonderful job offer.

"Oh, right, that was yesterday. I like Pie-Science Day, too. Did you bake, Sweetie Pie?" Michael asked with extra sugar to his voice at the end.

"Yes. And just for that sarcastic saccharine remark, I'm punishing you by saving a slice of pie for you."

"And how is that punishment?"

"It's from Linney's experimental coconut, peach, cranberry sauce pie." Even the mention of that unlikely

419

combination made Paige shudder in remembrance of the bitter odd pie with the crunchy burnt crust.

Michael gurgled. "You wouldn't! Did it taste anything like the unfortunate mixture of what you mentioned?"

"Worse. It was goopy and the crust was burnt. Even Bailey couldn't eat more than a few bites of it."

"And this is supposed to make me want to come to you sooner?"

"No. But this is." Paige took a large bite of the cherry bourbon crumb pie she'd made from scratch, followed by a dreamy utterance into the phone. "Mmm mmm." She described the morsel at length and quietly wrapped and hid the last two pieces in the freezer.

Michael's voice lowered. "Stop, you're making me hungry."

Paige let out a soft sigh, "Am I?" She took a long drink of water and upped the sultry tone to her voice. "I had *no* idea. Well, if you must know, I just hid the last couple slices of my cherry bourbon pie in the refrigerator for us. Oh, look, a cherry escaped on the pie pan." She nibbled the crumbs and licked the serving utensil she just used with an elongated moan of appreciation. "Mmm. Are those better incentives to arrive at my doorstep?"

"Excellent. I especially like the last part."

"Oh? Does *cherry bourbon* do something for you?" Paige asked, drawing out the R sound as she readied the vegetables for the roaster. She could hear Michael let out a long sigh.

"You do something to me, bourbon or no."

"Enough to encourage you to come back tomorrow?" she asked, trying to quietly wash and chop the root vegetables.

"You must know by now that the sound of your voice is enough for me fly to your side, Flee. Yes, I'll be in PA tomorrow, although I'm just now unpacking from the Columbia trip…" Michael spoke about the project and how "hands on" the team was, completing what could have taken a month in record time.

Paige listened with a few mmm hmms thrown in. By the time he finished, she had seared the roast, put it in the oven with the vegetables to slowly simmer, and was heading out of the kitchen.

"Oh, that's so wonderful," Michael blurted out.

"Huh? What is?" Paige asked, heading up the stairs to avoid Bailey's power tool noise.

"My bed in my clean room in my condo, here in Ohio."

"Mine, too. You'll never guess where I am."

"Your bed in that wallpaper less small room at the end of the hall past all the furniture?"

"Nope. My new, fully painted room. It comes complete with a vanity, old stuffed chair, and my grandparent's phenomenal refurbished dresser. Since you left, I moved rooms and painted the walls. Bailey and Linney fixed the dresser, and oh look, Bailey even put up the white trim work. Gorgeous. You remember the room? The one with the view?"

"The one that only had a twin mattress and the wide ledge where we…" Michael's voice trailed off to silence. He resurfaced with a soft growl to his voice. "What are you doing now in that room?"

The phone call seemed to be taking on a different tone.

"I was going to change out of my work clothes into

a yoga outfit. With the renovation projects, job offer, and café work, I may just want to read or rest a moment. Why?" She kicked off her shoes and opened her blouse. "Do you need to go?"

"No." His voice sounded husky, as it did when he whispered in her ear or nibbled on her neck. "Paige, why don't you strip down to your panties and bra for me. In fact..." She heard a clunk, a zipper, and in a moment, his voice again. "I'm in my boxers. My gray knit boxers."

"You are?" Paige's voice was a whisper. She stood in the middle of her new room, looking out her window where twilight coated the remnants of the snow with a soft pallet against the silhouetted shadows of the trees. She didn't pay attention to that. In her mind's eye, she saw Michael's handsome face with his long nose and high Native-American cheek bones set against thick gorgeous black hair. She envisioned more than that. His lean, muscled body V-ing down to his knit boxers, most likely burgeoning with what they held. She shivered at the thought.

"Yes. Tell me what you are wearing." Michael asked.

"My black slacks, white blouse, the thin black belt with the jeweled—"

"Paige?"

"Yes?"

"Get busy and get in bed."

She did. Without thinking, she quickly stripped, tossing her clothing onto a chair, and slid into the cold crisp sheets. She made a slight yip as the cold touched her naked skin.

"Are you in bed, in your bra and panties?"

"No."

"No?"

"I'm naked," Paige admitted.

He let out a hiss. His voice fell into a deep quiet as he coaxed her to touch her smooth belly. She moved from hugging a pillow under the covers to exploring her own form. She opened her eyes and looked out the window to the darkening sky. The tree scape brought her back to when she and Michael were touching each other, looking at that same view.

He whispered over the phone where his hands would touch her body and how his lips would follow. He was more travelled and experienced. This was new to her. She never had anything resembling phone sex, but the comfort of the bed and his lurid, deep voice lulled her into following his lead. Curled up under the blankets, Paige's hands were guided to open herself and press into that needful center. Soon, they forgot the phone and focused on their voices.

Mesmerized into a rhythm of soft yearning, Paige opened up and began to ask Michael to touch himself, picturing her hands on his smooth muscled chest. She was a fast learner.

With closed eyes, she made her words a honey sweet enticement. "Trace the length of your cock. All the way up. Grip it, for me. Imagine it's my hand sliding up and down, gently pumping you."

When asked, Paige found and held onto her toy, a small, thin bumpy shaft. His growled whispers urged her to rub it over her clit and slide it along her slit.

"Fill your pussy with it, for me." His deep voice graveled out the request.

She did. Moving, undulating, pleasing herself. His

voice beckoned her to continue. With a twist on the next few strokes, she plunged the toy in and out of her pussy, faster and faster. Each moan and sound fueled the other. Though hundreds of miles apart, they drove each other to the pulse-pounding edge. Crying out each other's name, they both came.

"Michael." Paige's eyes popped open. Her face was flushed, and her breathing ragged. She held onto his name as if it were a song. "Mi-Michael," she repeated into her cell, panting. She drew in a deep breath again. "Michael, it felt like you were…"

Michael said something in Oneida sounding like, "nay lak wa" and then let out a laugh. "Oh, Paige. I don't know about you, but mmm-mmm-mmm."

"Is that what you said in Oneida?"

"Yes, well sort of. I said *amazing*. But now I am—"

"Tired? Thirsty?" she said with a dreamy breathlessness to her voice.

"Yes, and yes. Plus, hungry," Michael said with a chuckle.

"Me, too," she admitted.

They lingered sharing sweet intimacies.

A beep went off on his phone. "No way. You have to be kidding me."

Paige heard clicking on his phone. He returned with urgency to his voice. "Paige. I really hate to go, but I have to take that work call. Sorry, Flee. Tomorrow—"

She lost the last of what he said when she dropped her cell phone into the twist of covers. He'd already clicked off by the time she fumbled to pick it back up.

His last word "tomorrow" rang as a promise to see

her the next day, which added to her pleasant afterglow. She yawned, rolled over, and napped a few minutes only to have a different kind of alarm wake her minutes later. Namely, Bailey.

He called up the stairs asking her about dinner. She sighed and rose. An oven filled with dinner and her grumbling stomach seemed to agree with his request. Her pillow and yummy bed would have to wait.

****

Paige was nearly sleepwalking by Thursday evening. She worked yet another shift at the café, though she'd originally been hired for about four shifts a week. Since she was leaving for a permanent job, the owner took advantage of working her as much as possible—and he did, more than double that. She returned home exhausted. She had also doubled down on keeping the house projects flowing and sifting through the *saved treasures*. She posted many of them for sale on auction sites or boxed them for antique shops. The remainder were set aside as house decoration projects. More projects!

Paige needed a break. Michael was missing in action—again. So, when Lucy texted her the location of the best Irish Pub and asked her to join them the next evening for St. Patrick's Day, she happily agreed. She even posted word to her barista friend, Paul, hoping he would connect with one of her new girlfriends.

That gave her pause. Her girlfriends. In Atlanta, most of the friends she knew were girlfriends of Davis's football buddies. It wasn't like that in PA where it seemed she was setting down roots on her own terms. She did miss a few of her friends, causing her to send them some texts. One friend pinged back, pleading with her to continue the tradition and "get out there" for St. Patty's day. Paige texted her not to worry and sent a picture of the bar she'd planned to go to with others.

Bailey interrupted all her texting. "What's for dinner?"

"I hadn't thought much about it." Paige put away her phone, still not getting a response from Michael. "How about something green?"

Bailey nodded noncommittally.

She dug in the veggie drawer, pulling out spinach, potatoes, and other items. "I can make some green pepper appetizer, green veggie patties, and green salad. An early St. Patrick's Day veggie feast. How's that sound?"

This time Bailey smiled. "Is Michael or Linney coming for dinner?"

Paige didn't hide her disappointment. "Haven't heard from Michael at all. I honestly thought he would be here by now. It's been a week."

Bailey, who oftentimes seemed oblivious to emotions around him, didn't miss this cue. "Let's call Linney. Maybe we can take a break and play that game you always lose at after dinner."

"Ha. Ha." But she smiled as she called Linney, using the speaker on her cell phone.

"Can't Squirt. After I finish here, I'm going out with George tonight."

Paige leaped for her phone to take it off of speaker. Bailey's hand stopped her. Their mumbled struggle became audible.

"Paige, leave the speaker phone on. Hey there, Bailey."

"Hi Linney. I just need to ask one thing. Is it a date

or to break up with him?"

"Both."

"Good. Good." Bailey beamed, returned to chopping where Paige had left off, and began to whistle.

"Linney, as hard as I try, I just don't always understand you." Paige shook her head.

"No need to, Squirt." Linney added loudly, "And Bailey, save me some leftovers in case George leaves in a huff before dinner is over."

"Will do. I'll even let Paige win in chess."

"What? Hey, I can play chess. Not too well, but… Hey, the potatoes and spinach go in the food processor like this. Bye, Auntie." Paige hung up, unsure if her aunt was still there.

****

Paige left another voice message for Michael. "It's late. When are you coming over? Dinner's done, and I even let Bailey win at chess. I'd like the encore to be with you—"

Michael's voice came to his phone. "Paige. Hi. Sorry."

"Oh, you're there."

"Yes, just checked in at the hotel. Had to get into my room. I've been setting things up for tomorrow's session."

"Hotel? I thought you were coming here."

"I said something to the effect I would be coming to PA, not to your place." Banging came over the phone. "Ouch! Stupid place for the hotel to put a waste bin. Bashed my leg. I already had a pounding headache from days of too little sleep, all the meetings, reports, and traveling. Eh, who cares? Even this rock-hard bed is going to feel good."

"Hmm. I could make it feel better. Do you want me to drive to you?"

"No! I mean no. Sorry, Flee. Give me one—"

"More day. Yeah, I know. I know." Paige's exhaustion fueled her less than understanding remark. She let out a sigh of frustration.

"Don't be like that."

"Don't be like that?" Paige tried to hide that she was becoming incensed.

"Impatient. Not now. I'm fried. Is it too much to ask for another day to see you? Oh, and I only need you to keep your job offer pending until early afternoon."

Paige had had enough. She was overdone, too, and blew a gasket. "Impatient? Please tell me you didn't say that. I have been nothing but patient. Tomorrow, your project's done, and I don't have a clue what your super-secret plans are from this point forward. For your information, I already took the drug test and completed the paperwork. I mentioned that more than once. Short of failing the drug test, which I won't unless having excess chocolate in my bloodstream counts, I think the job is mine. In fact, my confirmation and training instruction packet are due to arrive by the morning."

Michael was silent for a moment. "You signed on? What if my solution falls through?"

"Then we commute and take it from there."

"Don't you get it, Paige? I would be in your chain of command. I'm with *Monitor and Ventures,* too. Not your direct boss, but enough to cause difficulty if we were seeing each other. I asked you to hold off."

"Demanded you mean."

She fumed and her words stuck. Hot raw tears of

anger fell. Her voice faltered and repressed her drawl. "Maybe we should hang up before I say something I shouldn't say."

"Or maybe I should. You have no idea what I have been going through."

Paige nearly choked back the words, "That's the point. I don't know. I don't know anything of your confidential plans." Then she slammed her words out. "It's unfair, and you know it. Apart from your trip to repair the plant, you've kept me in some blind holding pattern. It makes me think you want me as a convenient sidebar. Oh no. Did I guess it? You didn't want me to take the job because you wanted me out of your hair?"

"Paige, no. That's not it—"

"Well, let me save you the trouble," she continued to speak right over him with a sob. "I'm saying goodnight. We can speak tomorrow if you are so inclined to give me any of your secretive ideas." She unsuccessfully snuffled back another sob and spoke in a quieter voice. "Good luck on your project wrap up. Hope it's a success. I know you worked hard enough on it."

"Paige, I'm just—" Michael's phone beeped with an interrupting call. He swore and clicked over to it.

"Goodnight Groundhog Man," Paige said to the void and hung up.

She'd been sitting in the dining room, unable to move. Tears rolled down her cheeks. Winky brushed her. She picked up the cat, "I keep losing him, Winky."

"No, you don't," Bailey said, turning the corner.

"I meant Michael."

"I know. I know." Bailey patted her shoulders. "C'mon, Squirt. Let's put both of you to bed." Winky

429

bolted. "Well, at least let's go. Food's put away."

"Linney didn't come back yet?"

They began to walk upstairs.

"Nopers. Just me and you kid."

Paige gave Bailey a long look as they reached the top step. He actually picked up on it. "Uh…not how I meant and you know it. Linney is my pulse-point. It looks like you and I both seem to be falling for some strong-willed people. Kind of fun though."

She stopped at her bedroom door. "Fun?"

"Worth the struggle in the end when you get 'em."

"*If* you get 'em," Paige added under her breath.

"There's always that." He smiled as he entered Linney's bedroom. "And we will. I'm working on mine. Yours is up to you, but I bet you'll get him. He's crazy about you." He closed the door.

Paige stood in her bedroom doorway. How had he done it? She just had a blowout with Michael, but she'd already stopped crying and felt kernels of hope.

She stepped into her room. The antique clock read just after midnight, officially St. Patrick's Day. Only a couple stars peeked out past the clouds. "You heard him stars. I want my love to come to me, today, on St. Patrick's Day and for things to finally fall in place." The clouds covered the stars before she got her whole wish out.

She texted three simple words to Michael. "Sorry, Groundhog Man."

Paige turned off her phone, leaving it to charge. It might not have been the three words he wanted to hear, but it was heartfelt. Surprisingly, sleep stole her quickly that night.

Chapter Fifteen

Paige took a deep breath the next morning and stared at her phone. She had hoped Michael would have left a message. Only he didn't. Nor did he call by later in the morning. With only two bars on her cell, she texted him a shamrock emoji and "Top o' the mornin' to ye."

A minute later, she regretted sending such an unsophisticated note. She paced and tried again, "Look, sorry. Already said so. Please call when you can. Any update or even a hello is appreciated. X Paige."

She wondered if that read as if she were an ex. So she added another text that read, "XOX" and thought that should get him to call.

He didn't. Remembering what high-pressure corporate days were like, she reminded herself he had presentations and busied herself with housework. It was the red-letter day when everything came together—or didn't.

Unable to help herself, she checked her email again. There it was—her offer in black and white. On the third email check, she saw that the finalized job offer package came from *Monitor and Ventures* complete with information about the orientation training session starting the week after next in Ohio. Hardcopy offer letter due by mail. Details followed with instructions and a request to reach them by day's end. Her heart raced. She forwarded it to Michael's private email, too excited to censure herself.

Paige read the offer again and again. Earlier in the week, she had already told her parents about the job and they were supportive of her, apart from "My baby will be so far away," followed by "She already is, Mother. Besides it's not final." It was final now.

She could do this job and do it well. Michael's hesitation was far from clear. Why shouldn't she take the position? In fact, by doing all the pre-paperwork, hadn't she? She, Amelia Paige Myers, had the job of her dreams in a field she wanted to be in. She excitedly typed her response.

Moments later, Paige found herself emailing her family. Then she texted groups of hometown buddies as well as her new friends, "It's official. They want me. I took the job."

Her phone lit up like a Christmas tree with texts. Girlfriends sent emojis with notes like "Double reason to celebrate," "Wahooo," and "No big surprise since you're smart stuff." Even Alfie, Michael's cousin, who threw the two of them together, responded quickly, "They're lucky to have you and so is my cousin."

In the middle of the storm of texts, Bailey entered the dining room, covered in sawdust with his hair in a man-bun knob and his beard in a surgical mask. He lifted his googles, motioned for her to stand, and hugged her to the point of breaking.

With ear plugs still in his ears, he shouted, "Linney told me to do that until she can congratulate you properly!" He broke from the hug, stepped back, and did it again, this time squeezing the air out of her lungs. "That's from me. Congrats!"

He stomped away, grinning, leaving Paige breathless and covered in saw dust, as was the newly mopped foyer.

The only person she hadn't heard from was Michael. "That tears it, Winky. Meetings or no, I'm calling him."

Winky twitched and seemed to almost have some kind of epileptic spasm.

"I don't care. He needs to know. Besides, what kind of relationship is it if he keeps me this much in the dark?"

Winky yowled and crashed straight into the lumber stack.

Michael didn't answer when she called. She left a voicemail, saying anything that came to mind. "It's nearly close of the business day. Silence hurts, you know. I thought you were better than that. Thought you would post me something, anything, during your breaks. I can't believe I let you string me along all this time." She paused, her voice showing her growing nervousness. "Okay. Right. Well. I took the position. I'm going out with the girls, who, by the way, actually want to celebrate my job. Oh, and Happy St. Patrick's Day, wherever you are. I don't know about you, but a drink sounds good about now."

She pushed the end call button hard, without having that satisfying noise from hanging up on a real phone.

Winky twitched nearby. Paige group texted her girlfriends. "I'm ready to get drunk tonight. Anybody want to pick me up?

"I'm not gay, but I'll pick you up, Amelia Paige," came Beth's text along with a time to be ready.

"Trust me. I'm ready now."

"In that case, I'm coming twenty minutes earlier. We'll get a head start. Wear green."

Paige looked down. She was wearing sawdust. She finished her housework quickly, or at least some of it. The rest could wait. She threw her phone on her bed as she quickly changed, pushing aside her distraught emotions toward Michael. She had some celebrating to do, didn't she?

****

Paige removed her coat and stuffed it under the bench in the wood paneled Irish Bar.

"Are you kidding me?" Patty grinned. The shamrocks on her headband bounced.

"What? It's green. Well, light green," Paige said, tugging on her blouse.

"You look like a nun," Patty snickered.

"A suppressed nun," Beth added. She was wearing an oversized felt top hat, green beads, green tights, green skirt, green everything. "Here, take my vest, Amelia Paige Meyers with the new job."

Paige started to put the sequin vest over her shirt.

"No, no. Go in the restroom and get rid of that convent look," Beth demanded. "We're out on the town and need to show some skin to go with the grin."

Paige did just that. Beth had worn the low-cut vest open over a top. Paige did not. She came out from the restroom with her shirt in her bag and the vest hugging her form. She'd pinned it to her bra, but the cleavage dip and large arm holes didn't leave much of her upper portions covered. With a deep breath, she approached their table. Paige looked to the mirror on the wall as she approached their table. Her butterscotch-honey blonde hair combined with the sequined vest caught the light readily as she moved.

"You sparkle," Patty exclaimed.

"Literally and figuratively." Lucy laughed.

"Do you think it's too much?" Paige asked Lucy, who was dressed slightly less conservatively than normal but was covered with strings of green beads.

A female bartender approached. "Absolutely not, honey. It caught those guys' attention, and they bought the first round of my special Green-O Mojitos for your table." The bartender put down four drinks. "And that's saying something. They're cheap as all get out, usually."

"Thanks, Heather." Lucy turned and waved at the two men, raising her glass in thanks.

Paige turned to follow her gaze across the room. Some women came in at that moment and started arguing with the men.

"Hey," Heather said, "it looks like their sweeties just came in. That means free drinks without their lewd remarks. Double win."

Amy and Sally arrived, asking for green beer and French fries with green ketchup.

Heather signaled her fellow barkeep for the drinks, and she returned with them quickly. "After this, table service will get real slow. Come around to the bar. Warning though, it's going to get rowdy tonight. Just come bug me or my handsome hubby, Kyle, if you need us. He'll be handling the music."

Beth honked a green horn when a man leaned in to kiss her cheek.

"Then again, maybe you're the ones we need to be watching."

Beth honked again, put beads on Heather, and continued her distribution of shamrocks, beads, and buttons.

By the time the second round of drinks and snacks were finished, the bar was packed to spilling. The music came on by the group called Tossers. It started with *Drinkin' All the Day*. Many of those in the bar raised their glasses during the song. Kyle rang a bell and announced over the mic that he wanted to see clapping and some better singing. He re-played the fast song version with more patrons joining in.

The music continued, with Paige's group laughing and shouting over some of the rowdier songs as the bar filled. They took selfie shots, posting them online. They even forwarded some to Paige, who in her haste, forgot her phone.

"Who forgets their phone?" Patty chided.

Paige felt sheepish, mumbled something about thinking it was in her handbag when she left home. The moment passed quickly with Sally's next alert for cute men.

"Black hair at five o'clock."

"Who's five o'clock yours or mine?" Patty asked.

"Both."

With only seats for four, the group of six women, took turns standing or squeezing in, laughter building.

The Emcee, Kyle, announced the next song, "*Drunken Sailor*." He said he would play it through twice. He wanted the men especially, to get their singing voices going for a contest coming up later.

"What's the prize?" someone called out.

"The tip bucket to charity."

That brought groans from the crowd.

"That and a kiss from one of those wee wonderful gurrhls over there," Kyle said with a fake Irish brogue and pointed right to Paige's group.

Beth honked her horn while Lucy, Patty, and Sally waved at the cheers from the crowd. Amy and Paige hid.

"They seem ready. Who's in?"

The bar roared their approval.

"One more ting," Kyle said, again in an increasingly strong fake Irish brogue. "I want to be seein' you fine lads buyin' a pint or two for all the marvelous ladies who ventured out tonight."

"What about the men?" one man shouted.

"You can be buyin' them one also, Brian. I have no qualms wit' whichever way you go," Kyle replied to a jabbing roar from the man's table.

The bar, which had been packed, became crushed with more patrons. Green pitchers of water sat out for those who needed it. Heather and the other two barkeeps miraculously kept up with orders. More drinks came their way, either bought or sent with lurid smiles.

Paige was no match for the pace of drinking. When asked, she happily traded her newly given Green-O Mojito with Lucy's water.

The pub was a chaos of happy, drunken green. Paige paced her drinking but felt a part of the spirit of it. She, surprisingly, even forgot about Michael's deadline decision day. Instead, she joined in, singing heartily to the chorus of *No, Nay, Never, No More*, a song she knew. Their group messed up on the clapping patterns, but they managed a slight harmony with Amy's help.

Contest time was announced. The fast song, *I Will*

Court Them All, played. It played again. Groups of men sang out when pointed to.

And there, from the corner, Paige heard it. It sent shivers down her spine. The unmistakable sound of a group bellowing in thick Southern drawls. She grew pale and turned to see none other than Davis and two of his buddies singing, I will court them all, I will. They pointed to Paige, who ducked lower in her seat, but Lucy was swaying a bit as she stood, providing little to no shielding.

"What hell are they doing here?" Paige asked to Lucy's dazed shrug.

"You know them? God, they're gorgeous," Patty exclaimed, rising for a better view.

"Hey, Paige. That's him, isn't it? Your big, handsome baby of an ex-boyfriend?" Beth pointed.

Paige sheepishly nodded, her mind reeling with questions. "How the hell did he find me?"

The women all shrugged and shook their heads, expressions sincere enough, though a bit dazed with interest when they looked at Davis and his friends.

"No idea, but I'm glad they came. Man, are they hot!" Patty stared.

Lucy just smiled and burped to Amy's giggle. The music changed to an instrumental song.

"Dibs on Davis," Beth announced.

"No way. I want the blond," Patty retorted.

"They all look blond," Sally said.

"Put your glasses on," Amy said. "There's a hunky, tall, brown-haired guy."

Sally surreptitiously peeked through her glasses and put them away.

Kyle announced Davis and his group had won the

kisses to a smattering of applause and jeers. The Atlanta men made their way through the crowd to the charity bucket.

The women at her table spoke at once.

"They won!"

"Which one should I go for, Amelia Paige?"

"I want the hot one."

"We all do."

"Just don't burp."

"Stop spilling, and I'll stop burping."

Paige tugged her vest in place before her breasts fell out. "They're all up for grabs."

She had been standing with her back to the room, facing her table of green-clad girlfriends—her increasingly drunk and happy, green-clad girlfriends. When they all stopped speaking at once, she finally turned around.

Davis stood behind her, grinning. He looked straight at her sequined chest. "Up for grabs? That's what I like to hear, Paigey. Knew you missed me." He winked and nodded hello to the table. "We paid big bucks for kisses, and looking at all of you, it seems worth it. Anybody ready for a kiss?"

"Yes!" both Beth and Patty said at once while Paige's jaw dropped.

Davis grinned ear to ear. He laughed. "Paige first, but I'll get to you two next. That is, if my friends don't get there first."

Paige rolled her eyes at the arrogance others took for charm. "Now, Davis, I don't think—"

Before she could voice her objections, or even her questions, he took her in his big arms, pulling her to a spotlight, and bent her over, kissing her with a big, showy kiss. She tried to push him away, but he wouldn't have it.

She relented, if, for no other reason, than they were in a party spotlight. That, and the kiss was over in a flash, without any zing felt on her part. The chemistry was surprisingly gone. Completely.

Davis grinningly brought her back upright. He no longer held her attention. In her tipsy state, she tried to process that thought as she looked on to see Patty and Sally being kissed by Davis's Atlanta buddies. The others looked on with Beth smiling straight at Davis.

Paige moved toward her table, noticing Paul, the barista/vet student, waving frantically from the corner. She waved back and motioned for him to join the table, but it looked more like she was pointing to Amy. He grinned with a thumbs up and began to push past others. She did a double take as she thought she saw Michael in the corner behind Paul, but the crowd blocked her view even when she was on tip toes. Thoughts of Michael flooded her mind.

By then, Davis had returned to her side, grinning. With a hand on her back, he pointed Paige toward Sally. Sally was still kissing Davis's friend in the spotlight. As the kiss ended, Sally jumped on her tall winner, wrapping her legs around his waist, and kissed him again to the cheers of the crowd. He laughed, held her up around his body, and kissed her another time.

Kyle said into the mic, "That's what I call being a good sport for charity. More of that later. After the next song, we have our jig dancing contest, ladies, so drink up, get ready, and figure out which of you is brave enough to try."

"I will," a man called out in a deep base voice.

"He said *ladies*," another man objected.

"How do ye know I'm not?" the base-voiced man said in a wavy falsetto. And with that, the attention was off Paige's group. A song, thick with Celtic drums, came on.

Paige continued to search through the crowd from where she stood but didn't see Michael. Davis said something. Beth laughed and touched his arm. Paige motioned she couldn't hear. Lucy burped and suddenly looked greener than the clothing around her. She swayed, burped again, but this time nervously held her mouth.

"Oh no! Come on honey, let's get you air," Paige said to Lucy and gave a worried look to Davis and Beth at his side. He seemed to understand and made a pathway for them toward the closest door. Beth motioned to the bar, mouthing "water" to Amy who rose to help.

Davis's buddies were unaware and made themselves happily at home with Paige's other friends at the table, all flirting so heavily, they didn't look up to see Paige and Lucy leave.

Chapter Sixteen

Lucy wobbled and stumbled out the bar door. Paige held onto her, leading her into a small brick alley next to the bar.

"I don't f-f-feel so good," Lucy slurred and burped out her words.

Music and a chaos of noise were still loud but muffled as they stepped farther into the tight, freezing alleyway.

"The fresh air might help," Paige said. Lucy inhaled and exhaled deeply but looked gaunt. "Then again, maybe not."

"Paige, we have to talk," came Davis's clueless words.

"I'm sort of busy here." She only glanced at him as she guided Lucy to a garbage can.

"I know. I heard. You have a job and you're getting another one. But we need to— Oh shit. Is she still going to blow chunks?"

His answer came with Lucy heaving on top of the half-full garbage can. Paige held her friend's hair back as Lucy gripped the can and threw up again.

"Just like home. You're always mommying everybody. We miss you. You can do this in Georgia, you know. It won't be as cold there." His comments grated on Paige. "Whoa! There she goes again. Look how green it is!"

"You're not helping," Paige said. Lucy stopped for a moment, and Paige rubbed her back and held onto her friend.

Davis took the opportunity to move in closer. "Why don't you come back with us? You gotta give me credit in findin' you. Okay, we're also up here for Dunkin's dad's sixtieth and thought maybe if you saw us…well, saw me, you'd come back with us."

He leaned in puckering his lips.

At that moment, Lucy lurched, grabbing for the can again. Paige was yanked forward and threw her elbow back to counter balance. Her elbow made contact, swift and hard contact. *Whack!*

"Shit, Paige! What da F did you do that for?" Davis cried out as he held onto his face. He drew his bloodied hand in front him and looked at it. "My nose! You hit me!"

"It was an accident," Paige yelled as Lucy hurled again, making loud heaving noises.

Amy and Beth turned the corner, carrying wet paper towels and water.

Beth shoved a water bottle at Amy and took some of the paper towels, rushing to Davis's side. "What happened? You poor baby! What did you do, Paige?" She glared at Paige.

"I saw. She accidentally elbowed the big guy here." Amy sneered back, pushing past him to Lucy. Both Paige and Amy attended to Lucy, who was shaking but finally seemed to regain color.

"Let me have a look." Beth took Davis's arm and had him lean on a compressor. She stood close to him, wiping his face with a paper towel. He flinched. "Hold still."

His eyes opened and travelled to her more than ample cleavage and down to her short green skirt.

"Isth it bwoken?" he asked with the voice of a small southern boy.

"Aww. Don't worry. I don't think so." Beth fussed over him and wiped his face, gently pinching his nose and tilting his head back to stop the blood flow. Paige saw, from her angle, that their eyes locked. Both patient and nurse smiled at each other. "Let me help you inside. You look like you could use a wee dram of Irish kindness." Beth said, seemingly unaware of anyone but Davis.

"'Anks. I 'ink *you* might be da Irish kindness I weally need, Beff." Davis walked, head back, holding his nose, allowing Beth to guide him.

Beth blushed, maybe at his remembering her name or just maybe because he had his handsome lug of an arm around her.

Paige stood shivering without her coat and grinned. She knew it was over with Davis Greer. She'd known it for some time. Their earlier kiss proved it. This was the cherry on the top. He was gone and maybe to Beth.

"I think I'm going to be sick," Amy said.

"You, too?" Paige quickly turned to Amy, eyes wide.

Amy shook her head and motioned toward Beth and Davis. "What a baby."

"Oh that. Yeah, I told you." They flanked Lucy while she took small sips of water. They watched Davis's friends join him at the end of the alleyway, firing questions at him.

"What happened Greerster?"

"Did you get in a fight?"

"Should we go deck someone for you, Davis?"

"It was an accident," Beth answered.

"Paige hit me," Davis agreed as he walked right into someone. "Hey, watch it, bub."

"Sorry," came another man's voice. "You said Paige. Where is she?"

Barista Paul came into view.

"In the alley, but watch out. She packs a wallop," one of Davis's friends said.

The women heard music and noise from the bar spill out from the open door.

"Hey, guess what? Paige punched Davis."

A cheer from inside followed and became muffled as the door closed again.

"Paige, you animal." Paul smirked as he approached. She rolled her eyes at the furry reference and hoped he wouldn't continue. He didn't. "I couldn't figure out where you disappeared to before I could even reach your table."

"We got kind of busy with a bad mix of mixed drinks," Paige said, motioning to Lucy before tossing out paper towels. Lucy was still leaning heavily on Amy.

Paul rushed to take Lucy's other arm. "Whoa. So, the green's got you green. Glad it's out of your system. It is, right?"

Paige nodded in agreement. She introduced them with a shiver and explained their connections and backgrounds to both Paul's and Amy's shared intrigue. She was careful to omit the barista's continual interest in all things furry, keeping it only to his interest in animals. Real animals as a vet student.

"I can drive somebody home, if you need it," Paul

offered looking straight at Amy. "Just gotta let my friend know."

"No car. Not yet. I need more fresh air," Lucy said, interrupting Paul's and Amy's magic moment.

"Well, there's a bench off to the right," Paige suggested, teeth chattering. "I'll stay with her."

"You don't have your jacket and seem to need it," Paul protested as he and Amy walked Lucy toward the bench.

Amy concurred. "Besides the music is too loud for me. I prefer acoustic."

"Acoustic guitar," Paul words overlapping Amy's.

Amy looked at him and said with innocence, "I play it…guitar and other instruments."

"No way." He beamed without sensing the double entendre and positioned himself in the middle, arms across the bench back. Lucy and Amy sat to either side of him. "I can cover for you, Paige."

Paige stood hugging herself on the particularly windy corner. She wasn't sure if she should leave her girlfriends or Paul for that matter. When she looked at Amy's urging expression, she had her answer. Amy made a surreptitious shooing motion. "Fine. I'll go and get my things."

"What about Michael?" Paul asked.

"What about Michael?" the women echoed. They had known about the issues Paige faced and how Michael went MIA.

"Sure. He's inside. Spoke to him briefly. I thought you knew."

"Michael? My Michael? I didn't see him or even hear from him today." Paige rubbed her bare arms faster.

"Well, text him so you can find him."

"Can't now. I sort of forgot my phone so I couldn't reach Michael if I tried. Besides, I'm not so sure."

"Just go." All three on the bench said at once. Even Lucy laughed and urged her, looking weak but more herself.

Paige turned and just about ran back to the bar.

"Go get your Groundhog Man," Paul called after her.

"I will if I can find him," Paige called back.

"Right here, honey," a very drunk man slurred near the door of the bar. He leaned into Paige, blocking her entrance.

"I wouldn't do that if I were you," Paul yelled. "She punches."

Paige shook her head and pushed the drunk out of the way. He staggered into his pals who scoffed and chuckled at him.

"Told you," Paul called out with a laugh.

****

Paige took a moment to catch her breath. The warmth of the bar washed over her as did the press of people and their off-key rendition of *Danny Boy*. She squirmed her way through the crowd. Her previous table was now filled with a mix of her girlfriends and Davis's Atlanta boys. Her coat could wait. She made her way to a clear spot near the music as the song finished.

"Well, look who we have here. The fighting spitfire herself," Kyle said into the mic.

She waved him away and looked all directions for Michael.

"I've got a song just for you, Amelia Paige," he

said into the mic, drawing her attention.

She crossed the bar toward him.

"It's the Fighting Irish song!"

She rolled her eyes. The music started to cheers from one direction and a commotion near the side door. She stood on tip toes and still didn't see Michael. She walked up to Kyle, squatting next to him so she could speak over the din. "Very funny about the song."

He smiled and pointed to his wife, who waved back. "It was her idea." He continued in brogue, "Better than trowin' you out on your arse for fightin', seein' the damage you done to that wee babe of a lad."

Heather came over with two water glasses. "I don't know if it was an accident or it was due. I shouldn't say this, but either way, good on you." She kissed her husband and hurried back to the bar.

Paige relished the long overdue drink of water and said, "Kyle, I need some help. I need to find somebody."

"It'll cost you."

"Fine, but my purse is stuffed somewhere over there by my coat near that huge *wee lad* as you called him."

Kyle asked for her favorite charity and agreed to help her at the end of the song, which came up.

"All right, pipe down all you fine drinking Irish people. I have a grand offer. This wee spitfire of a Celtic beauty wants to be makin' amends for her rough ways. We should be lettin' her, in all fairness, shouldn't we, now?"

Kyle let the crowd shout random responses both positive and negative before continuing. "She's offerin' a kiss for some green to be donated to the Charity Jar going to the Animal Adoption Center. That charity jar's sorely lacking. Any men up to the task?"

Shouts followed.

"Sure thing."

"I'm in!"

"She's hot!"

"Does an extra ten get extra kisses?"

"I'm first."

Paige panicked. Her voice carried into the microphone. "Wait, what? No! I only want to find my Michael!"

"You heard her. Any Michaels in the house ready for kissing?" Kyle asked.

"I'm Michael."

"No, you're not."

"Sure, I'm Michael if it means I can kiss her."

"Me, too, then!"

"Michael's me name."

"You bet."

A bartender hopped over the bar, grabbed the Charity Jar, and stood at the ready. He was big enough to hold back some of the crush.

Paige's heart raced. She was in fight or flight mode. Instead, her body chose deer-in-headlights as she froze on the spot, staring at all the drunken men claiming to be Michael. Panic chilled her reaction. Her mind raced with the adrenalin flooding her system. This was not what she wanted.

She closed her eyes and inhaled deeply to clear her mind. All she wanted, or could think of, was her Michael. All else suddenly didn't matter.

From behind her came a touch and a wish answered. "I got this, Flee."

"Michael?" Paige's amazed whisper was lost to the noise of the room, but her eyes spoke for her. They must have, because he flashed his grin.

"Sorry, my fellow Mikes, but she's all mine." He dropped what looked to be several twenties in the jar. "I'm buying out your kisses, but before you complain, I am handing this fine barkeep the rest of this green for beers for each of you." Michael turned to the barkeep. "Along with a green tip for you."

"And then some," the bartender said and added for crowd control, "We'll bring the trays to you."

"Hey, what about the kiss?" someone called.

"Kiss." "Kiss." "Kiss," became the new mindless party chant.

"You heard 'em. You still owe a kiss, Spitfire," Kyle said, smiling his pleasure to have things back under control.

Michael turned to her. He handed off the coats he was carrying. "Are you in, Paige?"

Her mind raced. He was hers. Whatever that meant, even if it were a night, a moment, a kiss, everything inside her was thrilled at the prospect of being with him.

She didn't answer. Instead, her arms flew around him, and she kissed him with a deep intensity of meaning. The room melted away. She inhaled the scent of his familiar cologne. Though they must have tasted of beer and drinks, all she could taste was home. He was home to her in that tender kiss. His strong arms enfolded her in a welcomed feel of his hard body against hers. Something tugged inside of her.

His eyes lit up as she let go of the kiss.

With only a half moment, he returned the kiss, with

even more fire, tongue searching, moaning hungrily. This kiss, this returned kiss ignited her with electricity. She wasn't cold anymore. In that instant in his arms, in the middle of an impossibly crowded noisy bar, she melted. Threads of heated need tingled and flew from her breasts, shooting deep into her core. A whimpered coo escaped.

They finally broke from the kiss, and the bar cheered. She was breathless. There was no dip, no flash, just that sincere sweet yearning deep inside that made her cheeks flush. She was in his arms, and it felt right. More than right.

"I'm all in, Michael."

He couldn't have heard over the Celtic drum music that came on. He didn't need to. He picked up their belongings and, holding her hand, led her toward the door. She smiled at her girlfriends as she passed their table and called out her quick goodnight.

Davis nodded. Beth smirked with a shrug. Paige gave her a quick smiling nod of approval. Beth beamed, holding to Davis as he pulled her closer.

She gave them at least a fifty/fifty chance. Much less for Dunkin and Sally. Some things were meant to be. Others not so much.

Michael was meant. She had even wished on a star for him.

Chapter Seventeen

The cold hit her face as Paige and Michael finally stepped into the night. Though it was warm by northern standards, she shivered. That, and she wore nothing on her arms, not to mention having already been out in the cold. He draped her treasured white coat around her shoulders without being asked. They moved clear of the bar, and she noticed the bench no longer held her friends but an intently kissing couple.

Michael and Paige both spoke at once. "I tried to reach you."

They exchanged words.

"Busy."

"Texted."

"Called."

"Forgot cell."

"Was that your southern boy you were kissing when I came into the bar?" Michael asked.

This was not where Paige wanted to start the conversation. She looked him straight in the eye, nodded, and said, "It just happened. Not my idea. I didn't really enjoy it."

He seemed to ruminate on her explanation.

Upon closer inspection, she saw he wore several strands of green beads, along with lipstick smears all over his left cheek. She raised an eyebrow and smiled. "And where might you have gotten those?" She pointed to beads. "And those?" She wiped off some of the lipstick prints.

He cocked up a smile. "It just happened? Not my idea? I didn't really enjoy it?"

She tried to look stern, but they both chuckled. She wanted to hug him and forget everything that'd happened this week, but somehow, they both knew more mending was needed. The ice was broken at least.

He gestured in the direction of his car, some blocks away. With his arm around her, they walked through streets filled with sidewalk traffic of St. Patrick's Day partygoers.

This time Paige opened the dialog. Several questions flooded out at once. "Are you mad at me about the job? Why didn't you text or call me? And how did your project go?"

Michael shook his head. "I did text. Check your cell. You have terrible reception. I even wrote you after a very long day. I reviewed the position terms you sent me. Everything's all in line. *Monitor and Ventures* gave you a solid offer, so take the job if you haven't already as I suspect you did. As for me, things didn't quite line up as I expected."

She stopped walking and looked at him. "Oh. Okay." She forced herself to a smile. "Well, at least I can see you in Ohio for the training."

"Most likely not."

She couldn't believe her ears. Her mind raced again, and her feet started moving. Suddenly, she was walking fast, dodging a young couple.

Michael rushed beside her. "Paige…"

She stopped and turned to him. "So, this…this is goodbye?"

The couple stopped and stared.

"What? No." Michael mumbled something in Oneida. He turned her to him, holding her, hugging her tightly. Tipping her chin so she looked at him, he gently added, "It's not goodbye. I want to be with you. Take any job you want. I just didn't want you to follow me to Ohio as a tag along and especially as an employee."

"He's right. You hold strong, girl," the female of the couple called out.

Michael turned to them. His expression gave more than a discrete plea for them move on. The male tugged his partner.

The female hesitated, walking very slowly and staring. "Wait. I want to see this."

Ignoring them, Michael softly kissed Paige's cheek.

The female gave him a so-so, mild, thumbs up, and said to her scoffing partner, "What? He can kiss way better I bet."

"So can we. C'mon," the man said and successfully pulled his partner away from the scene.

Paige had been lost in thought. She took in everything Michael said and wondered if she might have outgrown the tag-along relationship role.

Michael interrupted her thoughts. "Paige. Don't you see? I want to stay here. With you."

His words sank in. Michael wanted to stay. Her whole demeanor lightened, and she felt the corners of her lips tip up. He wanted to be with her for the long haul. Astonishment mixed with elation and her face lit up.

Michael smiled. "Anyone can see you are attached to the area and that hovel."

"It's not a hovel," she objected, grinning.

"Okay, the pre-renovated house. I love it here, too, Paige. More than I do in my condo back in Ohio. It's green here."

"I know. It's St. Patty's Day," someone called out with a laugh as a group hurried by.

Michael and Paige joined in the chuckle, easing tension. They started walking again. Paige listened intently as he spoke.

"I meant it's country here. I miss it. Something that became apparent when we skied. Not to mention, you know I need to check on my cousin, Alfie, every now and then. He needs someone in the family who can support his life choice until the rest come around. I travel a lot with my current job, especially with product roll outs or roll backs."

Michael continued, "Then, when you interviewed, I tried to leverage myself into a different position with *Monitor and Ventures*. I thought I could step back and run the plant. That way I wouldn't be your boss or in your line of command. No conflicts. That wasn't what happened today. Instead, I was offered the number two position at the plant."

Paige stopped walking again. This time, so abruptly that someone almost bumped into her.

"Before you ask, let me tell you, it's a mixed position. I will be sent out for retrofits while I still get day to day plant operation exposure. Maybe even on a project here or there. In essence, they promoted me into a newly created executive track garnering concurrent field and plant experience."

"Wow," Paige said in a hush of a whisper.

Michael nodded, unable to hide his pride in the

accomplishment. "Apparently, the rollout was well received. So was the redesigned retrofit I did in Columbia. I just didn't have time to tell you until the end of long work day when I showed up at your home."

"You showed up at my home?" Before he could answer, Paige threw her arms around him, and her coat slipped from one shoulder. "That's how you knew where to find me? My home? Linney told you?" Paige kissed his cheek.

"Not exactly. Bailey came to the door with a towel around his waist. Get this, I stood on a lower step as he told me you were at a bar but forgot the name. He started to gesture with directions. The towel fell off. The man didn't flinch. Stark naked. Just gestured away, his parts only a few inches from me. Hard to remember anything he said."

"Lucky you." Paige laughed.

"Not funny. I got lost since I only got part of the directions. Then I thought to look up all the Irish Bars in the area. Yours was the second one I tried."

"See? You are lucky because—"

Michael cut her off with a kiss. A delicious kiss full on the lips. All previous thought vanished.

"Congratulations on the job, Groundhog Man." She nearly hummed the last words in his ear. His reaction was instantaneous.

In a deepened growl, he said, "You, too, Flee. I'm impressed." He adjusted her coat, slipped it back over her shoulders.

"So, am I worth whatever you stuffed into that charity jar?"

They started to walk again.

"I don't know." Michael's gaze traveled to her

cleavage made more visible by one of the pins slipping. "Make that definitely."

"Horndog."

"Nope, I'm pure Groundhog Man."

She rolled her eyes and unsuccessfully tugged at her vest, thankful her coat covered her.

His arm slid around her as they walked. "So, you didn't ask me, but do I get to stay with you out in that wonderful ramshackle of a house you've been calling home?"

"You want to live at the farmhouse? Hmm...maybe." She hip-bumped him and continued, "Are you going to help fix up our home?"

Did she just use the words, *our home?* She flinched and quickly blurted out, "I mean Linney's home—the farmhouse...whatever."

He answered with ease. "Yes. All of it. Whoever's home it is. I can help more, but it seems you have things moving along."

"You'd be surprised what Bailey and I've done without you."

"Oh?" Michael teased.

"Not what I meant and you know it."

Michael nodded. "C'mon let's go home, for however long it's to be our home.

Paige took a few steps and stopped. "Oh no. One problem with that."

Michael's eyebrows immediately furrowed with concern.

"I think I left something back in the bar. Something I shouldn't have left."

"Your girlfriends?" he asked.

"No."

"Davis?"

"What? No. Definitely not. My purse."

Michael lit up and reached in his deep coat pocket. "I forgot. This one?"

She nodded and took it. "How'd you get it?"

"It was with your coat. When they announced your name, I saw someone casually picking it up along with a very visible puffy white coat. As much as I wanted to join you, I followed her to the door, distracted her, and got it back. Okay, maybe I lied and said my brother, the police officer, was coming back with my beer and that she could explain how she came by someone else's purse and coat to him."

"Impressive," Paige said and began to walk.

"Dishonest, but effective."

"What about my shirt?"

"You had a shirt?

"Yes. I'm wearing this vest at Beth's insistence."

He eyed it again. "Insistence, was it?"

"Yes. Well, encouragement."

"I like encouragement. That's how I got all those lipstick kisses."

They were nearly at his car. She screwed her face into an attempted glare.

Michael grinned. "What? It's St. Patty's day. I'm only part Oneida." A woman crossed his path as he spoke. "C'mon Flee. It's time to kiss an Irishman."

The woman said, "Okay," and planted a big kiss on him. So, did her male friend.

"What about me?" Paige called after them as they crossed the street.

An old lady stepped up and gave Paige a big "mwwah" on her cheek. "The rest is up to your fella there," she said.

Paige laughed. The old lady grunted as she shifted a bag. Michael took ahold of her package, helped the lady to her nearby car, and held the door open for her. He even kissed her on the cheek and helped her into her car. Another person walked by. She looked properly disheveled from a night out. She handed Michael a tall green paper hat for "Doing a fine Irish ting."

Paige shook her head and walked ahead. Michael caught up to her under a street light. And in that pool of light, he kissed her, he in his new hat, she in her shining sequined vest. This kiss was different. It was no peck. It lengthened into a simmer of the fire they held for each other. It also held a promise of something more permanent. The kiss said more than their discussion could.

Her coat slipped off her shoulders again, and her hair spilled over his arm. They lingered under the street light in each other's familiar, welcoming arms. She knew everything would hit on St. Patrick's Day. She just didn't know how much it would all crash before righting itself. It started to sink in that she was with Michael. Really with him. Nothing could get in their way now. And in that tender moment, his stomach growled.

He smiled sheepishly.

Paige giggled. "I have some pie waiting for you."

"Linney's or yours?"

"That depends on how good you are," Paige retorted. If it were Davis, he would have jumped on that line, saying something like "I'm better than good and let me prove it." That wasn't how Michael responded.

Michael pushed back a stray hair from her face and

held her gaze. "One universe, eight planets, seven seas, and seven continents. I am so fortunate to have found you, Paige. I'm not letting you go. Keeping you. *Atyenawast*. I love you."

She said the words, even though they both already knew. "I love you, too, Michael."

They stayed under that street lamp and kissed again. It was a sweet, endearing kiss, followed by one that gave her a relaxed longing, a familiar need to touch and be touched. It was a perfect kiss, lost to time.

Except it wasn't. It was caught by Paul and Amy on her cell. Amy sent it to the news station with the hashtag St. Patrick's Day Kiss Contest and included their names. Paige and Michael's private lingering kisses were no longer private. It was aired as the last segment of the news.

The male newscaster added, "What a sweet couple kissing. Now that's a fine St. Patrick's happily ever after kiss if I ever saw one."

The female newscaster beamed. "Aww. They're even walking away hand in hand. Oh look, he just did the heel kick, too. Best of luck to them both."

"Call in and tell us if you get married," her male counterpart added right before the credits rolled. The best part of all, they did.

Epilogue

About a year later, Michael and Paige sent the news station a photo of them holding a sign with the date of their wedding, taken on top of the newly re-built staircase of the farmhouse with their wedding guests pressed into the foyer below them. Bailey and Linney were front and center in the foyer. Davis was in the back with Beth at his side. Amy and Paul were in the foreground of the photo, holding a picture of the aired St. Patrick's Day kiss. Even Winky was in the picture—midair before he jumped off the new, immaculately hand-carved, stair railing.

For months and years to come, friends would all joke how Michael was forced to marry Paige at the news station's prompting. Paige and Michael knew better. The moment the Groundhog Day storm brought them together, they connected in a way that was just "meant to be." That and they had, *yotsistatsá·niht*, a strong fire and not just the kind in the refurbished fireplace, although, as Linney would argue, it helped. Everything helped except Linney's pies.

What happened leading up to the wedding or afterward was another story, one which Paige or Michael happily shared. Every Groundhog Day, they celebrated his birthday with far more than cake. Every year that it snowed on Valentine's Day, he painted the message in the snow, "I love you, Flee." And every

Ginny B. Nescott

year he stomped on it just enough to read something else like "I love you, Flu" or "I lice you, Flea." And, more than once, they carved their names on a tree in the forest just like her grandparents. Best of all, it was for the same reason, children.

Michael and Paige never grew profoundly rich. Family and the upkeep of the farmhouse made sure of that. But they learned and grew together. Everyone did, except Winky, and maybe Linney with her baking when she and Bailey were around. It didn't matter. Others could bake, and Winky was loved. They all were. They had each other and *yotsistatsá·niht*. Lots of *yotsistatsá·niht* heat.

About the Author

Ginny hides away in small town, in a home needing far more upkeep than she cares to admit, with her tall, Texan husband, her actor/artist son, and a large rescue dog. She loves a reason to celebrate and share a laugh with friends and family.

When she's not writing, she can be found cooking, at the theatre, dog walking, swimming, volunteering, reading, and laughing over games. Her goal is to bring a bit of laughter and hope to her readers and to encourage others to pursue their passions and find love!

~*~

Visit Ginny at

https://gbnescott.wixsite.com/ginnywrites
https://www.facebook.com/GinnyBeGoodToMe/

~*~

To chat with Ginny B. Nescott and other Wild Rose Press authors of erotic romance, join us at
www.groups.yahoo.com/group/thewilderroses.

Thank you for purchasing this
publication of The Wild Rose Press, Inc.
If you enjoyed the story, we would appreciate
your letting others know by leaving a review.
For other wonderful stories, please visit our
on-line bookstore at www.wilderroses.com.

For questions or more
information contact us at
info@thewildrosepress.com.

The Wild Rose Press, Inc.
www.thewilderroses.com

Stay current with The Wild Rose Press, Inc.
Like us on Facebook
https://www.facebook.com/TheWildRosePress
And Follow us on Twitter
https://twitter.com/WildRosePress